A BACKSTAGE BETRAYAL

Michael Ball OBE is a singer, actor, presenter and now author. He's been a star of musical theatre for over three decades, winning the Laurence Olivier Award for Best Actor in a Musical twice, he's also won two BRIT awards and been nominated for a Grammy. Michael regularly sells out both his solo tours and his Ball & Boe shows with Alfie Boe and has multiple platinum albums. *A Backstage Betrayal* is his second novel.

www.michaelball.co.uk

  @mrmichaelball

  @ mrmichaelball

  www.facebook.com/MichaelBallOfficial

Also by Michael Ball

The Empire

MICHAEL BALL

A BACKSTAGE BETRAYAL

ZAFFRE

First published in the UK in 2024 by

ZAFFRE

An imprint of The Zaffre Publishing Group

A Bonnier Books UK Company

4th Floor, Victoria House, Bloomsbury Square, London, England, WC1B 4DA

Owned by Bonnier Books

Sveavägen 56, Stockholm, Sweden

A CIP catalogue record for this book is
available from the British Library.

Hardback ISBN: 978-1-80418-230-7
Trade paperback ISBN: 978-1-80418-231-4

Also available as an ebook and in audiobook

1 3 5 7 9 10 8 6 4 2

Typeset by Envy Ltd
Printed and bound in Great Britain by Clays Ltd, Elcograf S.p.A.

Zaffre is an imprint of The Zaffre Publishing Group
A Bonnier Books UK Company
www.bonnierbooks.co.uk

A BACKSTAGE BETRAYAL

THE EMPIRE

Lady Lillian Lassiter .... widow of local industrialist, *Sir Barnabas*, co-owner of The Empire, step-mother-in-law of *Constance Lassiter*

Agnes de Montfort .... sister of *Sir Barnabas's* first wife, *Emilia*. Great-Aunt of *Edmund* and *Tom Lassiter*, co-owner of The Empire

Jack Treadwell .... *Lillian Lassiter's* natural son. General Manager of The Empire

Grace Treadwell .... wife of *Jack Treadwell*, playwright

Danny Moon .... doorman

Ollie .... sandy, wire-haired terrier

Ruby Rowntree .... composer

Tom Lassiter .... assistant to *Ruby Rowntree*, estranged son of *Constance Lassiter*, younger brother of *Edmund Lassiter*

Sarah .... landlady of *Ruby Rowntree*

Dixon Wells .... electrical engineer

Bridget Chisholm .... assistant to *Jack Treadwell*

Darien Burnside .... former assistant to *Jack Treadwell*

Harry the rat .... theatrical rodent

Flo Briggs .... cleaner

Little Sam .... carpenter and set designer

Frederick Poole .... front of house manager

Marcus .... apprentice to *Frederick Poole*

Milly .... assistant dresser

Ruben .... master of light

Pete and Jonah .... stagehands

Mr Porter .... bandleader

Mr Patterson .... foreman at Empire Records

Jeremy Fossil .... manager of quality control

Empire Records

Miss James .... worker at Empire Records

THE TALENT

Stella Stanmore .... West End star

Lancelot Drake .... film star

Clara Jones .... lead of touring review

Miss Gardiner .... lead of *The Two Ladies of Grasmere*

Miss Pritchard .... lead of *The Two Ladies of Grasmere*

Josie Clarence .... musical star

Harold Drabble .... pantomime dame

Marmaduke Smythe .... actor playing King Rat

Frank .... actor playing Idle Jack

Gordon .... actor playing Alderman Fitzwarren

Terrence Fortescue .... choreographer

Mabel Mills .... jazz trumpeter and bandleader

Tasha Kingsland .... aspiring chorus girl and nightclub hostess.

Friend of *Stella Stanmore*.

Real name *Ruthie Cook*

Mr and Mrs Cook .... *Tasha's* parents

Baby June Dudley .... singer

Mrs Dudley .... *Baby June's* mother

LASSITER ENTERPRISES

Constance Lassiter .... mother of *Captain Sir Edmund Lassiter*, and *Tom Lassiter*, running Lassiter Enterprises on behalf of her eldest son

Edmund Lassiter, Captain Sir .... grandson of *Sir Barnabas Lassiter*, titular head of Lassiter Enterprises. Currently in a sanatorium in Switzerland

Mrs Booth .... housekeeper to *Constance Lassiter*

Susan .... maid to *Constance Lassiter*

Mr Milner .... assistant to *Constance Lassiter*

THE BRICKLAYERS ARMS

Sally Blow .... widowed pub singer

Dougie Blow .... her son

Alfred Glossop .... landlord of The Bricklayers Arms

Belle Glossop .... *Alfred's* wife

Clive .... young accordionist

Mrs Parsons .... grocer

ROYALTY

Grand Duke Nikolai Goranovich Kuznetsov .... exiled playwright and member of Marakovian Royal Family

Vladimir Taargin .... Marakovian Ambassador to UK

Christian .... *Taargin's* ally

Ilya .... *Taargin's* ally

Crown Prince Stefan .... heir to the throne of Marakovia

Prince Andrei .... brother of King of Marakovia

Torstein .... one of *Stefan's* attendants

HRH The Prince of Wales .... heir to the throne of British Empire

Sir Gideon .... Foreign Office official

Colonel Osman .... expert on Marakovia

ALSO FEATURING

Joseph P. Allerdyce .... theatre impresario, fiancé of
Agnes de Montfort

Wilbur Bowman .... reporter

Ray Kelly... Highbridge crime boss

Sharps .... right hand man of *Ray Kelly*

Jason de Witte .... influential London critic

Detective Sergeant Orme .... Scotland Yard detective

Detective Sergeant Hatchard .... Scotland Yard detective

Fenton Hewitt .... butler at Lassiter Court

Gladys .... lady's maid

Mrs Young .... housekeeper at Lassiter Court

For Mum and Dad . . .
My first and still my best 'Producers'. Happy 90th birthday.
Mxx

1924

*C*hin up, Sally Blow.

The young woman pulled her woollen scarf a little tighter round her neck. At least now it was getting dark she could use it for warmth, rather than to cover the worn patch on the collar of her coat.

The sun was dropping behind the red brick towers and slate roofs of Highbridge, sending up one final flare of purple and gold, but the cold had come quick and fast as soon as dusk announced itself, and the damp was getting into Sally's bones from the feet up.

She'd been walking all day in pinching shoes, smiling her best smile in shop after shop, though she was half ragged with hunger by four o'clock. The café owners and shopkeepers, barmaids and doormen had shaken their heads at her. There was no work to be had.

I'll try again tomorrow, she told herself. Get up even earlier, wash her face harder and use her last scrap of lipstick, and brandish her comb with two teeth missing till her hair shone. Just this bit of walking to do now, back to her shared attic room and her little boy.

She'd not have turned past the theatre, as her way led up St Anne's Lane towards the cramped rows of workers' cottages to the east of the city, but she caught the smell of charcoal and baking potatoes a way ahead of her.

As a treat, she reckoned she could just stand by the brazier for a minute, as if she might be in the market for a potato, and warm up a bit before she headed off. The smell as she got closer made her stomach complain, and she fingered the coins in her pocket through her gloves. Mrs Griggs would give Dougie his tea, and Sally had paid the week through for his food. Should she blow sixpence on a good hot potato now, or make the pennies stretch? She inched closer to the glowing brazier.

'Fourpence, love,' the woman serving said. 'Take it now before my fella gets back and I'll put extra butter on it.'

Sally whipped out her pennies in a flash. There's being cautious, and there's passing up a good thing when you see it.

Easier to keep your chin up with warm hands and something in your stomach, too. The vendor hadn't lied – it was good country butter, and plenty of it. Well content with her bargain and her stomach quieted like a purring cat with her first bite, Sally heard a cheer.

'What's the commotion, then?'

'Opening night at The Empire, isn't it?'

'Is it?'

'It is, love.'

For two years the theatre had been a building site, after the old one had burnt down, but then its walls had started rising up slowly in a frenzy of hammering and brick dust. Sally had seen the stories about the fire in the *Highbridge Gazette*, but she'd had too much going on, what with her husband being ill, and Dougie teething, to pay much attention.

Sally munched her potato as the grandest car she'd ever seen in her life – a long, low beast, all burgundy and cream, with a silver angel on the front – rolled past them.

'Who has a car like that?'

'That'll be Lady Lassiter. She owns the theatre. Go along, love. Come back and tell us about the frocks.'

Sally glanced at the town clock. She'd still be home in plenty of time to fetch Dougie and get him to bed. Nice to have a story to tell him of fancy cars and bright lights. Her hands and heart warm from the potato, she followed in the wake of the Rolls-Royce and turned the corner.

The front of the theatre was ablaze with electric light; its twin towers, dressed in white stone, shot up like beacons in the deep dusk.

CAIRO NIGHTS was spelled out in golden bulbs, and the whole frontage seemed to glow like a jewel box. Velvet ropes held back a crowd of Highbridge citizens, wrapped up against the chill, and a red carpet was laid right out over the pavement. Ladies and gentlemen in evening dress were ambling into the lobby, and a tall thin man in a grey suit was bowing them in at the door. Sally had a confused impression of pearls and the sheen of satin as she joined the crowd outside the rope and, with a little shuffling, found herself a good spot near the front. The thin man looked pink with pride as he welcomed the theatre guests in. What a thing to be welcomed like that, with a smile and a 'good evening, madam'. She craned her neck a little. The lobby was gold and green, shimmering.

She had arrived just in time to see a woman step out of the back of the Rolls-Royce, as thin as a whip, and with blonde hair piled on her head and held in place with glittery combs. She had a dark fur wrap over her shoulders and a long slightly old-fashioned gown of midnight blue.

A photographer ducked under the rope in front of her. 'Lady Lassiter? If you wouldn't mind?'

The woman smiled and turned slightly while the flash popped and there was a little cloud of smoke.

'Who'd have thought she started off just like one of us?' a comfortably built woman next to Sally said. She was eating roast chestnuts out of a paper bag.

'Give over – she did not!' Sally said.

'I swear it. Started out working in the old mill at fourteen, then went to Paris and became a star. That's in France.'

'I know where Paris is.'

Sally stared as Lady Lassiter walked along the carpet and into the theatre, smiling right and left. She moved like a swan on the municipal pond.

'That's where she got her polish,' Sally's informant said, with authority. 'Lovely voice already, mind. Met old Sir Barnabas out there and he bought her the theatre as a wedding gift.'

'I got a new hat,' Sally said, and her new friend laughed.

An older lady and gent, done up to the nines, made their way down the carpet. A little parade of younger people followed them like goslings; the women had their hair cut short, and wore long straight dresses in gold and blue and had thick dark lines round their eyes.

The air fizzed with excitement, as if the lights of the lobby had something magic in them. Sally's potato was caviar, and the air champagne.

'I can sing,' said Sally.

'Oh, can you now? Alf, this girl says she can sing.'

A burly man with a face like a boiled ham, on the other side of chestnut lady grunted. 'Oh, well, in that case, do you want to order your car now, miss?'

Sally straightened her shoulders. 'Why not? I'll have one like Lady Lassiter's, but in green, and throw in a picnic, too. Quails' eggs and champagne in one of them wicker baskets, my good man. And it's Mrs. Mrs Sally Blow.'

Alfred snorted with laughter. 'I'll ring up your order now, Mrs Blow. And what's Mr Blow going to say about it?'

'Not much, he's been dead a year.' Sally sighed. 'I hear him, though,' she went on, half to herself and half to her cooling potato, 'when I'm down or my little boy is teasing me. "Chin up, Sally Blow," he says, and I carry on – on I bloody well carry.' The woman patted her arm. Sally lifted her chin. 'So who is that coming now?'

'Oh! Is it? Lord love us, it is! That's Lancelot Drake!'

The car drawing up was a little sporty thing, and it was the driver who got out this time. Sally held her breath. An actual. Real-life. Movie star. She'd seen him at the picture palace, fifteen feet tall and every inch of him gorgeous, but it felt wrong to be breathing the same air as him. The photographer popped his flash again and Lance beamed, then turned back to offer a hand to his companion. The woman had her hair cut short and wore a sheer white gown that looked like liquid starlight.

'And that's Stella Stanmore! She can sing even better than Lady Lassiter. Got a voice for those modern jazzy songs. Had her first big roles up here at The Empire, and a star of the West End now. And that's in London.'

Sally grinned, and savoured the last bite of her potato as Stella waved to the crowd.

A girl next to them squealed. 'Lance, Lance! Sign my book!'

Sally looked sideways. The squealer was nicely dressed, and Sally adjusted her scarf over the worn patch again. It was warm enough in the crowd to ignore the resulting draught which whistled down her neck.

The square woman with the chestnuts nudged the ham-faced man. He gave a sidelong look, then tugged his moustache.

'If your ladyship fancies a sing-song . . . Well, I'm Alf Glossop and I'm landlord at the Bricklayers Arms up on Victoria Road. Could do with some entertainment Friday and Saturday night. They're a rowdy crowd, and you'd be singing for tips.'

Sally considered. 'First night I'll do for tips, Alf. See if we get on. After that, if you want me back it's five bob *plus* tips. You need a barmaid the rest of the week?'

'You've got some sauce, Mrs Blow! Bloody hell, no, I don't. But if you can do your numbers, the grocer's on Albert Street is looking for a girl three days a week. She's putting a card up tomorrow, so get there early.'

Sally felt her heart lift. Maybe it was the potato, or the fizz from the theatre that made the air shimmer. 'Well, for that tip, Alf, when I open here, I'll get you tickets and a box of bonbons. Even give you a lift in my car.'

Alfred smiled and touched the brim of his hat to her, and the chestnut lady put out her hand. 'I'm Belle – Mrs Glossop.'

Sally brushed the last of the potato from her gloves and shook hands. When she turned back, her breath stopped. Lancelot Drake had made his way down the rope to sign the squealer's book. If Sally reached out, she could have touched him. Over the smell of chestnuts and potato she caught the whiff of cologne and brilliantine.

Then he looked at her. Right at her. Sally gawped like a goldfish. The lights of the theatre made his hair shine. She tried to say 'hello', but it came out as a sort of hiccup.

He smiled, then plucked a red rosebud out of his lapel and handed it to her with a little bow. Sally couldn't even speak to thank him before he was gone, waving and shaking hands all the way into the lobby.

Sally stared down at the perfect scarlet rosebud, cradled in the palm of her hand.

'Well, I never,' Belle said admiringly.

Alfred frowned, tilting his head to one side. 'Sally Blow, the Highbridge Rose. That's got a ring to it.'

Sally was still staring at the perfect bud. 'The Highbridge Rose. It does, Alf, doesn't it?'

Jack Treadwell, manager of the New Empire Theatre, stood centre stage just behind the curtain, pinching the velvet edges together with finger and thumb and listening to the low excited chatter of the audience as they settled into their seats.

His collar was pinching. It was brand new, like everything else in the theatre, from the crystal chandelier hanging from the central dome to the boards under his feet. Behind Jack, the set for the opening number loomed in the semi-darkness. An exotic bazaar, which would in a very few minutes be teeming with dancers in extortionately expensive silks and bathed in artificial sunshine. The theatre devotees of Highbridge would be magically transported to Cairo for an evening of high comedy, rich romance, and indecently catchy tunes.

Jack could feel the blood fizzing and thrumming in his veins, like the vamp of the orchestra waiting for the star turn to walk on to the stage. It was a pulse, inaudible, which seemed to unite him with every brick and board in the place. He could feel the whole theatre as if it were part of him, and he was part of it, from the traps ready to spring the genie onto the stage at the end of the first number, to the electric wires running to the follow spot above the gallery; from the ropes coiled in the wings, to the strings of the violins tuning up in the orchestra pit; from the dancers shuffling into position backstage, checking the straps and hooks of their costumes, to the front of house staff passing out souvenir programmes to the latecomers, from Danny at the stage door, humming the opening number under his breath, to their star, Josie, slipping into her silver tap shoes in the number one dressing room. They all moved to that same, insistent, invigorating, invisible rhythm. They were one organism tonight, one living whole, bound by brick walls and the shivering alchemy of performance.

'Darien!' Jack hissed sideways. A young man, dressed like Jack in black tie, trotted up to him with a benign smile. His watery blue eyes seemed, as usual, to be focused on nothing in particular.

'Yes, Mr Treadwell?'

'Are the dignitaries seated?'

Darien blinked; a tiny frown of concentration, or possibly confusion, appeared on his face – a slight tightening between the eyebrows with which Jack was becoming painfully familiar.

Jack's wife, Grace, had told him to try and be patient with Darien. His father, a bigwig on Highbridge City Council, had been terribly helpful with permits and the like, and Jack was trying – but then, so was Darien. His otherworldly lack of concern about taking or passing on messages had added greatly to the stress Jack had felt during these final frantic weeks. What was worse, while Jack had come home every evening, his clothes covered in paint and with flakes of gilt in some surprisingly intimate places, Darien remained pristine. He repelled dirt and paperwork to an equal degree.

'Yes, Lady Lassiter, and her late husband's sister-in-law Agnes de Montfort?' Jack explained patiently. 'The owners of the theatre? My wife and Ruby Rowntree, who wrote this musical? Their guests?'

Confusion cleared. 'Oh yes! They're here. With all those theatrical types.'

'You mean the cream of the profession we have tempted up to Highbridge for this very special evening?' Jack said, feeling his jaws clench.

'That's them! And I put up that nice picture of her and Miss de Montfort with you and Mrs Treadwell on the wall by the number one dressing room. Looks smashing.'

It was unlike Darien to do anything unless explicitly and repeatedly instructed to do so. Perhaps he was improving.

'Thank you, Darien.' Jack glanced behind him. The stage manager gave him the thumbs up. 'Off you pop, then, and tell Mr Porter to cue me in please.' Darien's frown reappeared. 'Mr Porter is the band leader, Darien.'

'Ah, right-ho! Now?'

'Yes. Now.'

Darien scuttled off. Jack closed his eyes and breathed in deeply. It already smelt like a theatre: sweat, sawdust and paint. This was it.

On the other side of the velvet curtain a long drum roll began. The audience were settled and silenced, the house lights lowered, then, at a blast on the trumpets, Jack swept aside the curtain and stepped out. He felt the heat of the spotlight on his face and opened his arms wide to the city's citizens: the theatre lovers, the star-struck, his friends, rivals, family, and the merely curious, all eager to be entertained. He took a second, scanning the myriad of faces. What a wonderful bunch they all were.

'Good evening, and welcome to the New Empire!' Again that pulse, the thrill of it – the whole company, the whole audience, like greyhounds in the traps, straining for the off.

'Ladies and gentlemen, what a feast we have for you tonight! A musical to set your hearts racing and your feet tapping. *Cairo Nights*, my friends, is a smash! So, with no more ado, settle in and put smiles on those lovely faces because, once again, after two long years, I'm delighted to announce . . . it's show time.'

He clicked his fingers. The follow spot snapped off and as the trumpet section blared out a triumphant brassy chord, he melted into the wings and the curtain opened.

Unnoticed, the framed photograph of Jack, Grace, Lillian and Agnes, on the wall next to the number one dressing room, trembled on its hook and fell to the floor.

CHAPTER ONE

NOVEMBER 1926

L illian Lassiter took her hand from the steering wheel, and gently shook the shoulder of the dark-haired gentleman sleeping in the passenger seat. He awoke with a start, rubbed his eyes and yawned before peering out of the windscreen.

'Lillian, my dear,' he said in a tone of mild surprise, 'this countryside is very beautiful. People in London told me everything north of Hampshire was black with coal dust.'

Lillian smiled. Nikolai's accent, with its round Slavic vowels and throaty consonants, made everything he said sound like poetry. Even 'coal' sounded like a rare gem. It was one of the first things she had noticed about him when they met at a party held by mutual friends in London. Then, as he turned the spotlight of his attention on her, she had noticed his looks, his intelligence and his charm. The next day he had sent her armfuls of pink roses, and taken her for supper with his avant-garde theatre friends. To her surprise, Lillian discovered she was, at the age of forty-six, being swept off her feet.

'Which is strange when London is itself such a dirty busy place,' he continued. 'I myself am glad to see some hills again.'

'Isn't it?' Lillian replied as her heart lifted with native pride. She had lived in Paris for some years, her star shining bright enough to dazzle even in the city of light, but Highbridge, where she was raised and had earned her first pennies sweeping factory floors, would always be her home. She'd said that to her companion, His Excellency, Grand Duke Nikolai Goranovich Kuznetsov the moment she'd felt herself beginning to fall in love with him, and when she had suggested he come with her to Highbridge for an extended stay, he had accepted with obvious delight.

She had chosen a route from Nottingham which took them across the Peak District, trusting her bull-nosed Oxford Tourer to handle the gradients without complaint, so Nikolai could see this very view. The sun had just risen, and the high pasture either side of them sparkled with frost. Ahead of them the road dipped, and the landscape opened out. Mist clung to the lower flanks of the valley, but the early gold of the winter sun picked out the hamlet of Pottersfield, with its ancient church, and the drystone walls dividing the fields.

'Is Marakovia as pretty as this?' she asked, changing gear and slowing slightly. It was the weather when sheep seemed to find the middle of the road the most tempting place to sit.

'Marakovia is bigger,' he replied thoughtfully. 'For a small country, we have a very big landscape. It is as if God was a little drunk when he made our crags and valleys. It is a country fit only for eagles and poets.' He put his hand on hers and squeezed it. Then he sat forward, like a hunting dog catching a scent, narrowing his eyes. 'But this is also very beautiful. Now, I must concentrate, because very soon we shall see Highbridge, I think, and it is very important to me to see your home town.'

She laughed. 'It'll take us an hour or two yet, Nikolai, we can't drive at more than thirty miles an hour on these roads. But I did so want you to see this view.'

He relaxed back into his seat and drummed his hands on his knees.

'And you knew that the view would be best at this hour. Ah, no wonder your friend Evie in London wanted your advice on her new production. She is a clever woman.'

'I admit it. You're not angry at me for making you leave the hotel so early this morning?'

This time, he lifted her hand from the gearstick to his lips. 'Not at all, Lillian. I admire your artistry.'

Lillian felt herself blush. *How strange.* She had expected to live out the rest of her life as a respectable wealthy widow; then she had met Nikolai, and everything had changed. Her heart now fluttered like a young girl's.

Nikolai squeezed her fingers and relinquished them, acknowledging – it seemed, with reluctance – that she needed both hands to drive.

'Tell me more about Highbridge, *milaya maya.*'

'It is an industrial city and sits in the river valley,' Lillian began. 'There is an old quarter round the stone bridge with some rather charming sixteenth-century cottages, but the new centre is further up the hill. That's where the town hall and the library and the theatre and the grander shops and restaurants are. My house is out of town, towards the north.'

'It is a very grand house, I think?'

'Quite grand. My husband was a very successful man, but his daughter-in-law, Constance, manages Lassiter Enterprises now.'

'On behalf of her son? Edmund? The one who you think is a *schartenmellich*, and was hurt in the fire?'

'I've no idea what that means, but it sounds about right.' She was pleased he had remembered the details. 'Constance is a *schartenmellich*, too, but she's managed the entire business very well since Edmund became incapacitated. Much better than he did. Thank goodness I have no interest in the business now. Agnes, the sister of my husband's first wife, and I own the theatre, and I have a few stocks and shares, but none in Lassiter Enterprises.'

Nikolai was frowning fiercely. 'There is another boy? Another Lassiter boy?'

'Yes – Tom, he is Edmund's younger brother.'

'*Schartenmellich*?'

She laughed. 'No, not at all, Tom's a darling, and he lives at Lassiter Court most of the time. His relationship with his mother is strained.' Lillian paused. Should she have tried harder to persuade Tom to reconcile with his mother? But then Constance had always treated Tom with undisguised disdain, and she had done her best to blackmail Lillian into selling the theatre. She owed the woman nothing. She shook her head, as if trying to dislodge the thought. 'Now, when we get to town, Nikolai, would you like to go to the house first, or the theatre? It has been a long journey, after all . . .'

'Lillian! We must go to the theatre!' He slapped his knee to underline the point. 'I will not rest until I have seen the New Empire. It is your heart. I will go nowhere else.'

Lillian laughed. 'We'll stop for lunch in Marsden on the way, then be in time for some of the matinee.'

'And shall I meet your son Jack, at the theatre? So romantic, to have the son you thought lost forever returned to you a war hero.'

'Jack would say he's no hero, but finding him again was the great gift of my life. He'll probably be at the theatre. If he's not there, you'll meet him at dinner this evening. You remember he and his wife are living with me at Lassiter Court?'

Lillian slowed the car to a halt to allow a shepherd to urge his flock across the road in front of them. The man carried a crook and wore a long smock of homespun cloth. When he raised his hand in greeting, it was like sharing a moment with the ancient past. When the sheep were gone, and Lillian let the car move forward again, Nikolai continued softly.

'I will be on my best behaviour, Lillian.'

'I know you will.' Lillian felt her throat becoming rather dry. 'Honestly, I've no idea why I am worried.'

'Yes! Why indeed? All you are doing is arriving at your home with a foreign man on your arm, a man recently exiled from his own country as a revolutionary, saying "Good afternoon, son, this stranger is my friend and will be living with us now." We all know from the stories, this sort of thing normally goes very, very well.'

Lillian snorted with laughter. 'I should have done as you said, and written.'

'But you are an actress and can't help making a dramatic entrance. Do not worry, my best beloved girl. I have no doubt that once we explain I am penniless, and then later, that we intend to marry, he will be delighted.' Lillian groaned slightly, while Nikolai looked out of the window, a broad grin on his face. 'My, what a lot of sheep there are in this country. I believed you all were beefeaters.'

Mr Poole, front of house manager of the New Empire, stood on the pavement outside the theatre, hands on his hips, and looked up.

'Right, Marcus!' he called. 'Switch it on!'

For one precious second, the sign above the theatre flickered on and lit the early morning gloom: THE EMPIRE. Then something fizzled and finally the *E* winked out sadly.

Mr Poole sighed. At least he didn't need to worry about the sign spelling out obscenities. That was a blessing.

'Oh, switch the bloody thing off again!'

The surviving bulbs dulled and went out. Mr Poole marched into the lobby and handed Marcus his coat and gloves. 'Thank you, Marcus. I shall call the electrician. Again.'

Marcus, a sharp-faced boy of seventeen and Frederick Poole's apprentice, backed away with unusual meekness. Whenever the sign was mis-firing – and that seemed like most days – his supervisor was prone to be cranky.

Mr Poole waited to be connected, and tapped his fingers on the polished counter top of the box office. The corner of his scrapbook, filled with cuttings about The Empire, both old and new, was sticking out. He straightened it with a forefinger and looked away.

The notices for the opening show had been marvellous, and *Cairo Nights* had played to packed houses for its whole run. Then the reversals, as Mr Poole referred to them, had begun. Mrs Grace Treadwell had suffered an illness, and Mr Treadwell had spent time away from the theatre taking care of her. Those with eyes to see knew she had lost a baby and was taking it hard, but no one spoke of it. More of the day-to-day running of the theatre had been left to Jack's assistant, Darien Burnside. Problems accrued. Then there was the whole farrago with the restaurant.

Like a man who cannot resist pressing on a bruise, Mr Poole opened the scrapbook.

Tutankhamen's Restaurant to Close

Though epicures in Highbridge greeted the opening of Tutankhamen's Restaurant, on the ground floor of the New Empire Theatre with delight, its passing will not be mourned. The unfortunate food poisoning incident last year put the first nail in the coffin of a venture which now seems over-ambitious and under-managed. Now it seems that the celebrated French chef, François Blanchet, misrepresented his qualifications and experience, and was in fact an army cook from Southend. Rumours hinting at his dubious heritage had been circulating among the Highbridge elite for some weeks after he appeared to lose his distinctive French accent during an argument with one of the waiters. We have the greatest respect for army cooks, and Southend, but the repetitive and lazy menu, poor service, and increasingly shabby cooking suggest Monsieur Blanchet was not a good representative of the profession or the place. Jack Treadwell, the inexperienced manager of the New Empire, seems to be losing his golden touch.

Nasty business, that, Mr Poole thought with a sniff.

'Yes, Mr Turnbull? My *E* has gone. Yes . . . Well, obviously there is a loose connection somewhere! But *where*, Mr Turnbull, that is the question!'

Mr Poole's eyes drifted to the cuttings opposite, while Mr Turnbull tried to explain himself.

Grace Treadwell's Play to Close Early.

All Highbridge citizens must share the sting of disappointment felt today by Mrs Treadwell, whose delightful drama 'The Price of Everything' was celebrated in her native city during its run at The Playhouse, but failed to find favour with West End critics. Jason de Witte, tastemaker of the London theatre world, referred to her work as 'the undercooked, adolescent, philosophical musings of a poorly educated provincial young woman, utterly lacking the sophistication necessary for the London stage'. His notice proved a fatal blow, and though the play received a warm welcome from theatregoers, the catastrophic fall off in bookings which followed the publication of de Witte's notice meant the run had to be cut short. We can only hope that Mrs Treadwell treats his opinion with the disdain it deserves, and returns to her desk assured of the continued support of her unsophisticated and provincial admirers at home.

Empire to Close for Two Weeks.

The world of theatre may be all about glitz and make-believe, but sadly no business establishment is immune to problems with the drains. Complaints have reached us that theatregoers' enjoyment of The Empire's lavish entertainments has been hampered recently by some unfortunate odours, and the problems have intensified after this weekend's heavy rains.

The Empire – Further Concerns?

The announcement of the new season at The Empire has met with a lukewarm response. Mr Treadwell seems to have struggled to bring any really first-class shows to Highbridge this year. Have rumours of the continued problems at The Empire reached the ears of London producers?

There were several pages of cuttings of a similar ilk. Mr Poole closed the book again, shuddering a little. Turnbull, the electrician, was still explaining himself with some vigour.

'Of course you need to send someone today!' Mr Poole interrupted. 'We look like we're closed again. The *Gazette* is printing the "assistant wanted" notice— Yes, again . . . and the advertisements for the new prices are on page three this morning! I am expecting a flood of visitors to my booth, and they should be greeted in a fitting manner.' He paused. 'Well, there's no need to take that tone.' Then he hung up. 'Marcus! I need tea.'

Someone cleared their throat and he looked up to see not his apprentice, but one of the messengers from the printing office. He had a parcel trolley with an alarming number of cardboard boxes on it.

'What on earth have you got there?'

'Cardboard boxes,' the messenger said, which was true, but not helpful.

Mr Poole exited his booth, tapping across the mosaic floor, and snapped his fingers, so the messenger, with a grin, handed over his clipboard with the paperwork attached.

'Programme proofs for *Ladies of Grasmere* – excellent,' Mr Poole murmured to himself as he read, then his eyes lit up with sudden enthusiasm. 'And the posters for the pantomime!'

'What are we having this year?' the messenger asked.

'*Dick Whittington*,' Poole said, tapping the man on his arm. 'And we have Harold Drabble for the dame.'

The messenger's grin broadened. 'Oooh, where's my tiffin?' he crooned. 'Why is that funny, Mr Poole? I've never worked it out, but it makes me giggle like a little kid whenever I think of it.'

'The ineffable mystery of comedy,' Mr Poole said wisely, opening the top box and pulling out the programme proof; then he frowned. Something else to add to the list of things to raise with Jack Treadwell, if he wasn't mistaken. The posters, however, looked splendid, and he was signing the paperwork with a vigorous flourish as Marcus tumbled back into the foyer.

'Mr Poole! Mrs Briggs needs a word, and Mr Treadwell is on the prowl backstage.'

Mr Poole blinked, returned the clipboard to the messenger, then pressed his palms together. 'Right! Marcus, get this lot into the lobby storeroom. I'll deal with Mr Treadwell.'

CHAPTER TWO

Jack Treadwell was at that moment creeping along the curtain
wall, stealthy as a ghost, towards the number one dressing room.
He paused at the picture of Lillian, Agnes, himself and Grace, which
had fallen off the wall on the night The Empire reopened. They had
put the picture straight back up again and assured one another it hadn't
been an omen.

Jack noticed a smear on the glass covering the photograph, and
rubbed it off with his sleeve. Mooning at pictures of him in happier times
wasn't going to help – he had a mission to accomplish, and whatever
else was going on at The Empire, he was damn well going to get some
accomplishing done. He steeled himself.

He crept closer to the number one dressing room. Clara Jones, its
current occupant, would still be in bed this early on a Monday morning.
She was a sweet singer, but rather miscast in the present production – a
flashy touring revue which could have done with some songs from Ruby
Rowntree and lines from Grace – and so deserved her beauty sleep. Poor
girl had been sending her love and passion into the half-empty stalls
for a week, and beaming at the desultory applause as if she was getting
an ovation. That sort of performance needed lots of rest – and lots of

steak suppers, too, judging by the bills coming in from the Metropole.

Her dressing room, though, Jack knew, was occupied. An evil influence had sneaked into his theatre and was causing further damage and distress. And Jack, finally, had a chance to do something about it. Ollie, the theatre dog, who was usually so good at identifying and discouraging unwanted visitors, had deserted Jack on this occasion. Jack had remonstrated with him. Ollie had turned over in his basket and huffed. Disappointing, but a man must learn to fight his own battles, and today Jack had the upper hand. He had only a minute before seen his nemesis – his enemy, the subtle snake fighting him for control of the theatre – slip into this very room. Jack had him cornered.

He reached for the door handle and flung it open, flicking the brass switch by the door as he did and flooding the room with light.

'You are trapped, you devil! Surrender!'

His nemesis was at the dressing table – or rather, on it. A large brown rat, sitting on his hind paws, and admiring himself in Clara's mirror while chewing on a stick of vermilion greasepaint.

Jack stared at the rat. The rat stared back. Jack realised that his plan of how to proceed from this point might have been a bit thin on detail. He had always been a man of action, though, and his training from three years of trench warfare in Europe kicked in. He opted for a full-frontal attack and so, with a blood-curdling yell, Jack pounced.

The rat did not flinch. It rather watched with curious detachment as Jack flew through the air towards it, then at the last possible moment, it dropped the greasepaint and skipped nimbly off the dressing table and into Clara's clothes rack. Jack swiped ineffectually at the empty space where the rat had been, then spun on his heel and made another grab for it. The rat skipped up onto the picture rail, just out of reach, and watched as Jack, fully committed but hopelessly unstable, sailed sideways into the rack, snapping it under his weight and dragging down Clara's Act Two ballgown – a feathery-looking monstrosity which was supposed to make her look like a peacock, but had a slight dyed chicken air to it – on top of himself. The broken rail slowly added to his distress as her silk pyjamas, nightclub flapper costume and wedding gown slithered on top of him, too, and then deposited her gypsy shawl over his head for good measure.

Jack floundered in fabric-clotted darkness, every inch of his six-foot frame tormented by aggressive coat hangers.

Jack didn't often lose his temper, but this was too much. Deploying some colourful language, he shoved the silks and satins aside, spitting out feathers and sequins until he could see again, and scrambled for purchase. An attempt to use the upright part of the clothes rack to haul himself up proved ill-judged, and resulted in some light bruising to the back of his head and another uncomfortable encounter with a clothes hanger. He shook his head, slightly dazed, and looked up. The rat was still there, and – Jack would swear it on the grave of his dear adopted mum – the damn thing was sniggering at him.

There followed a lot more language and some fist-shaking. The rat was unabashed.

'Goodness me, Mr Treadwell, what on earth are you doing tied up in Clara's bits?'

The rat, with a final insouciant flick of its tail, disappeared into the shadows, and Jack directed his attention towards the door and the source of the voice.

'Mr Poole! I very nearly caught the rat.'

Mr Poole put out his hand and hauled Jack to his feet. The coat hangers tinkled like cheap triangles as they fell from him.

'Did you now? Well, God loves a trier, Mr Treadwell, so I'm told. But I fear you may have met your match in Harry.'

'Harry?'

'Yes, Danny's named him after the American escapologist, Mr Houdini.'

'Has he?' Jack asked. So Danny was in on the conspiracy, too.

'Yes. Now, do listen . . . It is a tale whispered in most theatres, Mr Treadwell, that in every generation a rat is born who develops an insatiable love of cold cream and greasepaint. I believe I did battle with such a one in my salad days as a man of the theatre.'

'Did you win?'

Mr Poole leant forward to flick a feather from Jack's lapel. 'Not even close, Mr Treadwell. I was trounced.'

'So what does one do?' Jack asked in a despairing tone.

'One buys more cold cream, Mr Treadwell.'

Jack turned to stare at the place where the rat had disappeared. Where had it gone? Was it working with a team of lookout rats? Some sort of huge rat conspiracy gnawing away at the foundations of his theatre, his life! If he could only get his hands on the little—

'Mr Treadwell!'

Jack blinked and turned back. 'I'm sorry, Mr Poole, you were saying?'

'I was saying that the conveniences are blocked in the stalls again and Mrs Briggs's plunger has plunged its last. The smell is beginning to settle, and I think her arthritis is playing up. We need another girl to clean. The printers have delivered the proofs of the programmes for next week's performance of *The Two Ladies of Grasmere*, and Miss Pritchard's name is definitely a shade larger than Miss Gardiner's on the front cover. I've measured them. You know what Miss Gardiner will say about *that*. I have my suspicions that the printers have been corrupted. Apparently something similar happened in Deal and the company almost fell apart. The panto posters have arrived, Sir Toby wants you to discuss the new tram stop on the High Street, and there's a letter in the newspaper saying the old Egyptian restaurant is becoming an eyesore. The final *E* has gone out again, and Mr Turnbull is developing a tone. The Metropole are refusing to feed Miss Clara anything more substantial than a cucumber sandwich till their bill is paid, and I'm closing the gallery for the matinee this afternoon. Most of the audience will be schoolchildren.'

Jack sighed deeply. He was still staring at the clothes scattered around his feet, but Poole could see his mind was running through the reversals, just as his had done. 'We've got ourselves into a bit of a state, Mr Poole, haven't we?'

Frederick Poole was not a man given to gestures of intimacy, but so forlorn did Jack look at that moment, he risked a pat on the shoulder. Even though, with Jack being such a tall young man, he had to stand on his tiptoes a little to reach it.

'Now, Mr Treadwell, we all thought the Egyptian restaurant was a good idea, and I was just as taken in by that cook as you were.'

'Funny how he'd never speak to me in French, now you come to think of it, wasn't it?'

'He insisted he was practising his English, as I recall. And it's not your fault everyone's feeling the pinch these days. How is dear Grace's new play coming along?' Jack's expression made a verbal answer unnecessary. 'That is a shame. That notice *still* troubling her?'

'She can recite it, Mr Poole. Every nasty word of it, a whole year later. "Provincial authoress stumbles on West End stage . . ."'

'And so on.'

'I try and remind her of all the marvellous notices she's had, but it doesn't seem to do any good.'

Mr Poole's eyes travelled over the room. The paint was flaking near the ceiling, and the dressing table had folded theatre bills stuffed under one leg to stop it wobbling. But through it all, they had put on their best faces, convinced the audience they had been transported somewhere out of time and worry, sent them home smiling. Still, backstage the little disasters and compromises seemed to accrue like dust in the corners, and even Mrs Briggs, in all her fervour, could not drive them back. Especially if she had an inadequate plunger.

'Mrs Treadwell is a sensible woman,' Mr Poole said, 'but she is still an artist. And she has suffered blows.'

Grace's first miscarriage had been followed by a second. Again, they did not speak of it, but Mr Poole had charted it in Jack's behaviour. His happiness, then his worried distractions, his renewed absences.

Then Darien had buggered off to Switzerland and the rat had moved in. They stood for a few moments in silence, then Jack straightened his back.

'I'm going to buy a plunger and a really, really good rat trap at Bertram's, then pop into the Metropole with a cheque. Though I'm certain I've already sent one.' He ran his hand through his rather disordered mop of hair. 'Then I'll see Sir Toby about the tram stop at lunch, and speak to the printers on my way between the Metropole and the club. And once I find the account book, we can see about hiring a new girl for Mrs Briggs. Any new applicants for the job of my assistant?'

Poole forced his face into a tight smile as he remembered the various young men and women who had taken one look at the state of Jack's office and fled. 'None who seemed suitable, as yet.'

Jack scratched the back of his neck. 'Maybe the rat put them off. Once we get rid of it, they'll be queuing round the block.'

Mr Poole tried again.

'I admire your pluck, Mr Treadwell. You know I do. But be warned, a theatrical rodent will laugh – nay, scoff – at a conventional rat trap, even a top-of-the-range item. Far better, to me, to come to a sort of reasonable accommodation with the creature.'

'You think Clara will consent to sharing her face cream with a rat?' He pointed at the open jar, with a telltale paw-print on its surface.

The thought seemed to give Mr Poole pause. He picked up the jar and carefully wiped away Harry's signature. 'Perhaps we might persuade her he is a lucky pet?'

Jack gathered up an armful of costumes and rehung them with vigour. 'I'm not prepared to give up so easily, Mr Poole.'

Mr Poole tsked and removed the costumes from his grasp. 'We have to mend the rack first, Mr Treadwell, before we rehang. Now leave this to me, and off you go, if trying a trap will make you feel better.' Jack beamed at him. 'But the WCs, Mr Treadwell . . .'

'Yes,' Jack replied. 'The smell is settling! Thank you, Mr Poole.'

Mr Poole watched him charging off with his head up and a sense of renewed purpose, then turned to examine the clothes rail. He heard a squeak from the corner of the room but didn't turn his head.

'That's enough from you today, I think, Harry,' he said firmly, and after a slight scrabbling sound, he was left to his work in peace.

CHAPTER THREE

'Lillian, it is glorious,' Nikolai said, with a sharp intake of breath.

Lillian felt almost overcome with relief. The drive, the lunch, their arrival on the outskirts of Highbridge had all gone well, but this was the clincher. She had discovered with a shock, as they stepped out of the car, that all her future happiness rested on whether this rather marvellous, exciting, clever man liked a building or not. It was ridiculous, but there it was. She could not be happy with someone who did not love The Empire, and she was rapidly coming to the conclusion that she could not be happy without Nikolai either. She, Agnes de Montfort, Jack and Grace had poured their hearts into the project. It had once been a symbol of her late husband's love for her; now it was a symbol – no, a manifestation – of Lillian's love for her town, for her friends and her newly rediscovered son.

The high frontage of the theatre was faced with white stone, carved with sinuous reliefs suggesting vines. Among department stores and offices, with their pitched slate roofs, it looked remarkably modern, but still part of the city. The theatre was a prima ballerina, looking over her bare white shoulder at the city, supported by a chorus dressed in patterned brickwork. The glass canopy, which extended over the frontage like a tutu, was supported and complemented by cast-iron work in the art nouveau style. Nikolai was right – it was glorious. Only the frontage of the failed restaurant, now shielded with boards painted a dark green, looked a little off. Like a beauty mark on the face of a pretty woman, she told herself bravely, then took Nikolai's arm.

'Wait until you see inside,' she said.

They crossed the road, dodging past a mixture of motor buses advertising cough syrups and Fry's Turkish Delight, and horse-drawn carts piled with hessian sacks and wooden crates full of curious chickens, and Lillian pushed open the double doors to the lobby.

'Mr Poole! I'm home.'

'Good Lord,' Nikolai breathed, looking upwards. The lobby was huge, the ceiling made of delicate interlocking arches growing out of slender green pillars, the floor a smooth progression of marbled tiles in geometric patterns, circles made of squares, squares made of circles, in cream, black, terracotta and amber, and across the ceiling characters from myth and fairy tale, Shakespearean tragedy and antic comedy chased one another across fantastic landscapes. Lillian rarely saw Nikolai speechless. It made her terribly proud.

Frederick Poole emerged from his polished mahogany ticket booth and bowed.

'Lady Lassiter! How wonderfully jolly to see you!'

Lillian introduced him to Nikolai, whose expressions of delight with the interior made him flutter his eyelashes.

'The posters for the panto have arrived!' Mr Poole said, squeezing his hands together. 'We'll be papering the town with them next week, and lodgings are arranged for all the principals.'

Lillian patted him on the arm. 'Thank you so much for arranging that, Mr Poole. It should be the job of Jack's assistant, of course . . .' She hesitated. 'Have we had any more applications?'

Mr Poole snorted. 'Oh, plenty of applicants, but they take one look at the office and turn tail. That Darien . . . I know Mr Treadwell would bounce back if he only had a little more help. And we're in desperate need. I'd even go so far as to say . . .' His breath caught a little. 'Yes, we are in *dire* need, Lady Lassiter! You don't think that perhaps *Mrs* Treadwell would . . .?'

Lillian sighed. 'Grace would come and work here again in a heartbeat, Mr Poole, but you know Jack won't have it. He says she should be writing her next play, not taking messages for him, and he's quite right.'

Mr Poole's face became a mask of dejection. Things must have got worse while she was away. 'I'm home now, Mr Poole! I hope I can lighten the load a little.' He sniffed, bravely. 'We thought we'd catch the second act of the matinee,' Lillian added. She noted a look of nervousness. 'I assume there are seats available?'

'Indeed!' Mr Poole replied in strangled tones. 'Naturally! Only . . . That is, we offered a special for the matinee today, and we have a couple of large school parties in attendance. Nice boys and girls, I'm sure, but they seemed a little overexcited on the way in.' He cleared his throat. 'There has already been a little trouble with sweet wrappers being thrown into the orchestra pit.'

A cheer rose up from beyond the double doors leading into the auditorium, but Lillian, Nikolai and Mr Poole all frowned. It was not the cheer of an audience having a good time. It had a derisive, sneering sort of edge to it. The door opened and one of the ushers, her hair a little untidy, emerged.

'Oh, Mr Poole! Good afternoon, Lady Lassiter. The stage lift has jammed! On a tilt! Poor Miss Jones is stuck fifteen feet in the air halfway through her entrance, and the orchestra have been vamping for five minutes! Little Sam is out visiting his mother in Sheffield, and Pete and Jonah are on stage banging on the thing with rubber mallets, and the little devils in the audience have started throwing apple cores!'

'Where is Jack?' Lillian asked smartly. 'He knows the mechanics almost as well as Sam.'

'The club,' Mr Poole said, looking at his watch. 'I'll send Marcus.'

'But poor Clara!' the usherette said. 'She's up there in her peacock costume being *abused*.'

'I think our tour will continue backstage, Nikolai,' Lillian said. Nikolai snapped his heels together and bowed. Then she turned to the usherette. 'Run round the back, dear, and tell them to bring the curtain down at once.'

Danny, the stage door manager, was waiting in the yard at the back of The Empire, leaning on his cane, with the theatre dog, Ollie, at his heels. One side of his face was covered with a plain white mask, hiding injuries from the war in which he and Jack had served. The other side of his face, when Jack arrived, encumbered with trap and plunger, showed concern.

'How bad is it, Danny?' he asked, heading into the lobby and handing over his packages, then bending over to scratch Ollie between the ears.

'M-mayhem, Mr T.,' Danny replied, and Ollie huffed in agreement. 'Lady Lassiter and some foreign fellow, a friend of hers, are up a ladder trying to free Clara's feathers.'

'Lillian's back? Splendid. What foreign fellow?'

The side of Danny's face not hidden by his mask went a bit pink.

'Some sort of duke, I think. Lady Lassiter brought him up from London.'

'What, as a souvenir?' Jack asked. 'No, never mind. Take care of that plunger.'

He bustled through the 'company only' doors which led off the lobby and into the maze of corridors and staircases of the backstage area, then into the wings.

He stopped dead. The working lights were on, and the tableau they illuminated resembled a Rubens painting Jack had seen in Antwerp after the war, of Christ being fetched down from the cross. Dramatic lighting, taut muscles and tension all over the place – though, of course, Christ hadn't been smothered in peacock feathers.

The stage lift on which Clara was supposed to make her dramatic Act

Two entrance, descending like a goddess on her cloud while the chorus wafted great swathes of white muslin around her, was stuck almost at its highest point, and had tilted. Clara was hanging onto its upper edge, not in any immediate danger of falling, but hardly secure either, and obviously rather alarmed. Pete and Jonah, the stagehands on duty that afternoon, were banging rubber mallets at random points on the zigzag of jointed metal which held the lift aloft. This was doing nothing but further startling poor Clara.

The chorus, such as it was – three men and three women, at least two of whom should have moved on to character roles by now – were clustered at the foot of the lift, their white muslin abandoned, squeaking with alarm whenever Pete or Jonah struck a blow.

A ladder was leaning against the lift, and Lillian Lassiter, in her long buff travel coat and a wide-brimmed black hat, was at the top of it, trying to persuade Clara to take her hand. A dark-haired stranger stood at the bottom of the ladder, holding it steady. He glanced over his shoulder.

'Ah, Jack Treadwell! I am Nikolai. Lillian has freed the feathers, but Miss Jones is a little nervous.'

He released his grip on the ladder to offer Jack his hand. Jack shook it. The grip was restored.

'Understandable,' Jack said brightly. 'Pete, do stop that. It needs a shove on the right quadrant, from under the stage.'

'Clara, darling, hang on!' one of the chorus said in ringing tones. 'The machinery might crush you at any moment!'

Jack would have given the ass a poke with his plunger if he hadn't surrendered it to Danny.

'You lot, back to your dressing rooms now, please.' The speaker looked as if he was going to protest, but caught the look in Jack's eye and edged away. 'Right, Clara, let's get you down.'

The starlet heard her name. 'I can't move – I bloody well can't! I'm shaking that hard, and if I slip I'll break my leg, then I'll starve.' She tilted her head upwards, addressing the ineffable. 'Oh, Mother, you were right!'

Jack didn't have time to ponder her mother's prophetic abilities. 'Some sort of jump mat? Jonah, Pete, go and grab the tumble mats out of the store. Lillian, do come down, and I'll pop up. Clara, I promise I can hold you if you slip, but I'm sure you won't.'

Lillian, who had turned at the sound of his voice and waved, now started her descent. Nikolai put his arm round Lillian's waist to jump her down the last rung with an easy familiarity Jack didn't quite like, but he didn't have time to ponder that either at the moment.

'Afternoon, Lillian. How was London?'

She kissed his cheek.

'Splendid. Now do fetch Clara down.'

Beyond the curtain, the swelling jeers were increasing in volume, interspersed with cackles of laughter. The velvet curtain shivered slightly – a sign of something being thrown against it with some force.

Jack took off his jacket, rolled up his sleeves, then scrambled up the ladder and put out his hand.

'They're going mad out there,' Clara said. The train of her feathered gown was twisted around her ankles, and she was gripping the tilted edge of the lift with white-knuckled determination.

'Don't worry about them, angel,' Jack said in a voice which he hoped conveyed a brisk confidence. 'We'll just get you down, and they'll be lambs again later.'

Below him, the tumble mats were being moved into position either side of the ladder. They had cost a fortune, so Jack was almost pleased to see them in use again. Since he became manager everything in the theatre seemed to have a price tag attached to it, visible only to him.

'I'm frightened,' Clara said, her voice suddenly very small.

Jack took a long breath in and out and the familiar smells of the theatre – sweat, oil, paint and sawdust – steadied him. His feelings of irritation with the lift, the chorus, Pete and his rubber mallet, Clara and the foreign fella all dissipated. At least his job was never boring. He smiled, with genuine warmth.

'Clara, darling, you can't be brave if you're not frightened first, but trust me. Lillian got all your feathers unstuck, so if you just let go, you'll slide ever so gently into my welcoming arms and we'll be laughing about this in an hour. Come on, every accident in the theatre is a funny story just waiting to be told. You know that.'

The jeers had turned into slow handclaps. Jack could just hear a strangled yell from Mr Poole. 'Stop clambering on the furnishings.'

Clara looked him in the eye, and seemed to find some comfort there, because she slowly unhooked her fingers. Jack braced his knees against the side of the ladder and lifted his arms to catch her. She slithered towards him with a suppressed squeak, gathering enough momentum sliding across the top of the lift to make him stagger as she fell into his arms, and for a terrible second he thought he was going to go over backwards. No. His knees held. He steadied himself and Clara wrapped her arms around his neck.

'Got you! Now try not to strangle me and we'll have you down in a jiffy.'

Making his way down a ladder with a nervous girl covered in feathers in his arms proved a challenge. It was that unsettling moment when his and her weight all balanced on one leg and knee, as his other foot felt in the air for the next rung down.

It was at just such a moment that Harry decided to put in an appearance.

'Rat!' Clara screamed in Jack's ear, and pointed. Jack missed his footing and felt the terrible stomach-lurching moment of his fall. With a strange slowness, he half-twisted in the air and found Clara being taken from his arms. He heard Lillian cry out, and then felt a sharp jolt as he landed on his side on one of the tumble mats, at eye level with the rat. He lunged instinctively at it.

'Harry! You devilish little . . .'

The rat twitched its tail at him and exited stage right, as Jack scrambled back to his feet and considered giving chase.

'Oh, thank you!' he heard Clara say in breathy tones, and turned round to tell her it was nothing at all, only to find she wasn't talking to him. It appeared that Nikolai had plucked Clara out of the air, and she was now resting in his arms and staring at him with sudden devotion. He had longish black hair, a neatly trimmed beard and a very well-cut dark suit, and was smiling in a fatherly fashion at the rescued starlet. Jack did not warm to him.

'Jack, dear, are you all right?' Lillian asked, putting her hand on his arm. He brushed himself down.

'Perfectly, thank you. Right, clear the mats please, gentlemen, and let's get this lift moving. Clara, will you be able to carry on?'

Nikolai put the girl down and she seemed to slither, with a certain amount of reluctance, from his embrace.

'Of course, Jack,' she said firmly, then glanced down at her maimed costume. 'Though I might need five minutes to make myself decent.'

Milly, the wardrobe assistant, appeared stage right, her sewing basket over her arm. She took one look at Clara and clapped her hand over her mouth in horror.

'*Ten* minutes, Mr Treadwell,' she said. 'Now come here, pet, and let's sort you out.'

Now what?

Jack felt a slight thrill. There was something exciting about dealing with a real problem for a change, rather than paperwork and plumbing. 'Pete, Jonah, let's get under the stage and deal with the mechanics.'

'Jack, what on earth are we going to do about the audience?' Lillian asked. 'In ten minutes they'll have torn the place apart. And possibly Mr Poole, too.'

She was right: whatever was happening on the other side of the velvet curtain, it had left rowdy behind as a descriptor some time ago, and was verging on the riotous.

'Do we throw them out?' he asked. '*Can* we throw them out?'

'I suspect there would be casualties.'

Nikolai brushed down his sleeves, straightened his cravat, and addressed Jack. 'Your house band is good, yes?'

'The best,' Jack replied.

'Then leave it to me.'

Nikolai squared his shoulders and headed for the curtain. Jack thought of his arm round Lillian's waist, and decided if he wanted to throw himself to the wolves, he would allow it.

CHAPTER FOUR

As Nikolai was straightening his cuffs, Ruby Rowntree, the jewel in The Empire's crown, the musical equivalent of Leonardo da Vinci, Picasso and whoever made the London Transport posters rolled into one, was looking for a pencil. Her friend, former student and now secretary, Tom Lassiter, knew Ruby well enough to interpret that particular frown, as, eyes still staring unfocused into the air between the polished walnut of her upright piano and her nose, she reached vaguely for it.

Tom plucked a pencil from the bristling tin of ones he kept sharpened and ready for such eventualities, and placed it where her fingers would find it. They did, and with a small sniff of pleasure, she plucked it up and set to on the sheet of manuscript paper in front of her.

Ruby had a room dedicated to her use at The Empire, with an armchair, an upright piano and drifts of manuscript paper and hairpins over every available surface. Tom's table was always scrupulously tidy. If a hairpin ever drifted onto it, he simply returned it to another small pot on top of the piano.

'Will you check the proofs of "Midnight Bazaar" for me, Ruby?' he said when she put down her pencil again. 'I'm pretty sure I've caught everything, but there's an accidental on the third page I'm not sure about.'

She didn't answer.

'Ruby?'

She turned with a quick smile. 'Sorry, dear, I was still miles away.' She rested her fingers on the keys. 'I would think, now you have a degree in music, you could decide for yourself.'

She looked as she always had done, ever since she started teaching him to play piano when he was a small boy. She was a slight and short woman, with fiercely red cheeks and her greying hair piled untidily on top of her head. She had always been, in his opinion, quite brilliant, but in the last handful of years she had also made an impression on the wider public.

'I wouldn't dare. You're a rich and famous composer now, Ruby.'

She giggled, turned around and plucked the sheet from his hand.

'Oh no, I don't want that. Strike it out.'

Tom wasn't exaggerating her sudden fame and wealth – not that you could tell her circumstances had changed from looking at her. She wore the same clothes, ate at the same small tea shops and family-run restaurants, and lived in the same boarding house with a strict landlady and an ever-shifting collection of cats. The world was forced to conclude that she lived this way not as a result of genteel poverty, but simply because it suited her. Her two shows with Grace might have led to her being talked about in the same breath as Noël Coward and the Gershwins, but, she said firmly when asked, that did not mean she suddenly wished to socialise with them.

'So have you got another tune for me?' he asked, nodding at the manuscript paper she'd been working on.

'I do! But it needs words.'

'Shall I add a fair copy to the "when Grace is ready" pile?'

Ruby wrinkled her nose. 'Yes, do. It's getting to be quite a large pile, isn't it?'

'It is.'

She sighed. 'Are you busy this evening, Tom? I want a night in the pub.'

'Then a night in the pub we shall have. Where shall we go?'

'How about the Bricklayers Arms?'

Tom had spent most of his gilded youth in the high-end restaurants and nightspots Highbridge had to offer, or playing tennis, but these days he found he had a lot more fun accompanying Ruby to the pubs and working men's clubs of Highbridge. She liked, she said, to smell the sawdust and tobacco in the air, listen to the rhythm of the talk, and after a half pint of porter, she would talk to him about music and melody in a way which made his whisky taste like champagne.

'Done.'

He wrote a note to the publishers of her latest hit, with a summary of the corrections he had made, and pinned it to the sheet in question, then looked up again. Ruby was still frowning with concentration, but she was looking up now, with her head on one side.

'Ruby—'

She held up her hand. 'Shush, Tom. Listen.'

He did. The faintest thread of melody was drifting up from the theatre below them and in through the half-open window, just audible under the rattle of the trams on the High Street. It was a baritone voice, and the melody – the fragments of it they could hear – seemed unusual: something rich and sinuous.

'What is that?' Tom said.

Ruby stood up. 'I don't know, Tom. But it's certainly not the mid-act ballad of *The Sunny Times Revue*. Come along.'

She bustled out of the room and Tom followed.

'One, two, three – heave! One more time, lads.' Jack really put his back into it this time. 'One, two, three – heave!'

Something gave. In the depths under the stage a cog found its groove, and Jack and the stagehands jumped back as the lift lowered with a shudder, then into place with an obedient sigh, just as it should have done half an hour before.

Jack pulled out his handkerchief and wiped the back of his neck and his hands. Now that the heaving was done, he listened for signs of riot out front.

'Did they throw the audience out?' he asked. The men shrugged.

'Jack!' Lillian appeared on the spiral stairs leading back onto the stage. 'Do come and see what's happening! It's a marvel.'

He ran up the stairs towards her and as he did he heard music: a rich baritone singing in a foreign language, with a simple string vamp supporting it like a gazebo supports an explosion of climbing roses in summertime.

Lillian was beaming. She grabbed his hand and dragged him up the final steps, and he found himself jostling shoulders with Danny just inside the high, curved proscenium arch.

Nikolai was out on stage in front of the velvet curtain, singing in the beam of the follow spot, his arms wide. And nobody was throwing anything at him. He ended the line on a long, high note of syrupy richness.

'Did the children leave?' Jack asked.

Everybody shushed him.

'Now, keep going, Mr Porter,' Nikolai said, shading his eyes to peer into the orchestra pit. 'Are you ready, my starlings? Girls first. Same tune – I met my love in the mountains . . .' The children began to sing, with Nikolai prompting them with the words in English. 'Now the boys, please!' Same tune! It is a round, like "Frère Jacques".' The boys were a little unsteady at first, but Nikolai joined them for a moment until they had their confidence back, and the theatre was alive with the threaded voices.

'Good Lord,' Jack said under his breath. Nikolai was conducting the children, beaming at them across the footlights, and the rippling voices swelled as he encouraged first one group and then the other, arms wide. Jack peered out into the stalls. The children were on their feet, faces turned up, singing their little hearts out. Mr Poole was standing in the aisle looking utterly baffled; one of the usherettes was peering out from behind him, a handkerchief to her eyes. In the circle, Ruby and Tom were watching, Ruby leaning forward slightly. Jack thought he could see the sparkle in her eye from where he was standing.

'Well, I'll be . . .!' Clara appeared at his shoulder, her plumage restored. 'How the bloody hell am I supposed to follow that?'

CHAPTER FIVE

Grace Treadwell, playwright, wife of Jack and daughter-in-law to Lady Lassiter, was spending her afternoon knitting. Sort of. If she was absolutely honest, she was sitting in the morning room at Lassiter Court, staring out at the park which surrounded it, with a tangled ball of yarn in her lap.

She shoved the yarn onto the settee, stabbed it with the needles and stared at it reproachfully. Ruby had recommended knitting as a way to relax mind and body so that Grace's creative juices could bubble away unchecked. It had not worked. So far, Grace's only flash of insight had been that she really, really hated knitting.

She crossed to her desk – optimistically arranged by Lady Lassiter's butler, Fenton Hewitt, each morning, with clean paper and pens, a full ink pot and a small vase of flowers – and stared at it. Next to the desk sat the waste bin, which Hewitt discreetly emptied every night. Grace sat down and picked up her pen, unscrewed the lid, and the nib hovered over the cream foolscap. The house seemed to hold its breath. *Act I, Scene I*, she wrote. *The comfortable living room of Mrs Angelina Carstairs. A young man in evening dress, Jimmy, is pacing back and forth across the stage.*

She stared at the words she had just written. *What does 'comfortable' even mean?*, she wondered. *Comfortable for whom? Should Angelina have a* comfortable *living room or a* luxurious *one? Actually, would she call it a drawing room? Could it have a mezzanine level?*

She crossed out 'comfortable' and 'sitting room'. Jimmy was a bit of a boring name. She put a line through that, too. The page now looked more of a mess than her knitting. She groaned, screwed up the page, threw it in the bin, and started again. *Act I, Scene I.* Half an hour later, those unimpeachable words were still alone on the page. Eventually she abandoned words altogether and drew a series of rabbits instead, innocently going about their bunny business while a fox peered at them from the edges of the page. The fox, she realised, had the look of a certain London critic. She drew a drop of drool, hanging from the fox's jaw.

This was no good. She needed something to happen.

She closed her eyes and spread her fingers out over the paper, trying to conjure it into existence – the important *something* that would shake them all up, would shake her out of this tight, miserable rut.

Tyres crunched on the gravel outside. She put the cap back on her pen and looked out of the window. Lillian coming back from London was welcome, but not the really important something that Grace needed. She went out into the hall and Hewitt opened the door, so Grace walked out into the chill, damp air. Lillian stepped out of the driver's seat, as elegant as ever in a purple day ensemble under her fawn cape, in time to receive her daughter-in-law's embrace.

'Lillian, darling! How was town? How is Evie, and how is her show going? We must have tea and you can tell me everything.'

'Good afternoon, Grace! Tea would be lovely, and town, Evie and I are all very well.'

It was only then that Grace realised Lillian was not alone.

The passenger door of the car opened and out stepped a handsome, broad-shouldered man in his mid-forties. His hair was rather long, and very dark, his features aquiline, and he wore a loosely tied black silk cravat around his throat. In spite of the cravat and the hair, there was something military about the way he carried himself. He would, in form and figure, be an excellent illustration of the word 'dashing'. He smiled at Grace, showing perfectly white teeth, and the corners of his eyes crinkled charmingly.

'Grace,' Lillian said, indicating her companion with studied carelessness, 'allow me to introduce His Excellency, Grand Duke Nikolai Goranovich Kuznetsov. He is going to be our guest here for a while. Nikolai, this is Grace Treadwell.'

Grace blinked. This was certainly something.

'I have heard you are a very clever writer, Mrs Treadwell,' Nikolai said, approaching, then taking both her hands in his and shaking them. 'I, too, am a wordsmith. I so like that phrase "wordsmith" . . . so evocative of the process, banging them out in the dark one by one, like sword blades.' Grace looked up at him. He was as tall as Jack, and his eyes were very dark. 'We shall drink to the Muses together late into the night, you and I, Mrs Treadwell. I shall teach you the folk songs of my homeland, and we shall smash our glasses into the fireplace and summon Virgil himself from the flames.'

He said all of this while still holding her hands.

'Oh, are you Russian?' Grace said. *Perhaps Jimmy could be Russian*, she thought. *And not called Jimmy.*

Nikolai shook his head. 'No, my dear lady, I am from Marakovia. It is a beautiful country, full of romance and mountains, palaces and peasants. We are steeped in the most marvellously tragic histories. A gold mine for writers.'

He grinned, and Grace was decided. She liked him very much.

'I'm sure Grace would love the folk songs, Nikolai,' Lillian said. 'But shall we start with tea? Hewitt,' she added to the hovering butler, 'I hope you are well. Would you see to that, and then to the luggage? His Excellency will be staying in the green bedroom.'

Nikolai finally released Grace's hands, then offered his arm to

Lillian and accompanied her into the warmth of the house, while Grace scampered to keep up with them.

'Have you been to the theatre?' she asked, as Nikolai handed his hat to Gladys in the hall.

'We have,' Lillian said. 'Jack's bought a new rat trap and Nikolai prevented a riot.'

'Oh,' Grace said. 'Mr Poole's speech about the theatre rat didn't work, then?'

'Apparently not.'

'Wait a moment . . . Did you say Nikolai prevented a riot?'

'Tea, Grace,' Lillian said, passing her cape to the maid, 'and we'll tell you all.'

CHAPTER SIX

Some hours later, and a mile west of The Empire, in an attic room over the Bricklayers Arms, Sally Blow looked out of the window over the slate roofs and the moon rising, as fat as butter, over them, and shivered. Not that it was cold in her room – the coals glowed in the fireplace – but you could see winter coming in the air now. Blink and it would be Christmas, with all the fuss and fun that brought. The moonlight made the damp slates shine. A laugh, bouncing off the brick and cobbles up to the room, made her smile, then she twitched the curtains closed.

She was proud of the curtains. She'd run them up herself on Belle's machine, and the cotton was yellow with little blue cornflowers, so even when the day was dreary, they brought a little sunshine in with them.

'Not all the way, Mum,' said a voice from the bed.

''Course not, Dougie,' she said, and pushed them apart a little way so the glow from the street lamp could make its way in, then turned round to her son. He looked so small in the bed by himself, though some nights he'd toss and turn so much Sally was sure he was made of elbows.

'Now you get settled while I make myself pretty.'

He scooted down under the blankets and Sally seated herself at the table and brushed out her hair, listening to his breathing. He'd had an asthma attack that afternoon, and though she'd dosed him with light cod liver oil and spread Angier's Emulsion on his chest, he still sounded a little wheezy. And he wasn't giving her cheek, either, so he definitely wasn't himself yet. At least now she had the money to buy the potions and salves which helped him. Yes, life was a lot easier than it had been when she'd met Belle and Alfred outside The Empire two years back. She liked working for Mrs Parsons in the grocer's, and the five shillings and tips from singing on Fridays and Saturdays in the bar meant most weeks she had a shilling or two to put aside. They had this room in the attic above the pub, too, at a keen price, and the good cheer coming up through the walls made it cosy.

'What will you sing for them tonight, Mum?'

'Whatever they ask me to,' she said, plaiting her hair with quick fingers and pinning it up. It was an old-fashioned style, but Noah, her husband, had liked it; she could almost feel his hand on her shoulder as she slid the last pin into place. 'Lively ones early on, then something soppy at the end of the night. Got any requests?'

Dougie had the blanket pulled up to his nose. He shook his head. He was pale as the sheet. Had the Angier's Emulsion helped at all?

Chin up, Sally Blow.

She squinted into the mirror and pinched her cheeks to get some colour into them, then turned down the lamp.

'You'll leave the door open, so I can hear a bit?' Dougie asked. When she drew breath to answer, he rushed on. 'There's no draught, not really, and I like to hear you sing.'

'All right, then.'

She left the door open a crack. The light from the first floor leaked up and into the room and fell on a single dried rosebud in a thimble-sized vase. The one Lancelot Drake had given her outside the theatre that night. The Rose of Highbridge. Sally shook herself a little. Of course she'd been teasing with Alfred then, funning about her fancy car and her name in lights, but some small part of her had believed it. And yes, things were a thousand times better now, but . . .

People come to hear the songs, not me, she thought as she walked downstairs. They liked her well enough, but if another girl came to lead them into the choruses, they'd ask after Sally once, shrug, and then enjoy themselves as much as they ever had.

As she reached the bottom of the stairs, she put her smile on and lifted her chin. Alfred spotted her.

'Here she is! Sally, love, do you know "I'll Show You Around Paree"? Request from Bert.'

'The old Vesta Tilley one? I might make up a few of the words, but I know the chorus.' She came into the bar behind him, then ducked under the bar and headed for her corner, nodding at the regulars.

'All right, Johnny? How are you going, Fred? How's the grandkids, Marsha?'

She had her spot under the window by the piano. No sign of George today. She raised an eyebrow back at Alfred and he shrugged. Damn, they got better tips, no doubt, when he was along to bash out a few chords.

She lifted her hands. 'I'm on my own tonight, ladies and gents, so how about we all get warmed up with a favourite?'

She launched into 'Oh! Mr Porter', a cheeky silly tune with a chorus everyone knew, and it got them started. Lots of familiar faces in the crowd. Funny how even in a town the size of Highbridge, different wards had different populations. This was the corner where the railway workers and tradesmen lived – a different crowd from her old neighbours, who all worked at the Lassiter factories and lived in houses owned by the company. The thought of the day she'd got her eviction notice, the day after her husband's funeral, caught her out, and she almost missed her words.

Sally sang for an hour, then had a port and lemon at the bar. It was a busy night, foggy with warm bodies and pipe smoke, bursts of laughter, cries and cheers round the dartboard, and the late autumn winds cooling their ankles whenever the doors to the street opened and closed. As she sipped her port, Sally noticed a man in a flat cap, sitting alone and drinking his pint at a corner table. He had a thin face, with a long nose and deep-set eyes, but what was remarkable was the space everyone gave him in the busy bar. No one rested their drink on his table, or asked to share it, and the people near him seemed to avoid even looking in his direction. She leant over the bar as Alfred came close.

'Who is the bloke on his own behind me, Alf?' she asked, keeping her voice low, though she couldn't say why she did.

The landlord hardly had to glance up, and when he replied, it was in a mumble.

'That's Mr Sharps, Sally. Ray Kelly's man.'

She felt a shiver of fear. No wonder people were steering clear of him. Ray Kelly had his finger in every pie in town. Wherever there was fear, violence or corruption in Highbridge, you caught a glimpse of him, like the stench of sulphur the Devil leaves behind him.

'He came in last week when you were singing, too,' Alfred added, then he carried his freshly pulled pint over to a waiting customer.

Sally glanced back in his direction. Sharps was looking straight at her.

She finished her drink, and returned to the silent piano for another hour. Sharps stayed until the end, not cheering or clapping or singing along – just watching; then he got up and left while the rest of the crowd were still cheering.

It gladdened Sally's heart to see him go. She had her second port and lemon, trying to catch the eye of anyone slipping out without dropping a penny or two in her tin. Alfred called last orders and the crowd started to thin out.

As they did, Sally noticed a tall young man, dressed like a gentleman, with sandy hair swept back from his forehead, sitting in the snug with an older lady. He was watching her through the rippled and engraved glass.

Had he been there for her set? By the look of him, he could drop a crown in her tin and not bother about it. Sally was wondering about sashaying over there and rattling her tin right under his nose, when he got up and made his way towards her through the people leaving. Yes, definitely a gentleman. What was he doing in a place like the Bricklayers Arms?

He dropped a coin in the tin. He was too quick for her to see what it was, but it made a good hard *thunk*.

'Thank you, sir,' she said. 'Come again!'

The man nodded and looked as if he was going to turn away, then changed his mind. He was quite young, Sally realised – like her, nearer twenty than thirty – with high cheekbones and nice eyes.

'You have a lovely voice, Mrs Blow,' he said.

'So do you,' she replied, and blushed. She hadn't said it to be smart, but rather because it was true. His voice was light and warm and smooth, as if someone had polished it with beeswax. He smiled, a bit shy and off balance at that.

'I wonder . . .' He paused. 'What do these songs mean to you?'

She shook her head, confused. 'They mean what they mean – no great mystery about it.'

'But what do they mean to *you*?' He looked terribly serious as he said it. 'I've listened to lots of singers in my time, Mrs Blow. Not half of them had as pretty a voice as yours, but the ones who became really great, they sang songs that . . . When they sang them, you felt like they'd just sprung free from the core of them. You couldn't imagine anyone else ever meaning that song the way they did.'

Sally felt herself blushing again, as if he'd seen her in her dressing gown and curling papers, and sipped at her port. 'You mean they acted them out?'

He shook his head. 'Didn't even have to move a muscle. They chose tunes which meant something to them, and lived them inside out. Made it feel as if there was no distance, no space between them and the song, between the song and you. Listening tonight, I thought how wonderful it would be if you found a song like that.'

He seemed to realise he was looking at her more intently than was strictly polite, and put out his hand. 'I'm Tom, by the way.'

'You a musician, Tom?' she asked, shaking it.

'Sort of. I love music – I arrange it, I play it. But I don't create it. Sorry, you're very talented and it's none of my business. Just my friend over there . . .' He nodded to the older lady in the snug. 'She's a real musician, and when she's been talking to me about music, I get all het up. You understand what I mean?'

Lord, what lovely eyes he has. Sally realised she was still holding his hand. She released it quickly. 'I do, Tom,' she said quietly.

'Well, I hope you find a song like that, Mrs Blow. It'd be a thing to hear.'

'I'll think about it.'

Then, with a nod and a wave, he wandered off; the older woman he was with had stood up and was waiting for him. She had cheeks like apples. A musician, he'd said. Sally wondered who she was. Then Mrs Parsons tapped her on the shoulder to ask if she could come into the grocer's early on Tuesday, as she had an errand in town, and by the time Sally had agreed to it, the gentleman with the beeswax voice and the older lady were gone.

There *was* a song.

Sally said goodnight and took her tin upstairs, emptying it out on a napkin by the light of the low-burning lamp, so as not to wake Dougie. He had tied himself into a knot in the blankets, but there was a bit of colour in his cheeks now and his breathing sounded easier. She moved the coins about with her fingertip. A good night, and a crown piece in there. She'd lay odds that was from Tom. Sharps hadn't left anything; she hoped that was a sign he didn't mean to come back.

That song. It was a sentimental ballad she'd learned off her own mother when she was not much older that Dougie, about having a hole in your heart where your man should be. It had wound its way round her heart and hands in the hours and weeks after her Noah was killed. An angry, painful jewel of a thing, a thousand miles away from the sort of cheerful tunes and soupy old favourites she entertained them with downstairs. She tided the coins away into the old cigar box which held her everyday money, put the crown in the beaded purse with a drawstring her mother had given her the Christmas before she passed, and started singing it to herself.

When I feel the cold, when the mist
runs down the hills, the ghost of Johnny D
puts his hand on my shoulder
and I'm struck with what couldn't be.

She sniffed and thumbed the tears away from the corners of her eyes. 'What does he know?' she whispered. 'This Tom, who's seen lots of singers.'

She unbuttoned her good blouse and hung it over the door of the wardrobe to air, stepped out of her skirt, smoothed it flat, and sat at the chair to roll down her stockings.

Oh, what use your fairy gold,
what use grape and grain,
when my chance to have a heart that's full
can never come again?

She put out the lamp and got into bed, teasing free enough blanket to cover herself without waking her child.

They say I'll see him in Heaven
But what good is that to me
when the mist quiets the streets
and there's no place I can flee
To escape poor Johnny's ghost
And the grief and the old oak tree.

She'd give Tom back the crown in a heartbeat if he'd take the thought of that song back with it. She shut her eyes, and whether she wanted it to or not, the song sang her to sleep.

CHAPTER SEVEN

J ack looked out over the park from the window of the private sitting
room he shared with Grace on the first floor of Lassiter Court. The
moon was bright, reflecting off the frost on the grass, and turning
the bare trees into Gothic silhouettes.

'Get me a whisky, Jack, would you?' Grace said from the settee in front
of the fire. She had her feet tucked underneath her, and a shawl over her
shoulders. 'I need something to steady myself after all the excitement.
What a life Nikolai has lived!'

'I'll join you.' Jack twitched the curtains shut and went to the drinks
tray.

Clara had followed Nikolai's improvised intermission with aplomb,
and the children in the audience had been as good as gold for the rest of
the performance. Jack had stayed late at the theatre to make sure there
were no more problems with the lift during the evening show, then
returned to Lassiter Court to find his wife and mother swapping
stories with Nikolai – or rather, His Excellency, Grand Duke Nikolai
Goranovich Kuznetsov – over a splendid supper, and both looking
happier than he'd seen them in months. Even the servants seemed giddy
at the idea they had an actual duke to serve boiled greens to. Jack had

smiled and nodded away then, but in the privacy of their sitting room, his smile had grown ragged at the edges. He'd lived quite the life, too, after all. Serving in France, years in a prisoner of war camp, then working in Paris till he drifted back home, wandered into The Empire with a vague message from his late adoptive mother, and had been seized by the theatre bug. He'd found love, and his natural parent. He and Lancelot Drake had saved a girl from a burning theatre and almost got cooked in the process. That was as dramatic as anything Nikolai had done, wasn't it?

Grace was looking at him. 'Don't you like him, Jack? But you like everybody. What on earth do you have against the poor man?'

It was an uncomfortable question. He hadn't actually *said* anything against Nikolai. He handed her her drink and took his place on the settee next to her, his arm round her shoulders. She was still waiting for an answer. He wasn't sure he had one to give.

For a start, he thought, he didn't like *everybody*. He liked most people, that was true. But he did not like, for example, Sir Edmund Lassiter, grandson of the man who had built this lovely house in which he was living, and any number of factories around Highbridge. He didn't like Edmund's mother, Constance, either. Admittedly, after that Jack was a bit pushed to think of anyone who made his hackles stand up the way Grand Duke Nikolai did.

And he couldn't say why. Not because he didn't know, but because he was aware that it made him sound petty and childish. In the years since Lillian and he had discovered they were mother and child, he had been the apple of her eye. She was not effusive, and was respectful of the memory of his adoptive parents, but Jack had felt the diffused beam of her love and pride washing over him in a consistent and comforting manner. He had sensed it had shifted away from him slightly during the shenanigans at the theatre in the afternoon, and in the evening he had come home to find he was definitely sharing it with the oh so charming Nikolai. And his wife – his very own wife – was charmed by this man, too. He'd done everything he could to cheer and encourage Grace through her troubles

– their troubles – and she'd been terribly brave, but for the last year he'd sensed a veil of sadness round her. It made him feel as if he couldn't see her properly, and it broke his heart. Then when he'd come home and found her deep in conversation with Lillian and Nikolai about all the latest plays in London, she'd looked almost like her old self again.

He was irked, and felt badly for being irked. Nikolai's wholehearted, intelligent and sympathetic understanding as Lillian talked about the drains, the dwindling box office receipts and the damned restaurant, had irked him further. The irkedness compounded and made him itch.

'You *don't* like him,' his wife said. 'Honestly, Jack . . .'

He removed his arm from round her shoulders and leant forward, glowering at the carpet.

'Don't tell me I'm being unreasonable. I know I am. But the man swans in from God knows where—'

'From Marakovia.'

'Which is almost the same thing, and he's witty and well-read and energetic and horribly talented. You should have heard him on stage, Grace. I haven't seen anything like it for years. And you and Lillian obviously think he's marvellous.' He swallowed his whisky too quickly. 'I can't trust him. If he's so wonderful, why did they throw him out of his own country?'

Grace put her hand on his cheek, turning his face towards her. 'You know perfectly well why. He was supporting democratic reform, despite being an aristocrat. Gosh, he's put your poor nose out of joint, hasn't he?'

'He's probably just after Lillian's money.'

He regretted this as soon as he'd said it. One of the perils of being married was learning to recognise, with painful clarity, tiny expressions of irritation on one's beloved's face. He saw one now. Grace removed her hand, and his skin felt strangely cold without it.

'Nonsense,' Grace said stoutly. 'That's a despicable thing to say, Jack, and you know it. Lillian is a very beautiful, very clever woman and she has a spine of steel. If it wasn't for the scandal around your parentage getting out, she'd have had every man in Highbridge proposing to her.' That stung him. 'I'm very pleased she met Nikolai. And he's so fascinating!'

None of this was making Jack feel any better about Nikolai, or Marakovia.

Grace got up, taking his empty glass from him, and poured them both another drink.

'And I'm not sure Lillian has very much money anymore,' she continued, more gently. 'The Corot that was in the dining room has disappeared. I think she sold it to keep this place going. The theatre is just scraping by, and it's not like I'm bringing in any money.'

'I just wish she hadn't gone on so about the troubles at the theatre,' Jack said sulkily, accepting the drink. 'It made me feel about twelve.'

Grace wrinkled her nose and handed him his glass. 'Lillian doesn't blame you, darling. It's not your fault Darien was a liability, or the fact you've had all the building's teething troubles to deal with. She thinks you've been doing a magnificent job, considering. So do I.'

Something about that 'considering' made Jack feel very small.

'Then you've had me to deal with,' she added as she sat down. He set his glass aside and took her hand in both of his.

'You, my darling, matter more to me than everything else in the whole damn world. I am never "dealing" with you. My greatest ambition is to be half the husband you deserve.'

Grace rested her head against his shoulder, and her voice became a little clotted. 'I have taken you away from things, though, Jack. I know I have. I should have been braver about the play, and the babies.'

He wrapped his arms around her and held her close, feeling that horribly familiar shudder in her frame which meant she was crying a little. After a few minutes, she shook herself and put out her hand. Jack gave her his handkerchief and she blew her nose.

'You've been unwell, Grace. I wanted to look after you.'

'I have to pull myself together.'

'You don't have to do anything.'

She groaned. 'Yes, I *do*. I do think I'd feel better if I could at least write. Then at least I'd be making something, and I think then waiting for babies wouldn't be so hard. But I just keep hearing that notice in my head, then when I stop doing that I'm exhausted, and that's when all the sadness sort of falls in on me. I keep thinking of everyone else who has children and it makes me sick with envy. It's like being stuck in a whirlpool.' He closed his hand around hers. 'Honestly, I practically threw myself at Lillian when she and Nikolai arrived. His stories were a lovely distraction. Are you sure you don't want me to come and work at The Empire again?'

He leant forward and kissed her. 'You hired me the first day I turned up at the theatre. I can't have you there as my assistant. I just can't. You're a marvellous writer, Grace. It would be terribly wrong to take you away from that.'

'But, Jack . . .'

Her eyes looked huge in her pale face.

'Please just keep writing,' he said.

She sighed and settled against him. 'I wish it was that easy! You know today, before they arrived, I sort of prayed for something to happen. I need to . . . Oh, I don't know what I need. I hope it's talking to Nikolai about theatre, because it certainly isn't knitting.'

He took a long swallow of his whisky. 'Good Lord, Grace! That's a dangerous wish.'

She bit her lip, a glimmer in her eye.

'Yes, I suppose it was, but Jimmy was making me desperate. Still, if it's just a glamorous Marakovian coming to visit, that's not all bad, is it?'

Jack tucked a stray lock of her hair behind her ear and let his hand rest on her shoulder. 'As long as it stops there, I'll cope.'

CHAPTER EIGHT

The bookseller looked up with exaggerated slowness from the heavy, leather-bound volume on the counter in front of him.

'Ah, it's you, Ambassador Taargin,' he said with a certain sort of breathy reverence, once his confusion at being interrupted by a possible customer at this late hour had subsided. 'Good evening. Christian and Ilya are upstairs.'

A squall of wind drove the soot-stained London rain against the window. The bookseller slid off the stool, crossed the room between teetering but dusty piles of books, turned the sign on the door to closed, and lowered the blind on the darkness.

The man who had entered – a middle-aged gentleman of military bearing, with a salt-and-pepper moustache – tapped on the volume the bookseller had been studying.

'Anything interesting?'

'A collection of folk tales. Rather macabre, but some powerful imagery. I'll make tea, sir.'

'Do.'

'And may I be so bold as to enquire . . . Are the royal family well?'

Vladimir Taargin nodded. 'The king remains in good health . . .'

He paused. 'Considering his age. And the crown prince is as energetic as any young man.'

'And the king's brother?' the bookseller asked quietly.

Taargin smiled more warmly. 'Andrei rides every day. An inspiration.'

'I am very glad to hear that,' the bookseller said, lowering his gaze.

Taargin walked past the desk and climbed the uncarpeted stairs to a dingy room on the first floor. The two men waiting for him were seated on a pair of distressed dining chairs by a similarly scarred round table, empty but for a candle in a glass lantern, which cast wavering shadows across the walls. One man seemed to be of a similar age to the new arrival, though was more solidly built. The other was considerably younger, and both had that air which seemed to imply a uniform, even though they were in civilian clothes. They stood as Taargin entered and removed his leather gloves, his eyes travelling over the piles of books stacked in columns of varying heights like a ruined temple, mouldering into dust against the cobwebbed walls.

'He is bringing tea,' Taargin said, and went to the window. 'Do sit down.'

The unpleasant weather was to their advantage. Londoners scurried between the street lights along Charing Cross Road in search of shelter, so anyone pausing to watch the bookshop would have been easy to spot. Taargin was reassured. They waited in silence until the bookseller creaked up the staircase with a tray. Once the cups had been placed on the rickety table and the bookseller had absented himself again, he spoke.

'Kuznetsov has left for Highbridge.' He stepped away from the window and took the last available dining chair. 'Ilya, your information was correct. He has formed a liaison with this former actress, Lillian Lassiter, who owns a theatre in the city.'

The older man, who looked like a walrus, huffed like one, too. 'A man of royal blood. Taking up with an actress. I did not want to believe it.'

'It is distressing,' Taargin replied, 'though I do not know why we should continue to be surprised by the company he keeps.

'Perhaps we are finally rid of him, and he will rot in the English provinces,' the walrus added hopefully.

Taargin crossed his legs and drank his tea, his little finger carefully extended. 'I pray you are right, Ilya.' He shook his head. 'His ideas may wither without his rabble-rousing but we must encourage people, including our dear prince, to forget him. Or learn to hate him. That would be even better.' He set down his cup. 'And perhaps quicker.'

'Do you believe, sir, that Crown Prince Stefan is still fond of Kuznetsov?' Christian, the younger man, asked.

Taargin pursed his lips and placed the tips of his long fingers together, studying the dusty floor. The smell of decaying knowledge in the room made his nostrils flare.

'Stefan has not spoken his name, has not breathed a word of social equality, meritocracy or democracy, since Kuznetsov left the country.'

'That is a good thing, isn't it?' Christian said.

'Dear boy, a dwindling interest would be welcome, but this sudden change in the prince . . . it smacks of concealment. His rooms are searched daily for seditious literature, those close to him are watched for signs of sympathy with these dangerous beliefs. However, as yet we cannot pierce the veil and look directly into his mind. I have fears. I have doubts.'

He saw them reflected in the faces of the two other men.

'And there is the matter of Stefan's visit to this country in the summer,' Christian said. 'I understand the Prince of Wales intends to ask Stefan to accompany him on a tour of England.'

Taargin nodded. It had taken a great deal of work to place Christian at St James's Palace, but the information he procured was invaluable. 'What sort of tour?'

'Factories, schools, shipyards,' Christian said. 'Mention has been made of both Newcastle and Sheffield.'

'Keep me closely informed, Christian,' Taargin said. 'Sheffield is too close to Highbridge to be comfortable. This trip is ill advised, but the king will not forbid it for fear of offending the royal family here.'

'The General Strike in May ended in a victory for the ruling class,' Ilya said softly.

'The revolutionaries instigating it were handled with kid gloves!' Taargin snapped. 'The stain of socialism has leaked from Russia across our mountains, and lapped up on the shores even here.' He controlled himself, and finished the lukewarm tea in his cup. 'Nikolai Kuznetsov is a danger to our nation, and I dread to think what might happen to our poor country if the crown prince comes to the throne while still under his influence. Our friends will watch him in Marakovia. We shall keep watch here, and do all we can to show Nikolai in his true colours.'

'What if that does not work, sir?' Ilya asked, his voice low and heavy. 'What if on this visit—'

Taargin lifted his hand. 'We have a duty, my friends, to our country beyond anything else. We did not bleed on the battlefield to hand our lands to a rabble. I say again, we have friends, we have purpose. I pray we are never forced to choose between the prince and our country, but if that day comes . . .'

'For Marakovia,' Christian said.

'For Maravovia,' Ilya echoed, his voice hollow.

'Indeed,' Taargin replied darkly, and the shadows around them seemed to thicken.

CHAPTER NINE

'No, Grace, you shall have to explain it to me again. I think you are teasing me.'

Nikolai stared at Grace over his half-moon reading glasses, the script of *Dick Whittington* open on his lap, wearing an expression of profound bafflement.

'Now you are laughing at me, which is no way to teach a poor student!' He held up his hands. 'Start from the beginning. It is a Christmas entertainment, yes?'

Grace set down her teacup. The morning light, sparkling with frost, poured in through the windows of the morning room in Lassiter Court, over Grace's deserted writing desk, the wastepaper bin, the pale Turkish rugs on the polished parquet floor, the elegant art nouveau furnishing, and lapped around her neat ankles.

The week since Nikolai had arrived in Highbridge had passed very quickly. Lillian had taken him on tours of the local beauty spots, and he had found time to sit and discuss the theatre with Grace. Grace discovered that talking about writing was a great deal more fun than actually trying to do it, and as they talked she found herself beginning to uncoil creatively, just a little. She had been like a spring wound too tight, she thought, locked solid with the tension.

With rehearsals fast approaching, their topic today was pantomime, which Nikolai found a great deal more challenging than Chekhov or Ibsen.

'Yes, we open on Boxing Day – that's the day after Christmas – and hopefully we'll run until at least the end of January. Mid-February, perhaps, if it goes really well. The director is Archibald Flynn. He's directed a dozen pantos in the North-West over the years, it was an absolute coup to get him, and we have Terrence Fortescue as choreographer.' Nikolai nodded. 'Lillian has got Josie Clarence as the principal boy and Harold Drabble as the dame. He's marvellous. "Ooh, where's my tiffin?" Then there's King Rat, of course. He's marvellously evil, the children love him apparently, and Fairy Bow Bells. Gordon, who will play Alderman Fitzwarren, will double up as the King of Zanzibar.'

Nikolai leant forward, positioning himself on the edge of the green leather sofa, his brow deeply furrowed. 'This is very strange. I believe you are still speaking English, but I find once again I am at a loss to understand *many* of the words you are saying. And I do not think Zanzibar has a king.'

'Oh, that doesn't matter.'

'It might to the people of Zanzibar.'

'I doubt they'll hear about it,' Grace said. 'Panto is a British tradition. The key thing is just not to think about it too much.'

'That will be hard,' Nikolai said seriously. 'I think too much about everything.' He rubbed his hand over his neatly trimmed black beard. 'Lillian has promised she will attempt to teach me frivolity, but I am not sure even she could do that. Director and choreographer . . . These words at least I can comprehend, but the rest?'

Grace smiled.

'Remember, the principal boy is a girl and the dame is a man. The story's based on a fairy tale, or a folk tale, in this case, but always involves lots of local gossip and everyone talks to the audience. That script you have there is a sort of guideline. And it's mostly in rhyming couplets.

Oh, the audience talks back, too, and joins in with some of the songs. In *Dick Whittington*, Dick and his cat sail off to Zanzibar and save it from a plague of terrible rats, then return so Dick can marry his true love, Alice, in the nick of time and save his old boss Fitzwarren from bankruptcy.'

'This sounds . . . highly experimental,' Nikolai said doubtfully. 'I have believed my own work was avant-garde, but it appears I have been outpaced by pantomime.'

'They are always trying something new on stage, so I suppose it is experimental in a way. No two shows are the same. But it's as old as the hills, too.'

'Fascinating,' he said, his rich voice seeming to come up from his boots. 'Fascinating.'

The old front doorbell sounded with a clang, and Nikolai glanced at his watch.

'Ahhh, it is time for my interview! I am to meet a Mr Wilbur Bowman, as I am an "Interesting Visitor to Highbridge".' His dark eyes twinkled. 'Will I like him, Grace?'

Grace smiled. 'Yes, I'm sure you will. Wilbur is an old friend.'

Hewitt showed Wilbur into the room, and Grace settled in the window seat while the two men talked. She half-listened, and half-read the translation of *The Cherry Orchard* that she and Nikolai had been meaning to discuss before they got caught up by pantomime.

It was one thing to think about plays in the abstract, but as they had talked about the panto, she had seen herself walking the passageways of the actual theatre: heard the chatter coming from the rehearsal rooms, the scraps of song, the sawing and hammering coming from the workshops; seen the bundles of costumes; smelt the sawdust and starch. She felt a deep pang under her ribs. The Empire was *her* theatre. Surely Jack could cope with having her back as his assistant? Yes, he wanted her to write, but she was beginning to feel as if he had, in an excess of delicacy, exiled her.

'Marakovia is a wonderful country, small, but poised between many great nations,' Nikolai was saying, waving one of his black Turkish cigarettes in the air. 'We export plum brandy and romanticism, what little we do not consume at home.'

Wilbur made a note, then asked. 'Isn't it rather unusual for an aristocrat like you to become involved in the theatre?'

Nikolai shrugged.

'My family would have preferred a military career for me, that is true. But the heart wants what it wants, Mr Bowman. My mother was a very clever woman and gathered the most gifted and artistic of our people around her, so my youth was full of books, ideas, dreams – the sort of things military men tend to hate.' He laughed softly and Wilbur's pen scurried across the page. 'I was educated in Paris before the war, then Germany after it, then in 1920 I returned to Marakovia with a mission to bring fresh ideas of modernity and democracy to the people of my country, through drama and song.'

'And am I right in thinking, sir,' Wilbur asked, 'that you are a cousin of the current king, and have always acted as a sort of uncle to Crown Prince Stefan? He is quite a young man, I believe.' He flicked back a page in his notebook. 'Only twenty-two.'

'That is correct.' Grace blinked while Nikolai tapped the ash off his cigarette. She had had no idea that Nikolai was that close to his country's royal family.

'Crown Prince Stefan is due to visit England next year,' Wilbur said. 'Do you intend to see him while he is here?'

'I would always be delighted to see Stefan,' Nikolai said, and Grace abandoned Chekhov entirely. 'But his uncle, the king's younger brother, does not approve of me. I am certain, however, that Stefan, when his time comes, will always lead his people with wisdom and kindness.'

Wilbur's pencil bounced across the page.

'That's interesting, Your Excellency, but you didn't answer my question.'

'Do call me Nikolai.'

Wilbur smiled slightly. 'So, Nikolai, is it fair to say your efforts to share the ideas you gathered abroad with your people met with . . . some resistance?'

'Not from the people, nor from Stefan.' Nikolai put out his cigarette, got up from his chair and wandered over to the window, his hands in his pockets. 'Stefan came, in disguise, to several of my performances.' He turned round, frowning. 'Though I would rather, for his sake, you did not say that in your newspaper.'

Wilbur's pencil hovered over his pad. 'I might say he seemed supportive of your efforts?'

Nikolai nodded. 'Yes, you may say that.'

'Are you a communist?'

Nikolai laughed out loud, which made Grace jump, and Chekhov slid to the floor.

'No, dear boy, I am a democrat, a meritocrat! I believe in offering children a free education, for example, and opening up the institutions of my country to people without an illustrious pedigree such as my own, but I am no communist.'

'But it was your ideas which led—'

'Yes. These modest proposals of mine . . . The king's brother saw in my attempts to lift up the lower classes of my country, not ambition and fellowship, but sedition. He forced the king's hand. I was ordered to cease my writing, my play-making, or leave the country. I chose to leave.'

The sun was casting its last rays outside the window, outlining him with a slightly melancholic glow. Grace sighed.

'And now you're in Highbridge?'

'I am!' Nikolai beamed suddenly and spread his arms wide. 'What a wonderful city you have! So many places of culture and learning, such lovely scenery.' Wilbur said nothing and kept writing. 'I am ambitious to try something here myself, but first I shall immerse myself in the study of this extraordinary theatrical form you have here – the pantomime.'

Wilbur's pencil slipped.

'You want to study panto?' he asked, blinking.

'Naturally,' Nikolai said. 'It is remarkable, democratic, daring, improvisatory.'

You haven't lived, Grace thought, until you've heard someone say 'improvisatory' with such relish in a Marakovian accent.

'Lillian is producing *Dick Whittington*,' Nikolai went on, 'and I have begged to be allowed to watch rehearsals. I am certain I shall learn a great deal.'

'"Ooh, where's my tiffin?"' Wilbur murmured under his breath; then he closed his notebook and returned it to his pocket. 'Thank you, Your Excellency – my apologies . . . Nikolai. That's all I need. My editor will love that bit about you studying pantomime. If the photographer could visit you perhaps this afternoon?'

'Why not take the photograph at The Empire?' Grace said. 'Perhaps Nikolai could stand next to one of the new posters for *Dick Whittington* with Lillian and Jack.'

Nikolai beamed. 'An excellent idea, Grace!'

'And no doubt Mr Treadwell would be glad to see the poster in the paper,' Wilbur added with a slight smile, and Grace blinked innocently at him. 'No, that is a good notion, Mrs Treadwell.'

'Shall we go now?' Nikolai said. 'You can put your bicycle in the back of Lillian's car, Mr Bowman, and I shall drive you in.'

Wilbur agreed, and within a few minutes the two men were waving goodbye from Lillian's car as it disappeared down the driveway. Grace watched them go, her fingertips on the glass of the window, the longing to go with them so strong it made her bones ache.

CHAPTER TEN

M r Poole watched the photograph being taken: Lady Lassiter looked particularly lovely in a dark green day ensemble, and Nikolai beamed as they stood either side of the *Dick Whittington* poster. Jack's smile looked a little forced; then he immediately disappeared into the bowels of the theatre with a long to-do list and a harried expression. Lillian offered to show Nikolai the initial designs for the panto set in her office, Wilbur and the photographer returned to the *Gazette*, and Poole finished the tally of tickets sold for the previous evening's performance. A respectable house for the first night of *The Two Ladies of Grasmere*, but not spectacular.

He sighed, and felt an answering draught of wintry air as the door to the lobby was opened and closed. He looked up to see a young woman in a long tweed coat and gold-rimmed glasses stepping hesitantly into his domain. Two circle seats for 2/6, for her and a girlfriend, he thought.

'Good morning, miss! And how can I help you today?'

'My name is Bridget Chisholm,' the girl said, coming towards him. He revised his thinking. People coming in for tickets seldom gave their names. 'I've come to enquire about the assistant's job.'

Poole blinked. The last advert had resulted in not one single enquiry to date. He had begun to fear every qualified man or woman in the town had already applied, taken one look at Jack's office, and fled. 'Have you indeed?'

He ran an assessing eye over the young woman. Neat. A pleasant, round face with not too much powder or paint. Good clothes, modest but tasteful, and her red gloves were a nice touch. Showed a bit of personality. She opened her handbag. 'I have references from my previous employer in Leeds, naturally. Should I leave those with you, Mr . . .?'

'Poole, dear. I'm Mr Poole.'

'I assume I need to make an appointment for an interview with Mr Treadwell. I meant to write, but as I was passing the theatre, I thought I'd enquire first to see if the situation is still available.'

Miss Chisholm spoke with confidence and in an educated voice. Poole's hopes began to rise. He attempted to quash them – they had been dashed too often before.

'You might assume that. If you aren't in a rush, Miss Chisholm, perhaps you might have a cup of tea with me while I peruse your credentials.' He smiled. 'Marcus. Tea!'

Poole invited the young lady to take a seat on one of the polished benches in the lobby while he read the papers she handed him. The credentials looked promising: shorthand, typing, bookkeeping! Yes, this looked very promising indeed. So did Miss Chisholm herself. She didn't chatter or fidget as he shuffled the pages and read the very warm letter of recommendation, just looked around the lobby with a pleasant smile on her face. She thanked Marcus for the tea in a civil manner, and didn't slurp or smack her lips over it either.

'And what brings you to Highbridge, Miss Chisholm?'

'My former employer retired, and I fancied a change from Leeds. I heard Highbridge was a little smaller, but quite lively.'

'Do you have family here?' he asked.

'No, Mr Poole. I'm one of these independent women you hear about.' A twinkle in her eyes, too! 'My mother lives in Leeds, and we're fond of each other, but get along even better when we're not under each other's feet.'

Mr Poole had read about these modern women, and thought, as the father of daughters, that they sounded like a jolly good thing.

'You'll understand, Miss Chisholm,' he said after finishing the letter, 'that a theatre is an unusual workplace.'

'Naturally, Mr Poole,' Miss Chisholm said, setting down her teacup neatly on the little tray on which Marcus had delivered it. 'And some unusual characters, too, I should imagine. That must be very interesting. It sounds rather fun. Hard work, obviously,' she added, 'but I do enjoy a challenge, and there must be fresh ones every day in a theatre.'

Mr Poole's hopes suddenly shot so high, he could barely breathe.

'When might you be able to start?'

She looked a little surprised. 'Well, at once, Mr Poole. I have an interview with Lassiter Enterprises this afternoon, and another at Bertram's tomorrow.'

Lassiter Enterprises should not have her, Mr Poole decided. No, nor Bertram's, neither. *Be still, my beating heart!* he told himself. He must show her the task that lay before her; then, if she did not quail, he would bloody well hire her himself.

'Perhaps I should give you the tour and show you the offices, Miss Chisholm, as you're here.'

He fetched the keys from under the counter, then paused, remembering what the offices had looked like the last time he had put his head round the door. Mrs Briggs had stopped even trying to clean in there in mid-1925. It might be best to prepare Miss Chisholm a little. 'You aren't of a nervous disposition, are you?'

She stood up. 'I'm not. Is there a ghost or some such?'

'Oh, the theatre ghost is a dear stick,' Mr Poole replied brightly, 'and we were delighted that he decided to continue haunting the new theatre. His appearance is always a sure sign of a hit show.'

He led Miss Chisholm through the lobby doors into the auditorium, slowing his pace so the young lady could admire the luxurious fixtures and fittings. She looked up at the chandelier and mosaic of the Muses and smiled, then wrinkled her nose.

'What's that smell?'

Mr Poole picked up his pace. 'We haven't seen much of our ghost in the last year, I'm afraid. Not that the shows have been bad, but they've lacked a little fizz. And everyone is a little nervous about opening their purses at the moment.'

'But if the ghost is not a problem, why did you ask if I am of a nervous disposition, Mr Poole?

He decided to be honest. 'I only wanted to prepare you a little for the office itself. It's been sadly neglected since young Darien abandoned his career in theatre management. Well, it was sadly neglected before then, too.'

He opened the door from the stalls into the west stalls promenade, then escorted her up the narrow marble staircase which led to the manager's office suite, and the entrance to the royal box and retiring room.

'I'm not afraid of hard work, Mr Poole,' Miss Chisholm said firmly.

Mr Poole whispered a silent prayer that she would not go running off in a panic, turned the key in the lock of the outer office, and shoved it open with his shoulder.

Miss Chisholm followed him in, and for a second or two they contemplated the scene together.

It was worse than Mr Poole remembered. It looked as if a bomb had gone off in a very well-stocked library. Papers, envelopes, scripts, printers' proofs and correspondence of every sort was scattered over the furniture and silted in piles on the floors. The filing cabinet drawers were extended and overstuffed with unopened packages, and in one case what looked like a part-drunk bottle of whisky.

'Mr Poole,' Miss Chisholm said, in an admirably steady voice, 'I'm not going to find the body of Mr Treadwell's last assistant buried in here somewhere, am I?'

Mr Poole could understand why that might be a concern.

'No, we had a postcard from Darien a month ago. He's in Switzerland. He's taken up alpinism.'

Miss Chisholm frowned. 'You found a postcard in all this?'

'He addressed it to the front office.' She hadn't yet fled. Mr Poole thought this encouraging. 'Will you take the job?'

She raised her eyebrows. 'I don't need to meet Mr Treadwell, or the owners of the theatre first?'

Mr Poole thought of the offers she might receive from Lassiter Enterprises or Bertram's if he were to let her slip away at this point.

'You've seen the office and neither fainted nor burst into tears. Your letters of recommendation are fulsome. I am . . .' He trembled at his own bravery. 'I am confident that Mr Treadwell would wish me to hire you immediately.'

'You're very kind. Where is he?'

'Most likely backstage trying to outfox a rat.'

Miss Chisholm inhaled sharply, then shook her head. 'Suppose I make a start at once?'

Mr Poole's heart fluttered in his chest and he pressed his hands together. 'That would be wondrous. Would you like another cup of tea, Miss Chisholm?'

She set her handbag on the floor and removed her gloves.

'Yes, I think I should.'

Mr Poole heaved a sigh of relief and backed out of the room. 'Take that, Lassiter Enterprises,' he whispered, and went to make the tea himself.

Some hours later, Jack pushed the door open, stared for a second, then closed it again to check the name on the door. Yes, it was definitely his office. Well, this room was, strictly speaking, the domain of the manager's assistant, where Darien had refused to ply his trade. Jack's own office led off the back of it, but he hadn't managed to get that far in a month.

Darien's increasingly erratic filing methods had turned the whole room into a churned-up mess of uneven surfaces which had reminded Jack uncomfortably of no-man's-land. It did not look like that anymore.

He could see the carpet, for a start. And the assistant's desk was clean and empty – just the typewriter in its cover, and the telephone. There was still a lot of paper about, but much of it seemed to have been corralled into neat piles along a previously unnoticed bench under the window. It was as if Cinderella's helpers had been through with a bucket of fairy dust and a strong work ethic.

The door to his private office opened, and a young woman with round glasses emerged and smiled at him.

'Mr Treadwell, I presume? I'm Bridget Chisholm. Mr Poole hired me as your assistant this morning. I hope that's acceptable.'

Jack was still somewhat dazed by the sight of the carpet.

'Absolutely marvellous. Good Lord, you must have been working like a Trojan to get all this squared away so quickly. I'm delighted to meet you.'

He put out his hand and she stared at it. That made him look, too, and remember – for the first time since the sight of the carpet had so flummoxed him – that he was somewhat encumbered by a dangling melange of string and wood.

'What is that, Mr Treadwell?'

'Oh, it's my rat trap. A top-of-the-line model! But Harry, the scoundrel, just ate through a couple of wires at the back and the whole thing collapsed. Then he snaffled a nice bit of Stilton I'd laid in there as bait. Just yanked it out of the wreckage and swanned off without a care in the world.'

Miss Chisholm was frowning in concentration. 'Am I right in concluding, Mr Treadwell, that Harry is a rat?'

'That is correct,' Jack replied, looking around for somewhere to drop the remnants, but a little afraid he might antagonise her by doing so. 'A theatre rat.'

'If the rat has developed engineering skills, Mr Treadwell,' she said, a hint of amusement in her voice, 'perhaps you should be careful to avoid antagonising him.'

'To live in fear,' he declared stoutly, 'is not to live at all.'

Miss Chisholm shook her head. 'May I ask where you bought the trap?'

'Bertram's,' Jack replied mournfully. 'Haven't even paid for it yet. On account.'

Miss Chisholm nodded, then picked up her coat from the rack in the corner of the room and put it on. Jack felt a brief surge of panic. 'Are you leaving? I don't suppose the rat will bother you, unless you bring a lot of cold cream into the office.'

She hung her handbag over her arm, slipped on her gloves, then put out her hands.

'No, Mr Treadwell, I'm going to return the trap to Bertram's before they close and see The Empire's account isn't charged.'

'You will come back, won't you?'

'I will, Mr Treadwell, if my terms are acceptable.'

'What are they?' Jack said, knowing he'd fight tigers to keep her.

'Two pounds ten shillings a week.'

'Yes! Agreed.'

Miss Chisholm took the collapsed remnants of the trap carefully into her arms. 'Perhaps if you have some time in the morning you might explain a few things to me, Mr Treadwell. I'm afraid I couldn't make complete sense of the office diary.'

'Yes! Delighted to. We shall have buns at eleven, to celebrate your arrival.'

She smiled again at the mention of buns, and Jack's heart sang like a blackbird's on the first day of spring.

He bowed to her as she left, then popped into his private room, which lay to the rear of the larger office.

It turned out there was a carpet in there, too. With five minutes available to him and a sandwich to sustain his animal functions, Jack dashed off a letter to the *Highbridge Gazette*, under an assumed name, wondering if the arch-rivalry between the leads of *The Two Ladies of Grasmere* would be apparent in their performances this week, and if the citizens of the town would be able to resist being drawn into the feud on one side or other.

CHAPTER ELEVEN

Another week passed; the winter began to close in round Highbridge. Cold winds rushed down the dale, tearing the last dead leaves from the trees, and long sleety showers made the shoppers on the High Street dash between the storefronts. Even Lassiter Court took on a rather grey appearance, as if hunching its shoulders.

Grace had got her wish. Something had happened, but whatever intellectual jolt Nikolai had supplied, it had not been enough to get her working. The pages on her desk remained either empty, or filled with aimless doodles. Then Jack had come home, fizzing as if he'd spent the whole afternoon drinking champagne, and announced he had a new assistant and apparently she was absolutely marvellous.

Lillian and Nikolai spent the next day at the theatre, and returned to join in the chorus praising Miss Chisholm's work and her efficiency. On her second day she had found a large uncashed cheque, and worked her way through enough of the accounts to assure Jack that Mrs Briggs could have a new girl to help with the cleaning. Jack's stirring of rumours about the rivalry of the leads in the new play had led to what he referred to as a 'tasty' boost to the box office of *The Two Ladies of Grasmere*, and he was confident the second week of the play would do even better than the first. Grace had smiled, and gasped at the stories of Miss Chisholm's brilliance and initiative, and felt spectacularly miserable. She reluctantly admitted to herself she had been hoping Jack would relent and let her return to her old job. No chance of that now that Miss Chisholm had arrived to warm every winter's day with sunshine. She also knew that feeling sulky about the new arrival was no better than Jack feeling sulky about Nikolai. She had the unpleasant feeling of being hoist with her own petard.

A car horn sounded outside, and Grace got up and looked through the window, expecting to see Nikolai and Lillian returning from their latest outing.

The car approaching at high speed down the gravel drive was not Lillian's tourer, but a bright red Bugatti. It was approaching at breakneck speed when the driver wrenched the wheel sideways and stood on the brakes at the same moment, narrowly avoided the stone lions guarding the turning circle and swung to a stop, spraying gravel in all directions.

Grace walked into the hall as Hewitt opened the door, and Stella Stanmore, star of the West End stage, who had made her name performing in *Riviera Nights*, Grace and Ruby's first triumph, swung herself out of the driving seat and, moving almost as quickly out of the car as she had within it, ran towards Grace. She looked as if she was dressed for a nightclub rather than a drive, in a sheer silk evening dress with a white fur coat over her shoulders, and gold high heels.

'Grace, darling! I've come for a visit. I am welcome, aren't I?'

Grace opened her arms and received the embrace. 'You're always welcome, Stella, but what on earth are you doing here?'

'Oh, I decided I was desperate for some country air.' She turned her most show-stopping smile to the butler. 'Hewitt, dearest, I have a few things in the boot.' She threw her car keys in his direction and Hewitt, without moving a muscle more than necessary, grabbed them out of the air and handed them to the maid at his side.

'Please fetch Miss Stanmore's things and take them to the Blue Room, Gladys. Would you like some tea, Miss Stanmore?'

'Haven't you got anything stronger?' Stella glanced around her. 'Oh, it's morning, I suppose.'

Grace still had her arm around Stella. 'Darling, you're freezing! Have you been driving all night?'

'Yes, I . . . It was rather spur of the moment.' Gladys was removing two cases from the tiny boot of the sports car. Knowing the amount of luggage Stella normally thought essential for even the briefest of stays, Grace thought they looked rather inadequate. 'I should have told you I was coming. I'm a goose. I shall go away again.'

'You'll do no such thing,' Grace said, worried now. 'Hewitt, I think eggs and toast for Miss Stanmore, please, and one of those astonishing hot brandy drinks Mrs Young always makes me have when I have a cold. A large one.'

'Very good, Mrs Treadwell. On a tray in the drawing room, perhaps? The fire is lit.'

Hewitt stepped aside, and Grace guided Stella up the stone steps and into the hall, keeping hold of her arm until they were in the drawing room and Stella was deposited in an armchair in front of the fire.

'I'm sorry just to charge in like this,' she said, 'but I was terribly bored with London. Night after night and all the same faces, and I thought, what on earth am I doing? Lillian said I'd always be welcome at Lassiter Court, and perhaps Jack and Grace would like to see me and I could sit in your lovely sitting room, Grace, and read a few books. I'm told reading is wonderful once you get the taste for it. Do you have horses? Perhaps I could ride one. And shooting things?'

Hewitt arrived with a steaming glass and a tray with a domed lid over it. Grace mouthed her thanks, but Stella hardly seemed to notice him.

Grace picked up the brandy toddy and put it into Stella's hands.

'Stella, you can do all the riding and shooting you want to, though

I don't think you'd like it very much, but please do tell me – what on earth is wrong?'

Stella folded her thin hands around the glass and drank. A little spot of colour came back into her cheeks. Then she curled forward and began to weep. Hewitt discreetly replaced the silver dome over the eggs to keep them warm, and withdrew while Grace pulled out her handkerchief and put her arm around Stella.

'Oh, Grace, it's an absolute horror.' Her voice quivered. 'There was a girl, and the newspapers are saying I killed her!'

It took nearly an hour before Grace managed to get an idea of exactly what had happened. As she pieced the story together from Stella's random and distracted utterances, she persuaded her friend to finish the toddy, eat some of the eggs and get into a hot bath in her private bathroom. As Stella warmed herself in the huge, free-standing tub, a soup of soapy bubbles and misery, Grace sat on a stool beside her, and occasionally passed her the second half of the second toddy.

'So this girl Tasha was a nightclub dancer, Stella?'

'Yes.' Stella wiped her eyes and trailed her hand about in the water. 'At The Manhattan, then at The 43. It isn't one of the nicest clubs, but they let us in there at all hours, and she sat at our table once and we started chatting. She was a sweet little thing. She hadn't had much luck, but always tried to be cheerful about it.'

Grace passed her the toddy. She drank.

'Poor Tasha,' Stella went on, passing it back. 'She would fling herself at everyone involved in the theatre.' Stella wafted the bathwater around with her hand. 'I realised she was taking cocaine to help with staying up all night.'

'Cocaine, Stella?'

'Oh, it gives you the most terrific energy boost!' She sank lower under the water again. 'But one has to be careful. And Tasha wasn't.'

'And she had a heart attack?'

Stella was weeping now, perfect tears running down her cheeks as she talked. 'I think so. Found dead in the bathroom at her boarding house on Sunday afternoon, the poor thing. They had to break the door down. The police came and found her stash. She had a whole bottle of the stuff and was making it into packets to sell. They gave the news and her picture to the newspapers and, of course, they thought it was *Christmas.* "Nightclub dancer in sordid tragedy."'

'But why, Stella, is anyone accusing you?'

'Oh, I'm turning into a prune. Pass me my robe.'

Grace got to her feet and fetched the robe from the back of the door. If Stella had a robe, she hadn't packed it, but Hewitt had put one of Grace's on the back of the bathroom door. Stella stood up, her back to Grace. She was so slight, but the lines of her shoulders and steep curve of her waist made her look powerful, rather than weak. A dancer's body, and full of so much talent and just a little wildness. Grace held out the robe, and Stella took it and slipped it over her shoulders as she stepped out of the bath.

'We were friends. I took her to lunch a couple of times, and I suppose most theatre people knew we were friendly.'

Grace put her arms around her friend and rested her cheek on her shoulder.

'I'm so sorry, Stella.'

'It was the one thing the newspapers needed to really make the story pop,' Stella said, gently freeing herself and taking a towel from the neat pile on the stool beside her, then throwing it over her damp hair. 'One of the greasy monsters was at the stage door when I came out last night. Set off his flash bulbs before I even knew he was there, then shouted at me about corrupting a poor innocent girl. "Was it you who gave her the drugs, Stella?" That sort of thing. It was horrible.'

She paused and turned to look out of the window. Grace simply watched and waited.

'The first editions came through when we were in Argyll Street, recovering. I'm afraid I rather fell apart and I—'

'Leapt into the car and drove up here?'

Stella nodded. 'Do you think Lillian will mind terribly?'

'Of course she won't. Did you talk to anyone else? Your agent, or the police?'

Stella shook her head, her eyes large and frightened. Grace sighed. 'Stella, go to bed and sleep. Lillian is at the theatre with Jack, and I'll call your agent and tell her where you are.'

'I *am* tired as hell.' Stella walked out of the bathroom and threw herself down on the bed. The wintry light from the high windows fell across her, the shadows of the panes slicing her into little pieces.

'Don't worry, darling. We'll look after you.'

Grace left the room and closed the door softly behind her. Stella was crying again, but more quietly now. Grace rested her fingers on the door for a moment, then sighed and made her way down into the hall. The incomparable Hewitt was waiting for her.

'Hewitt, I shall call Miss Stanmore's agent, and perhaps we'd better call the theatre and see if we can find Jack and let him know what's happening. Has *The Times* come this morning?'

'I've put it on the desk in the morning room, Mrs Treadwell,' Grace could see from his expression that he had read it. He cleared his throat. 'Mrs Young and I are fond of Miss Stanmore. Is there anything she requires?'

Grace sighed. 'I'm guessing from her packing she'll probably need quite a lot. Ask Gladys to raid my wardrobe for a few things suitable for country living, will you?'

Hewitt nodded and withdrew, and Grace returned to the morning room, pushed her page of foolscap aside, and unfolded the newspaper.

CHAPTER TWELVE

Jack hung up the telephone receiver and picked up his own copy of the newspaper, then hissed between his teeth. Poor Stella. It made her sound like a monster.

Jack whistled.

'Well, I'll be b—'

'Marcus!' A call came up from the street, and Jack recognised Mr Poole's voice. 'The bloody '*I* has gone now! Fetch the stepladder, pronto!'

The last time Mr Poole had tried, in an ecstasy of frustration, to deal with the wayward signage himself, he had ended up dangling from the art nouveau ironwork extending over the balcony. Jack threw up the window, and leant out.

'Mr Poole! Hold hard! Let me come and have a look.'

He bounced down the stairs and by the time he reached the pavement, Marcus had positioned the ladder under the *I*, and was waiting for him with an expression of wide-eyed respect on his sharp little face that Jack was beginning to think was satirical.

'Right then, you hold the bottom, Marcus,' Jack said, and looked up. The chilly wind which ruffled his blond hair smelt of damp coal, then around the corner came a young man, a suitcase in his hand, wearing a shabby coat and a rather battered fedora. Jack turned and found the man gazing at him with frank curiosity – the sort of frank curiosity which seems to necessitate some sort of response.

'Our *I* is gone,' Jack said, waving upwards.

The young man approached. He was clean-shaven, and looked to be about Jack's own age, with very dark eyes, pale skin and a slightly sunken look. He smiled, and the sudden warmth it gave to his features made Jack blink. The man set down his suitcase on the pavement and looked upwards.

'Would you like me to take a look?'

Jack was dubious that this stranger could tangle with the strange complexities of the sign which had so befuddled Turnbull, the electrician, for years now, but Miss Chisholm had restored, to some degree, his faith in humanity.

'Be my guest, Mr . . .'

'Wells – I'm Dixon Wells,' the young man said vaguely as he looked upwards, rubbing his hand over his chin. 'Are you Jack Treadwell?'

'Yes, I am,' Jack supplied, and the young man abandoned his chin to shake his hand.

'I saw your picture in the newspaper.' He looked at Jack for a long moment, frowning, then seemed to shake himself out of his reverie. 'I'll need a spanner, and probably access to the area behind the sign.'

'Of course,' Jack said. 'But are you sure you know what you're doing? It's not a pleasant day to be scampering up ladders, either.'

'Oh, yes. I know about wires and current at any rate. Generally, I'm a little bit more at sea.' Dixon looked up at Jack with a searching gaze. 'I don't mind the cold, and I'd be very happy to help you.'

Jack knew better than to look a gift horse in the mouth, and the state of the sign couldn't get a lot worse, so, with an admonition to Marcus to keep a close and solicitous eye on their new friend, he retreated out of the cold.

*

Jack didn't want to go too far while the stranger guddled around in the electrics, so he bought a box of macaroons from the bakery and idled in the lobby, catching up with Poole and hearing about the achievements of his brood of daughters, then discoursing on the virtues of Miss Chisholm, whose mix of good sense and sass was making Jack's days considerably brighter even as the evenings drew in. Their pleasant discussion was only occasionally interrupted by muffled banging coming from above their heads. Having an assistant who actually assisted was a revelation for Jack. He felt as if, after years of trial, he was becoming imbued with almost godlike powers. Every morning he arrived at The Empire and found a neat summary of his diary, calls he should make and 'matters arising' on his desk, correspondence to read and check – often with a suitable reply typed out and attached with a paper clip to the original.

The feeling he had had for the last two years – of being constantly on the back foot while vaguely aware there was something absolutely crucial he had forgotten – lifted, and he felt as if he were floating. There was time to think. Time to be inspired.

The staff of The Empire, both front of house and backstage, had also embraced Miss Chisholm, but were slightly afraid of her, as were the theatre's suppliers. It was a marvel. Rather than making Mrs Briggs rely on the new plunger, Miss Chisholm had discovered the name of the original plumbers, and an insurance policy on the works which resulted in the stalls smelling sweeter than summer meadows without causing further damage to the bank account.

Jack and Mr Poole had hardly began to rehearse the many wonders of Miss Chisholm when they were interrupted by the reappearance of Dixon Wells.

'The *I* is working,' he announced.

'That's marvellous, Mr Wells,' Jack said, and introduced the two men, but Mr Poole smiled with world-weary sadness.

'Indeed, Mr Wells,' he said. 'I do appreciate your efforts, but I'm afraid your success will be short-lived. The minute the *I* is back on, the *M* goes. It's a hellish cycle.'

Dixon removed his damp and shabby hat, and held it in front of his chest. 'No, no, I think it should be good now. The original wiring was rather bodged, I'm afraid. A pigeon looking at it funny would have been enough to set something off, but it's happy now.' He sounded apologetic. 'If you want to try it out, you can step out on the pavement and check. I can flick the sign on and off a few times.'

Jack and Mr Poole exchanged glances, then skirted the ticket booth and stepped out onto the pavement together, as suggested. They stared up at the sign, and Jack gave Mr Poole the nod.

'On!' he called.

The sign flickered into life – complete, constant, and somehow rather brighter than it had ever been before. Mr Poole gasped.

'Off!' Jack said.

The sign blinked off.

'Now is the real test,' Poole said, his voice trembling with anticipation. 'On!'

A moment of suspense, then THE EMPIRE shone out in all its glory.

'Oh!' Mr Poole pressed his palms together, and Jack laughed. 'Oh, my goodness! Off! On! Off! On!'

The sign obeyed. They hurried back into the lobby and took turns at shaking Mr Wells's hand very hard.

'You're a miracle worker!' Jack said. 'A saint among men!'

'Are you a Highbridge man?' Mr Poole said eagerly. 'I do not think I've seen you at the theatre, but you do seem a little familiar.'

Dixon scratched the back of his neck. 'I've just arrived in Highbridge.'

His face went slightly pink. Jack had taken some time to settle back into life after the war, and wondered if this man was in a similar sort of position – though how he had washed up in Highbridge was a question for the Fates.

'Are you in need of work, Mr Wells?' he asked. 'I'm sure Turnbull would give his right arm to have a man of your skills on his staff. Though I'm not sure we shouldn't just hire you ourselves.'

'I don't need work, but I've always thought a job would be nice,' Dixon said, and offered up that remarkable smile. 'I'd like to spend some time here, if I may.'

Jack blinked, and he looked the man over again. The battered hat and coat suggested abject poverty, but perhaps they were, in fact, actually the strange shabbiness sometimes affected by those who were very wealthy indeed.

'Then a job you shall have. Go over every wire in the place. Mr Poole will grant you access and introduce you to our lighting people.'

'But first, Mr Wells,' Mr Poole said, his voice heavy with emotion, 'I *insist* on you having a macaroon.'

Jack went out once more to admire the glow of the sign in the hazy afternoon then returned to his office to find Miss Chisholm sorting through yet more piles of paper. Her concentrated efficiency gladdened his heart.

'The sign is working,' he declared.

'How marvellous,' she replied with genuine pleasure. 'Did Mr Turnbull—?'

'No, we've had another stroke of luck. An itinerant electrician has appeared like a fairy godmother, waved his spanner as a wand, and we're all aglow. Appropriate with panto season almost upon us,' he replied, tossing his hat and feeling a performer's pleasure as it landed neatly on the prescribed hook. 'His name is Dixon Wells.'

'Where did he come from?'

'Fairyland, obviously. I've told Mr Poole to let him loose on the whole building. You'll see him about.'

He sat down on the chair in front of her desk and crossed his long legs.

'Shall we have a run-through, Miss Chisholm?' She nodded and picked up her pad. '*Ladies of Grasmere* closes this week, then we have a show that's having its pre-London try-out next week while the rehearsals for the panto get into gear, then we go dark to prepare for the show. Technical rehearsals and set building till Christmas Eve, then the first show will be on Boxing Day. By the way, Lillian will be having a party at Lassiter Court on Christmas Eve. Can you arrange for a charabanc to bring the cast and crew up from the theatre? I do hope you'll be joining us as well.'

'I should be delighted.'

'And Stella Stanmore is staying with us. Seems there has been some sort of bother in London. We'd rather keep it out of the papers, so if anyone calls and enquires . . .'

'The Empire has no comment on the whereabouts of our dear friend, and we join with all of the theatre world in mourning the tragic death of the young lady in question . . .?'

'Exactly. So you've read the newspaper, then?'

'Of course I have.'

The telephone rang and Jack watched with a sense of blissful ease as Miss Chisholm picked it up.

'The Empire Theatre, Mr Treadwell's office,' she said, in a voice which exuded calm and efficiency. Then a tiny frown appeared between her brows. 'I'm sorry, you have lost whom? Of course I know who that is – he's due to start rehearsals for the panto next week.'

CHAPTER THIRTEEN

The song was still nibbling at Sally Blow.

She enjoyed working in the grocer's shop up the road from the Bricklayers Arms. She'd come in early and sweep out while Mrs Parsons had her breakfast, then be busy all day weighing up the fruits and vegetables, twisting the paper bags full of beans and radishes, and on Fridays Mrs P. would give her a good deal on anything that looked as if it wouldn't last over the weekend.

When she had come in that Tuesday morning, though, Mrs Parsons seemed much less disposed to chat than usual. Sally wondered if the increasing chill was making her rheumatism flare, so she'd shrugged her shoulders, taken her apron from the hook on the back of the door and got busy with the broom. She needed to keep busy, what with the song bothering her, and then Mr Sharps had turned up again on Friday night at the Bricklayers Arms and he, without doing anything, bothered her too. He'd arrived half an hour before she started and left again after her last song, when the crowd were still clapping. Every time his eyes rested on her she got a chill in her bones.

It was only at the end of the day, after the factories had let out and the girls who worked in the mill had been through, picking up odds and ends for their suppers, that Mrs Parsons cleared her throat.

'Come into the kitchen, Sally. Have a cup of tea.'

Sally had hardly ever been into the kitchen. For the most part, she had her bread and cheese at lunch in the storeroom, among the bags of flour and sugar. Mrs Parsons liked to keep her privacy, so there was something in the air.

Mrs Parsons poured, and pushed the cup and saucer towards her.

'Sally, dear,' she said, 'you've been ever such a good worker.'

Sally's stomach flipped. 'Thank you, Mrs Parsons.'

'So this pains me,' Mrs Parsons went on, her eyes fixed on a little ceramic donkey on the mantelpiece over the range. 'My sister's daughter needs work, and I can't afford two girls.'

'Oh,' Sally said.

'I doubt she'll be as good as you.'

'Don't hire her, then!' Sally said quickly. Her eyes were getting all hot. Mrs Parsons reached out and patted her hand.

'She's family, dear. You know how it is.'

'Can't say as I do, Mrs Parsons,' Sally said, staring at the pattern on her teacup. 'My boy is the only family I've got. And he's six, so not much good at getting me employment.'

'Now, Sally,' Mrs Parsons replied, her voice getting firm. 'Like I said, you're a good worker. You'll have no problem getting another job.'

The injustice of it made her skin hot. 'Easy for you to say, Mrs Parsons. I was down to my last shilling when I met Belle and Alfred. I'm only just feeling like I'm back on my feet.'

Mrs Parsons withdrew her hand, and folded it together with her other one on her lap. 'I'm sorry to hear that. But it cannot be avoided. Susan will be starting tomorrow morning.'

'*Tomorrow?*'

'No use hanging around when there's a decision to be made.' Mrs Parsons stood up quickly and fetched an envelope from behind the clock. Sally recognised her own name carefully written on it, though her vision was getting a bit blurry. She blinked hard. Mrs Parsons handed the envelope to her. 'Now, there's a ten-shilling note in there, as well as a reference saying you're honest and hardworking.'

Sally took it and looked up at Mrs Parsons. Her eyes looked a bit red, too. Sally thought of her little store of savings, her attic room and her yellow curtains, her mending basket and the heavy old bed where she and Dougie could curl up through the winter and make up stories. If she couldn't get another job – and sharpish – how long would Belle and Alfred let her stay there? A thousand recriminations leapt to her lips. What was the good of working hard, of showing some loyalty and pluck, if it could all be whipped out from under you in a second? But what was the point? Every time life let you get a bit comfortable, it sneaked up in your blind spot and swept your legs out from under you. A couple of weeks before she'd been admiring her curtains, and now she was thinking how long it would be before she had to pawn them for rent or Dougie's medicine. She felt her breath catch.

'Thank you, Mrs Parsons.'

She stood up, carefully took off her apron and laid it gently over the back of the chair. Mrs Parsons' nose twitched. Perhaps she had been hoping Sally would make a fuss. That way, she wouldn't feel so bad.

Sally let her shoulders droop, picked up the envelope and turned towards the door with a sigh. She'd bite back the words, but she wasn't above twisting Mrs Parsons' conscience a bit. Not that it was an act, either. She'd never been let go before, and losing a job – even if it was to Mrs Parsons' niece – felt like a failure, as if she was being judged and found wanting.

'Sally!' Mrs Parsons said, getting to her feet. 'Would you clean? My cousin is looking for someone to char.' She looked guilty. 'It's not as pleasant as shop work, I know, but it's better than the mill or laundry.'

It was a straw. Sally clutched at it.

'I'm not too proud to clean, Mrs Parsons.'

'Well, go along and see her. Mrs Briggs at The Empire.'

The Empire. What a turn-up.

Sally dropped her eyes to the envelope in her hand and she thought of that night behind the velvet rope, watching the great and good arrive at the theatre and imagining herself in one of those sleek cars, pulling up to the red carpet, stepping out in an evening gown to the sound of popping flash bulbs and people calling her name. Now here was reality, coming to give her another nip. She'd go to The Empire, but in an apron, not a silk dress, and go in through the side door and be greeted with a grunt. If she ever got on stage, it would be to sweep up the flowers thrown at the real performers. Well, there you are.

Chin up, Sally Blow.

She straightened up and turned, her hand on her hip. 'Thank you for the tea, Mrs Parsons,' she said, 'and for the tip. I'll take it. But I hope you'll miss me and your niece spills the sugar at least once.'

CHAPTER FOURTEEN

Stella slept all day, and Grace's pages remained blank, or messy with odd loose words adrift from any sense. She glanced down at the page without any clear memory of what she'd been writing at all, and saw, with a terrible sort of grief, that the page was scattered with words from that damn notice. Jason de Witte. Jack had offered to find him and punch him in the jaw when it had first appeared, and Grace had been strongly tempted to let him.

Stella's agent, usually steely and unflappable, had been rattled when Grace spoke to her on the phone. She understood why Stella was upset, but fleeing London seemed an excessive reaction. She was sure that the gossip in the newspapers would die down in a matter of days, and The Lyric, where Stella had been appearing, would be happy to have her back on stage at once. On the other hand, a pair of detectives from Scotland Yard were eager to talk to her, and would make the journey to Highbridge the day after tomorrow.

Grace screwed up her latest piece of foolscap and tossed it into the wastepaper basket, then picked up a shawl from the back of her chair and went out through the house, and through the French windows leading from the drawing room to the terrace at the rear. The sleet had stopped, but it was a damp and misty evening. She pulled the shawl more closely around her shoulders and walked along the gravel path between the turned earth of the flower beds and breathed in. Wet grass, straw, woodsmoke. They would be getting ready for the evening performance at the theatre now: the principals in their dressing rooms; the stage crew checking and coiling the fly ropes; the musicians arriving and hanging their coats in the band rooms, exchanging greetings; the chink of the glasses in the bars as the staff slid them onto the shelves and polished the brass fittings. God, she missed the theatre, and The Empire in particular, but there was no way to get back to it other than by writing this damn play. And she could not write. She should have been a great deal more specific in her prayer, she realised. She should have asked for something to happen which would get her home, put the boards under her feet again.

The French windows rattled behind her and she turned. Jack and Lillian were stepping through them onto the terrace, in the midst of what looked like a fierce argument. Nikolai was following a few paces behind, staring off into the middle distance with the expression of a man who is making it clear he is trying not to listen, even though he obviously cannot avoid doing so.

'No, Lillian, absolutely not,' Jack hissed at his mother as they came within earshot. 'You can't possibly ask her!'

'Ask me what?' Grace asked, alarmed at Jack's slightly wild look.

'Well?' Lillian said to her son.

'I'm not having it.' Jack ran his hand through his hair. 'Before I tell you anything, Grace, you have to know that.'

Grace was really worried now. 'Jack, do just tell me.'

He inhaled. 'Very well. Archibald Flynn, our director for the panto, has disappeared.'

'He's done *what?*' Grace gasped.

'We got a call from his agent this afternoon, telling us that he is unavailable.'

Grace's hand flew to her mouth. 'Oh, Lord! Is he ill?'

'That's what I asked,' Jack replied. 'His agent wouldn't say, so Lillian has been calling people in London this afternoon.'

'Evie said there's been a rumour doing the rounds in town that he got involved in a tax avoidance scheme,' Lillian said with a sigh. 'The authorities apparently got wind of it and Archibald has fled the country.'

'Whatever the ins and outs,' Jack said crossly, 'the long and the short of it is, we start rehearsals in a week and we have no one to take the helm.'

Grace stared between them. Lillian looked a little pleased with herself – strange for a producer in her position – and Jack looked furious. 'So what were you two arguing about?'

Lillian adjusted the fur wrap around her shoulders. 'I told Jack we have an excellent director at Lassiter Court.'

'You mean Nikolai?' Grace asked, then noticed that gentleman vigorously shaking his head.

'No, Grace, you goose,' Lillian replied. 'I meant you.'

Grace recoiled slightly. 'But, Lillian, I've never directed a panto!'

'Neither have I!' Nikolai exclaimed. 'I have not even seen one, whereas you, Grace, have seen many productions while you worked at The Empire, I think.' He caught a black look from Jack, lifted his hands, took a step back and pretended to be very interested in the flagstones of the terrace.

'That's exactly what I said, Grace,' Jack said. 'You can't possibly do it. You haven't been well and you're writing. It's a ridiculous idea – the strain would be enormous. What, just a few days to prepare, then be thrown in at deep end with a vast cast! No, ridiculous. We'll find somebody else, of course we will.'

Lillian pursed her lips. 'Everyone experienced is already booked! Grace knows the theatre back to front – good Lord, she helped build it – and half the cast. She's directed comedies and written musicals. Honestly, I don't know why we didn't hire her to direct in the first place!'

'She's not well!' Jack said again, his face pale and jaw set.

Lillian met his gaze, but did not reply. Nikolai cleared his throat.

'Perhaps we should let Jack and Grace discuss this in private, Lillian,' he said eventually. 'Let me mix you a Martini.'

Lillian lifted her chin, then, without further comment, she turned to the terrace and allowed Nikolai to lead her back into the house.

'There's nothing to discuss,' Jack shouted at their retreating backs.

Grace took a step towards him. 'Of course there is, Jack. You know as well as I do, every experienced panto director in the country will be booked. Who do you mean to hire?'

'We'll muddle through, darling,' he said, trying to smile as he patted her arm. 'You aren't well and you want to write. You've always wanted to write. I can't let the latest of my muddles get in your way. Perhaps Harold would like to direct as well as being the dame. Nikolai might assist him . . .'

A terrible thought struck her. 'Jack, do you think I can't do it? That I'm not capable?'

'No! You're an excellent director, Grace. Clear, and actors love you, and you're terribly organised. But you haven't been well.'

She bit her lip. 'Do stop saying that, Jack. I'm not sure that staying at home is making me any better. Perhaps I should do it. The doctor says I'm healthy as a horse physically.'

'No, Grace! What about your writing?'

'Jack, I want to be at The Empire!' His face looked drawn and confused. She took hold of his wrist, feeling the taut muscles under the suit jacket and shirt, stroking the inside of his wrist with her thumb. The quiet darkness seemed to lean in towards them. She stepped forward, so the light from the drawing room windows fell across her face. 'I've felt so terribly lonely, and now here's a chance for me to come back to the very heart of things for a while.'

'Grace, you're very brave, but the strain of directing a panto . . . It's the biggest production of the year!'

'I've just told you, the doctor says I'm perfectly well,' Grace snapped, pulling back from him and only just managing to prevent herself from stamping her foot. 'And I know what staging one is like just as well as you do. I saw five of them through from casting call to first night before you even knew The Empire existed.'

He carried on as if she hadn't spoken. 'You'll have to do all the preparations and plan the rehearsal schedule. Of course, Nikolai has offered to assist you and Lillian says she'd be happy to supervise the set design.'

'Excellent.' Grace felt a flare of excitement. 'It will be difficult . . .'

'Exactly! I won't have Nikolai and Lillian bullying you back into the theatre. Lillian has the best address book in theatre land. We'll find someone.'

'Jack Treadwell, just stop and listen. I know you think you're protecting me, but you aren't! You're standing in my way.' That brought him up short. He blinked at Grace as if seeing her clearly for the first time since he'd barrelled into the garden. 'Jack, you've been treating me like I'm made of china for months, and sometimes it's very nice to be looked after, but this is too much. Look at me, darling.'

He did, and some of that flare of excitement must have shown on her face.

'Are you sure, Grace?'

She laughed. 'No, it's a terrifying idea, but I'd do pretty much anything to be back in the theatre again.'

He wrapped his arm round her waist. 'You've missed it so much?'

'I have. I was beginning to get very jealous of Miss Chisholm.'

He laughed softly. 'How unfair, when I've been gritting my teeth about you reading stirring dramas with Nikolai. Is this another product of your prayer, Grace?'

'I hope not.'

They walked back up to the terrace, hand in hand.

'How is Stella?'

'Still asleep. Her agent said she'll be welcome back at the Lyric any time, but we need to get her through the next few days first. Jack, a pair of detectives from Scotland Yard are coming up to question her.'

He groaned. 'If ever the thought crosses your mind to wish for something to happen again, you must promise me you'll go outside and spin and spit.'

'I promise, I will,' she said with conviction.

He opened the door for her and the sound of the gramophone greeted them in the hallway. He immediately brightened. 'What's that?'

'Evie sent some records over from New York. That's Louis Armstrong playing "Muskrat Ramble".'

Jack's eyes narrowed. 'Sounds like the sort of tune Lillian puts on when she's celebrating. She knew you'd say yes, didn't she?'

She kissed him. 'Lillian is a very clever woman. Try not to hold it against her.'

'Grace, are you absolutely sure?'

She leant against him, listening to the music. 'Yes. I feel like you've invited me home.'

CHAPTER FIFTEEN

Sally was not the sort of person to hang around. Chin still up, she caught the tram at the end of the street and was at The Empire an hour after sitting down with Mrs Parsons. It was dark, and the November evening was getting chilly. A modest crowd of well-dressed Highbridge citizens were making their way into the lobby to see – Sally squinted at the poster – *The Two Ladies of Grasmere*. She'd better wait. If she popped in now, they'd think she had money spare for a seat and an idea of spending it, and she didn't like the thought of that confusion.

She walked slowly round the edge of the building. In the two years since the theatre reopened, she'd never seen a show here. Friday and Saturday nights she was singing, and after work she mostly liked to take Dougie for a walk to the park. She'd been to the pictures a couple of times, but getting dressed up to go to The Empire felt like it wasn't for her. What if she spent her money, got all the way here and didn't like the show? She'd feel a right fool then. And the chemist was always recommending something new for her to try for Dougie's breathing. Wooden frames with posters in them were screwed into the side wall of the building at intervals. The pantomime! *Dick Whittington*, it said. Dougie would like that. Maybe if she got the cleaning job, she'd get a deal on a ticket. She turned the corner and saw an alleyway leading to a yard, and a sign saying STAGE DOOR. The smartly painted blue door below it was held open by a brick. It all looked very modest in comparison with that grand lobby. Should she go and ask for Mrs Briggs? Oh, she'd been foolish to come down in the evening like this, all in a rush of hurt pride and fluster! Theatres were cleaned during the day, after all. And maybe she *could* get a job in Bertram's, now she had her letter. She was quick with her numbers. She hoped Mrs Parsons had written that down. Shop work wouldn't be as rough on her hands as charring either. Cleaning other people's homes had worn her mother out. It was a silly idea, coming here with her feathers all ruffled.

She was about to go when her eye was caught by some movement just above the brick. A furry snout with a black button nose poked out into the night air and sniffed, and a second or two later a small, cheerful-looking terrier emerged and trotted across the yard to meet her.

Sally crouched down and offered the dog her hand to sniff, and he graciously allowed his ears to be scratched.

'What a good boy!' Sally said, cheered by the soft warmth of his fur. The dog wagged his tail with great enthusiasm, then the stage door swung open, and light spilled out into the yard, falling over Sally and the dog like a spotlight. Sally shielded her eyes against the sudden glare.

'Ollie? What are you up to?' a male voice asked.

Ollie yapped, though he didn't move from Sally's side, and instead butted gently against her hand as she paused the scratching. Sally saw the man who had spoken standing in the doorway. He was leaning on a cane.

'Good evening, miss!' he said, spotting her and stepping out into the yard. 'Is Ollie bothering you?'

Sally stood up. 'Not a bit. He's given me a hearty welcome as it happens, cheered me right up.'

As the man came towards her, Sally noticed half his face was covered in a white mask. Hurt during the war, no doubt. The half not covered seemed friendly enough.

'Has he now? And wh-wh-why did you need cheering, if you don't mind me asking?'

Sally felt embarrassed to say, but the little terrier was pushing up against her ankles.

'I've just lost my job, and I heard there was an opening for a char here. So I came straight down, and then realised I was being daft turning up at this hour. Then this fella found me.'

The dog barked and the man shook his head and laughed, then put out his hand.

'I'm Danny Moon, doorman here, and this is Ollie. By the l-l-looks of it, I'd say the job is yours. We all take Ollie's opinions very seriously.'

Sally grinned, and bent down to stroke Ollie's ears again. 'Well, thank you, Ollie! I'm not sure if I should take the job, though. More shop work might suit me better.'

Danny looked between her and the dog for a second.

'Ollie looks quite determined. Have you got a minute now? Come backstage and take a look. Then you can decide if it would suit you or not.'

Sally glanced towards the open stage door. Half an hour having a look around in a real theatre wouldn't do any harm, and it'd be a chance to warm up after standing around in the misty chill of Highbridge.

'That's nice of you, Mr Moon,' she said, following him back towards the golden glow of light spilling out of the door. 'If it's not an inconvenience to you, I'll have a look about.'

Ollie gave a contented huff, and Danny smiled and gave a little bow as he ushered her inside.

Sally had never seen any place like it. The second she stepped through the door, she began to feel music in her head – a sort of jaunty, jumping jingle on a piano, which meant a really good tune was about to start. The lobby behind the stage door was a neat little space, with pale green walls and a polished rack of pigeonholes for messages on the wall behind a wooden counter. The space behind it looked cosy and neat, with a stool, an armchair and a dog basket, and even a telephone with a message pad right next to it. But before she could even start to take it all in, Danny was climbing up a short flight of stairs and pushing open a double door with COMPANY ONLY painted on it in swirling cream letters. Sally trotted up the steps behind him. As she stepped through the door, she heard a rushing noise, like the waves retreating from the beach – a sort of sigh. The audience, she realised, settling into their seats. A thrill ran up her spine. That smart crowd she'd seen milling around on the pavement outside were on that side of the curtain, but she, Sally Blow, was behind it.

Corridors reached off in confusing directions all around her. On the walls were posters and photographs, and arranged against them were tea chests with the address of the theatre stencilled on the sides.

Danny nodded towards them. 'Deliveries for the panto,' he whispered. 'All sorts of things sent up from London – materials for the costumes, some of the p-p-props.'

Sally peered into one as they passed and got a glimpse of a cloud of pink netting, all sewn with sequins. Danny was off again, and she followed along a corridor marked TO THE STAGE in huge letters.

She heard actual music now – an elegant air played by piano and violins, drifting towards them. Danny pointed with his cane. 'Down those stairs are the workshops and the electrics room, the cane flicked upwards, 'and up those stairs are the rehearsal rooms and Lady Lassiter's offices.' Sally saw herself setting a cup of tea down on a fancy desk, and that woman she'd seen arriving at the theatre two years before looking up and saying, 'Thank you, Sally.'

'And along here are the dressing rooms,' Danny said as they passed by doors, some shut, some half-open to allow glimpses of mirrors, make-up and racks of costumes. She could smell sawdust and cigarette smoke. 'And now, if we're quiet, we can watch the opening from the wings.'

Sally's heart started tripping along to the music in her head as she followed Danny out of the corridor and into an area of deep darkness, with just the faintest glow coming from shaded lights fixed to the walls. A few men in shirtsleeves stood about, leaning on the back wall, and an older woman, in an old-fashioned dress with a corset and bustle, stood on the edge of the darkness, her head down. The fingers of her right hand were tapping against the heavy fabric of her dress, as if she was playing a tune of her own. Sally felt looking at her was like staring at someone praying, so she looked up and almost stumbled. It was like standing in the middle of a cathedral and looking up into the spire. Floating ghostlike in the air above her were huge hanging panels of scenery, and among them long straight lines of rope which ran from coils on the back wall and disappeared up into the darkness, like the rigging of a huge pirate ship. On the stage, a dining table, laid with plates of wax fruit, stood in the shadows, the silver candlesticks catching the occasional glimmer in the dark, and right in front of her was a sudden patch of brilliance. She blinked, and realised she was looking out on to the actual stage, and the heavy red velvet curtain itself. The house lights were coming down, and the velvet shone like late summer roses in the sun. The music finished with an elegant flourish; the men backstage exchanged nods and hauled on ropes, and the curtain swung open. There was a pause, as a thousand people seemed to hold their breath, then the older woman lifted her head and walked out into a wave of applause.

'What a thing,' Sally whispered to herself, 'to be waited for like that.'

Sally couldn't see what the woman was doing from here, but it must be something funny, because a warm wave of laughter rippled through the audience and across the stage. Sally felt it wash around her. It sounded different up here – not like when she was in the crowd at the flicks; more like music. Another woman, of a similar age to the other, and with her iron-grey hair piled high on her head, stepped into the wings next to them and tutted.

'Always overplays her first bit,' she hissed. 'Terrible technique. Been doing it since Bognor Regis.'

Then she swept on to the stage and, in a high fluting voice, announced 'Miss Bransome, you have discommoded the fishmonger once more!'

The audience laughed and applauded as if they were greeting an old friend. A thrill seemed to creep up from the boards, through Sally's shoes and all the way to the top of her head. She had never drunk champagne, but she was pretty sure this fizzing, golden feeling would be what it was like. She realised Danny was watching her. When she caught his eye, he leant towards her.

'Still want to work in a shop?'

Sally caught her breath. 'Not bloody likely. If Mrs Briggs wants me, she can have me.'

Danny looked pleased, and Ollie sat on his haunches, as smug a terrier as ever caught a biscuit.

CHAPTER SIXTEEN

Grace sat on the wrought-iron garden bench on the terrace, enjoying a brief interlude of winter sun and marking up her copy of the *Dick Whittington* script, twirling her pencil between her fingers. Miss Chisholm and Jack were sending postcards and ringing agents to inform the cast of the change of director. If any of them had protested, they had decided not to tell Grace.

Stella sat next to her in her white fur coat and huge dark glasses, smoking and watching Lillian and Nikolai while she showed him the garden.

'What on earth am I going to say to the policemen?'

Grace made a note on her script. 'Tell them the truth, of course.'

Stella pulled her coat a little more tightly round her shoulders, and Grace noticed that the fingers holding her cigarette were trembling, and her nail varnish was chipped.

'After that, you're going to have a nice stay with us until the newspapers get bored, and then get back to work.'

Chipped nail varnish was not like Stella at all. Neither was the silence that followed Grace's words.

'Stella, you haven't been . . . using too much cocaine, have you?'

Stella flicked the ash off her cigarette. 'No.' Then she paused. 'It's very hard sometimes to keep being "Stella Stanmore" all the time. Being wild and free-spirited is absolutely exhausting, and I'm getting so old.'

'But, Stella, you're only thirty!'

Stella's shoulders hunched in her wrap and she stared at the butter-coloured flags of the terrace with deep concentration.

'All the other girls are nineteen! Lord, I used to make fun of the singers and actresses who still wanted to play the ingénue at thirty-five, and I'm going to become one of them. The young ones . . . they're so eager and shiny, like puppies and kittens. They make me feel like an old cat, and snow does perk me up.' She shuddered. 'Though one often feels dreadful the next day, and sometimes it means spending time with people one would usually avoid, just because they have the good stuff.'

'But you have experience, Stella!'

Grace could see the sharp frown behind the dark glasses. 'No one wants experience in a showgirl, Grace. Well, not *that* sort of experience, anyway. No, I think it's time I left the stage entirely.'

Grace set her script aside.

'Stella, what on earth are you talking about? You're at the absolute height of your career. Your name is enough to open a West End show! You have years as the romantic lead ahead of you.'

Stella shook her head and her voice quavered. 'I've lost my stomach for it. I'll stay here, or find some dull rich man to marry, if you won't have me. And don't ask me to help with the panto.'

She ground out her cigarette and immediately lit another one. Grace bit her lip. The idea that Stella's career was over was ridiculous, but there was obviously no point in telling her that now. She must have cared deeply for this Tasha to react in this way, not matter how she talked in her free and easy way. But why should grief for the girl turn into repudiation of the theatre? And Grace *had* been hoping for her help.

'You're welcome to stay here as long as you like, but we're all going to be busy with the panto. If you don't get involved, won't you be bored?'

Stella's face was almost invisible behind the fur coat. 'Perhaps. But I'd rather be bored and alone than out there at the moment.' Grace sighed. 'Out there' seemed to encompass the whole world other than Lassiter Court. 'I can't talk about it any more.'

'But, Stella—'

'No, Grace,' she said sharply, then shook herself. 'Tell me what you think about Nikolai and Lillian. Are they lovers? I mean, I've always thought Lillian was rather too refined for anything like sex, but perhaps that's just because I keep thinking of her as Lady Lassiter.' She wriggled slightly, and Grace snorted in spite of herself. 'Have you noticed a spring in her step since Nikolai turned up?'

Stella leant forward, her long legs crossed and her chin in her hand. She sent a smooth column of smoke out into the still air, in the direction of the older couple, like a finger pointing.

'Absolutely. It's strange, I've always thought of her as a slightly tragic widow. Then as Jack's birth mother – another tragic story. Being abandoned by the father, then having to give Jack up. Then stoic and noble, with how she rallied everyone after the fire. But Nikolai is glamorous and fun – and a revolutionary, for goodness's sake.'

Stella tapped her ash off the end of her cigarette. 'I celebrate Lillian embracing her romantic comedy side. We contain multitudes, after all.'

Grace looked at her sideways. 'You're quoting poetry now, Stella? That's Walt Whitman, isn't it?'

Stella laughed, alarming a blackbird foraging in the winter shrubbery. 'I haven't a clue, but I did have a fling with a rather darling undergraduate this summer who couldn't get through his champagne supper without reciting something. Some poetry stuck to me.' She pursed her lips. 'What if they intend to marry? What would Jack think of that?'

Grace hadn't thought that far ahead. 'I'm not sure it would go down very well. He's been a bit sulky about Nikolai.'

'Is he worried they'd have brats? Surely Lillian is too old for that nonsense!' Grace looked back at her script and Stella put out her hand.

'Oh, Grace, I'm sorry. I'm an absolute twit. I didn't mean children would be a nonsense for you.'

Grace couldn't quite look at her. 'I know you didn't.'

'I know it's the absolute thing for some women. The maternal type. Not that I'm saying you're the maternal type – you're an artist. Unless you want to be the maternal type. I'm sure you'd be marvellous with baking and handkerchieves and all that. Oh, I'm such a disgrace of a human.'

Even through the cloud of mink and cigarette smoke, Grace could see Stella's distress was sincere. 'I know what you meant, Stella. Stop getting yourself into such a knot.'

She leant back. 'Getting myself into knots is my thing at the moment. Has it been foul, Grace?'

Grace thought for a second before answering.

'Yes. It has rather. And I know it's put Jack off his stride at work. I keep trying to be happy and confident it will work out next time, but it's as if the ground isn't solid. I'm walking along feeling quite ordinary, then I take a plunge, like I've fallen down a hole. You've never wanted children?'

'Never!' Stella shuddered. 'No, darling, I am one of those women who was born to be a disgraceful influence on the younger generation, not wipe its nose. Though if I do have to marry, perhaps I'll have to be a mother, too. There are nannies, I suppose.'

Grace would have laughed at her, but her talk of giving up the theatre was unsettling.

Nikolai and Lillian were coming up the garden path towards them now, still arm in arm. Nikolai said something and Lillian smiled, looking up at him sideways.

'I'm sure they're lovers,' Grace said. 'Lillian's always had a glow, but I swear it's a . . .'

'Sexier glow?' Stella grinned.

'Exactly.'

Stella laughed.

'Ladies,' Nikolai said as they came within speaking distance, 'Lillian and I would like to invite you to the Metropole this evening. Lillian means to introduce me to Agnes de Montfort, and I believe that the Mabel Mills Jazz Band are playing.'

Grace felt Stella stiffen beside her, but she could not be allowed to spend her entire time at Lassiter Court.

'We should be delighted, Nikolai. I'll call Jack.'

CHAPTER SEVENTEEN

The London detectives arrived the next day at exactly the appointed hour. Grace felt no urge to rush out to greet them, though. She put her chin in her hand and observed them as they got out of the taxi and paid the driver. They were an odd pair. The one who got out first was exceptionally tall, with stooped shoulders and a long face, with wisps of hair touching his collar, and a precise manner in his movements. He looked as if a horse had put on a mackintosh and been taught to walk on its hind legs. His companion was round – a snowman with a ruddy face and a thick sandy moustache. Both were well bundled up against the cold.

The bell clanged and Grace heard the front door open, but did not move until Hewitt had shown the men into the library and come to fetch her. Grace had thought carefully about where to receive them, and the library – a generous-sized but businesslike room, with the great portrait of Sir Barnabas in his civic regalia looking down on them – felt right. She came into the room expecting them to be seated in the chairs set out for them by the fire, but the snowman was peering out of the window, and the horse was reading a volume of Catullus he had pulled off one of the shelves.

'Mrs Treadwell?' the horse said, glancing up from his Latin. 'Is Miss Stanmore here?'

'She'll be with us in a few minutes,' Grace said, hoping that was true. 'She has asked me to be here while you talk to her.'

'We'd rather speak to her alone,' the horse said darkly.

'Now, now!' the snowman intervened. 'If the lady is more comfortable having a friend with her while we speak to her, that's quite understandable.' He bustled forward and offered his hand. 'I am Detective Sergeant Orme, Mrs Treadwell, and my lugubrious companion there is DS Hatchard.'

Grace found her hands enveloped in Orme's. They were fleshy and dry, and the handshake was surprisingly strong. Hatchard merely nodded at her.

'Now this is quite a business! Though I must say it's a delight to be out of London for a while, isn't it, Hatchard?'

'No,' Hatchard replied, and Orme laughed, slapping his hand on his ample thigh.

'Isn't he a card? So Miss Stanmore fled up here the moment she learnt about the tragic death of drug seller Tasha Kingsland, I understand?'

Grace blinked.

'Stella didn't flee,' she said. 'She had bad news and an unpleasant run-in with a reporter, so she came to visit friends. Will you sit down?'

'Oh, happy to stand for a minute, Mrs Treadwell. This is Lady Lassiter's home, is it not? Your husband's natural mother? And I believe you have a visitor from Marakovia staying here as well?'

'You are remarkably well informed,' Grace said, taking a seat near the fire.

'Assume, Mrs Treadwell,' Hatchard replied in a voice which sounded as if it were emanating from an abandoned tomb, 'that we know everything.'

Grace felt her jaw clench a little. 'Well, that must make your job very straightforward.'

Orme laughed uproariously at this, and was still wiping his eyes when the door opened and Stella finally made her entrance. She was wearing a houndstooth skirt – an old one of Lillian's – and a white shirt with a Peter Pan collar: the perfect costume for a young lady whose day might take in horse riding, a game of tennis and some light Bible study.

Orme bounced forward. 'Ah, Miss Stanmore! What a pleasure to meet you, albeit in a sad set of circumstances. I'm Detective Sergeant Orme, and this is DS Hatchard.' Both men finally settled into the chairs set out for them and as Stella sat next to Grace, Orme took a notebook from his pocket.

'How long had you been acquainted with the deceased, Miss Stanmore?' he began.

Stella crossed her long legs and sat back slightly in her chair. 'A little over ten months, I think. She was acting as a hostess at a club I sometimes go to with friends, then moved to another I also go to quite often. She recognised me – she was a great theatre fan – and we talked.'

'Where do you get your drugs from, Miss Stanmore?' Hatchard said bluntly. 'The place you sent Tasha is notorious for cocaine sales.'

'What? I didn't *ask* her to go there.' Stella tossed her head slightly. 'And I never bought dope from her.'

'I'm not thinking you bought it *from* her,' Orme said. 'I'm thinking maybe *she* was selling it on *your* behalf.'

'What?' Grace said.

'Wholesale,' Orme went on remorselessly. 'You would give it to her a bottle at a time, and Tasha would divide it into little packets that she could sell, easy as pie, out of her evening bag at the club. Probably didn't see any harm in it. A way to get a little extra pin money and fund her own habit. But it's boring work, dividing that stuff into packets. Probably decided to sample a little to get her through the night, but she took too much and her heart gave out.'

'Why in God's name would you think I gave it to her?'

'She came to see you at your dressing room the day before she died, didn't she? Came in looking glum, the doorman said. Left looking more cheerful. Did you give her the cocaine, Miss Stanmore?' said Orme.

'No,' Stella snapped.

'What did you give her?' Hatchard asked.

'A little money, and some words of encouragement.'

'Profitable business, selling drugs in nightclubs, if you have the contacts to do it in volume,' Orme said, addressing the air above Grace's head. 'Now, you might think Hatchard and I are being unreasonable. Perhaps we are. But there's a few things about this case that have got our noses twitching. Shall I tell you what they are?'

'I wish you would,' Grace said, 'because you seem to be talking nonsense so far. Why would a woman as successful as Stella sell drugs?'

'Well, Mrs Treadwell . . . Now, you might not be aware of this, but some bad people – nasty types – they bring in these drugs from abroad. A lot, I have to say, comes in to Limehouse, as much a den of iniquity as in the high days of Sherlock Holmes! But a considerable amount also comes in to . . .' He waved his pen, then pointed its nib in a westerly direction. 'Liverpool! Did you know that?'

'Of course not,' Grace said sharply.

'Of course not. Well, we know it. Interesting thing. The naughty people who bring it into the country, they buy from different people on the continent, and bring it in in different ways. Now normally, when we catch a girl like Miss Kingsland selling the stuff in clubs, we have no way of knowing where it came from, but of course the poor lass died while splitting her bottle into packets, see? And Orme and I . . . Well, we looked at the bottle and we said, "That's not Limehouse."' He scratched his nose with the end of his pencil. 'So we called up our colleagues in Newcastle and described our bottle.'

'And?' Grace asked, her throat feeling a little dry.

'And, Mrs Treadwell, the bottle rang a bell.'

'Loudly,' Hatchard added.

'Now, it may come as a shock to you to hear that there are some bad people in this very town.' Orme's voice had grown suddenly soft. 'Yes, even in Highbridge! Very naughty fellows. One lot in particular, run out of this city by a man named Ray Kelly. Heard of him?'

Grace felt a chill crawling up her spine, and she had a nasty feeling Hatchard was watching her.

'No,' Stella said. She got up and crossed to one of the side tables under the window, flicked open the silver cigarette box, took one and lit it. 'I've never heard of him.'

'Are you sure?' Orme said. 'Mrs Treadwell has, I think.'

Grace wet her lips. 'Everyone who lives in Highbridge has heard of him.'

Orme rubbed his chin again. It was starting to look pinker than the rest of his already pink face. 'Is that so? Now, now. We know that men like Ray Kelly – frightening, clever men – they can make these arrangements seem attractive. Your theatre's had some rough times of late. If you let Ray Kelly use it as a way to sell dope by the bottle to actors and actresses, like Miss Stanmore, I'm sure he'd see you right.'

Grace had heard enough. She stood up. 'Mr Orme, you're wasted as a detective. You should have been a dramatist. Please leave and take your ridiculous insinuations with you. If you need to speak to Miss Stanmore again, you may make an appointment with our solicitors.'

Hatchard and Orme exchanged glances. 'Now, that's a shame! We had hoped to pierce the veil with the help of you ladies.

'Oh, for crying out loud!' Stella said. 'Whatever I am, I am not a drug dealer. Tasha was a sweet girl and . . .' Her voice cracked. 'And you're *idiots.*'

Grace wished she could have scripted her a better exit line, but Stella did deliver it with absolute conviction. She stalked out of the room and slammed the door behind her.

'We've outstayed our welcome, Hatchard,' Orme said over his shoulder. 'I suppose we'd better be off.'

'I'm sorry you've had a wasted journey,' Grace said, sounding not very sorry at all.

'Wouldn't say that.' Orme placed a card on the table. 'Tell Miss Stanmore to call us if she changes her mind.'

CHAPTER EIGHTEEN

S ir Gideon walked across the park, his copy of *The Times* tucked
under his arm, and took a seat on a bench in the rose garden, not
far from the Serpentine, enjoying the brisk, frost-sharpened air after
the fug of the Foreign Office. London, once the sun got through the coal
smoke, looked positively pretty from here. After a few minutes perusing
the classified advertisements, he heard someone settling on the bench next
to him, and looked sideways at his new companion as he turned the page.

'What news upon the Rialto?'

'I wish you wouldn't quote Shakespeare before I've had my lunch,'
the new arrival said. 'It makes me bilious. If by "upon the Rialto",
you mean from Marakovia, then there is a lot, and very little of it good,
I'm afraid.'

Sir Gideon folded his newspaper and looked more carefully at the man
sitting next to him.

He was a handsome chap, long-limbed and rangy, with chestnut hair
and large blue eyes. He had his legs crossed and his arm thrown out
along the back of the bench. His fingers were tapping on the wood.
Colonel Osman had had an excellent war on paper – the youngest colonel
in his regiment's history, a fistful of medals and the appreciation of a

grateful nation. It had left him a bit nervy, however, and contemptuous of authority. Not the sort of man Gideon would have chosen to send wandering in central Europe to gather information, but beggars couldn't be choosers. Osman's father was a viscount who had fallen for a very beautiful – if rather free-willed – Marakovian. His dubious heritage had given Osman valuable language skills and connections in her native country, while his father made him acceptable to Gideon's masters.

He returned his attention to the slumbering rose garden.

'Well?'

'The expulsion of Grand Duke Nikolai has put Andrei, the king's brother, in the ascendancy. He's been consolidating his power in the capital, and Crown Prince Stefan is increasingly isolated.'

Sir Gideon sniffed. 'Prince Andrei seems like a stabilising influence to some of us.'

'He's a fascist,' Osman said simply.

'And how is Nikolai Kuznetsov being spoken of?'

'The newspapers are full of bile,' Osman replied, with a frown, 'but I believe the people still think of him fondly. Listen, Gideon, I want to know whose side I'm on here. Have you seen what Mussolini's lot are doing in Italy? You can't want Marakovia to go the same way! There is a chance with Prince Stefan to establish a stable democracy, if he's given the right encouragement . . .'

'And you think the right encouragement will come from Nikolai?' Sir Gideon scoffed. 'Did you see the picture of him with that woman in front of the theatre?'

'With the pantomime poster? Yes, I saw it. *The Times* syndicated it from the local paper. And, yes, I know Kuznetsov's politics are not to your taste,' Osman continued as Sir Gideon arched an eyebrow. 'But at least he is a democrat.'

'Who the Marakovians choose to kick out of their country is up to them. And when one can make friends on both sides of the political divide, one should, shouldn't one, Osman?'

'No, Gideon. Not if it means making friends with people like Andrei.'

Sir Gideon folded up his newspaper and tucked it under his arm. 'Don't leave the country. The Prince of Wales wishes to hear from someone who has more current knowledge on the conditions in Marakovia than I, in advance of the Crown Prince's visit next year.' He delivered the news with the smallest suggestion of a sneer. 'You are to accompany me on our next briefing. When His Highness can fit us in between rounds of golf.'

Sally liked the municipal gardens in the centre of Highbridge. It was a bit of a walk for Dougie to get there, but they could get the tram back if he looked tired. It was a neat space, laid out with walkways and benches, flowerbeds that were a burst of colour in the spring and summer, and even with December on them, the holly and laurels looked cheering on a cold day and the paths had a frosty crunch to them. There was a pond where the children of the richer inhabitants sailed model boats, and though the weather was a bit too cold for them to be splashing about now, there were still the ducks to look at.

It was nice to spend the day with Dougie, too. She'd be starting at The Empire next week, so this was a holiday for them both. Knowing there'd be money coming in had made her easier in her mind about spending a shilling from her private purse on going out and about.

Next to the white park house, where they sold ices in the summer, was an aviary, built by Sir Barnabas Lassiter to celebrate Queen Victoria's Jubilee, and the birds which lived in it – cockatoos and budgies, parrots and finches – seemed to have taken to the Highbridge air. Dougie liked to whistle at them through the wire.

As they turned off the yew avenue, he spotted the cages and went tumbling off to see them. It wasn't good for him, running like that in the cold weather after their walk, but he looked so eager and happy as he dashed towards them, Sally didn't have the heart to call after him and tell him to slow down.

Just as Dougie was reaching the aviary a male figure, his head down, turned the other corner. Dougie barrelled into him, making the man drop his package, and fell back on his bottom on the path.

Sally started forward, expecting to hear a shout and Dougie crying, but the male figure had bent down and was helping Dougie up, ignoring his fallen package, and was brushing off the boy's trousers instead. Sally hurried towards them, and by the time she arrived at the cages, filled with perches and nest boxes, the boy and man were next to each other by the wire, pointing at the fluffed- up birds. She heard Dougie laugh.

Sally bent down and picked up the parcel. It was tightly bound in brown string and addressed to Francis, Day & Hunter Ltd: music publishers in London.

Sally brushed the grime from the package, and the man talking to Dougie turned round. It was the fellow from the pub – the one who had put the song in her head. He almost fell over himself when he saw her.

'It's you!'

She laughed. 'It is me. That's my lad who almost sent you flying. Did you apologise to the gentleman, Dougie?'

'Yes, Mum! He's called Tom. And he said it didn't matter and he used to run to the cage when he was my age, too.'

'That's very nice of him.'

Dougie had moved on to more important things. 'The one that talks,' he said to Tom, pointing out a blue and yellow parrot which was cracking nuts with its terrible-looking beak, 'is called a macaw. It's from South America.'

'Well, I never. And where is South America?' Tom asked.

Dougie grinned, enjoying the game. 'It's on the other side of the Atlantic Ocean.'

Tom stood up and straightened his heavy winter coat. He was taller than she remembered, with a good six inches on her, and his brown eyes were very dark, with heavy eyelashes.

'Apparently the first one they bought for the aviary had a very colourful vocabulary,' Tom said. 'They had to retire it to a pub in Liverpool and get this one. Much more respectably brought up.'

The macaw regarded them with a certain wary detachment, while Dougie hung on to the wires with his fingers and stared.

Sally handed Tom the package. 'Here you go. It's not too messy, I think.'

He took it and tucked it under his arm. 'Oh, I wrapped it tight enough to withstand a few knocks. Do you remember my friend in the pub? This is her music I'm sending to town.'

'And they'll publish it?'

'Oh, yes. She's Ruby Rowntree. They publish lots of her music.'

Sally had heard of Ruby Rowntree. 'Glad I didn't know that when you and her were in the pub. I'd have been nervous.'

'She loved you,' he said, looking her straight in the eyes, then he blushed a little. A long moment stretched between them, and the frost seemed to sparkle as if a brighter sun had passed over them.

'Can budgies talk?' Dougie asked.

Tom turned and chatted to him about the birds, and their different abilities. He seemed, Sally thought, to be having a genuinely good time talking to her son, and when the excitements of the aviary were exhausted, it felt natural to walk on together. Dougie told Tom about his favourite subjects at school, and how he liked drawing maps, because he was going to be an adventurer, then found a stick and became absorbed in dragging it through the frost, or battling some invisible dragon with it. Tom and Sally walked on together, he making general observations about the weather and she replying. She mentioned how it got on to Dougie's chest, and found herself talking about his asthma. He asked sensible questions, and seemed to listen to the answers. She felt strangely aware of him – the dulling winter light falling over his shoulder, the faint smell of tobacco and hair cream – and this strange crackling energy between them. They were almost at the gates back into town when he cleared his throat.

'And what does your husband do, Mrs Blow?'

Sally felt the familiar pang, like a lightning strike going though her from shoulder to toe.

'Noah was a factory worker. Died when Dougie was only a baby. And do call me Sally.'

'I'm sorry to hear that,' Tom said, stopping just as they reached the pavement. It was as if, Sally felt, they both wanted to stay in the garden a little longer, before they got swept out into the world and all its worries again.

'Feels like a lifetime ago,' Sally replied. She turned. Dougie was still battling ghosts on the frosty grass. 'Dougie! Come on, now.'

Dougie ambled towards them, dragging his stick.

'I don't have much family,' she went on, half to herself. 'And Noah's mum and dad are in Sheffield, so we were very glad when Belle and Alf took us in. We feel like a family in the Bricklayers Arms now.'

He smiled – that warm, golden smile. 'The accidental families we find are sometimes the best. That's how it feels to me, anyway.'

'You not got family, Tom?'

His expression became a little sadder. 'My mother is alive, but we're not very good friends, I'm afraid.' Beyond the garden, the skies were beginning to darken. The street lamps glowed in the hazy gloom and the rattle of a passing tram seemed distant and muffled in the evening fog. Dougie came up to them, took Sally's hand and shivered.

Tom pulled off his scarf, and wrapped it round Dougie's neck. 'Here – for when you go exploring in the Antarctic, like Shackleton.' Then he turned up his own collar.

'He can't take that, Tom!'

'Of course he can. Anyway, I have a confession.'

She frowned, her head on one side.

'Go on.'

'I came to listen to you last week, then I had to go for supper and didn't manage to get to your tip jar before I left.'

She laughed. 'I didn't even see you! Well, in that case it's owed and you're lucky we don't take your gloves, too.'

Tom bent down and he and Dougie compared hand sizes.

'I don't think they'd fit, Mum,' Dougie said solemnly. 'I'll keep my wool ones.'

'In that case . . .' Tom got to his feet again. 'I'll wish you a good afternoon, Dougie, Sally.'

She shook his hand and he headed off down the street. She watched him go, his tall slender frame disappearing into the fog, thinking about how it had felt to hear him say her name.

'Mum?'

Sally shook herself. 'Right, let's get you home.'

CHAPTER NINETEEN

Grace arrived at the theatre an hour before rehearsals were due to start, to hear the sound of music from the large room where the chorus would be going through their numbers. She peered round the door, to see Tom in his shirtsleeves at the piano, and her chorus of ten men and women in the midst of a group number, tapping away in a tight phalanx. Watching them for a moment, Grace had the distinct impression they were all trying to dance behind one another – even the dancers in the front row, which seemed a bit of a challenge.

'Enough! Tiny elephants! Cease!' called a thin male voice, and something thumped on the floor. The dancers came to an immediate halt and stared at the floor. 'Mrs Treadwell, do come in.'

The invisible person spoke with unquestionable authority.

Grace stepped into the room. Terrence Fortescue, the choreographer, was sitting on a low wooden bench in front of the mirror. He wore long, loose black trousers, which stopped just above his ankles, and a thin black sweater. His chin rested on the top of a solid-looking black cane. His hair was the colour of old ivory, plentiful, and coiffed. Grace was reminded of a particularly delicious syllabub she'd once had at the Metropole.

He turned his perfectly round face to Grace; his small eyes were almost invisible within the caves of their sockets.

'The read-through begins at ten,' he purred, 'is that correct, Mrs Treadwell?'

'It is, Mr Fortescue.'

He smiled, thinly. 'I am putting them through their paces. They are acceptable.'

Grace glanced at the chorus members. They looked sweaty and mildly alarmed.

'I'm delighted to hear it.' She turned to go, then looked back over her shoulder. 'Please don't break them.'

His smile widened, but he made no promises.

In the main rehearsal room she found Nikolai sharpening pencils, and two men chasing each other round one of the trestle tables set out for the read-through.

As Grace stood in the doorway, the older of the two men reached across the table and hauled the younger man across it towards him, then dealt him such a blow around the ears he spun round. As he did, he straightened his legs, which caught the older man by surprise and threw him to the ground. He rolled over and saw Grace staring down at him.

'Morning, Mrs Treadwell.' He sprang back up and spoke to the young man on the table. 'That's it, Frank. You've just got to sell the spin, I'll sell the fall.'

The younger man pushed himself off the table. 'I get it, Harold. We'll pop it in if Mrs Treadwell approves.'

Grace walked over towards them, hand outstretched. Frank, the younger man, was cast as Idle Jack, and Harold Drabble was their star - Sarah the Cook.

'I absolutely approve.'

Harold beamed at her. Though he moved with rubberish agility, he was a barrel of a man. As he took her hand between his own, Grace felt she was being welcomed into her rehearsal room by a courteous grizzly bear.

'Young Frank will charm their socks off. God, I love the first day of rehearsal. All these new faces, and such drama to kick us off with. Is it true Archibald Flynn absconded with the Sudley Baldington wardrobe budget?' He towered over her, teeth bared.

'I believe it was something to do with his taxes, Mr Drabble. Welcome to The Empire. Are your digs comfortable?'

'Call me Harold, dear. Yes, very nice.' He swung away from her and sauntered off towards the tea urn with a strange rolling gait, as if he had a beach ball between his knees. 'Taxes! I sympathise!' he called over his shoulder. 'Well, I think we shall all get along famously without him. Directing panto is mostly about remembering everybody's names.' He poured his tea and returned. 'I think I'd better use the line at once, don't you think? On my first entrance.'

'Ooh, where is my tiffin?' Nikolai supplied proudly in his rolling Marakovian accent, from the pencil sharpening station. Harold raised an eyebrow and looked him up and down.

'Just so, Your Dukeyness. Don't wear it out.'

Nikolai became immediately very serious. 'I shall indeed, not wear it out.'

Before Grace could say anything, the door opened and Marmaduke Smythe made his entrance. His face – narrow, with a long nose and large, dark eyes – gave him the look of a suspicious crow rather than a rat. He looked around the room, turning his head and taking them all in, then lighted on Grace like a spotlight.

'Mrs Treadwell,' he said, crossing the space between them. 'I am distraught for you, to be cast in such a demanding role at a moment's notice.' He clasped her offered hand in both of his own. 'I am more than willing to support you in any way I can. I have a few little ideas, gleaned through my many, many years of experience. All of them, I place most humbly at your feet.' He released her hand and bowed. 'The Rat, you see, in my interpretation, is an aristocrat, a creature of great sophistication forced out of polite society by petty rules, now maddened by the cruelties visited on him.'

'How fascinating!' Grace said.

'I shall look forward to chasing you with a rolling pin,' Harold announced from the tea urn. Marmaduke ignored him, his attention still fixed on Grace.

She fluttered her eyelashes a little. 'That's most wonderfully kind of you. I am so grateful to be supported by an actor of your experience. And you know,' she leant forward and put a hand on his arm, 'we have Terrence Fortescue for the choreography. He's already putting the chorus through their paces next door.'

'How wonderful,' Marmaduke said in a voice which made the floorboards vibrate. 'Though, of course, King Rat does not cavort.'

Miss Chisholm came into the room, half hidden behind a stack of mimeographed copies of the script. She set them down on the table, then began to arrange them. The brass butterfly clips in the corners glimmered.

Josie Clarence pushed the door open, already in her playsuit. 'Grace, is it true that Stella Stanmore is in Highbridge? Do I still have a job?'

Grace turned towards her. 'Josie, darling, of course you do. You are our Dick! Stella is only visiting us.'

Josie frowned, then tossed her hair. 'Fair enough. As long as she's not *sniffing* after my job.'

Grace froze, then stared at Josie till her cheeks went a little pink, and spoke quietly.

'Josie, dear, you're our star, just as you were in *Cairo Nights*, but if I hear you say one word against Stella – to anyone – or mention that terrible business in London, I'll put your understudy on in a heartbeat. Do you understand?' Josie looked as if she was about to protest, then caught the steeliness in Grace's expression, and simply nodded. 'Good. Now go and sit with Harold.'

The rest of the cast made their entrances, then just before ten the befuddled chorus were led in by Terrence Fortescue. Like a goose and his goslings.

Grace joined Nikolai at the head table. 'Are you ready, Grace?' Nikolai asked quietly.

She breathed in. Marmaduke Smythe needed to be flattered, and Josie Clarence checked when her nerves made her spiteful. Harold Drabble would be a collaborator and friend; Terrence Fortescue needed respect and room to work. The characters of Jimmy and Mrs Carstairs, and Grace's months of misery trying to write, seemed to disappear. Here she was with her cast settling into their seats, the wintry light streaming in through the tall windows. She looked between them, imagining each face in make-up, each costume, from Fairy Bow Bells to the cat, to the King of Zanzibar, to Josie – Dick Whittington himself – and Alice; then she looked down at the script in front of her.

'Yes, Nikolai,' she said. 'I'm ready.' She lifted her eyes. 'Good morning, everyone, and welcome to The Empire. We'll begin with a read-through. If you could hold your comments to the end, please. The rehearsal schedule is on the blackboard behind me, as is a list of available times for your first wardrobe visits. For all administrative matters, please speak to Nikolai here first. For anything about the show, come to me. Now, shall we begin? Nikolai, if you'd be so kind.'

Nikolai cleared his throat. 'London,' he read, with such enjoyment that even Josie smiled. 'May Day celebrations outside the shop of Alderman Fitzwarren. As the alderman readies himself for breakfast, the apprentices pass behind him carrying large sacks and barrels labelled "Wine from France", "Eggs from Essex", and "Broadcloth from Highbridge".'

At the mention of the town's name, the company cheered.

'Enter Dick Whittington with stick and bundle over his shoulder,' Nikolai finished.

'So this is London!' Josie exclaimed from the other end of the table. 'And to think that I was told that all the streets were paved in gold!'

'Enter Alice Fitzwarren and her father.' Nikolai's delight was infectious.

Harold leaned in towards Josie, touching shoulder to shoulder, and she grinned. King Rat nodded once.

And they were off.

CHAPTER TWENTY

Sally Blow tied the handkerchief over her hair a little tighter, then pushed open the door to the rehearsal studio with her shoulder, rolled in her mop and bucket, and looked around. It was an aching sort of pleasure to be here at the end of the day and to guess at where the mess had come from, picturing them all at work.

Mrs Briggs was a decent boss and the pay was no worse than the shop, but it was hard physical labour, and Sally's hours were full of cold dirty water and the slap and slide of her mop. Her favourite hour was half past three when she took round the office teas. Bridget Chisholm would be rattling away at her typewriter, not even looking at her fingers as they flew about. Jack Treadwell was hardly ever at his desk, and half the time when she went to collect his cup for washing, it would still be full, or only half drunk. When Sally had brought Lady Lassiter a cup of tea on the first day, she'd asked for her name and said, 'Welcome to The Empire.' The next day, Lady Lassiter had looked up from her papers as she took her cup and said, 'Thank you, Sally' – proving that dreams can come true, as long as you keep them small enough. The company for the pantomime had their own tea urn, so she didn't see much of them, though Mrs Treadwell smiled at her in the corridor.

Very slowly, Sally was learning the mysteries of the theatre and its personalities. She felt as if she was an explorer, like Dougie wanted to be, and this was a strange continent she was mapping, bit by bit. The different departments had different names, hierarchies and their own ways of doing things. Mr Treadwell was the manager of the whole theatre, but, she thought, he was like an emperor with lots of kingdoms under him – the chop shop, wigs, wardrobe, the stage crew, the lights – and then there was front of house, Frederick Poole's kingdom, which covered the lobby, auditorium and bars. Sally went back home every night and whispered her new discoveries to Dougie as they curled up in the big bed.

Coming into the rehearsal room at the end of the day made Sally's heart swell and tighten in the same moment. She was so close to this theatrical magic, but still a little separate from it. The blackboard showed the scene they'd been working on and what they planned to do the next day. Mrs Treadwell always forgot to put the chalk back on the sill under the board itself, and Sally found it twice among the scrambled-up notes on her table. These were always lists of things she needed to do and remember. As soon as Mrs Treadwell had ticked them all off, she'd tear the page into four and drop them in (or sometimes near) the wastepaper basket. Sally took a moment to fit them together.

Better joke for Act I Scene 2
Water effects for Act III
Milly on Zanzibar costumes 4 o'clock. More gold?

Then she sighed, dropped the pieces of paper in the bin, and got to work mopping the floor. She'd be singing in the pub the following night. Maybe, if the crowd wasn't in a boisterous mood in the first hour, she'd try 'Then You'll Remember Me'. It was a cosy sort of tune which made her think of warm fires, and the feel of rabbit fur against your skin, with a bit of a swoop to it which could squeeze your heart if you hit it right. Sally's mother had had a rabbit fur collar on her Sunday coat. When the coat fell apart, she'd made Sally a toy bear out of the scraps. She'd never dared hug it; she'd just stroke it till she wore little bald patches between the ears.

She mopped to the rhythm in her mind, then began to hum. Finding she liked the way the tune bounced around the walls, she sang as she worked along the floor under the windows, where the dancers' tap shoes had scuffed the pine, then into the middle of the room, carefully avoiding the coloured marks on the floor, which showed the edges of the bits of the set. When she caught a movement, she saw in the mirror there was a man standing in the doorway behind her.

She spun round. 'What the bloody hell are you doing here?'

It was Tom. Sally's hand flew to the kerchief around her hair and her cheeks grew hot.

'I knew I recognised that voice!' he said, grinning at her. 'Same as you, I think. I work here.'

'Tom who has heard lots of singers . . .' Sally said. 'What do you do here, then?'

He pointed at the piano, and she noticed he had sheets of music in his hand. 'I assist Ruby Rowntree. She has a room here.'

'Oh,' Sally said. 'She doesn't drink tea.'

'No, she doesn't.' He walked towards her, avoiding where she'd mopped, and put his hand out. 'I realise I never introduced myself properly, in the pub or the park. I'm Tom Lassiter.'

She wiped her hand on her apron before shaking his. 'Lassiter? Like Lady Lassiter? Who owns the theatre?'

He smiled. 'Yes, she's my step-grandmother, believe it or not.'

She blinked. 'I saw you were a gentleman, but I didn't know you were Highbridge *royalty*.'

'More like the court jester. When did you start working here?'

'Just a week or so ago. Ollie sort of recruited me.' That was a daft thing to say.

It made him laugh, though. 'Ollie and Jack Treadwell run this place.

If Ollie approves of you, you're destined for great things.' He put the song sheets on top of the piano. 'Did you think of a song, Sally? That one you were singing as I came in sounded a bit more like you meant it.'

Sally gripped her mop handle and looked away from him. 'I can't sing sentimental stuff in the pub. Alf and Belle don't want people weeping into their beer.'

He shrugged. 'You're allowed to do both, but every singer needs a signature tune. Sure you haven't got one?'

'Maybe I have,' she said with a sigh. 'But singing it would be like going up there without my clothes on.'

'You've got to take a risk sometimes. Find a way to let the audience know who you really are. It's like Harold and his catchphrase.' He beamed with sudden excitement. 'He's amazing, you know. He can have us all weeping one second, then he's clowning again and you think your sides are going to split. You'll see when we start rehearsing on the main stage. Just watch him. Or what about the Metropole? See how the singers there switch the mood about.'

His eagerness irritated her. *All right for Mr Lassiter, isn't it? With his soft hands and his ideas about what I should do.* 'I can't afford to go to the Metropole! I'm barely keeping a roof over my boy's head as it is!'

'I'm just saying, be brave.'

Easy for him to say. Sally felt foolish suddenly, and ashamed for looking at Mrs Treadwell's notes, and felt as if, somehow, it was Tom's fault.

'Yes, I can see how you've really struck out on your own, Tom. Working in the theatre owned by your family.'

He blushed a bit. 'That's fair, I suppose. Sorry. I know it's none of my business.' He took a step back towards the door. 'Thing is, Sally, I love music, and I get all carried away when I meet people who have real talent. I just haven't found my way in.'

'Be brave. Take a risk.'

He looked stung, turned and began to walk away, his shoulders hunched.

'Tom!' He turned back. 'I'm sorry. I'm not usually such a cat, you just caught me unawares.' He turned back to her, cautiously. 'It's nice, you taking an interest.' Now he smiled again – that slow, warm smile. 'It's hard to take a risk, though, when there's nothing to fall back on.'

'I suppose it must be. How old is Dougie?' he asked.

She was touched he'd remembered the name. 'Dougie's six now. He was two when Noah died.' She swallowed. 'Noah worked at one of your family's factories.'

There, that was said now. The words seemed to sweep over them both like a cold wind.

'What happened?'

'He got his sleeve caught in the grinding belt. Broke his arm and then he got . . . what do you call it? Blood poisoning.'

'Sepsis.'

She looked at him. 'That's it.'

'I'm sorry. I've never had much to do with the factories myself.'

Tom looked down at his expensive shoes, at the bottom of his expensive trousers. Why did this feel like a tragedy? As if a great chasm had opened up between them on the half-mopped floor. What was the point, she wondered, of a crackle in the air and the fact Dougie liked him, when she was mopping the floors and he was a Lassiter? He knew nothing of her life, and she could never know anything of his. But he looked so mournful standing there, with his big brown eyes.

'I'll try out that one I was just singing at the pub tomorrow. See how it goes over.'

She squeezed out her mop and slapped it onto the floorboards.

'If they don't like it,' Tom said, 'you can knock me over the head with the mop next time you see me.'

'Can't think that would be good for my employment prospects.' She grinned.

'Don't be too sure. You got Ollie's seal of approval – that means you can bash us all about a bit.'

For some reason, that made her eyes sting. She half nodded, and returned to her mopping.

The pub was busy that Saturday. The Highbridge Wanderers had won their match and it had put all the men in a high old mood. The women in the bar had a loose and happy air to them, too. They had a little money in their pockets, the fire was warm, and when the men were grinning rather than scowling, the air felt lighter. Hardly the time to try out that sentimental number, Sally decided. Maybe she'd just lean on the old favourites again. An image flitted through her mind of Tom Lassiter looking disappointed.

'You get up and sing then,' she murmured.

'What, Mum?' Dougie said. He'd had a good week and was sitting in bed with a story paper. Ruben, the lighting technician at the theatre, bought them twice a week for his little boy, and had offered to pass them on to her. Dougie's face had lit up when she brought him in a stack that afternoon. It was hard for him, not being able to run about with the other kids on the street, but she felt her heart lift with pride, seeing her boy with his nose in the stories like a little scholar.

'Nothing, pet. I'm arguing with people in my head, which is as silly a way to spend your time as I can think of. Now, if I leave you to yourself, do you promise not to read too late?'

Dougie beamed and nodded.

'All right, then.'

Sally kissed the top of his head and made her way downstairs. The fight with Tom was not over in her head, so when Alfred spotted her and nodded to the corner of the bar, and said, 'You've got a visitor,' she half-expected it to be him, badgering her about sad tunes and looking at her with those big eyes.

It wasn't Tom. The crowd parted and Sally saw Ruby Rowntree sitting near the saloon door. She had a battered black case on her lap, and a tartan shawl round her shoulders.

'Miss Rowntree, isn't it?' Sally said, approaching and offering her hand. 'It's very nice of you to come and hear me again, miss. I do so like your songs.'

Ruby smiled, patting the bit of bench next to her, and Sally sat down. 'I'm glad, dear. Most of the tunes I've published are for the stage, you know – music for rich people to hum as they drink their cocktails. But I do enjoy music hall songs, too, and the old folk tunes. They have more bounce and grit to them.' She put her head on one side like a robin watching someone dig an allotment. 'Like a football crowd. Or the look on a woman's face as she's getting through the laundry and wondering if the bread will stretch.'

Sally had never heard a tune described like that. It made her laugh. 'Maybe you're right.'

Ruby wrinkled her button nose. 'I'm always right, dear. About music, anyway. Any sign of your piano player tonight?'

Sally peered around the jostling crowd. On the other side of the room a woman laughed, and a man slapped a friend on his back, making him spill his beer.

'No, the bugger's let me down again. Still, I can carry it on my own.'

'You can, I've heard it.' Ruby opened up the case on her lap. 'But I thought I might join you.'

Sally looked down. In the case was a polished wooden squeeze box, with ivory buttons.

'No! Really? Well, if you like, Miss Rowntree. But you play piano, don't you? Why not play on that?'

'Call me Ruby – and this is much more fun, I think. I don't get to play it often, and it's a nice instrument for the bar. Got a wheeze in it, like it's been smoking a pipe by the fire all afternoon.'

'Why have you taken the trouble to come and play with me, Ruby?' She bit her lip. 'Did Tom say something?'

'You might have come up in conversation once or twice recently,' Ruby said. At the bar someone delivered a punchline and a roar of laughter went up. Ruby waited till it had died down a bit before she carried on. 'I hear you're working at the theatre now?'

'Just charring with Mrs Briggs.'

'I bar Mrs Briggs from my room,' Ruby said cheerfully. 'A nice woman, but I'm afraid she'll try and tidy me up and I'll never find anything again. Anyway, Tom said your pianist wasn't here when he popped in a second time. So I thought I'd come along and take another look at you. And play, if there was a chance. It will please me, Sally, to do it.'

'That's very good of you, Miss Ruby. Tom was kind to my boy, in the park,' Sally said, not sure why she was telling Ruby that, other than it felt good to say his name out loud again, somehow.

'He is a kind man.'

'Easy to be kind when you're rich,' Sally replied with a sigh, then blushed, feeling Ruby's careful assessing gaze on her.

'Yes, Sally. But it's easier to be cruel, too. Tom isn't. Don't judge him by his mother or brother.' Her voice became brisk. 'You'll be singing the songs you did the other week, will you?'

'And the like.'

'Tell me the name and hum me the first bars, and I'll be able to follow you.'

Sally hesitated. She'd been arguing with Tom about not singing anything sentimental, but now . . .

'I was thinking maybe I'd try "Then You'll Remember Me", too,' she said.

Ruby nodded. 'I know it. You give me the nod when you think the moment's right, and I'll back you up.' She tucked the case under the bench. 'Shall we, then, Sally?'

Sally felt herself blush furiously, but Ruby was already making her way through the crowd, tapping on men's shoulders to let her through. Bert Hargreaves turned round and almost jumped out of his skin when he found himself looking down into Ruby's little red face. Then he doffed his cap and escorted her to the corner like a maître d'. The crowd made room for them, and those nearest to the corner settled themselves to pay attention.

'Shall we start with "How Do You Do"?' Sally asked.

Ruby nodded and played the starting note quietly on her squeeze box. Then Sally turned to the crowd, and Ruby's fingers bounced over the tune, giving a bit of an introduction, the way the organ players did in church, ready for the people to come in.

And Sally started to sing.

Sally had had various pianists bashing out chords for her before. George was her favourite because he didn't complain about splitting the tips sixty–forty in Sally's favour, and mostly kept an ear out for what tempo Sally wanted, but singing with Ruby was something different.

After 'How Do You Do', they went on with 'A Little Bit of Paradise'. Ruby played a simple sort of jogging rhythmic line under Sally's voice, and it felt like they were getting to know each other. The crowd started paying attention, and after Sally rounded that one off and thanked Miss Ruby for her help, the lads banged their fists on the tables a bit.

Sally went next for 'A Lassie Up in Lancashire', which had one of those choruses you can't help singing along to; Ruby's squeezebox started rippling up and down scales and made it feel jollier than ever. Sally half watched her, getting comfortable and confident now. It was like dancing, but not like dancing with Noah, who had liked music but was too self-conscious to let himself go. With Ruby playing, Sally felt as if the music itself was swirling her around on the dance floor, and, magically, that the music was listening to her. Sally stretched her hands out and led them into the chorus and Ruby bent over her squeeze box, working it back and forth with her wrinkled hands.

Sally felt as if she was being lifted – carried up into the air. It was a thrill, like being in love, or that rush Sally had felt when the midwife put Dougie in her arms and told her the little mite of a thing was her son. Not just lifted – flying.

They finished the first hour to cheers twice as loud as usual. Someone had bought them a port and lemon each, and set them on the table nearest the piano. Bert shoved a couple of young fellows off their seats to give them a place, and Sally saw Alfred and Belle at the bar, both with grins splitting their faces from ear to ear.

'Shall we have a go at "Then You'll Remember Me" when we get back.' she said.

Ruby's eyes twinkled. 'Are you sure that's the one you want to do, dear? You have them in the palm of your hand now. How about being *really* brave?'

'He listens too much, that Tom,' she said, plucking at her dress. 'There is this ballad. But I can't. It kills me to sing it.'

'Like going up there with no clothes on?'

Sally blushed. 'He told you that, too?'

'He did. He was kicking himself for not finding the right words to say, to encourage you to give it a go. That's why I'm here.'

'But, Miss Ruby—'

'Don't "but Miss Ruby", me, dear. They're all ready, and you've got me this evening. When will you have a better chance to give it a go?'

Chin up, Sally Blow.

'Oh, very well. And if it all goes to rags, we'll just wake them up again with "Burlington Bertie".'

'That's the spirit, Sally. Now hum me the melody.'

Sally leant over, and very quietly sang the first lines into Ruby's ear. Her skin smelt of lavender talc. The expensive sort.

'I have the shape of it,' Ruby said after a minute or two. 'Shall we, then?'

Sally took a huge swallow of her port. She had never been so scared in her life. For one thing, when Ruby took her place on the piano stool with the squeeze box on her lap, the crowd in the pub settled and turned their way, nudging one another to quieten down; then, when Ruby played the first note – a long drawn-out and swelling sigh – the words seemed to go out of her head. Then she thought of Tom as the song rose – what he'd said about being the song – and the words started unfolding from inside her. She didn't need to look at Ruby; she knew Ruby was watching her, feeling her way around the tune Sally was singing and building something round it, like a frame. With her old fingers and squeezebox she was fashioning some kind of golden cup, like they had at church, to hold the song in, even as it spilled straight out of Sally and into the room. Her mind flickered to Noah holding Dougie in his arms, pleased as Punch, laughing as the baby held his finger, then back to the days they were courting, and he'd get up at dawn on his day off to pick flowers for her from the hedgerow outside the town. *Why hadn't I pressed those? Because I'd always thought there'd be more.* And she thought of him in the weeks before the accident, worn down and nervous-looking, but always trying to smile back at her when he caught her eye.

She was aware of the crowd, somehow in her blood, without thinking of them. She could see through her memories, the women leaning on one another, foreheads touching as they watched. She saw Alfred had gone still, halfway through pulling a pint; saw a young man's Adam's apple bob as he swallowed hard, Bert thumbing away a tear from the corner of his eye. And she saw out in the street the snow falling in the glow of the gaslight, and felt that old squeeze box putting her on her toes.

She let the last phrase fall, as if she was laying it at their feet. Ruby's squeeze box sighed into silence and for a second, everything was absolutely still. Then Belle started to clap, tears running down her dear old face, and that set them all off.

'Now give them a lift,' Ruby said, playing the opening of 'Burlington Bertie', and Sally launched in while the whole pub sang along, only pausing to shout their orders at Alfred, till he was red-faced and sweating with all the business.

CHAPTER TWENTY-ONE

As far as Jack could tell, rehearsals for the pantomime were going well. Wilbur Bowman had done a nice article for the *Gazette* – 'Grace Treadwell steps in to save the day' – and Grace herself was coming home every evening looking happy and distracted. Jack was still dealing with the transformation in his own life Mis Chisholm had brought about. In an indecently short period of time, he had gone from being exceptionally busy – constantly dashing from one crisis to another – to having leisure to think. He was now in danger of getting bored.

He sought out Lillian in her office and they talked about the sorts of shows they wanted to see at The Empire in the coming year; then, pleased to find they were very much in agreement, they talked about the new productions in London and their favourite mutual topic – the brilliance of Grace.

'You were right, Lillian,' Jack conceded. 'She's doing a brilliant job. And she's so much happier than when she was writing the play.' His mother, elegant as ever behind her desk, with its neat pile of plays and basket of correspondence, only smiled, but looked pleased. Jack realised he owed her a more grand and extravagant gesture of thanks. He offered the best gift he could by adding, 'And I understand Nikolai has been helpful.'

'I'm very glad,' she said, and Jack could tell she was. Lillian was a superb actress, but there was a certain gleam in her eye which only appeared when she was sincere. 'You know, he thinks almost as highly of Grace as we do.'

That was certainly a point in Nikolai's favour.

Lillian returned to her play and papers and, his hands in his pockets, Jack wandered the corridors, dreaming, until it occurred to him he hadn't seen anything of Dixon Wells for some time. He enquired of Little Sam, and was told Dixon had been provided with a cupboard next to the carpentry shop below the auditorium, and was apparently very happy there.

As Jack approached the half-open door, he could hear Dixon whispering to himself, accompanied by the little metallic clicks Jack had come to associate with delicate tools and the mercurial power of the electron.

He knocked on the door and Dixon looked round guiltily. He had made himself quite at home. His disreputable coat hung on the back of the door and a leather roll of tools was laid out in front of him. He appeared to be in the process of rewiring a small lamp from the prompt box.

'Jack! I've been meaning to come and ask you about setting up in here. I'm not in the way, am I?'

'Not at all, Dixon. You seem very comfortable. Where are you sleeping?'

When Jack first arrived at The Empire, he had used a camp bed in the lobby, which was now Danny's domain. He couldn't really criticise, then, if Dixon had found a place to sleep in the theatre itself, but he had a vague idea it shouldn't be encouraged.

'At the Metropole,' Dixon replied.' Jack's eyebrows shot up. 'I should get a room in a boarding house, I suppose, but the Metropole is very convenient.'

Jack blinked. Dixon was moving in a rather odd fashion, leaning over the desk in an exaggerated way that made Jack think he was hiding something.

'What's that behind you, Dixon?'

Dixon, not very casually, propped up a copy of the newspaper behind him and stretched in the most obviously fake yawn Jack had ever seen. 'Oh, nothing.'

Jack raised his eyebrows and, while Dixon looked increasingly miserable, leant over and plucked away the paper. It was hiding a small wooden box which had been lined with straw and a thick square of tartan cloth, not unlike Ollie's old blanket.

'What on earth?' Then Jack noticed, on a small tray next to the box, a tub of cold cream.

'Dixon! What is the meaning of this?'

'Meaning of what? The cold air of the season can dry one's skin terribly, you know.'

Jack was not convinced.

'Dixon Wells, you are harbouring Harry! You are giving succour to the enemy!'

'Harry's a very nice rat,' Dixon replied stoutly. 'And I bought the cold cream myself.'

Jack wondered if he should be firm, but there was something about the way Dixon was sticking out his chin which made Jack feel oddly fond of him.

'As long as Harry behaves himself, I suppose . . .' He leant up against the table, which was scattered with all manner of lengths and spirals of copper and mysterious coils. 'Dixon, it's jolly having you here, but I should know a little more about you. How come you ended up in Highbridge? You must be a man of means if you can stay at the Metropole.'

Dixon stared at the table top. 'My father controls all my money. He says I'm not fit to look after it.' He glanced up quickly at Jack, then picked up one of the tiny screwdrivers from his roll of tools and twisted it round his fingers. 'But I've saved a lot from my allowance. I'm not causing any trouble, am I?'

'My dear chap, you're doing the most fantastic work. Things that flickered have given a steady light. What was too bright has subtly dimmed, what was turgid now sparkles. There's no question that we're very glad to have you, but we really should be paying you . . .'

Dixon's eyes widened. 'Oh, I don't want to be *paid*, Jack. I've been having such fun. Ruben on the lighting is a very nice man, and Mr Poole keeps giving me macaroons.'

A man resistant to be being paid for his labour was somewhat out of Jack's experience. He cast around for an explanation. 'Are you a fan of the theatre?'

Dixon moved some of the coils around on his desk. 'Yes . . . well, to a degree. I like *music* very much. I've even designed some of my own microphones, you know, for gramophone records. The theatre's a bit . . . too much for me on occasion, but I enjoy being down here.'

Jack studied the man. The theatre did attract all sorts: people of talent and ambition, like Lillian; people who were born or adopted into it, like Grace; people who stumbled in and fell in love with the whole business, like Jack himself. Then there were the occasional waifs and strays who couldn't find their place in the world in general, or found they were living at an odd angle to their peers, who found a snug gap somewhere between all the make-believe, grand personalities, stress and drama, and were suddenly completely at home.

Jack certainly didn't want to drive Dixon away, and something about the way he had made himself comfortable and bonded with Mr Poole, Ruben – and even Harry the rat – made him feel oddly protective.

'As long as you're happy, Dixon.'

'I am. I saw your picture,' Dixon went on. 'In the newspaper with Lady Lassiter and Nikolai. I thought you looked kind.'

Could that be all it was? Jack wondered.

Dixon glanced back up at him again with that peculiar smile.

'And you take in all sorts here, don't you?' Dixon went on as if he had heard Jack's own thoughts. 'There's Danny and me, and that man who sits in the upper circle in old-fashioned clothes. Well, I've only seen him once, yesterday, but he looked very at home.'

Jack straightened up at once. 'Did he have a sort of floppy cravat on? And a surprisingly long nose?'

Dixon nodded, then blinked in surprise as Jack whooped and punched the air. 'Dixon, that's marvellous news. That's the theatre ghost. The pantomime will be a hit. I'll just go and tell Grace and the cast. And remember, it's the Christmas Eve party at Lassiter Court tomorrow. Do join the charabanc and come along.'

Dixon nodded. 'Yes, I'd like that.'

Jack strolled out and wound his way up staircases and along corridors to the stage, to share the joyous news of the ghost's appearance with Grace and the cast.

CHAPTER TWENTY-TWO

The Christmas Eve party at Lassiter Court was one of the great events of the season in Highbridge. The upper echelons of the town's society were delighted by the chance to sip champagne in one of the best houses in the area, and the thrilling addition of theatre folk gave the evening a spice of devil-may-care revelry. The fact that Lady Lassiter was harbouring the scandalous Stella Stanmore and exiled royalty in her home meant that local matrons fell over themselves to secure an invitation. One or two, who had perhaps blotted their copybooks with unfortunate remarks around the history of Jack Treadwell's birth, took the precaution of block-booking tickets for the pantomime into late January, in the hopes that Mr Poole might put in a good word for them.

Grace was absent during the preparations, watching the technical rehearsals for the pantomime, her nails bitten down to the quick, then having a final run-through of the lighting cues. Christmas Day would be spent visiting local hospitals with the cast, entertaining the nurses and patients with carols and handing out gifts, then on Boxing Day they'd have the dress rehearsal and the opening night. Going over her notes in these final hours, Grace found her heart beating fast and her chest tight. She felt, finally, absolutely alive.

She was still absorbed in her plans when Jack drove her to Lassiter Court to change for the party, so it wasn't until Grace was back downstairs that she had a chance to look around and appreciate the transformation to her home. Great quantities of greenery had been carried in from the gardens and park, and every picture frame and doorway was lined with swags of holly, yew and mistletoe. Artful displays of bare branches renewed with spirals of ivy spilled across the occasional tables, and squat candles nestled among them on silver dishes. Everything glowed with warmth and promise, and the romance of Christmas.

Grace ran her fingers over the polished table tops in the hall, then turned in to the dining room and found the grand mahogany table had been spirited away to make room for comfortable clusters of chairs at intervals around the walls. At the end of the room stood the Christmas tree, hung with dozens of glass ornaments – snowflakes, sailing ships, globes and teardrops – shimmering among silver drifts of tinsel, and more candles in individual glass lanterns. Under the tall leaded windows which looked out onto the drive, a luxurious buffet had been set out. Grace, discovering she was suddenly extremely hungry, spotted platters of devilled eggs and anchovy toasts, and in the centre the caviar sat in a silver dish, surrounded by ice, with a thin golden spoon sticking out of the pot and plates of immaculately cut and buttered triangles of brown bread beside it.

'Do you like it?' Lillian asked, coming in behind her.

'It's absolutely wonderful,' Grace said sincerely. 'The old cats of Highbridge will find nothing to disapprove of, and their husbands will bless you for the anchovy toasts.'

Lillian laughed. 'I worried I was perhaps becoming a little too pagan with the decorations, but Hewitt assures me the spirits of Christmas are on my side. And I did so want Nikolai to see a proper English Christmas. I bought fountain pens as favours this year, and the usual packages of gingerbreads. I think we shall send everyone home happy.'

Grace hesitated. 'Lillian, can we afford all this?'

'No, not at all,' she said with a shrug. 'But it's important to put on a good show. I have faith in our prospects for the New Year, Grace. We have the panto to set us up, Jack has Miss Chisholm, and Nikolai and I have been burning oak leaves in the fireplace in the library.'

'Oak leaves . . .?' Grace asked as Hewitt glided into the room with a tray of brimming champagne flutes, and Lillian and Grace both took one.

Lillian laughed. 'Thank you, Hewitt. Yes, dry ones, harvested from the woods. It's an old Marakovian custom, apparently. Burning them casts sparks of inspiration and good luck into the house, which will make all our fortunes.'

'I'll drink to that,' Grace said with enthusiasm, and did.

'Grace, darling,' Lillian said as Hewitt retreated, 'I have a favour to ask you.'

'Anything,' Grace said, overcome with firelight, greenery and her first sip of champagne. Lillian hesitated before she spoke, which was most unlike her. Grace frowned.

'I'll be making an announcement this evening.' Grace thought she noticed the suggestion of a blush on Lillian's perfectly powdered cheek. 'Might you take care to perhaps be close to Jack when I do?'

'Of course, but—'

Before she could ask any more, Tom sauntered into the room, a glass of champagne in his hand. 'Lillian, I've set up the gramophone in the library as requested, and I'm happy to play carols on the piano in the drawing room whenever you give me the nod.' He paused to admire the tree. 'Good Lord, that's a stunner.'

'Marvellous. Is your mother coming this evening, Tom?'

He grimaced. 'Oh, yes, and I'm expected to share her Christmas ham with her tomorrow.'

'I do wish you and she got along better,' Lillian said.

'Lillian,' he protested with a slight laugh, 'Constance was a monster to you.'

'She was,' Lillian conceded. 'But I am so happy this evening, my goodwill extends even to her. Any news of Edmund?'

Tom lowered his head over his champagne glass. 'Nothing that makes me think we'll see him in Highbridge any time soon.'

There was something in his expression which made Grace want to ask more, but a horn tooted outside. The charabanc from the theatre was approaching along the drive. 'Oh,' Tom added. 'I've been observing Nikolai preparing his Christmas cocktails. I suspect this party will go with a swing.'

It swung. An hour later, Jack was ambling through the hallway with a glow in his blood that was half plum brandy, and half a reflected glow of pleasure from those around him. Harold Drabble had led a singalong at the piano that had left Lillian's guests pink with delight. Terrence Fortescue was sitting in the middle of the dining room, with the now devoted girls and boys of the chorus lounging at his feet, as he leant on his stick and delivered a mixture of cryptic advice in oracular fashion. Ruby and Mrs Poole occupied a settee with a good view of the Christmas tree, and Nikolai plied them both with his Christmas cocktails while Mr Poole, not quite able to give up his front of house role, walked between the rooms, greeting regular patrons of the theatre and occasionally twitching the evergreen displays when he thought Hewitt wasn't looking.

Jack bore down on him with a fresh glass of champagne.

'Mr Poole! Season's greetings!' Mr Poole took the glass with an appropriate murmur. 'How are the bookings looking?'

Like the illuminated sign outside the theatre, Mr Poole had been looking a lot cheerier in the past few weeks. His cheeks were filling out a little and there was a distinct sparkle in his eye.

'It's absolutely marvellous, Mr Treadwell,' he said, then sipped his champagne and wrinkled his nose as the bubbles hit. 'We're entirely sold out for the first fortnight, and healthy numbers for the week after, too. I think that article Mr Bowman did about Mrs Treadwell gave everything a boost.' He sipped his champagne again and sneezed very delicately. 'Our patrons have wanted to show Mrs Treadwell their support, you know, ever since that horrid notice, and they haven't had a chance. Really, Archibald being driven out of the country by the taxman was an huge boon.'

Jack realised Mr Poole had been overheard. Constance Lassiter was standing a little way from them in desultory conversation with Sir Tobias Seymour, but on hearing Mr Poole's comment she had gone still, then turned to look at them over her shoulder while Sir Tobias took the opportunity to sidle away into the crowd.

'Good evening, Constance,' Jack said, adopting a polite smile.

She looked him up and down, then turned and moved away.

'Rude!' Mr Poole said, though by his expression, the moment had delighted him.

'Yes,' Jack said thoughtfully. 'Not everyone shares our delight in The Empire's good fortunes. Have you seen Miss Chisholm, by the way? I want to make sure she gets her fair share of Lillian's caviar. God knows she's earned it.'

'Yes, Miss Chisholm is certainly here. When I last saw her, Marmaduke Smythe was explaining the motivations of King Rat to her.' Jack felt a spasm of concern, but Mr Poole leant towards him. 'Don't concern yourself, Mr Treadwell. She seemed wryly amused.'

The chink of a fork on a champagne flute summoned the attention of the crowd to the stairs.

'Ladies and gentlemen, if we might have your attention for a moment.'

Lillian was standing halfway up the first flight, with Nikolai at her side. The bannisters were festooned with holly, and in her pale turquoise dress, a sheer tulle shawl over her shoulders, she looked like a fairy queen in her bower. Guests drifted in from the other reception rooms, and Jack found Grace taking his hand as the crush thickened.

'Welcome to Lassiter Court, everyone, and Merry Christmas,' Lillian said, resting one hand lightly on the banister. 'I do so hope to see you all at the pantomime. I would just like to thank our wonderful cast for all their hard work preparing what I know will be a wonderful show this year, and of course, I am particularly thankful to dear Grace, who has stepped in as our director and been doing magnificent work—' She was interrupted by a chorus of 'hear, hear', particularly from the cast. Jack glanced down at his wife and squeezed her hand. Her eyes were dancing, and he was torn between delight in her pride and pleasure, and concern she might be overstraining herself. Loving people meant always being in a state of mild worry. He thought back to his adoptive parents. He missed them terribly, but at least, when the Spanish Flu took them, they'd known he was in a prisoner of war camp, not lost like so many young men, forever on the fields of France. On the edge of the crowd he spotted Miss Chisholm, standing with Ruby and Mrs Poole, and near the door to the library was Dixon, wearing an ill-fitting dinner suit, his bow tie a little crooked. On the edge of the crowd, Lillian's business partner Agnes and her fiancé Joe Allerdyce were standing with Charlie Moon, the previous manager of The Empire, who had helped Jack so much when he'd first arrived in the town. That was before Jack had uncovered the mystery of his birth – or partially uncovered it, at any rate. Looking around at his family, Jack felt no need to meet his father. Whoever it was had seduced, attacked and abandoned Lillian under a false name. Jack had long ago decided he'd rather never know the scoundrel's identity. Seeing those familiar faces around him, he knew that he was truly blessed among men. Lillian had started speaking again.

'And I hope you will forgive me for making a personal announcement on this happy evening. I am honoured to tell you, my dear friends, that His Excellency, Grand Duke Nikolai Goranovich Kuznetsov has asked me to be his wife. And I have accepted.'

Jack froze as Lillian's guests applauded and raised their glasses. Grace nudged him and, as Lillian's gaze sought him out in the crowd he managed – just – to smile.

CHAPTER TWENTY-THREE

Tom decided, as he scraped out the remains of the pot of caviar and spread it on a piece of bread and butter with the back of the golden spoon, that he was pleased Lillian was marrying again. He liked his aunt very much, and wanted her to be happy, and Nikolai seemed decent. He himself was not full of festive cheer. He had been bizarrely deflated not to see Mrs Sally Blow step out of the theatre charabanc, then cursed himself for his stupidity. The invitation to Lassiter Court extended as far as the cast, the Pooles, of course, Miss Chisholm and Dixon Wells. Not to the stagehands, or the chars and usherettes. Anyway, she'd be singing at the Bricklayers Arms tonight. He thought of the look on her face when he'd said he didn't have much to do with the factories. In fact, he didn't have anything to do with them, but he knew that as well as churning out cutlery and fancy goods, they were the source of the quarterly income deposited into his bank. Sometimes he envied people who had to work for a living; surely putting bread on the table gave them a purpose he was lacking at the moment. Then he imagined saying that to Sally Blow, while wiping caviar off his fingers, and blushed.

How was Sally going to spend her Christmas, he wondered. Might he drop by, after seeing his mother? He could take a package of Lassiter Court gingerbread for Dougie. He scowled at himself. Sally thought he was just a spoilt, overgrown schoolboy. His turning up uninvited at her home on Christmas Day would look ridiculous. He might take one of the little parcels of gingerbread with him anyway, though, just in case the opportunity arose to pass it to her casually, in an offhand manner, at the theatre. He went in search of Ruby, and, as she was sitting with Mrs Poole, got her to tell the story of playing with Sally in the pub one more time.

'She had 'em then, Ruby?' Mrs Poole asked, her pretty, round face sparkling with amusement. 'I might pop along to listen with my sister one Friday while Mr Poole is working.'

Ruby sipped her sherry. 'She did. You'll hear it, Esmé, there's real talent there.'

'And when I have, I promise I'll come and tell you all about it, Tom,' Mrs Poole said with a wink. So she had got the idea Tom had a particular interest in Sally, too. Well, so he did, though Sally didn't seem to think much of him. Tom felt both embarrassed and touched, and with a shy smile, excused himself to circulate, pacing through the reception rooms in search of something, as the someone he was looking for was three miles away in the middle of town.

As he paced, he saw Stella passing from room to room, talking very brightly to all the townspeople, though she seemed to be avoiding the theatrical lot. He noticed her offering Lillian and Nikolai her congratulations; then she disappeared. It troubled him enough to lift him out of his preoccupations and stop Grace in the hall.

'How is Stella?' he asked.

Grace bit her lip. 'Oh, Tom, I hardly know. The police haven't called again, and I know her agent has telephoned and sent telegrams asking when she will go back, but she won't answer them. The newspapers are apparently too busy fretting about the shortage of coal in London to write about her, now the inquest is over.'

Tom was a little shocked; he hadn't even known the inquest was taking place.

'What was the verdict?'

'Death by misadventure,' Grace said, twisting the long chain of her necklace between her fingers.

'But . . .?' Tom prompted.

'But Stella spends all her days reading or walking around the gardens in one of my old tweed skirts.'

'Stella?' Tom almost choked on his champagne. 'Reading?'

'I know,' Grace said with a sigh. 'It's so unlike her. I half-expected her not to come down at all this evening. Hewitt says she's still sleeping half the day, and the maids have heard her crying. I've been selfish, just concentrating on the pantomime. I feel we've rather deserted her.'

Tom shook his head. 'You've been saving our collective bacon, Grace.' She did not look entirely comforted. 'And anyway, once opening night is out of the way, you'll be able to keep more of an eye on her, won't you?'

'Yes, that's right,' she said, pulling so hard at the chain of her necklace, Tom feared it would break. 'She must have cared terribly for this girl, but even so, I still don't understand why that would mean she'd insist on retiring from the stage.' Tom became aware of the introduction to one of the panto tunes coming from the drawing room. 'Oh, that's Harold's song!' Grace exclaimed. 'I'd better get in there and make sure he doesn't exhaust his voice.'

'Go on,' Tom said, and she hurried off. He made his way into the library, where he was fairly sure he'd seen Hewitt heading with a tray of devilled eggs. Instead he found Dixon Wells, on his own, bent over the gramophone. The fire crackled. Tom had seen Dixon round the theatre, been introduced, and marvelled at the brighter atmosphere inside and outside the building, but had not had time for any long conversations. Feeling he'd rather be here, missing the presence of a woman he barely knew, rather than missing her in a larger crowd, he dropped into one of the comfortable leather armchairs by the player. It was a rather beautiful object, housed in a chinoiserie cabinet. He found himself wondering what Sally would think of it – the question he asked of everything that fell under his eye at the moment.

'Dixon!' He roused himself. 'How are you? Enjoying the party?'

Dixon started and blinked at Tom for a few seconds, as if trying to remember where he was. 'Yes, I've been listening to the gramophone.' The embers glowed in the grate. 'Did I tell you I made my own microphone last year?'

'You did not.'

'I think it sounded rather better than whatever was used to make *these*. I went as far as making a record with my mother and sister.'

Tom smiled. 'I'd like to hear it some time.' He opened his silver cigarette case. Dixon refused one, but Tom lit up and sat back. 'Where are your people?'

'Mother and Lila live in Surrey. Father is mostly in London. He works for the Foreign Office, but he goes home for weekends sometimes.'

'And what do they think of you coming to Highbridge?'

'Oh, they don't know where I am,' Dixon said. Tom must have looked concerned, because Dixon frowned and hurried on. 'They know I'm in good health. I've been fighting with my father about money. I needed to get away and stay away. It's all very dreary.'

'I'm sorry to hear that.' Tom felt difficult relationships with family were one of his few areas of expertise.

Dixon shrugged and focused his attention on the gramophone again, in a way which suggested he wished to drop the subject. Tom followed his lead. 'Dixon, if you can make better microphones than the ones they use already, why don't you work for one of the manufacturers?'

'I wouldn't have macaroons or a rat like Harry if I worked for one of those companies. They're all in London, and I don't like London. I'd much rather set up on my own. That's where the dreary fights with my father come in. He has had doctors say I'm not fit to look after my own capital.' His expression became suddenly fierce. 'It's not even his money!

It comes from my mother's father. And I know I'm a little strange at times, but I . . .' He tailed off.

Tom considered the burning end of his cigarette. 'We're theatre people. You don't seem strange to us.' Dixon smiled. 'So they only record in London?'

'Some travel around in motor cars and record singers elsewhere, but they're all based in London.'

The fire crackled.

'Dixon, do you happen to know how records are made?'

'Of course, I've been into it all quite deeply. Even if I am a little strange, I'm not stupid.'

'Dear fellow, of course you aren't. Can you tell me about it?'

Dixon brightened further and began to explain the process to Tom in some detail. He was miming the mysteries of sound waves, with rippling gestures in the air, when Jack came into the room and greeted them.

'Jack, come over here and sit with us for a minute,' Tom said. 'We're talking about gramophone records.'

With a sigh, Jack sat down in one of the leather armchairs next to the fire. 'Really? We've just had some terrific ones sent over from New York.'

Tom felt something spark within him, like the flare of a struck match.

'Dixon has designed his own microphone,' he said slowly.

'Of course he has,' Jack said, lighting a cigarette and winking at the younger man, who blushed, but looked rather pleased.

'And he knows a lot about their manufacture—'

'Only theoretically,' Dixon mumbled, still blushing.

Tom leant forward in his chair, his elbows on his knees. He thought of Sally's words: 'Take a risk.' 'Jack, would you be open to a new enterprise? Now you've got Miss Chisholm helping at The Empire?'

Jack frowned. 'I might be. What are you thinking, Tom?'

'Yes, what *are* you thinking, Tom?' Dixon said with more alarm, sitting forward so the light fell across his face.

'Nikolai, are you in here?' Lillian came into the room, then stopped, her hand flying to her chest. 'Oh, I . . . Mr Wells!' She cleared her throat. 'I do hope you are having a pleasant evening.'

'I've been listening to gramophone records,' he said simply.

'Anything we can do for you, Lillian?' Jack asked, twisting round in his chair. 'Is Grace all right?'

Lillian looked between him and Dixon, then smiled rather distractedly at them all. 'No, it's nothing. And Grace is being marvellous. I only wanted to ask Nikolai to make another batch of his plum brandy cocktails. Hewitt refuses to take responsibility.'

Tom watched her go, wondering why she appeared so shaken at the sight of them, but Jack reached forward and tapped him on the knee.

'Come on then, Tom. Tell me all.'

Tom scratched his chin.

'Have you thought of any use for the old restaurant, Jack?'

Jack shook his head. 'I haven't. It haunts me.'

'I don't really know what I'm thinking at the moment,' Tom confessed. 'But here we are. Dixon knows all about records, I know about the music business and publishing from working with Ruby. You, Jack, could sell coal at the pithead—'

'Thanks very much,' Jack said, then added after a slight pause. 'I think.'

'Well, you could,' Tom replied.

'I don't understand,' Dixon said. 'Why are we selling coal?'

Tom went to the side table where the whisky decanter was sitting and poured generous measures for them all.

'We aren't.' He handed Dixon his drink. 'But I wonder if we might sell records.'

They talked long into the night. Hewitt interrupted them briefly to tell them he had prepared the green bedroom for Mr Wells, and laid out some of Mr Treadwell's clothes for his use. When Jack finally stood up and wished them a good night, Christmas Day was already a few hours old.

'We'll pop into the Metropole tomorrow,' Tom said, as he showed

Dixon to his room, 'to pick up the record you made. Then after Grace and Jack have done the tour of the hospitals with the cast, and I've seen my mother, we'll come back here for our late Christmas lunch and listen to it.'

Dixon glanced behind him at the comfortable room, the clothes laid out for him and the fire glowing behind its guard. 'Am I imposing? Mother told me I have a habit of imposing. Sometimes I don't notice if people want me to go away.'

Tom squeezed his shoulder. 'Not at all, dear chap.'

'Do you think Jack likes me?' Tom was slightly startled by the question, and by the intense, pained look on Dixon's face.

'I'm certain he does, Dixon. So do I.' He was rewarded by one of Dixon's slow, shining smiles. 'I'll say goodnight, then.'

'Tom?'

'Yes, Dixon?'

'You said you were having Christmas lunch with your mother, too. Does that not mean you will be having two Christmas lunches? Can that be healthy?'

Tom was inclined to laugh out loud, but he remembered the hour. 'My mother celebrates Christmas like Scrooge before the ghosts visited. I'll be lucky to get more than a slice of ham and some very cold looks. I'll have appetite left for a Lassiter Court feed.'

Dixon stared down at the polished floorboards. 'Families are terribly complicated, aren't they?'

'They are, Dixon,' Tom replied, and found himself thinking of Sally Blow. He wondered what sort of man her husband had been. He thought of introducing her to his mother, to Lillian and Jack. 'Indeed they are. Goodnight, dear chap.'

CHAPTER TWENTY-FOUR

Constance had not enjoyed the party at Lassiter Court. She had gone with certain expectations, and had been disappointed. The fact that Lillian was her late father-in-law's widow meant the two women attempted to appear civil in public. They would never attempt to do so in private, but it was easier for them both to keep up the pretence, if not of friendship, then at least chilly civility. Lillian occasionally graced the classical concerts Constance and Lassiter Enterprises sponsored in the town hall with her presence, and Constance visited Lassiter Court for events such as the Christmas Eve party. Over the last eighteen months she'd derived a certain vicious pleasure in spotting, with the expertise of a long-time observer, the little stresses and strains in Lillian's world. Enquiring about the restaurant had been fun the year before; then watching Grace blink back tears as Constance sympathised about the closing of her play during their last Christmas party had been particularly delicious. Not that she had anything against Grace, but she was married to Jack and living with Lillian. Constance held both responsible for her son Edmund's injuries during the fire, and the ruination of her own plans. As a result, it was indeed pleasant to see Lillian and Jack witnessing Grace's distress, and to gloat over their inability to do anything about it.

Constance had been looking forward to a little more panic, and a little more fraying at the edges that evening, and was bitterly disappointed to find everyone apparently having an extremely good time. Even noticing the missing Corot painting had not made her feel any better.

She let herself into her house with her own latch key, and was surprised to see Susan, her maid, waiting for her on a stool in the hallway.

'Good evening, Mrs Lassiter,' Susan said in a whisper. 'There's two men come. Older one says he's a friend of yours, though he doesn't look friendly. I didn't know what to do. Shall I call the police? Or get Philips to throw him out? The older gentleman, he's got a manner to him. What with Mrs Booth being away, I didn't rightly know what to do. They're in your study. The older one just poured himself a whisky and sat down like he owns the place.'

Constance paused for a fraction of a second as she pulled off her gloves, then handed them and her purse to Susan.

'That's perfectly all right, Susan. I know the gentlemen. You may go to bed. Tell Philips the same when he has garaged the car. I shall lock the front door myself when my visitors leave.'

'But, Mrs Lass—'

'Go to bed, Susan.'

The maid bobbed a curtsey and waited in the hall, her eyes cast down, until Constance had put her hand on the crystal door handle which would admit her to the study, and turned it.

Ray Kelly was sitting in one of the armchairs at the small table under the bookshelves opposite the desk, a cut-glass tumbler of whisky at his elbow, amber in the low light. By the window, almost completely hidden in shadow, stood his man Sharps, as thin as a flick knife.

'Constance,' Kelly said, waving his hand towards the empty armchair on the other side of the table. 'Take a seat. We do hope you had a pleasant evening. Will you take a drink?'

'A whisky,' Constance said, sitting down. 'I hope you are well, Mr Kelly.'

Her relationship with Kelly was mutually advantageous, but she was a wise enough woman to treat him with great care. People who displeased Kelly had a habit of disappearing as completely as the flame of a snuffed-out candle – a trace, an absence which resolved quickly into nothingness.

Her son Edmund had run up gambling debts with Mr Kelly – debts which would have crippled even Lassiter Enterprises at one point – and though Constance had greatly improved the health of the company books, there was still work to be done. Around the time of Edmund's accident, she had allowed herself to associate with Kelly more closely. One of her managers was also on his payroll, and she was well aware that the trucks which rolled out from Lassiter Enterprises factories often carried more than china and tableware. One hand washed the other. As well as not having to worry about the debt being called in, Constance was in the enviable position among Highbridge business people of never having to worry about organised labour at her manufacturing sites. Any workers who started to talk about their rights too loudly would get a visit from Sharps or one of his minions, and would soon discover the welfare of their family was better served by their keeping their heads bent over their work stations and their voices down.

'I am middling well, Constance,' Kelly said with a sigh. Sharps poured Constance's whisky into another of her tumblers and set it silently on the table, before withdrawing to his post by the window. 'But only middling, which is why I've left my comfortable fireside in the dale, where I'm all snug for the winter, to pay you a visit.'

Constance picked up her glass.

'I'm sorry to hear you've been disturbed, Mr Kelly,' she said carefully.

'We're touched our comfort means so much to you,' Kelly replied, his voice suddenly a low growl; then he picked up his glass and twisted it so the lamplight made the liquor in it glow. 'There's been a pair of London police in town. Came to visit Miss Stella Stanmore.'

Constance tutted. She had seen the woman at the party this evening, flirting with the blustering and blushing gentlemen of Highbridge. Kelly raised an eyebrow and Constance cast her eyes down.

'Yes, we know how you feel about those theatrical types only too well. Don't we, Sharps?'

'We do, Mr Kelly.' As he replied, Sharps drew a knife from his pocket, flicked it open and began to trim his nails by the thin rays of moonlight coming through the tall windows. Constance struggled to suppress a flicker of disgust.

'We've been amused on occasion,' Kelly continued, 'watching you play silly buggers with them. Heads in the clouds, haven't they? Think themselves so worldly, but naive as children.'

Constance said nothing.

'But . . .' Kelly set down his glass and leaned towards her. 'You've overstepped, Constance. You buggering about has brought London coppers to my town. And I don't like it.'

The wheels turned in Constance's mind, and clicked together like the tumblers of a lock. Her mouth went dry. 'I see. I'm very sorry. That was never my intention, Mr Kelly.'

He put his hand out, quick as a snake, fastened it round the back of her neck and pulled her towards him, bringing her face so close to his she could feel his cold breath on her cheek.

'If I'd thought it was intentional, dear, you'd be dead already. And who'd give a shit if you were?'

His fingertips, dry and hardened, dug into the back of her neck; the sheer power of them was terrifying.

'You stole from me, Constance. Not a lot. But there's a principle there. You think I don't count my goods as carefully as your best foremen? Think I don't keep accounts?' He gave the back of her neck a shake and she felt a paralysing, animal fear. 'Didn't you? Say it, woman!'

'I did steal.' She gasped, closing her eyes, willing herself to be calm. 'How can I apologise?'

Kelly released her, a slow smile spreading over his gaunt features, and he sat back in his chair. 'Sensible woman. Always thought you a sensible woman, Constance. Apart from your little feud with the theatre. Haven't we always said so, Sharps?'

'We have, Mr Kelly,' Sharps replied. He hadn't even looked up from cleaning his nails.

Kelly folded his hands in his lap and crossed his legs. 'We're not unreasonable. We've valued our relationship. But, Constance, you've been warned. You don't have many friends – be careful to keep the ones you have.'

CHAPTER TWENTY-FIVE

'So it is no longer singing loudly into a big trumpet?' Nikolai asked. The denizens of Lassiter Court were scattered around the drawing room in the sort of comfortable haze which comes from a busy day followed by a large meal, and the gramophone had been moved into position by the piano for Dixon's demonstration. He had brought one of his microphones with him, along with his record, and it had been passed round the room with the sherry and mince pies. Stella was currently studying it, curled up in the corner of the settee like a cat, her head on one side.

'No, Your Excellency. These microphones turn the sound waves into an electrical signal, so performers can sing more softly, and you can hear all the individual instruments. It sounds much richer and sharper.'

Nikolai leant back in the leather armchair and crossed his long legs.

'Do call me Nikolai.'

Jack glanced at him. His face was sore from all the polite smiling he'd been doing since Lillian had announced their engagement. Lillian had every right to be happy – that was what Grace had said to him, quite firmly, between spells singing carols to invalids that morning – but the self-assurance of the man, his optimism, set Jack's teeth on edge.

'So then what happens, Dixon?'

'The vibrations are engraved onto a master disc. They are made on beeswax. Then that is used to make a metal master, and that presses all the rest. It's quite straightforward. And also terribly difficult.'

'Perhaps we could hear the recording, Dixon?' Jack said, getting up from the sofa and putting his hands in his pockets.

'Ah, yes. Of course.' He lifted up a velvet bag, from which he produced a record about eight inches in diameter, and set it on the turntable. 'I created the master with my microphones and my equipment at home, then had half a dozen copies pressed.' He began winding the gramophone handle with gusto. 'I'm afraid I didn't have access to any great musicians in my village. Just my family. My sister plays the violin, you see, and my mother the piano, and our gardener has a nice voice, so we got him in to sing. He leans a bit close to the microphone at times.'

'Do you play an instrument, Mr Wells?' Stella asked kindly. Dixon blinked rapidly at her. 'No. Well, I did have a banjo once, but Mother took it away, because I learnt the one tune I liked and kept playing it.'

He faltered into silence.

'My friend . . .' Nikolai began. Something about his accent, Jack thought, made him sound as if he was about to say something rousing and meaningful every time he opened his mouth. He remembered the fake French chef whom he had hired to run the defunct restaurant and wondered, bitterly, if Nikolai was actually from Grantham. 'My friend, we are not here to judge the musicians, but the recording. Please, let us listen.'

Dixon nodded, released the brake on the turntable, then lowered the stylus onto the disc. He hadn't really needed to speak at all. The music did all the talking for him.

'Goodness!' Stella swung her feet to the ground and leant forward. 'It's as if they're in the room!'

The musicians were attempting 'A Wand'ring Minstrel I,' from Gilbert and Sullivan's *The Mikado*. The singer began bravely, but was rarely absolutely in pitch or in time, cleared his throat occasionally and had a tendency to over-breathe. The violinist tried to play quietly when her fingers were unsure of the notes, and the piano was played with great confidence, but without any perceptible sense of rhythm. Not for want of trying, the pianist was whispering '*one*, two three, *four*, five six,' to herself throughout – all of which the astonished group in the drawing room could hear.

The recording ended. Dixon looked around them and fingered his collar nervously. 'It has to be done all in one take, of course. This was the fourth attempt. And I couldn't persuade Mother to count in her head, or Tonbridge to stop panting, and they were getting tired, so I hope . . .'

'Remarkable,' Tom said. 'I mean, it's an awful arrangement, and not well played, but the recording is incredible.'

Jack polished off the last of his sherry as Grace, Lillian, Stella and Nikolai crowded round Dixon, shaking his hand, which made him flinch, and asking to see the miraculous microphone again.

Grace turned towards him.

'Jack, darling! It's a marvel, but what on earth are you and Tom planning to *do* with it?'

'It's a secret, dear heart. Dixon, Tom and I are plotting, but we're all sworn to secrecy until after the opening of the pantomime. Give us a few days to get our ducks in a row.'

He noticed Grace frowning, and turned to see Hewitt handing Nikolai what appeared to be another Christmas present – a long flat cardboard box tied with a white ribbon.

'What on earth is that, Nikolai?' Lillian asked.

'I do not know,' he said, pulling at the thick white ribbon. 'Hewitt tells me it was delivered from town.' The ribbon gave way, and he lifted the lid. Jack caught a glimpse of newsprint and Nikolai went still, scanning the page without lifting it from the box, then setting the box down on the table.

'Nikolai?' Lillian asked, a note of concern in her voice.

He shook his head. 'It is nothing . . . Please excuse me.' He got up abruptly and left the room.

Dixon leant forward, his head on one side, and peered at the page.

'Oh, that's not very nice,' he said.

'Dixon, what on earth is it?' Jack asked.

'The Daily Bulletin,' Dixon said. 'The largest newspaper in Marakovia.'

'Dixon,' Stella said, with a half-laugh in her voice, 'can you read Marakovian?'

'A little,' he said shyly. 'My father was stationed there for a while.'

Lillian stood up and rested her hand on the mantelpiece. 'Can you tell me, Dixon, what it says?'

Dixon blushed. 'Not exactly, but "Grand Duke worsens disgrace" I think would be accurate. He leant over the paper, avoiding touching it, as if it might be poisonous. 'Claims to like – support, perhaps – workers . . . Consorts with actors and drug addicts.' He glanced, unfortunately, at Stella. 'Oh, there's a picture of you all at the Metropole.'

Grace stepped over to the box, replaced the lid and rang the bell for Hewitt. When he glided into the room, she handed it to him.

'More kindling, Hewitt,' she said firmly, and he bowed over the box with the merest suggestion of a raised eyebrow.

'It is to be expected, of course, that the newspapers in Marakovia would write nonsense about Nikolai,' Lillian said. 'But how on earth did they get the picture? Do you remember it being taken?'

'They were taking pictures of Mabel Mills,' Jack said slowly, 'when we were there the other week. And I thought I saw some in the *Highbridge Illustrated*, in their social diary section.'

'But who on earth would send a copy of a Marakovian paper here?' Stella said with a shudder. 'And on Christmas Day?'

'They didn't just send it,' Dixon said cheerfully. 'Somebody hand-delivered it when they knew you were all out.'

The thought was not comforting.

CHAPTER TWENTY-SIX

Boxing Day dawned, crisp and bright, over Highbridge. After an early breakfast, Jack and Grace motored down to the theatre for the dress rehearsal, with Tom and Dixon in the back of Jack's car, and Lillian and Nikolai following behind them.

Jack had banned all discussion of records for now, and Lillian had declared she wanted to hear nothing about the newspaper. Jack glanced at his co-conspirators in the back seat, and wondered if Tom suspected Constance had gone to the trouble of procuring and sending the newspaper out of spite. He shook his head, took his hand from the wheel to squeeze his wife's, and she glanced back at him with a tight, nervous smile.

'Remember, Grace, we have the blessing of the ghost,' he said. 'So whatever happens at the dress today, it will go splendidly this evening.'

She only nodded, and then turned and looked out of the window as the country verges disappeared, and they passed between the neat villas at the northern edge of town before approaching the heart of Highbridge.

Miss Chisholm was waiting outside The Empire for them, looking appropriately festive in her green coat and red gloves. The sign sparkled, and the banner announcing opening night flickered in the light breeze.

Grace stepped out of the car and Miss Chisholm walked forward.

'How are we looking, Miss C.?' Jack asked.

'Sam is asking for Lady Lassiter, and Mr Porter would like to double-check some of the tempi with you, Mrs Treadwell.' Grace nodded her thanks, and hurried into the theatre. 'Did you have a good Christmas, Mr Treadwell?'

'It was a delight from beginning to end,' Jack said, not entirely truthfully. 'And you?'

'Very pleasant,' she said in a voice that discouraged further conversation.

'Right.' Jack rubbed his hands together. 'Let's get to work.'

Tom discovered Sally in the promenade bar, polishing glasses and humming to herself, her hair tied up in a yellow kerchief. He watched her from the threshold for a second, the light sparkling on the glass as she worked, casting diamonds of light around her.

'Good morning,' he ventured eventually, and she jumped slightly and looked up at him.

'Mr Lassiter,' she said. 'I hope you had a good Christmas.'

Her voice sounded strangely formal. 'I thought we'd agreed you'd call me Tom,' he replied, making his way into the room.

'Perhaps in the pub,' she said, returning her attention to the glass, 'but it doesn't seem right at work.'

Tom took a package of gingerbread out of his pocket and set it on the polished bar next to her. 'From the party at Lassiter Court. I thought Dougie might like it.'

She bit her lip and didn't say anything, only nodded; Tom thought that there was something about the way she was holding herself that suggested she might cry at any moment.

'You're not angry with me, are you, for suggesting that signature tune? Ruby said you were absolutely wonderful.'

She shook her head. 'Just leave me alone. Please, Tom.'

Tom felt his heart squeezed so hard he couldn't quite breathe for a second. *Have I made a complete fool of myself?*

'I . . . Of course. I just wanted you to know, I did listen to you. I'm going to do something with myself rather than wait about—'

'Please, I just need to get on with my work,' Sally said sharply, and turned away.

Tom's heart plummeted. Surely there was something he could say or do. Some way to find out what he had done to offend her. He looked at the straight, stiff line of her back and whatever it was, he couldn't think of it.

Through the open doors of the auditorium the pantomime overture began. The tune, full of frivolity and cheer, was so at odds with his mood, he couldn't bear it. He turned on his heel and left, feeling dark and miserable. He would push on. He went to Lillian's office to make use of her telephone, a sense of hurt and hunger like a void under his ribs.

The dress rehearsal was a disaster. When Grace gathered the cast and crew on stage afterwards, they looked variously miserable, terrified, or, in the case of Terrence Fortescue, icy with rage.

Mr Porter ran through the missed and bungled music cues first, then Fortescue spent twenty minutes tearing each of the chorus to shreds, and another five sneering at the principals. The seam on Josie's very tight jerkin had ripped, King Rat's tail had been cut off by a trapdoor shut too soon, and Alderman Fitzwarren's robes had got paint on them. In the process, the backdrop to the May Day Fair, which opened the show, had become somewhat blurred. Milly, the wardrobe assistant, was breathing into a paper bag. Little Sam and the stagehands were staring fixedly at their shoes.

'. . . and if I could take my name off the programme at this stage, I would!' Fortescue concluded, spitting each syllable out as if they had left an unpleasant taste in his mouth.

A heavy silence fell and Grace felt the eyes of the company turn towards her. *Provincial author stumbles* . . . she thought. She could almost see the fox that looked a little like Jason de Witte, the critic, weaving its way between the flats at the back of the stage.

She cleared her throat and stood up from her stool, her notes of all the missed lines, bungled jokes, sloppy exits and fluffed scene changes between her hands.

'And that is why we have dress rehearsals,' she said. Harold smiled wryly and Josie looked up. 'These are my notes for you,' Grace went on, holding them up above her head. Then she ripped the pages apart and dropped them onto the stage.

Milly put down her paper bag and the chorus huddled together a little closer, like baby birds in an ice storm.

'You don't need these,' Grace said firmly. 'You all know exactly what went wrong. And that's why I know you are going to get it right this evening. Not just because you're frightened of Terrence here . . .' Some of them risked a smile. 'Not just because you know how hard Josie's been working, or the joy Harold's going to bring to the people who come to see us tonight, or because we want Nikolai to finally understand pantomime . . .' A few risked a light chuckle. 'But because I have seen how brilliant you *all* are,' she continued, 'and I know that that's what the audience is going to see tonight. Now we've got the nonsense out of the way, go and relax. Eat, sleep, take a walk in the municipal gardens, and then come back here and let's give Highbridge a truly brilliant show. From the first note to last curtain call. And congratulations on all of your hard work. I am really terribly proud of you.'

They looked comforted, but still nervous. Harold hauled himself to his feet, came over to Grace and put his arm round her shoulders. 'Bless you, my love. Now people, we'll do it for Grace, shall we? Give yourselves a kick up the arse and I'll see you at five.'

Jack took Grace's hand as the overture began and felt the bones of his fingers nearly snapping under the pressure of hers, but he was convinced the ghost was right and they had a hit on their hands. There was a lightness in the air, a general enthusiasm. Lillian and Nikolai sat alongside them in the royal box, with Stella, Dixon, Miss Chisholm, Tom and Ruby in a line behind them, while Agnes de Monfort, the co-owner of the theatre, and Joe Allerdyce, her long-time fiancé, grinned at them from the directors' box opposite.

Jack had felt it – that simmering pleasure – as he'd walked through the theatre as the audience began to gather outside. He'd seen it in the nervous smiles the chorus exchanged as they practised in the corridors, in the care with which the stage crew re-coiled the fly ropes, and the way the prop master rearranged the candy-coloured rolling pins, pie tins and spoons on his table, in the glint of the treasure chest filled with outsized doubloons. He'd seen it in the whip of Milly's needle as she added just one final crop of sequins to Alice's wedding gown, in the way the trumpeter taped the sheets of music together on his stand, then polished the bell of his instrument on his tie, in the skip in Mr Poole's step as he carried a stack of souvenir programmes from one side of the lobby to the other, in the flick the waiter in the promenade bar gave to his cloth as he polished a champagne glass. In the corridor backstage between dressing rooms, he paused, hearing it in the competing vocal exercises coming from Harold Drabble's and Josie's doors. But it was the magic the audience brought in through the doors with them that clinched it: the strange shimmer in the air which arrives with a thousand men, women and children gathered together in full expectation of a really good time.

Act I, scene 1. Dick and his cat arrive in London on May Day. Jack leant forward, his elbows on the edge of the box, and watched.

Grace had filled the stage with colour and movement. The chorus were a surging crowd, Dick lost and dazzled among them and joining in awkwardly with the dance of a city street, till he was caught, transfixed by the sight of his one true love, Alice. There was a lovely bit of business with the cat teasing a chorus boy in character of a spaniel, and a warm surge of laughter rose up like a wave through the stalls. Fitzwarren came on stage to lament in bouncing couplets about his failing fortunes to his daughter, Alice. The audience oohed and aahed in sympathy. Then, in a hooped skirt that extended a good two feet in every direction from his considerable bulk, Harold appeared at the back of the stage, borne forward by the chorus. His wig rose a foot from his head, bound round with a red kerchief. The May Day crowd, Alice, Dick and Fitzwarren dispersed, and Harold turned to the audience, making them wait. They held their breath.

'Oh, where's my tiffin!' he declared, hands on his hips, and the audience erupted into happy cheers. 'Good evening, boys and girls! I'm Sarah, Fitzwarren's cook. Now, are you having a good time?'

Jack leant over to his wife, ready to whisper some encouragement or reassurance, but at that moment she relaxed the pressure on his fingers and sighed. She knew.

CHAPTER TWENTY-SEVEN

'So, here we are then!'

There was quite a party assembled outside the doors to the old Tutankhamen Restaurant. The first week of the pantomime had been a huge success, and they were all, Jack knew, a little giddy with it. The *Highbridge Gazette* had called the show a triumph, and it looked as if it would run to full houses throughout January, and if their luck held, well into February. Now 1926 was behind them, and they had welcomed in 1927 at the Metropole to the strains of Mabel Mills. The sight of his wife laughing with Josie at one of the tables round the edge of the dance floor, while cascades of multicoloured streamers fell around them, was an image Jack was keen to fix in his mind – a talisman for the coming year.

While Grace worked with the cast to iron out any final problems with the show and incorporate into its fabric whatever extra bits of business the presence of an audience had inspired, Jack, Tom and Dixon had been at work. Standing on the grey pavement outside the old restaurant, Jack wondered if they had done enough, but he couldn't delay sharing their plans any longer.

Grace had been at The Empire to watch the matinee, and Stella,

Tom, Lillian and Nikolai had motored in from Lassiter Court with Dixon. At Lillian's invitation, Dixon had abandoned the Metropole, and another of Lassiter Court's many comfortable bedrooms had been made available to him.

Jack turned the key in the lock, pushed open the door and ushered them into the restaurant, then turned on the lights. They illuminated, rather too brightly, a sorry scene. He'd been so proud of the dining room and nightclub when it opened, and it hurt to see it looking so dusty and dishevelled. The street entrance led to a slightly raised level where arrivals could be greeted by the maître d', in full view of the diners and dancers, then led down a short curved staircase to the main floor. Half of the room was filled with tables and two rows of booths; the other half consisted of the dance floor and a low stage for the musical entertainment. The columns which held up the roof were in green marble, with gold palm leaves at top and base, and around the walls marched friezes of Egyptian pharaohs and gods.

It had looked absolutely splendid when it opened, but the gilt on the palm leaves had started to flake and the tables, without their linens and crockery, looked naked and ashamed. The dust had settled into the soft furnishings; the air was musty, and the chairs were stacked in the corners like wallflowers at a very unsuccessful ball.

'It does look like a tomb,' Nikolai observed, unhelpfully.

Grace rested her hand on Jack's shoulder for a moment, and prevented a slump.

'Jack, it's huge,' Dixon said in a whisper. 'I hadn't realised it was so big.'

Jack straightened his back and rubbed his hands together. From the ashes of the restaurant, a phoenix would rise – if he could just get them all to believe.

'We propose setting up a record company,' he said.

'You propose *what?*' Lillian said, and glanced at Nikolai, but he only blinked, his expression one of polite interest. Grace's expression,

Jack noticed, remained cheerful, but he suspected the smile was rather fixed. He hurried on.

'Tom and Dixon and I had a sort of brainwave on Christmas Eve, and that's it. All the recording companies are in London, and we've got singers and songs that deserve an audience up here, too. You've heard the recordings – Dixon will be in charge of all that. Tom's going to manage the manufacture of the records, and I'm going to sell them.'

'What has this got to do with an old restaurant?' Stella asked, running a finger along the dusty brass balustrade.

'This isn't a restaurant!' He jogged down the stairs and opened up his arms. 'I present to you . . . the Empire Recording Studio and Music Emporium!' The looks he was getting were still a bit blank. 'Look, just imagine it. If we put up a wall here, we can divide the space between the shop and the recording area. It will need to be soundproofed, naturally, but we can manage that. Two rooms, one for Dixon and his equipment, and one for the musicians.'

'You won't fit an orchestra in there,' Stella said, blowing the dust off the balustrade, then leaning on it.

'We can do that in the theatre,' Jack said. 'But for singers and small bands, we could do everything here, couldn't we, Dixon?'

Dixon sneezed. 'It would need to be dust-free, but yes. I don't need much room for my equipment. A room with drapes and a carpet, say forty by thirty feet in total? Will that fit?'

Jack nodded and Dixon smiled shyly.

Jack rubbed his hands together. Grace bit her lip, but the fixed smile had gone and she had a sort of sparkle in her eyes. 'Now for the shop. We can sell records from EMI or whoever, as well as our own, and sheet music, pianola rolls! Even instruments. And look at those booths we spent so much money upholstering. What if we could have a gramophone on every table? We'd have some records behind the service counter which customers could borrow and play, so they can check they like it before they spend their hard-earned shillings.'

'Wouldn't that end up making the most awful racket?' Stella asked, walking down the stairs to join him.

He shook his head. 'Not if we put padded barriers between them, and used the wind-up portables. It will be . . .' He paused. 'A merry conflagration of sound.'

Grace came trotting down the stairs to join Stella and Jack. 'I see it! We could have racks of records there. And a cashier's desk. And perhaps we could convert the bar, Jack? Serve coffee and cakes, like the Lyons teashop.'

The dusty space shivered in Jack's vision and he began to see it full of young people, drinking their coffee and listening to records.

'So we record the masters here, and sell the records . . . Dixon, might the recording studio have a window?' Jack asked. 'So customers can see the musicians playing?'

'If we can soundproof it.' Dixon was grinning now, too, wandering round the old dance floor while his fingers worked gleefully at the frayed cuffs of his coat.

Jack looked up at Lillian, who was still standing with Nikolai and Tom by the old maître d's station.

'What do you think, Lillian?'

'I think it sounds terribly expensive, Jack! I know you're all excited, but this building work and all the equipment! How much do these portable players cost? Then we must pay for all the manufacturing and stock before we even begin!'

Jack took the hurdle at a leap. 'I've been through the figures. I think seven thousand pounds would cover the conversion, recording equipment and initial stock, and see us through the first year with staff.'

Lillian gasped, but the tingle would not be stilled. Jack lifted his hands towards her. 'Lillian! We'll find a way, I know it. There's what Grace and I put aside from *Cairo Nights* for a house. And I'm certain the bank will extend our line of credit.'

'Jack . . . The money you put aside for your house?' Lillian exclaimed. 'Hadn't you better consult your wife on that?'

Grace picked up one of the chairs, dusted the seat and sat on it, removing her gloves. 'Blow the house, Lillian. I'd rather have a record shop.'

Jack went down on his knees to kiss her cheek and she laughed.

'Oh, honestly, children,' Lillian sighed. 'Jack, do get up, the floor is filthy. I suppose it's possible that Mr Fiell would like to buy rather than rent the grazing land to the north of Lassiter Court. Though the income has been rather useful.'

'We'll get more income from a record shop,' Jack said. 'I can feel it in my bones, Lillian!' He bounced to his feet and dusted off his knees. 'It's just the shot in the arm The Empire needs. Just think of the excitement!'

A long silence.

'Nikolai,' Lillian said at last, 'what do you think?'

Nikolai offered her his arm and they made their way down the stairs and joined the others at the table. His lips were pursed and his head down. *Man knows how to milk a dramatic pause*, Jack thought, with a mixture of resentment and admiration.

'I come to this country with nothing . . . almost nothing.' Jack felt his jaw clench, but caught Grace's warning look and said nothing. 'I come with only my father's signet ring, and this diamond tie pin.' He removed the pin from his cravat and, as the silk round his neck gracefully unfolded, he stared at it. 'But I lay this down to contribute to the enterprise. Record the voices and songs of your people. Share them with the world.'

He placed the pin down on the table in front of them.

Lillian sighed. 'I guess we are all in then, Jack.'

Jack whooped and performed a creditable shuffle on the wooden boards. 'If I might . . .' Dixon said. 'I've saved something from my allowance. I have two thousand pounds I hoped to invest.'

Nikolai discreetly picked up his tie pin again.

'Goodness, are you quite sure, Dixon? I keep thinking you are on your uppers.'

Dixon followed the direction of his gaze. 'My coat, you mean?'

He fingered the material. 'I'm very fond of it. Mother keeps trying to persuade me to wear one of the new ones, but the cloth is so itchy.'

Lillian held up her hands. 'Very well! I admit a shop for music and records here might work, and I was as impressed by Dixon's recordings as anyone. But did you say manufacturing? Tom?'

Tom was still standing at the top of the stairs, looking rather shy. 'We should make the discs in Highbridge, too, Lillian. So much faster than sending the masters to London, and we'd have control of the quality that way. That's where I come in. I want to make the records.'

'Tom,' Lillian said slowly, 'it's been an awfully long time since I talked about factories and the like with your grandfather, but setting up an enterprise to actually make the records! It makes setting up a recording studio and a shop look like child's play.'

'I'm aware. But I have some thoughts. And this is in my blood, somewhere, Lillian.'

Lillian turned. 'Jack . . .'

He held up his hands. 'Lillian, I felt the same, but Tom's convinced me he knows what he's doing. And this was all his idea in the first place.'

Grace sat forward in her chair. 'Are you sure?'

'I'm convinced I want to try, Grace,' Tom said. Jack watched him; he certainly had a glint in his eye. 'And my mother's attempts to make me learn accountancy had some benefits.'

'But the costs . . .' Grace said.

'I have capital,' Tom said. 'I'll invest that, and borrow the rest from Lassiter Enterprises.'

'Tom, dear,' Lillian said, putting out a gloved hand towards him. 'What about your mother? You're not twenty-five yet, so she controls your capital, and I can't see Constance investing in any scheme which involves us.'

Tom gave a slightly crooked smile. 'I know what my mother is like, Lillian. And I think you can leave her to me.'

Lillian still looked unhappy. 'But, Tom, suppose you do persuade her . . . What if things go wrong? You could lose everything. What would you do then?'

'I suppose I should have to work for a living, like everybody else.'

Lillian turned to Jack. 'Jack, can you allow this?'

Jack thought carefully before responding. 'I've always earned my living, Lillian. And I was sent off to fight when I was younger than Tom is now. It's an enormous risk, but I think it's up to him whether he takes it or not.'

Lillian lifted her hands. 'Very well. Tom, Jack, Dixon, you have my support. Now I have two questions. Is there any serviceable champagne in the building, and who is going to explain all of this to your aunt Agnes?'

The street door opened, and Miss Chisholm appeared as dusk gathered behind her.

'Oh, thank goodness you're all here. Mrs Treadwell, Lady Lassiter, something awful has happened. I'm afraid we're going to have to cancel tonight's performance.'

Grace ran upstairs towards her, Jack at her heels. Miss Chisholm looked distinctly unwell. 'What on earth's happened?' Jack asked.

'I hardly know. The Metropole sent round a buffet tea for after the matinee today, and . . . Oh, dear. I'm afraid you'll have to excuse me.' Her colour changed from pale to ashen, and she fled back in the direction of the theatre.

CHAPTER TWENTY-EIGHT

They followed Miss Chisholm through the lobby and into the stalls, where she disappeared in the direction of the ladies' powder rooms. The new girl, Sally Blow, was standing in the aisle, holding a basin for Mrs Briggs.

She glanced round as they appeared, and addressed Jack. 'It was the chicken salad, I think, Mr Treadwell. It had walnuts in it, which I can't abide, but lots of the others had some.'

Jack's heart sank.

'Who is down and who is up, Mrs Blow?'

'Mr Poole is confined to his cubbyhole, King Rat is groaning on his sofa, and Fairy Bow Bells has gone back to her digs. The chorus all went to the Dog and Duck with the band for Mr Porter's birthday, so they're all right, just a little tight. And Josie is on a bread and water diet since she split her jerkin, so she's fine, too. The cat's as sick as a dog, though.'

Mrs Briggs groaned.

Jack looked at his wife. She had removed her gloves and tucked them into her handbag. 'Harold is the thing,' she said, with a briskness and purpose to her tone. 'How is he?'

The man himself staggered onto the stage. 'I can go on, Grace.'

She looked at him. 'Are you quite sure?'

He shook his head decisively. 'Nothing wrong with me the sound of an audience can't cure. I think Samantha from the chorus can manage the cat. But we'll need a fairy, and a rat.'

Grace turned. 'Stella, could you? It's a matter of flying in at a couple of key moments and you can have the script.'

Harold nodded. 'Just say it's your magic fairy scroll.'

Stella lifted her hand and stepped back; she'd gone almost the same colour as Mrs Briggs. 'I can't . . .' Her voice was tight and tangled. 'I'm never going on stage again. I simply won't.'

'But, Stella—' Grace said.

'No, absolutely not,' Stella said, as she turned and walked out of the auditorium.

Harold watched her go, his face heavy with concern. 'She's got a bad case of the wobbles, hasn't she? Anyone got any more ideas?'

Tom stepped forward. 'Perhaps Sally—' he began, but before Jack could ask him what he meant, Lillian had interrupted.

'I shall play Fairy Bow Bells, Grace. Though I think given how long it's been since I ventured on stage, perhaps I should walk before I attempt to fly. Nikolai, you've been at every rehearsal. Do you think you could manage King Rat?'

'I should be honoured, if Grace thinks it possible.'

Grace was still looking at the space where Stella had been. She shook herself. 'You'll be wonderful, Nikolai. Mrs Blow, how is Milly?'

'Her mum came and picked her up, Mrs Treadwell,' Sally said. 'And Mrs Briggs's daughter is coming for her in a bit. I can stay on and get the lobby tidy, I think. Danny is bad, but I think Ollie has the same opinion on walnuts I do. He's sitting by the stage door and growling at anyone who looks too poorly to work.'

Grace nodded. 'Thank goodness you don't like walnuts. Jack, could you check we have enough crew to run the show?'

'I can pull a rope,' Tom volunteered.

'So can I,' Dixon added.

'Good.' Jack was reminded of the first time he had ever seen Grace, poised and perfect, backstage, snapping out questions and commands with her eyes gleaming. He was lost in awe of her at that moment, and had to shake himself to concentrate on her actual words. 'Jack, then have Marcus put up a sign to advise of the cast changes. Nikolai, see what of King Rat's wardrobe you can use.'

'As long as I have the ears and the tail, I shall manage,' he said stoutly.

'Lillian?' Grace went on. 'The girl playing Fairy Bow Bells is a good six inches shorter than you.'

'All I need is my wand. I have a couple of gowns in the office. Harold, I think you'd better lie down until you need to dress.'

'I rather think you're right, Lil,' he mumbled, and exited the stage again with his hand over his mouth.

Tom was swept up for the next hour in the general whirlwind of activity. The band, like the chorus, were in good health, but he and Nikolai rehearsed King Rat's big number in the second act in the upstairs rehearsal room, and Fairy Bow Bell's solo lines in the finale with Lillian, then went to help Marcus and Jack fix notices to the lobby doors. Miss Chisholm had retired to the offices, and Marcus was ready to sell the standby tickets. Dixon was being trained on the follow spot after Ruben was found groaning miserably in the lime box.

Hurrying back to the rehearsal rooms, an hour before curtain up, to see what he might help with next, he found Sally scraping the suspect chicken salad into a slop bucket.

'Can I help?' he asked. She thrust the bucket at him.

'Yes, take this out to the back yard, and make sure it's not anywhere Ollie can get hold of it. Though I think he's got enough sense not to eat it.'

He took it from her.

'Tom, you were on the point of saying I should go up there, weren't you?'

So I'm 'Tom' again. Is that good?

'I was – you'd be marvellous.'

She scowled. 'That stage isn't for the likes of me!'

'Why on earth not?'

'Oh, don't be so daft.'

'What's daft about it, Sally?'

'Why are you pushing me? I should never have taken this job. Ollie has a lot to answer for. And Miss Ruby, too. Gets me to sing like that, then she's back here and I'm rinsing down the tiles in the WC again, and now every Saturday they're expecting miracles of me in the bar. And I don't know what to do.'

She shook the last of the salad into the bucket. It did smell a little ripe.

'You don't need to perform miracles – you are the miracle. Just be yourself, Sally.'

'Oh, for crying out loud! And who exactly is that? I'll tell you. I'm a widow, and a cleaner with a sick little lad and rough hands. You and Ruby, shaking me about. And for what? This isn't a fairy tale and you're not Prince Charming come to fix everything.'

Tom slammed down the bucket, coming dangerously near to slopping it. 'Of course it's a fairy tale! That's what theatre is all about. It's why we all end up here.'

'No. It's your fairy tale. People like me are here to clean it. Second Mrs Briggs is back on her feet, I'm handing in my notice. It's not fair, being this close, but still on the other side of everything.'

'Of course it's for you, too! Lillian swept factory floors before she became a star. Jack worked in a department store. Harold's mum took in laundry. Sally, what's happened? You're special.'

'I'm not!' He was shocked to see tears spilling from her brown eyes. 'I'm just Sally Blow. My husband, Noah . . . *he* was special. He had a smile that could make your day and he was a good man and *your family killed him.*'

Tom felt a chill spreading from the base of his spine. It made his blood feel thick and his mind slow. 'What?'

She wiped her eyes with her sleeve. 'They killed my Noah! I didn't know! I'm that stupid. They said it was just an accident. Then Noah's parents came to see Dougie on Christmas Day, and they went a bit strange when I said I was working here now, and they told me.'

'Told you what, Sally?' He felt his heart breaking for her.

'About Noah! He went to a couple of meetings about unions, that was all, but the bosses at Lassiter's found out, and the steward started picking on him. Giving him the worst and most dangerous jobs in the factory, driving him half-mad with worry, and he tried to hide it from me, what with Dougie being so little, and I just thought he was tired with the baby being fractious, but they were wearing him down! No wonder he was tired enough to make a mistake at the machines. Is it still an accident? Or is it murder then?'

'Sally, I don't know—'

'And what do I do? Make eyes at the heir, and sing that song for him. Even if you weren't there, I was singing it for you, and then I wash out your bloody lavs. And you think I should be on that stage! Lady Lassiter didn't even hear you—'

'Sally, darling!'

'Don't! Look at you. With your nice job, and your nice clothes, and it's all paid for with my husband's blood and the blood of the men like him.'

'It wasn't like that in my grandfather's day.'

'I don't need a history lesson, Tom. I need to get away from here, and I'm only staying until I can find another job.'

Tom was dumbfounded. Some small, ridiculous part of his brain had heard those words about 'making eyes' at him and Prince Charming; then there was the terrible story she was telling.

'Sally, I—'

'Just take the bloody bucket and go, Tom! I can't bear to have you look at me.'

He carried it away and added to the slops from the chop house, well out of Ollie's way. He had been so pleased with himself just a few hours earlier, ready to invest his money in his brave new venture. Money made from men like Sally's husband. He turned on the yard tap to wash his hands. How could he get them clean? He hadn't been lying, though. It hadn't been like that in Sir Barnabas's time.

'Tom?' He turned and saw Jack, his tie askew and his eyes alarmingly bright. 'Nikolai wants to have another run at his song. Isn't this exciting? The news that Lillian is appearing on stage seems to have spread. The queue for standbys is down to Bertram's!'

CHAPTER TWENTY-NINE

S ally would have loved nothing more in the world than to slink
home after all that had happened and hide in her room with
Dougie. They could have curled up in the bed, under the quilt
her mother had made her for her wedding, and she'd have watched him
read and let everything from the last few days just settle through her, like
water sinking through the sand on the beach at Blackpool. The hard,
biting truths her in-laws had told her, and the feeling she'd just made a
terrible fool of herself in front of Tom.

Her in-laws didn't come to Highbridge often, but they made
a special effort round Christmas to see Dougie. They'd had tea in
the pub, then gone for a walk in the park so Dougie could feed the
ducks, and when she told them about her job in the theatre, they'd told
her about what had happened to Noah. Not that they'd had it from
him – he wouldn't have wanted to give them cause for worry. He'd
confessed how hard things had got to his brother, just a week before
he'd been killed.

She pushed on with her work, trying not to think of that look of
pain in Tom's eyes, or the burn she'd felt when he started to say her
name, then Lady Lassiter had volunteered. She couldn't have done it.

Wouldn't have done it. But still, that half-hearted way Tom had spoken, and the way they hadn't even heard him, had scorched her. The usherettes and waiters started to clock on, all twittering about the notices on the wall, and she looked at the clock over the bar and realised she had five minutes to get out of her apron and run a brush through her hair before Belle and Alfred arrived with Dougie to see the show. It *would* be tonight they'd arranged to come, with her all disordered, and chaos both backstage and front of house. She shut the broom and dirty linens in the cupboard, then hightailed it to her locker behind the secret door near the WCs in the stalls, then was out of the side door to find her boy. The look of joy on his small face just about wiped her misery away.

'What's this?' Belle whispered to her as they made their way up to the circle. 'Everyone outside is saying Lady Lassiter is going to be on stage tonight!' She was pink, as if she'd run all the way from the Bricklayers Arms. 'Lordy, and I almost sent our Bill down in my place so I could stay and keep an eye on the pub.'

The usherette in the circle winked at them and showed them to their seats, right in the middle among the gentry of Highbridge. Mr Poole had looked after them all right.

'What a spot!' Alfred said as they sat down. 'Never thought I'd sit among the nobs like this. What do you think, Dougie?'

Dougie was a little pale, with pink spots on his cheeks. He put his chin on the velvet top of the barrier at the edge of the circle and looked down at the red curtain.

'It's . . .' He paused, looking for the right word. 'It's grand . . .!'

'You breathe slowly, Dougie,' Sally told him, 'through your nose, like the chemist said.' He nodded, eyes shining like gas lamps, and Sally pulled a packet of aniseed balls from her pocket. 'There you go, lambkin. And there's an orange, too, if you're good.'

'Can I share with Belle and Alf?'

Her heart squeezed. 'Of course you can. It's been madness this afternoon,' she told them over Dougie's head. 'So I've no idea what it'll be like.'

'It'll be something,' said Belle. 'I'm sure of that.'

When the overture started, Grace was holding a bucket ready for Harold. He was pale and sweaty even under the paint, which was an inch thick tonight. The chorus ran on in a sprightly fashion, and started their business. Grace glanced round. Nikolai was standing in the wings, wearing evening dress and twirling his tail. Lillian was rereading her script by the prompt light, wearing one of her long velvet evening gowns to which Fairy Bow Bells' wings had been sewn on – a little crooked – by Grace herself. Fitzwarren and Alice, thank goodness, had opted for high tea at the Lyons teashop after the matinee, so at least some of the cast had a rough idea of where to stand. The chorus, all a little twittery after an hour in the pub, promised to guide Lillian and Nikolai about as best they could.

Jack approached her in the darkness, carrying a pitcher of water. 'To wash with or drink, depending', he whispered, setting it next to her. 'I'm on props. How are you holding up?'

Grace looked at him. 'It's exciting, isn't it? How is Miss Chisholm?'

'Lying on the floor of the office with a copy of *The Gramophone*. I told her about our plans for Empire Records. That's all right, isn't it? It seemed to take her mind off her troubles briefly.'

'Yes, of course – now do get into position, Jack! There's a lot to do in the first act. Are you ready, Harold?'

He held up one hand, the other over his mouth, and Grace readied the bucket. Then he gave a sharp nod.

The overture ended, and with a blast on the trumpet, the curtain rose.

'So this is London!' Josie announced, and the audience – bless them, Grace thought – gave them a round of applause for getting that far.

Grace had never been skiing, but she'd seen pictures in the *Illustrated News*, and that evening she had some fellow feeling with a person hurtling down a slope, unsure if a crevasse or a rock or a tree was going to bring them to a disastrous halt, or if they would skip past the hazards and, through a mixture of luck and momentum, reach their destination intact.

Lillian's first entrance was greeted with loud cheers; leaving Harold on a stool, clutching a bucket, Grace watched from the wings. Lillian was still a magnetic presence on stage; knowing the whole audience was in on the joke that she was appearing, she flirted shamelessly with them and with Josie. Josie, to her credit, did not try and compete, and as Lillian kicked her heels on her first exit, and glanced over her shoulder, she applauded along with the rest of Highbridge.

Nikolai's accent became considerably thicker as he snarled at the audience and skittered from one side of the stage to the other, eliciting delighted shrieks from the children and dodging Harold's rolling pin with aplomb. As Harold tumbled off stage, tossing the pin at Jack, then collapsing into his chair again, Grace began to think they might actually get away with it.

For Act Three the stage was transformed, a little unsteadily, into the court of the Royal Family of Zanzibar. The chorus as the plague of rats, with added ears and tails, managed their ballet of destruction with a great deal of noise and mess, most of which was planned. Nikolai made another triumphant entrance, sauntering in, tail twirling and clambering onto the table and driving off the King and Princess with satisfying shrieks, then Grace heard a stifled yell from the prop table and turned to see Jack, poking around among the wedding props with Fairy Bow Bells' wand.

'Jack!' Grace hissed. 'What on earth are you doing?'

He looked at her, eyes wide with dismay. 'Harry's here!'

On stage, the vamp for Nikolai's victory song began. Grace gasped as she spotted Harry nosing curiously around the edge of the stage. She grabbed a clean basin and lunged, trying to cage him under it, but Harry spotted her coming and dodged expertly right and left, then fled onto the stage itself.

The audience began to laugh.

Nikolai missed his cue; the orchestra manfully continued the vamp while Grace and Jack stared in horror from the wings as the rat reached the middle of the stage and stood on its hind legs.

'Grace! This is a disaster! Do I chase him off?' Jack asked, stretching forward like a greyhound spotting a rabbit.

Grace grabbed his arm. 'No, wait, Jack.'

'Ah!' Nikolai said. 'What news, my friend?'

Grace put her hand over her heart, not sure what she was praying for this time, but praying for it very hard indeed.

And Harry squeaked.

'Then our triumph is complete!' Nikolai replied, and the crowd cheered as he launched into the song. When it became clear Harry was not going to leave any time soon, Nikolai began singing the song to him. On the final chorus, Nikolai got off the table, knelt and offered his hand to the creature. Harry hesitated, then ran up his arm and perched on his shoulder. The audience whistled and whooped.

As she watched from the circle, Sally's determination to leave The Empire became clouded with regret. Dougie was practically bursting with excitement beside her, laughing at every joke, booing King Rat so vigorously that the rather grand-looking lady behind them broke into smiles. Belle and Alfred beamed at each other, at her and Dougie, and at the stage. By the time they got to the singalong at the end, they all looked misty-eyed with delight.

Jack Treadwell came onto the stage at the curtain call and made a handsome speech thanking Nikolai and Lillian for stepping in, praising Harold's fortitude, and saying how none of it would have been possible without all the staff of The Empire pulling together. Dougie turned to Sally, his little face bright with pride at that. Then Jack thanked the audience for joining in and they had a final chorus of 'I'm Sitting on Top of the World', before the house lights came up. As they filed out of the circle, Dougie describing everything they had just seen to Belle again, Sally noticed Ruby Rowntree perched on the usher's stool by the door. Ruby caught her eye and beckoned her over.

'Did you have fun, Sally?' she asked. 'I couldn't resist coming in to see how they managed. It went rather well in the end, didn't it? Lillian has *such* a lovely voice – I'd forgotten. I saw her sing in Paris, you know, before she became Lady Lassiter.'

Sally smiled. It was impossible not to when Ruby looked at you in that robinish way. 'Did you now? She does. Feel the weight come off my shoulders when I listen to her, but I think the rat might have stolen the show, Miss Ruby.'

'Have you seen Tom today? He's been so busy this week with the new enterprise, and then today he's been caught up in these shenanigans.'

Sally lowered her eyes. 'I did. Ran my mouth at him, too.'

'Good for you. Keeps him honest. I don't suppose he'd even have had these ideas about a record company if you hadn't given him what for.'

'A record company?' Sally felt a flame of pride, somehow. Then squashed it. She'd have no more dealings with Tom Lassiter.

'Yes, didn't he tell you? It's very exciting. He's throwing everything he has into it.' She looked to where Belle and Alfred were standing with Dougie, and waved at them. 'Come and see me soon, Sally. I've done an arrangement for you of your oak tree song, and there's another tune I have I think will suit you.'

Sally shuffled to one side, to let a laughing couple in evening dress pass them. The woman was holding the hand of a little boy about Dougie's age. He had a collar and tie, and his hair split with a razor-sharp parting. The woman bent down to wipe crumbs from around the boy's mouth with a snowy white handkerchief.

'Miss Ruby, I'm not sure. I'm leaving The Empire as soon as I can find something else, and you shouldn't waste your songs on a girl who does the occasional singalong in the pub.'

The old lady tilted her head to one side. 'I'm not. I'm offering my advice, and my songs, to someone who I think has the talent to make them famous.'

Sally felt a fierce heat in her cheeks. 'There's . . . circumstances, Miss Ruby. I'm not sure I can.'

Ruby studied her with slightly narrowed eyes. 'Sally, dear, you must make your own decisions, but please don't decide to be small and dress it up as a scruple. We all have to make our way against the current sometimes. I . . .'

Her voice disappeared, and she seemed to be seeing something in the shadows Sally could not.

'Miss Ruby . . .?'

She blinked and returned her gaze to Sally's face. 'I'm getting old, dear. Sometimes the bravest thing to do is to live quietly, and we all have to make our own rules. Trust me, I do know that.' She reached out and took Sally's hand, holding her fingers with surprising force. 'But don't let yourself be bounced out of the life you want because a voice inside you says you can't, or you shouldn't. A little defiance, Sally. A little grit.'

Sally felt her eyes getting hot.

'I can't, Miss Ruby. There are other things to consider . . . I would be betraying . . . if I carried on this way . . .'

'Ah, that's a big word, betrayal. Big enough to become a shield to hide behind, if we let it.'

Then she released Sally's hand again and sat back in her seat. 'All this excitement. I'm quite drained. I think I shall sit here a little. You go with your friends, and your little boy, dear. But come and see me.'

A fresh covering of snow had fallen in the valley during the evening as The Empire family fought its way through the performance, so by the time they drove back to Lassiter Court, the applause still ringing in their ears, the fields at the edge of town had been transformed into a shadowed fairyland of greys and silvers, the frost firing like opals in the moonlight.

Lillian was as happy as she could ever remember being, except for the day she realised her son had not died in the war, as she'd believed, but washed up at her theatre, ignorant of who she was, but absolutely, miraculously, alive. That had been a painful, confusing day, too, though, mixed through with guilt and grief. This, by contrast, was purely joyous.

Next to her in the passenger seat, Nikolai was humming the King Rat victory song and chuckling to himself. He had refused to take off the ears or the tail for now, and Lillian was still wearing the dress with the improvised fairy wings.

'I think,' he said, pausing his song, 'that I now understand pantomime.'

Lillian laughed. 'It was wonderful, wasn't it? And Harry! I wonder why he hasn't joined in the performance before.'

'I think, like his friend Dixon, that Harry is a very clever creature,' Nikolai said, swirling his tail. 'He knows that Marmaduke would never share the limelight and the applause. I, on the other hand, am willing to be generous.' He twisted in his seat. 'A magical moment, Lillian. I met the eye of a wild beast, an untamed creature, and we understood each other. It was . . . an experience.'

'And extremely funny.'

He grinned. 'Yes. And singing with you was also very nice. Might you perform again, Lillian?'

Lillian slowed the car, taking the turn into the long carriage drive of Lassiter Court, following the tracks left by Jack, who had left the theatre in his car with the others just ahead of them.

'I don't know, darling. It never seemed appropriate when I was married to dear Barney.'

'But now you are marrying a disreputable exile, perhaps you will be more free?'

'You are still a grand duke.'

Nikolai tutted dismissively, and stroked his ears as she halted the car, then, with a distinct scurry, jumped out and ran round the front to open the door for her.

They were only just behind Jack. He and Grace, Dixon and Tom, were handing their coats to Hewitt and Gladys and calling for champagne.

'I think we deserve it, don't we?' Jack said quickly.

'Oh, we certainly do,' Lillian agreed. 'Hewitt, do you like my wings?'

'They are splendid, Lady Lassiter,' he said very calmly. 'Though may I suggest His Excellency is more careful with his tail? The Tiffany lamp on the hall chest is precarious.'

Nikolai snatched his tail closer to him with an expression of deep contrition and Hewitt's upper lip very nearly twitched into a smile. 'Miss de Monfort and Mr Allerdyce have just had a crate of Pol Roger delivered, Lady Lassiter. I understand they were in the audience this evening.'

'Oh, let's have those, then,' Lillian said. 'And Hewitt, will you see if Miss Stanmore is awake, and invite her to join us if she is?'

The champagne that Joe and Agnes had sent was excellent. Lillian looked round the room, at the flush and animation in Jack and Grace's faces, at Tom's broad grin, at Dixon, with his warm smile and obvious, gentle pleasure at being included in the jokes the others were sharing. Perhaps the record shop would be a success, perhaps it would be a disaster; her magic wand had only limited powers off stage, after all. But she made a new resolution: that she would at least try to enjoy it.

The door opened, and they all looked round expecting to see Stella, the stories of their nerves and triumphs springing to their lips again in anticipation of a new audience, but instead in came Hewitt. He carried an envelope which he offered, with a slight bow to Grace, then stood back. They watched as she opened it.

'Oh,' Grace said almost at once. 'It's from Stella. She's gone.'

Lillian leant forward. 'Gone? Do read it, Grace.'

'Sorry, darlings. I am being an absolute drag on you. Off to London, then away for a while. Have read enough books.' Grace frowned and turned the page over. 'That's it! Honestly . . .'

'I've always liked Stella,' Tom said. 'But she has been terribly strange of late. Grace, do you think she was actually in love with the girl who died?'

Grace handed the note back to Hewitt. 'If you could leave that on my desk, Hewitt. Did she say she was leaving?'

'No, Mrs Treadwell. She declined any supper when she came back from the theatre in a taxi cab, and went to her room. Her suitcases have gone.'

'Thank you.'

Hewitt departed and Grace sipped her champagne. 'I don't know, Tom. I don't think so. Did she seem struck by grief to you? Or broken-hearted?'

Tom blushed slightly and shook his head.

'I keep thinking of what she said to you when she arrived, Grace,' Jack said. 'That the newspapers said she'd killed the girl. I mean, they were awful, but they didn't say that as such.'

'You should have seen her when the police detectives accused her of supplying Tasha with drugs,' Grace said, looking into the fire, then around at the rest of them. 'Of course, she's a wonderful actress, but I'm sure that her indignation and shock were quite genuine. So not grief, not guilt over supplying her with cocaine . . .'

'Lillian,' Nikolai asked, 'you have known Stella a long time, too. What do you think?'

'I'm not sure.' She took his hand. 'It's quite possible it is just Stella being Stella, but I can't help feeling it looks more like guilt than heartbreak, even if she had nothing to do with the drugs.'

Grace nodded thoughtfully and Jack interlaced his fingers in hers. 'I think perhaps you are right. But her worst sin is she has deprived us of someone new to describe our cleverness to. I shall fill up our glasses, and we shall tell each other one more time, I think.'

CHAPTER THIRTY

'I don't care if you're paying the "going rate"! What bloody good is the going rate if a man works sixty hours a week and still can't afford to feed his bairns?'

Tom, sitting outside his mother's office at Lassiter Enterprises' main site to the west of Highbridge, glanced at his watch. Just after half-past four. He had achieved more since ten o'clock that morning than he had in the whole of the period since he graduated. That wouldn't mean much if this meeting didn't go well, however.

He could hear Constance's reply just as distinctly. 'Perhaps your union could do something useful in these "education" lessons of yours, and teach the men how to budget,' she said. 'I will not bankrupt this company or rob our shareholders because they waste their earnings in the pub. Three pounds and ten shillings is the going weekly rate for a machine worker. If your members don't like it, they can leave. You know there are dozens of men at the gate every morning who'd be very happy to take what we offer.'

Tom looked around. His mother's new secretary – a very smooth-looking young man – and the other clerical workers in the outer office did not seem to be paying any attention. Tom had to assume these sorts of confrontations were not unusual.

'Want to keep your foot on our necks? That's it? There will be a reckoning, Mrs Lassiter. One day.'

'Are you threatening me? I would advise against it.'

'Why? Because your friend Ray Kelly might pay me a visit?'

A couple of heads flicked up at that, then quickly down again. Tom had heard rumours, or the faintest breath of a rumour, that Constance and Edmund had got entangled with Ray Kelly in some way. Kelly, Tom knew, was king of the Highbridge underworld, lord of all the darkness that churned away behind the city's elegant facades. Was the man right? Edmund had definitely been struggling with money at times before his accident, Tom knew that, and that Ray Kelly was a loan shark – or a captain of loan sharks – among his other sins.

'Good day,' his mother drawled. 'So sorry we are unable to oblige you.'

The man flung open the door and stared round the office, his face flushed. Tom thought of Sally's husband and felt a sense of shame creep over him, heavy and hot.

'You know I'm right,' the man said. 'You all do.'

Then he stalked off with a quick, stiff-legged stride.

Constance appeared in the doorway behind him and watched him go, her arms folded across her chest.

'Milner, see to it that man is fired today, please. And make sure the workers know why.'

'Certainly, Mrs Lassiter,' the smooth assistant replied. 'And your son is waiting to see you. He doesn't have an appointment.'

Constance noted Tom sitting by her door with his hat in his lap. She looked at him without warmth or enthusiasm.

'Good afternoon, Tom. Give me one moment, I have to finish a couple of things and catch the post. Milner, bring in the Manchester contracts, will you?'

Tom nodded his agreement and waited. Fifteen minutes passed, then he was summoned in.

Constance had taken over the office which had been used by her father-in-law, Sir Barnabas Lassiter. Her son, Edmund, during his tenure as chairman of Lassiter Enterprises, had officially had use of it, but had spent most of his time at his club. After he was so badly injured in the fire which had destroyed the old Empire Theatre, Constance Lassiter had invoked the proxy he had given to her while he was serving at the front in the Great War, and moved in. She had now been in complete control of the running of Lassiter Enterprises for almost four years, and had seen the company move from the edge of bankruptcy to renewed profitability.

The office still retained its very masculine air. The walls were panelled in wood and hung with a portrait of the founder and a variety of hunting prints. The desk at which she worked was large, and covered in cracked green leather, but lent her authority, and though Constance Lassiter had never smoked, somehow the air smelt of cigars and money.

Tom sat down in the chair opposite her and waited for her to finish writing whatever was in front of her. She picked up a brass bell on her desk and rang it, and the smooth Mr Milner came into the room and took the proffered page without comment.

Tom waited patiently, familiar with his mother's games. The message was simple. Her every moment was packed with important activity; his was without value.

'What can I do for you, Tom?' she said at last, taking another letter from the pile of correspondence beside her and beginning to read.

'I have a business proposition, Mother,' he said. She glanced up, very briefly, but said nothing. 'I am going to make use of my capital, and enter into an agreement with Lassiter Enterprises. I shall take a lease on Shed Number Four at the north river plant. I know it's empty at the moment. You'll give me the lease for fifteen years at a generous discount, and lend me two thousand pounds for start-up costs. The interest rate will be fixed for two years at current base rates.'

She looked up at him now. 'Will I? How generous of me. And what will you do in Shed Number Four?'

Tom knew Constance had always disliked Lillian, ever since her father-in-law Sir Barnabas had brought her home. Constance thought of Lillian as a usurper, and a gold-digger. That Lillian had proved a devoted wife through twenty years of marriage had only increased the animosity between them. Then Lillian, newly widowed, had outfoxed Constance and Edmund, taken over The Empire, and claimed Jack Treadwell as her son.

After the fire, Constance's dislike for everyone associated with the theatre had deepened into loathing. The fact Tom spent his days there, and his nights at Lassiter Court, had only made her more bitter towards them, and contemptuous of him. Constance had only ever had enough love for one human being, and that person had been her older son, Edmund. He had her cruel streak, but, unfortunately, little of her intelligence. Tom was the cleverer son, but his more gentle, curious nature had earned his mother's dislike before she'd even noticed that.

Tom kept his voice very even then. 'I'm going into business with Lillian, Jack and a gentleman named Dixon Wells. We will produce, manufacture and sell gramophone records.'

Constance's expression became an ugly sneer.

'What utter nonsense, Tom. We will not lease you the building, nor lend you money to start off such a hare-brained scheme. Now do go away, I'm busy.'

'Perhaps I shall ask Edmund.'

'You are free to write to him, whenever you wish.'

Tom had written to Edmund on a number of occasions, and each time had received a typewritten reply with a scrawl at the end which could have been Edmund's signature. It had made Tom suspicious, especially since Edmund's letters to the board all seemed to support his mother's plans for the company entirely. Perhaps a minor adjustment here or there, nothing more. The letters sounded reasonable, considered. Not at all like the selfish, bullying and impulsive brother Tom had grown up with. He had made enquiries.

Tom crossed his legs, and stared out of the window. 'I thought I'd ask Edmund in person. It's quite a trek, but I haven't seen him since he left the hospital here. And I am his heir, after all, Mother. Now I've left university, I think I should take more of a direct hand in his personal affairs. You, Mother, naturally, would continue running everything here. You've been doing magnificently.'

Constance put down the page. 'I am in constant communication with Edmund. Why would you feel the need to visit him?'

'I know about your communications with Edmund, Mother,' he said with a pleasant smile. It was his best card, and required a certain finesse to play it. 'I don't suppose you ever had any dealings with the fellow, but Darien Burnside, who worked in the theatre, told me he was planning a tour in that part of the world and I asked him to pay a visit to the sanatorium.'

Tom watched his mother and thought of a drawing of a snake in a children's book, which had terrified him as a child. The caption – 'a hooded cobra hypnotises its prey' – had been one of the first sentences he had ever learnt to read.

'And did he visit?'

'Yes. Said it's a beautiful place. Absolutely top rank. But . . . Well, let's just say it left me eager to visit Edmund myself. If I could find the time.'

Darien might have been a terrible assistant, but he was not a bad chap, and he and Tom had grown friendly during his disastrous stint at The Empire. He had visited, and seen Tom's brother. Sir Edmund Lassiter, Darien reported, would never leave the sanatorium, and was kept in a deep haze of opium. Darien wrote that, given his injuries, he hoped and believed that Edmund had been aware of very little since his accident. He was certainly not capable of dictating long letters to his mother, or the board.

Constance smiled. It was not a smile which suggested fondness, let alone love, but Tom could tell that this was one of the rare moments of his life when he had impressed her.

'You might be too busy to visit if you were engaged in this new enterprise, however.'

'I might, for the moment,' Tom conceded.

She continued to examine him, then picked up her pen, twisting it between her fingers. Tom watched her cautiously, willing himself to stay still and keep a pleasant smile fixed on his face. Constance made her decision.

'What terms do you propose for the lease?' she asked, suddenly brisk.

Tom took a folded sheaf of paper from his pocket and passed it over to her.

'You've had the agreement drawn up already, Tom?' she asked, taking it from him.

'I was sure, Mother, I could convince you it was a worthwhile plan.' He paused, wondering how much honey to add. 'I'm very glad Edmund has been taking your advice recently.' She unfolded the papers and started to read. 'You'll see that Lassiter Enterprises will receive a two per cent share of the annual profits of Empire Records, to compensate for any wear and tear on the site.'

She raised her eyebrows at that, but read on.

'And you have the loan agreement with you, too, I suppose? And a letter to the bank authorising the release of your capital?'

'You have it all there.'

'Perhaps I should telephone Edmund and consult him?' she said as she finished reading. 'I expect, as your brother, he'd wish to encourage you, but I'm sure he wouldn't want you to overstep either.'

Tom straightened up in his chair. 'I have no interest in overstepping. You must do as you think best, but as his mother and proxy, and as his brother and heir, I'm sure we can be confident he would approve whatever we decide.'

Constance read the agreements again, then signed them and rang the brass bell. Milner returned. 'My son will be leasing Shed Number Four on the upper valley site, and Lassiter Enterprises will be lending him some capital. The details are here. Make the arrangements with the bank and give him the keys.'

'Yes, Mrs Lassiter.'

'Thank you, Mother,' Tom said, getting to his feet.

'Good luck,' Constance said. 'You've grown up a little bit, haven't you, Tom?'

'I have,' he replied, and when it was clear she meant to say no more, he left the room.

Tom did not break into a run when he left the yard, or perform a soft-shoe shuffle as Jack had done, but he was aware of walking with a slightly increased speed, as if he feared some breath of hellfire would follow him.

'Did she go for it?'

Ruby Rowntree was waiting for him on the far side of the factory gates – lurking, in fact, behind the high brick pillar, with Dixon Wells at her elbow.

'She did! Honestly, Ruby, there was a moment there I thought I was going to crumble into dust, but I held firm and I have the documents signed!'

'Well done, Tom!' Ruby said warmly, and punched him on the top of his arm with surprising force.

Dixon grinned. 'Looks like you've had a better afternoon than that man over there, Tom.'

'Ow! What?' Tom turned. The man who he had seen storming out of his mother's office was leaning against the wall on the other side of the entrance, his head tilted back to the sky.

'Shall we go and have port and lemon to celebrate?' Ruby asked.

Tom would not be like his mother, or his brother. Not now, not ever.

'Yes . . . Actually, give me one moment.' Tom crossed over to the man and put out his hand.

'I'm Tom Lassiter. I think my mother just fired you.'

The man stared at Tom's proffered hand, then turned away, rubbing his nose on his sleeve. Tom realised with a slight jolt he was near tears.

'She did. Just readying myself to go and tell my wife about it.'

'How long have you worked for my family, Mr . . .?'

'Patterson. I started as a lad and came back to it after the war. Been a shift foreman at the bank factory since twenty-two. Where we make the forks and knives,' he added, seeing Tom's confusion.

Tom put his hands in his pockets. 'Did you like the work, Patterson? Take pride in it?'

A look of pain crossed the man's face. 'I liked it well enough, and a man has to take pride in what he does, doesn't he? But you can't eat pride. God knows what me and the wife will do for bread now.'

He tilted his head backwards, his gaze reaching up beyond the high brick walls of the Highbridge manufacturing district that surrounded them. Arrays of chimneys sent thin columns of smoke upwards towards the clouds into the slate-grey January sky; behind and around them resounded the clanks of hammers on metal, the distant hiss of steam; the air thick with the smell of oil and coal dust. It was hard to believe that such a thing as a tree existed, when standing here.

'Would you work for me?' Tom said quietly.

Patterson looked at him in surprise, then laughed. 'Work for you? I'm not a car mechanic, Mr Lassiter, if it's your fancy automobiles you're worried about. Not a tennis coach either.'

'Men can change, Mr Patterson.'

'Not rich ones. Why should they?'

Tom shrugged. 'Fair point.' He nodded towards Ruby and Dixon. Patterson looked at them and frowned. They were obviously not the sort of people he expected to see with Tom Lassiter: a grey-haired lady in a tartan shawl, and a man in a shabby coat. 'But I don't want a mechanic or a tennis coach. Come and have a port and lemon with us. Let us tell you what we propose, at least.'

Patterson eyed him suspiciously. 'I thought your sort only drink champagne.'

'I prefer champagne,' Tom said, honestly enough, 'but I wouldn't risk ordering it at the Dog and Duck, and that's where Ruby wants to celebrate our new venture. You coming or not?'

Patterson shrugged himself away from the wall and joined them. Two ports later, Empire Records (Manufacturing) had its first employee.

CHAPTER THIRTY-ONE

The pantomime had to end some time. The cast dispersed, a new touring company came in, and Grace began, with Jack's agreement, to lend a hand on the Empire Records project. After a morning spent going over contracts in Lillian's office, she got up from her desk and went looking for Ruby.

'Ruby, why does your office look tidier now that Tom is working in the factory all the time?'

She grinned. 'Tom liked to feel useful, you know. He enjoyed finding things for me, so I never put any effort into keeping things tidy. I've always known where everything is.' She slipped a sheaf of manuscript paper into a folder. 'Do you think he ever wonders how I managed when he was away studying? He's a man, of course, so probably not.'

'I worry about him,' Grace said, leaning against the wall next to the piano. 'Making an enemy of his mother and sinking all his money into manufacturing records. Do you think he's doing the right thing?'

Ruby pulled the patchwork quilt that hung over the back of her armchair free, shook it, and began to fold it.

'His mother was his enemy already. And he's taking a risk, of course, but he's young, so now is the time for it.'

Grace found one corner of the quilt shoved into her hand, and began to fold.

'Ruby, are you leaving us?' Ruby tied a strap around the quilt, and added it to what Grace realised was a growing pile of her possessions.

'I'm not leaving you, dear – you don't work here.' Grace flinched. 'And I'm only going as far as Shed Number Four. I think Tom could do with someone to lean on as he sets things up. Grace, dear, what have I said?'

Grace swallowed. 'I'm a goose. It's about me not working here. You're right, I don't. Jack is happy for me to lend a hand with the shop, but I still feel on the edges of things. He has the marvellous Miss Chisholm to make all his phone calls now. And I don't feel any more inspired to write than I did before the pantomime. I know I can be useful with the business side of Empire Records – contracts and so on – which gives me an excuse to be here, but that's not exactly thrilling.'

'Is Stella going to record?'

'She's left us. Just flew off after we asked her to step in for the panto. Honestly, Ruby, she seems determined to leave the stage.'

'I'm sorry to hear that. And you'd better come up with a new project if you aren't going to write. I think we can abandon knitting, even though we gave it a good try.'

'But what?'

'Goodness, Grace. I'm a composer. Why you young people insist on treating me as if I'm some sort of oracle, I have no idea.'

'Because you're terribly wise, of course,' Grace said.

Ruby snorted. 'Nonsense. I'm a foolish old romantic, always have been.' She paused suddenly. 'That's it! Foolish romantic things are what you want to hear. That's why you come to me.'

'Now that sounded very wise indeed,' Grace said, and Ruby giggled and tapped her arm with a rolled-up sheaf of manuscript paper.

Grace was still miming terrible injury when someone knocked at the door. Grace recognised the face peering round into the room as Sally Blow.

'Oh, sorry to disturb, I thought you were alone, Miss Ruby.'

'Sally! Don't mind Grace.' Ruby sat down on the piano stool and began riffling through another pile of papers before digging out a small sheaf. 'Here you are. There's an arrangement of "The Old Oak" there, and three new tunes. One cheery and the other two rather mournful. The words are only moderate, as my usual lyricist,' she cast a black look at Grace, 'has rather let me down recently. But they'll do very nicely.'

'I can't take them, Miss Ruby,' Sally said. 'I told you, they're wasted on me.'

'And I told you that was nonsense. I shan't take no for an answer, Sally.' She clambered off her stool and thrust them fiercely into Sally's pocket. 'They're yours. Sing them, don't sing them, but they're yours now.'

Sally bit her lip as if she was fighting off tears. 'Thank you, Miss Ruby. I wanted to say goodbye. I won't be cleaning at The Empire any more, and I wanted to say, singing with you . . . Well, it was some of the best hours I've ever had, that's all.'

'I loved every second of it myself. Haven't had so much fun in years.'

'You sing at the Bricklayers Arms,' Grace said delightedly. 'Tom's mentioned you. I didn't realise you were also the same Sally who is Mrs Briggs's new favourite. I'm sorry to hear you're leaving us. Is there anything I can do or say to get you to stay. Not that I work here,' she added, glancing at Ruby, 'but I do know you'll be missed.'

Sally swallowed. 'I . . . Thank you, Mrs Treadwell.'

'You said something after the pantomime the other night, Sally . . . About circumstances,' Ruby prompted. Then she pointed at the stool she used when she had students in. 'Can you tell us about it? Think of it as payment for the songs – satisfy my curiosity. "Betrayal" was the word you used.'

'Well, I suppose it makes no odds.' Sally sat on the edge of the stool, folded her hands in her lap and, with her eyes cast down, told them about Noah and what had happened to him, and how she had found out all the ins and outs of it over Christmas.

'So I can't carry on, not hearing the Lassiter name flying about everywhere. See, since my Noah died, I've always felt him urging me on, telling me to keep my chin up. And since I've learnt exactly what happened in those last weeks—'

'You don't hear his voice anymore?' Grace asked.

Sally half-laughed. 'Oh, I hear it right enough, Mrs Treadwell, but it hurts me.' She laid her hand over her heart and looked up, and Grace realised for the first time what a strangely pretty face she had. She was not beautiful in the way Stella was beautiful: her nose was a little too long, and her jaw too square, but she had the most wonderful eyes, and a twist to her lips that was sad and funny at the same time. 'I know you and Mr Treadwell have nothing to do with the factories,' Sally went on, 'nor with what happened to him, nor Lady Lassiter either, but . . .'

She looked at her hands again.

'The theatre was bought with Lassiter money,' Ruby said sadly. 'And then there's Tom.'

Grace raised her eyebrows, but Tom's transformation – and his sudden sense of purpose – made a little more sense.

Sally sniffed, wiped the corner of her eyes quickly with her thumb, and nodded.

'Yes. So there it is. Now I know exactly what happened to Noah it feels poisoned. I've got morning shifts cleaning at the Metropole – don't worry, I shan't eat the chicken,' she added. 'So me and Dougie will manage. He loved the panto so much.' She glanced up at Grace. 'We were there the night Lady Lassiter and Mr Kuznetsov were on. He thought the rat was terrific.'

'I wish we could persuade Jack of Harry's virtues,' Grace replied. 'And I'm glad. Bring him any time.'

'Thank you.'

Ruby studied her for a second. 'Sally, I have a pupil, a ruffian but a natural musician, to play with you in the pub. He has his own accordion.

Name of Clive. I'll send him along, if I may. You and he will work well together, and he'll give you a bit of support. See what you can do, but don't let him near your tip jar unsupervised.'

'Thank you, Ruby. I'd be glad to know him.'

'He's not as good as me, of course,' Ruby said comfortably. 'But I can't be there all the time, and he'll be better than a pianist who never turns up.'

'There is really nothing we can do to persuade you to stay?' Grace asked. The more she looked at Sally, the more interesting she became.

'I'd rather you didn't, Mrs Treadwell. It's not easy to go, but I do feel like I'm betraying Noah working here, and that hurts me.' She put her fist to her chest again. 'Hurts me here. Like I can't deserve any good thing because of it. Might sound daft, but there it is.'

She stood up, took the pages that Ruby had shoved into her pocket and folded them more neatly. 'And thank you for this, Miss Ruby. I shall think of you whenever I sing them.'

Then she left, quickly. Grace studied the panelling of the door as it closed behind her.

'Betrayal . . . It's a terrible word, isn't it, Ruby?'

'Yes, my dear, it is. But you're not thinking about poor Sally now, are you?'

'No, I'm thinking of Stella. What's behind this refusal of hers to step on the stage, even to help us out. And then to run away.'

'You think it might be something like this?'

'Perhaps,' Grace said, folding her arms and staring at the polished floorboards.

Ruby returned to her piles of manuscript pages and printed music, neatly organising the stacks. Grace realised she'd become still for a second.

'Ruby?'

'Nothing, dear. A bit of a turn, that's all. You know, it might be a terribly selfish thing to say, but I'm rather glad Stella didn't step in, I'd forgotten what a wonderful voice Lillian has. And it fits so beautifully with Nikolai's. It's given me an idea.'

'What idea is that?'

'I've been collecting my material, like a pigeon building a little creative nest, dear. The day the lift broke, seeing Mabel again at the Metropole and hearing Lillian. Come along to the rehearsal rooms tomorrow afternoon. We're going to try something out, and I think you might want to hear it.'

'I'll be there. Oh, and I forgot to say why I came to bother you in the first place. We're going to the Metropole to celebrate the launch of Empire Records. Mabel has agreed to record for us, once we've built a studio and a factory, and a shop . . .' She swallowed. 'Well, anyway, she'll announce it this evening from the stage. Can you join us?'

'I should be delighted, dear.'

'Marvellous. Seven o'clock.' Grace put her hand on the doorknob. 'Poor Sally, though.'

'"Full many a flower is born to blush unseen, and waste its sweetness on the desert air"' Ruby quoted as Grace left, her mind already elsewhere. Then she heard Ruby add in a murmur, 'And we can't be having that.'

CHAPTER THIRTY-TWO

Agnes de Montfort nodded to the maître d' at the Metropole and surrendered her fur coat to the hat check girl, then took the arm of her fiancé, Joseph P. Allerdyce, and processed with him to her table where many of the rest of the Empire family were gathered.

Heads turned.

Agnes and Joe were a striking couple, both large, on the upper end of middle age, and sumptuously dressed. Joe, brought up in music halls and now the owner of a number of theatres and sundry places of entertainment in Highbridge and beyond, lived in his new modernist mansion, while his fiancée remained in her rambling farmhouse and continued to train racehorses. Neither seemed intent on setting a date for their wedding.

Joe had seen The Empire slip from his hands not once, but twice – first into the hands of Lady Lassiter's late husband, and then again into the firm grasp of his beloved and her sister-in-law. He told anyone who would listen, however, that he was pleased with the bargain he'd made, valuing her above any theatre in the country.

Their engagement had marked Agnes's period of late blooming in Highbridge high society, and a distinct change in her style of dress. The youth of the city were now as likely to copy her in their choices as to ape the London magazines. As Agnes was a woman of intelligence with firm opinions, but who cared very little what anyone thought of them or her, she had also gained a reputation as a devastating wit.

Lillian stood up from the table to receive them both and Jack watched as Agnes greeted Nikolai with considerable warmth, then immediately summoned a waiter to order steaks and Martinis for herself and her partner. They had met at the Christmas party of course. Jack wondered if Agnes and Nikolai had friends in common. She had more aristocratic blood than any of the rest of them, and sometimes it seemed to Jack that these families with ancient lineages formed a sort of international club.

Joe greeted his fellow guests, shook hands with Nikolai, then waved towards the bar, where the citizens of Highbridge who wanted to listen to the music and dance, but who couldn't afford dinner, had congregated in chattering groups. A painfully thin man with a collar too large for him jogged up immediately.

'Terry, well, here he is. Nikolai, this is Terry Sheldrake. He's the manager at The Playhouse and has been squeaking like a rabbit since he heard you were in town. Can you take five minutes to hear what a genius you are?'

Nikolai nodded, and replied with great seriousness. 'Out of respect to you, Mr Allerdyce.'

Joe's mouth twitched into a reluctant smile, then he found a chair next to Jack and lifted up his Martini in his large paw-like hand.

'What are you doing dining here, Jack? They poisoned half your crew only the other week.' He chuckled. 'Cracking night you got out of it, though.'

'Which we toasted gleefully with your champagne.' Jack rubbed his chin. 'Not a lot of choice in Highbridge, though, if you want a decent feed and a good band. Though I did my best. No, the chicken salad was supposed to be chucked away, then got sent round to us by mistake.'

'What are they doing feeding you anyway?' Joe asked as his steak – bloody and the size of a railway novel – was set in front of him.

'They've never sent anything to my theatres I didn't 'ave to pay through the nose for.'

'An admirer of Harold's, apparently. It made for a hell of an evening, but now we're offered the best tables and an astonishing discount, so I think we've come out rather well from it.'

Joe began slicing his steak. 'I'd been for thinking you'd lost your ability to land on your feet at every turn. Seems it's coming back to you. Gramophone records now, is it, then? Novelty of running a top-tier theatre worn off, has it?'

Jack could never tell if Joe was teasing him or not. He suspected Joe knew this.

'A man's allowed to seize the day, isn't he, Joe? Or seize the man, in our case. I practically kidnapped Dixon Wells off the street, then Tom realised the extent of his talents and the opportunity they represented. I see the new shop as a complement to the theatre.'

Joe arched an eyebrow in a manner which would have destroyed any of his employees. Jack was made of sterner stuff, but it still made him uncomfortable.

'Do you think it's a bad idea, Joe?'

That tempted another half-smile from Joe. 'You mistaking me for a fortune teller, lad? It might succeed, it might not. It's how you go at it that counts. And I'm at the age now where I like seeing you try. Glad to see Tom taking the initiative a bit. Agnes is fond of him, but thinks he needed a bit of a kick.'

'Yes, he's gone flying at the whole thing. The rest of us are just trying to catch up. Well, we can't mess it up as badly as I did the restaurant,' Jack said with a trace of bitterness. He had nothing against the Metropole, even after the chicken salad, but when he saw it as full and bustling as it was this evening, he couldn't help resenting its success.

'No! You can't do worse than that, so that's summat.' Lillian and Grace had always taken so many pains not to make feel Jack feel guilty about the failure of the restaurant, so Joe's candour made him feel oddly better. 'And Tom's a decent piano player, so even if he loses his shirt, he won't starve.'

'What about you, Joe? The season at The Playhouse this year isn't in your usual style.'

The waiter arrived with Jack's partridge, and he started sawing at it with a will. Partridge was his culinary nemesis. He liked the taste of it, but always forgot how fiddly the bits were to pull apart. He tried not to glance enviously at the steak.

'Chekhov and Strindberg not to your liking, Jack? Well, not mine neither, but there's a fashion in these plays for sex problems and drunks. If someone goes mad at the end, they only like it better. You ever seen any of Nikolai's work?'

'No. Any good tunes?'

'Ha! His last was called *The Slum Doctor of Prague* and had a chorus of the unfortunates. They all wore masks and moaned throughout.'

Jack was horrified. 'Not quite *Riviera Nights*, is it?'

A ripple of applause started around the stage, which built to a roar as Mabel Mills and her jazz men took the stage for their main set. The crowd around the bar surged onto the dance floor, and Ruby Rowntree, sitting a couple of places down from Jack, between Tom and Nikolai, clasped her hands together, then sat forward with her chin in her hands, blissful as a child.

Lillian was watching her fiancé talking to the manger of The Playhouse, and felt a buzz of pride under her ribs. How strange that in those blank years of her early widowhood, she had thought all the excitement of her life was gone. Now she had Jack, and the theatre, and Nikolai. Then, after not performing in public for more than twenty years, she had found herself on stage again and had loved it. She was grateful to Stella for giving her the opportunity – or, rather, by her strange behaviour, turning opportunity into a necessity. But Stella was obviously deeply unhappy. Perhaps Grace would have been able to find out what was troubling her so much, given time. Lillian's own efforts to enquire had been shut down. Of course Stella was upset about her friend, but she was sure there was more to it than that. Guilt: a terrible thing, and Lillian had largely lived her life free of it. Regret, yes, and shame, after she'd given birth to Jack and handed him over to be raised by another woman, but she'd known then she was doing the right thing for him, so no guilt.

And now there was this recording scheme. Tom and Jack had taken her over the figures in the weeks since they first announced the idea, and it seemed plausible. Not sound, exactly, but plausible, perhaps, if they were extremely lucky. She found herself staring across the table at Dixon Wells. The boy was sweet, strange, but certainly brilliant in his way, and Jack and Tom both seemed to like him very much, so why, when her eye fell on him, did she feel so uncomfortable?

'Wool-gathering, Lillian?' Agnes said, between mouthfuls of her steak.

'A little. Agnes, have you ever had the feeling of being afraid when you look at someone? Someone who doesn't in any way seem frightening, but you find yourself terribly on edge when he's around.'

Agnes followed the direction of Lillian's gaze, and raised an eyebrow. 'No, but I've seen horses do it.'

Lillian put down her glass. 'You'll have to explain.'

Agnes swallowed, and washed down her steak with the last swig of her Martini, before signalling to the waiter for another. 'I made a bad mistake in my early days as a trainer. Hired a man who seemed as if he knew his business, found out in a week that he was mistreating the horses, so I got rid of him, of course. A year later I hired a different lad, and though he was perfectly civil to the beasts, they wouldn't go near him. Turns out he was the half-brother of the first man. They saw the likeness, even when I couldn't.'

Lillian had been lost in a London fog once – only for a moment – when her then husband, Sir Barnabas, had stepped away from her to find a taxi. The murk had been so dense she had lost sight of him, and for a terrible vertiginous moment, she felt as if the entire world had gone with him, leaving her in a nightmarish limbo, where monsters might surround her at any moment. Now, the world she knew seemed to disappear and drop away from her again, leaving her lost, disorientated and alone with this new, terrible thought.

'Lillian . . .' Agnes's voice was low. 'Lillian, my dear, are you ill?'

Lillian concentrated on the table top. *I must not faint. Here is my glass, here is my knife, and my fork, and my buttered Dover sole.* 'I am well.' She forced herself to concentrate on her own breathing. 'Agnes, do you know anything of Dixon Wells's family?'

'No,' her friend said slowly. 'I think Jack hinted he is at odds with his father, who is something in the Foreign Office.'

Lillian swallowed. 'Yes, he mentioned that. Agnes, might you enquire a little further, discreetly?'

The waiter set down the Martini glass in front of Agnes, and she pushed it towards Lillian. 'Here, you take that one.'

Lillian grasped it gratefully. 'Thank you.'

'Not at all, my dear. Not at all. And yes, I'll make enquiries.'

'And now,' Mabel Mills said from the stage, 'I have a very special announcement . . .'

Lillian composed her face into an excited smile, but the fingers that clenched the stem of her borrowed Martini glass were white.

Vladimir Taargin wondered if he should speak to the bookseller about the upstairs room. The damp of the winter had leached in through the warped windows and there was a distinct smell of mould. No doubt, he considered, any attempt to make the place more comfortable would draw attention from the neighbouring properties, and that, he would rather avoid.

He stood where the light of the gas lamps cast enough light through the dusty panes of glass to read by, and opened the envelope the bookseller had handed him. More photographs from the Metropole of Kuznetsov and his fiancée. Useful, but . . . Ah, here was one of the Grand Duke and

Lillian Lassiter in conversation with a group of American jazz musicians. That could prove useful. The notes were also interesting. So Nikolai was lecturing about modern theatre. He had some people at the Daily Bulletin who would be able to make something of that.

The door behind him opened and Christian entered, shaking the London rain from his umbrella onto the dusty floor.

'I am sorry I am late, Your Excellency,' he said at once. 'My superior asked me to speak with him, and I feared refusing might cause suspicion.'

Taargin slid the notes and photographs back into the folder.

'You were correct to comply, Christian. Any news?'

Christian joined him at the window and peered into the street below. 'The Prince of Wales has decreed his tour with Prince Stefan in the north will be extended for two more days,' he said. 'He says he wishes to take Stefan to play a round at the Birkdale Golf Club on the north-west coast. Near Southport, but as far as I can tell, no firm arrangements for those days have been made.'

'Really? The Prince of Wales is a profoundly frivolous person. Golf!'

'Sir . . .' Christian cleared his throat. 'Southport is only eight kilometres from Highbridge.'

Taargin twisted his head sharply. 'Eight kilometres?'

'The Prince of Wales has made no mention of Highbridge. Nor of Kuznetsov. And it is, apparently, a very fine golf course.'

'Yet it feels a little too close to be a coincidence,' Taargin growled. 'Are you certain, Christian, there has been no private communication from Stefan requesting this alteration?'

Christian looked baffled. 'I handle all the correspondence at St James's Palace, sir. I have seen nothing which looked suspicious.'

'And neither have our friends at home.'

'And so?'

'And so, Christian, our hands are tied. The newspaper stories about Nikolai and his extravagances are having some effect among the people. While the king toils day and night for their comfort and security,

Nikolai cavorts around on stage dressed as a rat. There we have had some success. But be vigilant, Christian.'

'Sir, there is something else.'

'Go on.'

'The Foreign Office has put an appointment in the prince's diary with this gentleman. An expert on Marakovia, apparently, called . . .' He took his notebook from his pocket and turned the pages. 'Here it is.'

Taargin glanced at the page, and for the first time since they had met, he smiled.

'Yes, I remember Sir Gideon. One of these sybaritic Englishmen their Foreign Office would occasionally foist on us. I shall take him to dine at the Ritz. As I recall, his politics, such as they are, are not dissimilar to our own.'

'And another gentleman, a Colonel Osman? The prince requested his attendance at briefings.'

'I have never heard of him, but I'm sure the Prince of Wales will listen to Sir Gideon.'

CHAPTER THIRTY-THREE

The weeks Dixon Wells had spent at The Empire, and lodging at Lassiter Court, had been the happiest of his life. People had given up commenting on his coat – largely – though he didn't notice it, because the staff at Lassiter Court had been repairing it overnight, and their furtive piecemeal attempts had resulted in it looking a great deal better.

The old restaurant had become his particular domain, and while Little Sam and his crew worked to construct the recording studio to Dixon's specifications and designs, he ordered boxes of coiled wires and electronics from a variety of specialist firms in Manchester and London, and set about them with a will and his set of tiny screwdrivers. He had almost electrocuted himself once, and literal sparks had flown on a couple of occasions, but progress was being made.

Little Sam was not just supervising the construction of the recording studio. He had also been charged with the other works necessary to convert the restaurant into a record shop with a small café. Dixon was amazed how he and Jack could stand together in the middle of the space and see what it could be. Dixon knew he was not blessed with that sort of imagination, but he had his own creative spark: sparks of real electricity turning noise into a fluctuating current, then into a physical form – a shape cut by a stylus into a beeswax master. The moulding and casting and pressing was Tom Lassiter's remit, but then the process was reversed and the shape became sound again. Sound in a physical form. Sound you could carry to your friend's house; sound which would live on – not be lost in the air like every other song sung, tune played, or word spoken from the beginning of time. Sound which would stay, the way stories did in books.

Dixon was savouring this thought for the thousandth time during his second week of residence, when he happened on the Lyons teashop a hundred and fifty yards from the theatre. He had been ordered out for a walk and some proper food by Jack, and now he was in smelling distance of the café, he was glad of it. Some sort of meaty soup, it smelt like, and warm bread.

He pushed open the door and blinked until his vision cleared, and when it did, smiling up at him over her book in a corner of the shop, was Miss Chisholm. She invited him to join her, and he did. It became a routine. For some reason they never walked from the theatre together, but every day when he arrived, there she would be with a pot of tea. After a week the staff began to recognise them and offer them their usual: Miss Chisholm had a cheese sandwich, Dixon had the soup and a roll. The days filled further with variety and wonder. The day after he had dinner at the Metropole, he was brave enough to ask her her first name.

'Bridget!' she replied cheerfully. For some reason, she didn't have a book today but a roll of plans.

'What are those?'

She tucked them into her handbag. 'I'm trying to get to know the theatre a bit better. Mr Treadwell wants to serve milk shakes at the record shop, and I think there's space in the basement for a cold room. It'll need a way into it from the shop, though, and a hatch in the street for the ice man, so I'm trying to see how it might fit.'

'Are you an architect as well as a secretary?' he asked. She studied him suspiciously for a moment, then grinned.

'You say exactly what you mean, don't you? No, Dixon, I am not. I'm just interested in all sorts of things.'

The waitress arrived with their food and Dixon twisted the plate slightly so the Lyons' emblem was at twelve o'clock on his dish and side plate, then set about buttering his roll.

'Jack is a nice man, isn't he?'

Miss Chisholm nodded. 'Yes. Perhaps a little cavalier sometimes, but certainly good-hearted. Why do you ask?'

Dixon immediately wished he hadn't, remembering the morning he had seen the picture of Jack, Lillian and Nikolai in the newspaper on the breakfast table in his mother's home. He had come to Highbridge with a question because of that photograph, and now it was impossible to ask. She sensed his discomfort. 'Do tell me how things are going on in the studio. When will you be ready to record?'

'Very soon, I hope. It's a matter now of finding the right song. But Grace told Jack today that Ruby is planning something, and I understand she's terribly clever. They seemed very excited at the idea.'

Bridget asked intelligent questions, and Dixon responded with detailed answers. 'I suppose everything will be on hold for a little while for the wedding. They have set a date, haven't they?'

'The ninth of April,' Bridget confirmed. 'I've been sending out invitations.'

CHAPTER THIRTY-FOUR

G race led Jack along the rehearsal corridor, her eyes dancing. 'Ruby has had another triumph.'

As they approached, faintly through the closed door they could hear Lillian and Nikolai singing together.

Grace went to open it, but Jack stopped her. 'No, Grace, let me listen.' He frowned. 'It's the song that Nikolai sang, isn't it? From the day Clara got stuck.'

'So I'm told,' Grace replied. 'I wasn't here that day. But isn't it wonderful?'

'It is.'

Nikolai's baritone and Lillian's alto voice wrapped around each other like vines, supported by strong minor chords on the piano. There should have been something discordant about it – certainly, the sound was not as smooth and pleasant as many of the tunes Ruby had written – but then this was infused with Marakovia. What had Nikolai said in his newspaper interview? 'Plum brandy and romanticism' – that was it. Grace could feel it vibrating through the door, then – miracle of miracles – Mabel Mills's trumpet joined them: a line of longing, clean as spring water, bursting between their voices and reaching high and wide.

Grace realised Jack was staring at her, his jaw hanging slightly open. He took her hand and squeezed it hard.

'God, she's brilliant!' He frowned. 'What's it called?'

'"The Sunrise Song". Do you think it will work, Jack? As our first recording? I mean, we'll have other tunes, too. But this could be our calling card – The Empire Records announcing its arrival.'

He nodded. 'It's perfect. What else have we got?'

Grace leant against the wall of the corridor and counted on her fingers. 'I haven't been completely idle. Mabel Mills and her Jazz Band will record for us, and so will Josie. She'll do some of the numbers from *Cairo Nights*. Her agent is thrilled, it's exactly what she needs at the moment. That will give us our first ten, then I think we could have the house band record some dance tunes. There won't be a lack of music, I promise.'

'None of this would be possible without you, Grace. You know that, don't you?'

'I do,' she said, trying to sound more pleased than she felt. 'Now we've just got to get Dixon to record it all, Tom to press it, and finish building a shop to sell it all in. Have you had an idea for a picture story for Wilbur yet?'

'Perhaps,' he said. 'Gosh, it really is a very special tune.'

'Shall we go in and congratulate them?'

He nodded, though his face had that slightly tight look it tended to take on whenever he was going to have to be polite to Nikolai. 'Dixon's on course, I think, but I'd better go and see Tom myself. My picture idea relies rather heavily on him.'

Grace patted his arm, and an idea drifted through her head. That line of poetry Ruby had quoted in her room the other day when they had talked to Sally. It was becoming more solid, so she could just catch the edges of it.

'What is it, Grace?'

'Nothing,' Grace said as the idea disappeared again. 'Go and see Tom, and take Ruby with you.'

*

When Jack and Ruby arrived at Shed Number Four, Tom and Patterson were waiting for them – forewarned by Miss Chisholm, of course. The shed was a long, low box of corrugated iron on a steel frame, constructed hurriedly in the early days of the war. Tom had given it a fresh lick of paint – the same cream that many of the cottages in the dales were painted – and someone had put potted plants next to the office door.

Tom ushered them into the office area with all the pride of a new wife showing off her first home to her in-laws. There was a neat little lobby with a counter and chairs to wait on, and Tom's office led straight off it. Jack couldn't help noticing it was a great deal tidier than the old restaurant.

'Nice view,' he said.

'Bit of a perk,' Tom admitted. The office had two desks in it, a large leather-covered one in the centre, and a smaller one tucked in the corner at which Ruby Rowntree took her place. She had turned the corner into a rough approximation of her room at The Empire, with a cork board above it and drifts of manuscript paper. One of her patchwork quilts was slung over an armchair tucked between a filing cabinet and the window.

'Ruby! Gosh, you've made it positively cosy. But what will you do here?'

'Jack, dear, I'll be composing, naturally. And providing moral support to Tom and Mr Patterson.

'You don't need a piano?'

She tutted. 'Good Lord, no, though Tom insists on having one put in.'

'That's for me as much as anything, Ruby. I'd like to keep arranging as well as running things here, so I'll need it. I can't just play it all in my head, the way you do.'

'I've just heard "The Sunrise Song", Tom. It's sensational.'

'I know. Ruby's a genius.'

'Thank you, dear,' Ruby said vaguely. 'Yes, I'm rather proud of it. Circumstance rather slotted it together. The tune is traditional, of course, but the arrangement came together well. Now, where's my pencil?'

'Behind your ear, Ruby,' Tom said. 'Now come on, Jack. Let me show you the rest.'

The office had a second door which led directly out to the factory floor. It was a clean, bright space, divided into different areas, Tom explained, for the creation of the masters, electroplating, casting, pressing, smoothing and finishing.

'No, no, no! Patterson? Miss James has found another one!' An irate gentleman in a foreman's coat, with a startling head of red hair, was waving a disc in the air. 'If the hole isn't in the very centre, every singer sounds like a drunk! Recalibrate!'

'Who's that?' Jack asked.

'Jeremy Fossil,' Tom said. 'I pay him a lot of money to tell me what idiots my workers and I are. 'I'm discovering new things that can go wrong every day, from a careless hand mixing the shellac to warping. Jeremy is explaining all of them to me one by one, and why each fault is my responsibility.'

'You've started pressing records?' Jack asked, eyebrow raised.

'Test runs. We bought a couple of masters from one of the London firms to test the equipment, and I'm very glad we're doing them. Sensitive little devils, these records. The lady standing next to him is Miss James. She stays at the same boarding house as Ruby and is going to be our head of quality control. Once we have some quality to control, that is.'

He sighed, and Jack studied him sideways. 'How are you doing, Tom? You've taken on a great deal very suddenly.'

Tom pursed his lips. 'I'm discovering there are a lot more hours in the day than I knew, and each one seems to throw up a new problem. But I'm enjoying it, Jack. I'm enjoying it a great deal. It's a different thing, isn't it, going to bed dog-tired because you've actually been working all day?'

'Yes, it is.'

Jack looked around him. It was clear Tom's days over the last couple of months had been very full indeed.

The vast space was full of half-unpacked boxes, metal drums, machinery with packing straw still clinging to it, tea chests piled on wooden pallets. It reminded Jack of the backstage at the theatre when a large musical was getting in, and it had the same air of busy excitement. Workers moved back and forth, whistling warnings as they manoeuvred wheelbarrows and trolleys over the painted concrete floors. Shouts and commands as the great industrial presses were calibrated and adjusted. The air was sharp with smells of hot chemicals – a clear astringency with an undercurrent of oil and sweat.

'We have twenty on staff now,' Tom went on. 'And Miss James will have a dozen girls in her department, polishing and checking the discs and adding the labels . . . when we have them. How are things going in the studio?'

'Dixon and Little Sam are blood brothers. I can get no more detail there than the fact "it will be ready soon". But I heard the electric company sent the wrong cables, and one of the microphones exploded yesterday morning. I'm sure it will all work out wonderfully.'

'And what of Harry?' Tom asked.

'We're keeping out of each other's way, for now. But Dixon is so fond of the creature, and working so hard on the studio, I really don't have the heart to say anything.'

'And Miss Chisholm?'

'Has worked out how we can offer milkshakes to the record-buying populace. It is a marvel what a difference she's made. And I still have enough time to scurry about drumming up business for the theatre. The last couple of touring plays we've had in did rather well.'

'No more snags, then?'

'I wouldn't say that. Only, with Miss Chisholm's help, I'm managing to get out in front of them a bit more. And I told her to keep an eye out for Ray Kelly and any of his associates, in case they start sniffing around the theatre again.' Jack saw the expression on Tom's face and stopped. 'They're still only rumours, you know, about your mother being involved with him and his people.'

Tom nodded. 'But I've been rather slow to make the effort to find out if they're true or not, haven't I?'

'Understandable, old chap.'

They walked back into the office to find Ruby in her chair, one of her notebooks open on her lap, and a broad grin on her round, red-cheeked face.

'Look at you both – I'm so terribly proud of you.'

Jack was surprised to find he was blushing. 'You might not be in a second, Ruby. I've had one of my plans. For the opening day at the shop.'

'Do tell . . . Actually, wait a moment.' Tom leant out of the door. 'Fossil! Patterson! Miss James? Could you possibly join us for a moment? Treadwell's had an idea, and if it's anything like his usual ones, it might be best if you hear it from him, rather than blame me for it later.'

Jack found himself facing a slightly larger crowd than he had intended.

'Lovely to meet you all,' he said, 'I'm hoping to enlist you for a bit of a stunt on the opening day for the shop. We're intending to open at four in the afternoon, twenty-fifth of March, and stay open into the evening, and . . .' The whole enterprise was feeling more and more ridiculous with every syllable he uttered. 'Well, I want the newspapers to get a proper story out of it, so I thought . . . what if we make a recording in the morning, of this wonderful new song of Ruby's, sung by Nikolai and Lillian?' They stared at him. 'The press could take pictures of the whole process, you see, from cutting the master to rushing it here, to checking the finished discs and getting it on the shelves at the shop. It makes us look . . . very modern.'

The clock on Tom's wall ticked loudly.

'Utterly impossible,' Fossil said, his voice as flat and hard as granite.

'Utterly impossible, or just extremely risky?' Jack said hopefully.

Patterson had taken a pencil out from behind his ear and was making quick calculations on a piece of Tom's elegant stationery. He sucked his teeth. 'It's theoretically possible, Mr Lassiter.'

'Practically, highly unlikely!' Fossil protested, looking around at his fellow workers as if they had gone quite mad.

'It's an excellent idea, Jack,' Ruby stated. 'We must rise to the occasion, Mr Fossil. Do a favour for an old woman. I'm very fond of that song.'

She fixed him with an expectant, hopeful stare. She had something remarkably kittenish in her manner at times, and looked as if she very much hoped Fossil would be kind enough to wave a pretty ribbon for her to chase.

It happened. Stone melted.

'I suppose we can try.'

She beamed at him.

'But, Jack . . .' Tom lifted his hand. 'The other recordings Mabel's and Josie's, and the tunes from the theatre band. We'll have those in well before opening, won't we?'

Jack's thoughts flitted back to a fierce debate about a hatch between the instrument room and the musicians' den, as they were calling it. He wondered if it would still be ongoing when he returned.

'Yes, absolutely. No problem at all. Dixon suggested Josie do the ballad from *Cairo Nights* first. Your arrangement for piano and violin.'

Ruby pressed her palms together. 'A good choice for Josie.' She wrinkled her nose at Mr Fossil. 'She can be marvellously expressive in her lower range.'

'We shall take good care of it, Miss Ruby.' Mr Fossil sounded flinty again. 'I shall return to my shellac, Mr Lassiter.'

CHAPTER THIRTY-FIVE

It took another week. A week of long days and evenings of sweat and sawdust, things fitting together and things refusing to fit, wires not quite reaching, fabric not cut to the right lengths, and doors rehung. The shop area was still almost entirely empty apart from the old booths and the beginning of the serving counter for teas and coffees, but Little Sam and his crew had done a magnificent job on the studio section. The box-like structure was built of double-layered pine, and Bridget had come up with the idea of placing all sorts of greenery and ferns on the roof between its ceiling and the double height ceiling of the restaurant. It gave it an almost tropical feel, and the deep greens of the foliage complemented the green and gold on the walls.

The box was divided into two, a smaller room for the recording lathe and Dixon, and a larger one for the musicians. In the musicians' den, the interior walls were lined with curtains of heavy cotton to damp any reverberations, and the wires from the microphones led through narrow drilled holes in the connecting wall. The hatch had been designed and installed in the shared wall so Dixon could slide it open to confirm a performance had been successfully recorded, or interrupt the musicians if something had gone wrong.

Dixon was horribly nervous. The den felt too large, the hatch too small, and the air too thin. He felt Jack's hand on his arm just as his vision began to darken round the edges.

'Breathe, Dixon,' he said softly. 'We're all friends here. Just let them know when you're ready.'

Dixon checked everything one more time, studying voltage meters as the musicians warmed up next door. His earphone would not give him a perfect idea of what he had available to record, only a guide, but Josie's warm laugh at something Jack had said seemed to ripple up the wires and enter directly into his bloodstream.

On the table in front of him was a postcard with a four-leaf clover, a horseshoe and a garish rainbow on it. On the back was written *Good luck, Dixon! With all best wishes, Bridget.* He set it straight on the board in front of him. He was ready.

He slid the hatch open and found himself peering into the den. Josie stood in the centre of the space, with Tom at the piano, and Mr Porter had his own microphone. Dixon frowned.

'Where's your music, Tom?' he asked.

'We've all learned it, Dixon,' he replied cheerfully. 'Don't want any sounds of papers turning on our first day. And we've sent Jack out to wait in the shop. He couldn't stop fidgeting.' Dixon smiled. He glanced over at Ruby, Lillian and Grace and they smiled back at him.

'When the red light goes on, we're recording,' he said, pointing at the dull bulb mounted on the wall just above his hatch, and began to close the slide again, then paused. 'And thank you.'

He retreated back into his cubbyhole, breathed out through his nose, switched on the lathe and clicked on the red light. Tom struck the opening chord. They had become Dixon's friends over the last few weeks; they had trusted him with their money, their time and their talent. It was the least he could do, to make them immortal.

They got it on the first take.

*

They all followed in procession to the factory, with Lillian tooting her horn and laughing, with Ruby, Josie and Nikolai crammed in beside her. Tom was driving with Jack, and Dixon was cradling the master on his lap. Jeremy Fossil had to ask him twice before he was willing to release his grip on it. It was treated with the reverence due to a communion wafer.

They watched the electroplating and pressing like nervous parents.

Miss James passed the finished record to Fossil, who handed it to Patterson, who passed it to Tom, and Tom finally put it into Jack's hands. He held it lightly by the edges, watching the light beam across the grooves. EMPIRE RECORDS, the label said, gold on a deep green background. 'My Love Awaits Me'. (Treadwell/Rowntree) Josie Clarence and the Empire Musicians.

'Can we listen to the bloody thing now?' Josie asked after Jack had spent a good minute staring at it.

He placed the record on the turntable, clicked the switch and placed the stylus down.

The song began.

Josie's shoulders had dropped; Grace had her arm through Ruby's, and was smiling. Fossil and Tom were leaning forward towards the horn, like game dogs at attention, trying to hear any imperfections in the sound.

Mr Porter had his arms folded across his chest, and he was nodding. Lillian and Nikolai were holding hands. Jack put his arm around Dixon's shoulders.

'You've done it, Dixon. You've only gone and bloody done it.'

He inhaled; the factory smelt of vinegar and fresh paint, and everything in it seemed to shimmer. Heaven, he was sure, would feel something like this.

Lillian suggested taking the record to play to Agnes and Joe. They telephoned from the factory, and Agnes said she would meet them at Joe's house, as he had the better gramophone. Ruby said she was a little tired, and Mr Porter and Josie volunteered to run her home, while the others went to hear judgement pronounced.

The house built by Joseph P. Allerdyce was acclaimed by the leading architects, aesthetes and modernists of the country to be a masterpiece, and his housekeeper spent half her days showing groups of awe-struck tourists of the intelligentsia around its white marble halls. Agnes loathed it, but Joe's pride in the house had softened her attitude somewhat. It looked as if it had been fashioned out of chalk, almost dug out of the gentle slope which shielded it from the disapproving gaze of her own ramshackle farmhouse. Mature trees seemed to hold it in a gentle embrace from above and to the sides, while steep manicured lawns extended from its glass and concrete frontage to a perfectly rectangular lake which seemed to draw down the sky and lay it at the mansion's feet.

Inside, Joe had ditched the rich flummery of Victorian decoration – a feature of his entertainment venues – and replaced it with walls of white, punctuated with large windows, so the house appeared to be decorated by nature. The cold effect was softened by honey-coloured floorboards, and a scattering of modern sculptures, which stood like attendants or guests in the corners of the rooms.

The main reception room was filled with sofas in green leather, glass tables artfully scattered with magazines, elegant card tables surrounded by chairs with straight backs, and green leather seats which were, Jack found to his surprise, remarkably comfortable.

Nikolai was entranced.

'Mr Allerdyce, sir,' he said, accepting a whisky from him. 'This is a masterpiece. A triumph!'

Joe looked pleased. 'Aye, well. I admit I like how it turned out. Once you are married, we'll give you a dinner here. You'll spend the evening here if we do that, won't you, Agnes?'

'As long as you keep your excellent cook,' Agnes replied. She was standing by the gramophone with the record in her hand. 'Now shall we listen? I fear Tom may have a stroke if we do not.'

'Go ahead.' Joe nodded, and Tom set the record on the turntable, released the brake and lowered the needle. It sounded, if anything, better here than it had done in the factory. Agnes nodded, and patted Tom on the shoulder.

As the chorus began for the second time, Agnes caught Lillian's eye and, with a slight tip of her chin, indicated she would like a word in private. Lillian moved quietly to her side and they retreated a little way from the gramophone and the others.

'I have made a few enquiries about the family of Mr Wells, Lillian.'

Lillian braced herself, looking across the empty marble space at her fiancé. 'Go on.'

'His father is Colonel Sir Gideon Wells. He does indeed work at the Foreign Office, and spent a little time in Marakovia. He married a rather stupid woman a cousin of mine was at school with, almost certainly for her money, and the general consensus is he treats her badly.' Lillian glanced at her sharply. 'The cruelty, I understand, has been mental rather than physical. They lead separate lives now, and she is active in her local church. They have a daughter, Dixon's older sister, who seems likely to be a spinster. A rather mousey creature, but devoted to her mother.'

'I see,' Lillian said. 'Did you find out anything else about him, Agnes?'

'Come and admire the garden with me,' Agnes said, moving closer to the window. 'It looks its best in the evening.' Lillian followed her and realised her friend had placed her so she could pretend to admire the view, but in the reflection of the glass, keep an eye on where everyone else was.

The garden did indeed look lovely; the pristine lawn was lined on both sides with wild borders of Queen Anne's lace.

'I found the following, Lillian. The old girl network was not complimentary. Sir Gideon has always had an unpleasant reputation with women. Maids were chaperoned when he stayed in the country houses of some women I know. Need I say more?'

'You do not.' Lillian's mouth had become uncomfortably dry.

'I also presumed to find out where he was in 1896.' Agnes stared out into the gentle dusk. 'He had been married two years by then. His wife's parents made some efforts to get him away from their home, and sent him to manage some of their properties in Northumberland. He returned before he was expected, and they found him a sinecure at the Foreign Office.'

For a dark moment, Lillian was back in the private dining room of a squalid establishment near the centre of Newcastle, fighting her own grief and fear during the brief painful minutes of Jack's conception. She looked at the reflections of Joe's other guests in the dark glass: Dixon, receiving Joe's praise with his shy and kindly smile; Jack and Grace, beaming with pride.

'Lillian?'

'I can't be sure, Agnes. It was so long ago. And the man in question gave me a false name.'

Agnes pursed her lips, and sniffed. 'But would you recognise the man who attacked you if you saw him again?'

'Yes. But I was hoping I would never have to do so.'

'No. I see that,' her friend said with a sigh. 'But you had better prepare yourself.'

Lillian darted an alarmed look at her, and Agnes drank her whisky. 'My friendly network of informants extends quite a way, dear. I have a message for Nikolai from his cousin, the Crown Prince Stefan. With a little subterfuge, aided by the Prince of Wales, he hopes to add Highbridge to the tour he is undertaking with the prince later in the year. They will visit a factory or two, and take in a show, but of course the primary aim will be to meet with Nikolai.' Lillian gasped. 'You must say nothing, Lillian. Only you and Nikolai can know anything of this. I mention it because it is likely Colonel Sir Gideon Wells, as an old Marakovian hand, will be part of the Prince of Wales's entourage. Then you will know if it was he who attacked you, or not.'

Lillian could not speak, but for a few minutes at least, she did not have to. The record was put on again and by the time it had finished a second time, Lillian was ready to face the room.

When the others had left, Joe walked Agnes back through the woods to her own house along the wide gravel track he had caused to be built for just this purpose. They walked arm in arm in easy silence, till, through the last trees and across the lawn, Agnes could make out the twinkling windows of her own ramshackle cottage.

'You told her then?' Joe asked.

'I did. And I impressed on her the need to keep the secret of Prince Stefan's visit from anyone but Nikolai.'

'Good. They're a pleasant bunch – Jack, Grace, Tom and the rest. But still young, like puppies. Too inclined to trust. Lil has had enough hard knocks, though.' Agnes could feel rather than see his smile. 'It was a fine thing to hear her sing again, though, wasn't it? And now she's going to release a recording. Things do change.'

The air was heavy with the scent of damp earth, a new spring to come. With each year that passed, Agnes valued that scent more deeply. 'They do. I only hope their bad luck is over. They've had more than their fair share over the years since The Empire was rebuilt.'

'They have!' They crossed the lawn together, and Agnes opened the door with her latchkey, releasing the familiar smell of her house – baked bread and horse blanket. 'I used Turnbull's in my refurbishment and Hallam's for the drains, and never had an issue—' He stopped suddenly on the threshold. 'Now then, I wonder . . .'

'What is it, Joe?'

'Might be I just have a nasty habit of thought. When do they mean to open the shop again?'

She pulled him gently into the hallway, crowded with galoshes and damp wool coats. 'Towards the end of the month. Jack has some stunt planned. They'll record the Sunrise Song in the morning, and have it on the shelves for the four o'clock opening.' He was still lost in thought. 'Come and have a nightcap and tell me what you are thinking.'

He shook himself. 'I will.'

Agnes did not think that Joe, when he slowly unfolded his suspicions, was being foolish, or overly cynical, or alarmist. She had, after all, known the principles involved for many years. The next day she left her horses to call at the Empire and had a serious conversation with Tom at the factory, then with Jack, Grace and Lillian at the Empire.

She left Tom, to her disquiet, distressed, Jack angry and Lillian pale with shock. Before she left, Grace took her down to the shop and she tried a milk shake and admired the general industry of the workers getting the shop ready for its opening.

'I wish you the very best of luck, Grace,' she said as she left.

'You and Joe must think we're all very foolish not to have seen it,' Grace said.

'Not at all, dear,' Agnes replied. 'I think you're a good person. That's a very dangerous thing to be in a naughty world.'

CHAPTER THIRTY-SIX

Tom switched on his torch. He had not known what or who to expect, but still, seeing his mother's suave assistant in the beam, the key to Shed Number Four in one hand, a large brown bottle in the other, did not come as surprise. The man blinked, and attempted a smile.

'Oh, Mr Lassiter, I was just passing. I thought I saw someone sneaking around the back of the shed and I thought I better come and check. Such a big day you have coming up tomorrow.'

'What is your name again? Milner, wasn't it?'

'That's right. Do you, err, know how to use that?' Milner said, nodding towards the shotgun that lay across Tom's lap. He had dragged Ruby's armchair onto the factory floor, just outside his office. A packing case at his elbow held a book and a glass of whisky. There was no ashtray. Smoking was strictly forbidden on the factory floor.

'I do. A long time ago, Mr Milner, I had nothing better to do than travel around to country houses and shoot things. Can't think why it amused me back then, but it did. But this . . .' He waved his hand behind him. 'This is not an amusement – this I take very seriously indeed.'

'So I see.' Milner attempted a light laugh. 'Well, obviously there's nothing for me to worry about. I'll be off.'

'This will go a lot faster if you stop lying, Milner. Don't worry, I know who sent you, so I'm not going to ask you anything. But I'm tired and irritable, so if you must say anything, don't lie. Do you understand?'

'Yes.' Milner smoothed his hair back with a trembling hand.

'Good. Now put down the bottle and the key.'

He did so, the glass clinking on the concrete. 'Tell me, Mr Lassiter, were you here last night?'

'And the night before,' Tom said.

'Don't you have to sleep some time?' Milner's smile became unpleasant.

'I might. If I do, one of the stable hands from my great-aunt's stables will be here, so you will have no possible reason for any further night-time visits.' Tom's right hand rested on the stock of the shotgun. 'Do you understand?'

Milner nodded.

'Now leave. And, Mr Milner, as you consider your future in Highbridge, keep this in mind. My mother has risked your liberty and your life to sabotage her son. Does that sound like the action of a leader to whom you should entrust your career? I would, if I were you, think very carefully about what you've done in the past, and what you do next.'

The man hesitated for a moment, then turned and left. Only when the door to the outside world had closed behind him did Tom unload the shotgun and go and check the bottle Milner had left behind him. He whistled through his teeth.

CHAPTER THIRTY-SEVEN

Wilbur Bowman had been a reporter long enough to know a stunt when he saw one, but he had to admit that this one had a bit of the old Treadwell stardust about it.

'Do you think so?' Jack said brightly when Wilbur told him so on the pavement outside the restaurant. Along the High Street, the town clock struck nine.

Jack waited for the photographer to capture him turning the key, then ushered them inside. The transformation was complete. What had been the dance floor was now home to a series of low polished shelves, a bar was set up to serve tea, coffee and buns, and the old booths had their walls raised so they were a series of independent little units, each with a wind-up portable gramophone screwed to the table.

Between the shelves and the booths were a series of scattered tables, all dark polished wood. No starched linen and fresh flowers, Wilbur noticed, but clean and pleasant nonetheless. Even empty, it had an atmosphere: something younger and more informal than the Lyons teashops, more homely than a nightclub.

'And that,' Jack pointed to the far end of the room, 'is where we record. Everyone's waiting.'

'Why did you have to unlock the door, then?' Wilbur asked.

Jack didn't even blush. 'I thought it might make a nice picture. Did it, Pete?'

'Aye.'

Mabel Mills was drinking coffee with her fellow band members; Lillian and Nikolai were in the musicians' den while Dixon moved microphones backwards and forwards a few inches. Wilbur flipped a page on his notebook.

'Miss Mills, how have you found recording with the new microphones?'

She sipped her coffee. 'You'll never get the heat of a performance in a club on to a disc, that I know. But Mr Wells gets us close. Come and sit with us, Mr Bowman.'

She patted the chair between her and Lillian and Wilbur sat down a little nervously while the photographer took more frames of them, a bristle of microphones at their backs.

'Now, Lillian and I were just speaking of the something extra these microphones can bring to our music, weren't we?' Mabel leant forward and spoke softly.

'And what is that?'

'Intimacy,' Lillian said in a low whisper. Wilbur's pencil slipped. 'Even with the whole band playing, I can sing like I'm sitting this close to you.'

'Works for the players, too,' Mabel added. 'We don't have to project to the back of the stalls or the club. We can be softer.'

Softer, Wilbur wrote with a trembling hand.

'Or mix it up. We can play like we're setting the street on fire, then Joshua, my crooner, can sing like he's whispering a lullaby to our baby girl, and when you play the record, you'll hear us and him both fine. One of our new records is "Mabel's Lullaby", and it's ready to go on sale today.'

Lillian waited until Wilbur had taken that down, then stood up. 'But this morning we are doing something rather special. Nikolai and I are going to record "The Sunrise Song", as arranged by our own Ruby Rowntree, and featuring Miss Mills.'

'It is a celebration of our upcoming wedding,' Nikolai said, 'and of this new enterprise.' 'Not unlucky, though?' Wilbur asked. 'I understand you sang it to prevent a riot in The Empire when the machinery broke.'

There was an awkward silence.

'We're reclaiming it as our victory song!' Jack declared, clapping his hands together. 'Now, Wilbur, come and see the recording lathe.'

Wilbur would write many stories in his career that were more important; he would write many more that were more important that year. He very rarely wrote one which was as much fun.

The recording process itself was fascinating. Dixon explained it to him – and so to his readers – and after the master was made, Jack drove them up to the Lassiter's site like the Hounds of Hell were after them. And after a breathless few minutes, while the master was being checked and no one would talk to him, Tom Lassiter took over to give Wilbur the tour of the plant.

Jack retreated into Tom's office.

'How is it going so far, Jack?' Ruby said from the desk. 'Lord, you look worn out. Sit down. Have the comfy seat, dear.'

Jack fell into her armchair and pulled her patchwork throw around his shoulders.

'I was up all night guarding the shop! No sign of any trouble. What about here?'

Ruby reached out and patted him on the shoulder. 'We had a visit. From Constance's secretary. He had a bottle of vitriol with him, and the key to the shed.'

Jack threw off the quilt. 'Good God! Did you call the police?'

Ruby shook her head. 'Calm down, Jack. And I shan't say anything more until you settle again.'

The armchair was very comfortable. With a show of reluctance, he settled back down into it and pulled the quilt over him. 'There. I am cocooned as ordered.'

'Good. No. He claimed to be checking all was secure, and as the landlord's representative, he has a right to be holding the key. We've changed all the locks, though, and given him warning the factory will be guarded at night. Tom dealt with him.'

'So . . .' Jack yawned. 'I suppose that means Joe was right, that Constance is behind some of our reversals?'

Ruby made a note in her book. 'Yes, it does. And Tom is rather heartbroken. He knew his mother didn't like him much, but to actively attempt to sabotage the factory . . . Honestly, Jack, I don't have the words. As I understand it, if this man had added the vitriol to the mix, it would have just looked as if the shellac had failed.'

'I'm very glad Tom has you, Ruby,' he said, and yawned again. 'So she probably bribed someone at Turnbull's, and at Hallam's, to sabotage the work at the theatre. And the chicken episode, I imagine, too.' He felt his eyelids begin to close. 'I wonder if she had anything to do with our director getting run out of the country, but how on earth would she manage that?'

Grace had to sit on her hands to stop herself from biting her nails. An hour until opening, and there was nothing else for her to do. It was torture. The empty shelves had been stacked with the Mabel Mills recordings, popular favourites brought in from EMI, and a dozen of Ruby's songs. The great speeches section included an old friend, Ivor French, doing 'To be, or not to be. . .' and Miss Pritchard and Miss Gardiner's reading of extracts from *Sonnets from the Portuguese*.

There were two prominent display stands at the front of the shop, one filled with copies of 'My Love Awaits Me' from *Cairo Nights*, and the other still empty, waiting for the freshly pressed copies of 'The Sunrise Song'. Miss Chisholm sat next to her, and even in her usually calm demeanour, Grace sensed a tremor.

'It'll be splendid,' Grace said firmly, and Miss Chisholm shot her a shy smile.

'I do hope so. Did you see the telegram from Miss Stanmore?'

Grace had. And it was the second time Miss Chisholm had asked. It had given no indication of where Stella was, or if she intended to come to Lillian and Nikolai's wedding in a little over a week, and consisted of only three words: *Good luck, darlings!*

'I did.'

'I'm so terribly sorry to hear about Mrs Constance Lassiter,' Miss Chisholm said in a whisper. 'I went to the Metropole first thing, and Bertram's. They aren't sure who she might have been dealing with. I had to be rather vague, of course, but they assure me dealings with The Empire will be handled only by their most trusted employees in the future.'

'Thank you,' Grace said. 'And for your discretion. It is a terrible thing. I honestly think there is nothing Constance would not do to harm us. A rather terrifying thought, considering Lassiter Enterprises still manufactures armaments for the government.'

'Goodness!'

'Don't worry, Miss Chisholm,' Grace said. 'I'm beginning to think that Constance is a little mad, but I don't think she'd risk a violent assault. She's a businesswoman, not a soldier.'

'Indeed. I suppose that's some small comfort.'

The girls on the cash desk and coffee counter wore dark green aprons with gold trim, and a small sign standing next to them advertised MILKSHAKES! THE AMERICAN SENSATION! Small cakes and tiny pork pies sat waiting for the peckish under large glass domes, and the tea urn was already steaming.

'Mrs Treadwell, have you looked outside recently?'

Grace looked up to see Mr Poole bending towards her, hands behind his back. He looked terribly serious.

'Oh, has no one turned up? But we spent an absolute fortune on announcements! We offered coupons!' She looked at her watch. Still forty minutes till they opened.

'Perhaps they're waiting until the last moment?' Miss Chisholm suggested.

'Oh, the final photographs will look terrible if it's just an empty shop!' Grace groaned.

'No, it's not that,' Mr Poole said. 'Lord, you and Mr Treadwell are always jumping ahead of a person! Do come and see for yourself.'

He led the two women up the stairs, past the old maître d's station, unhitched the chain wrapped around the doors, and pulled it open.

Grace blinked. The pavement was heaving. Dozens of men, women and children were gathered around the entrance in a great mass. They were not the usual habitués of the theatre, Grace noticed, but older women in plain coats holding the hands of small children, young men in caps and without collars. Girls and boys hardly out of the schoolroom.

'Oh, my! Any word from the factory?' Miss Chisholm asked.

'They're checking and packaging the records, according to Marcus, who seems to be in constant communication with Mr Lassiter's boy there. I can't imagine what the girls at the telephone exchange think of them. Anyway, sounds like they shan't be long.'

'We meant to have the crates of "The Sunrise Song" and the customers come in at the same time,' Miss Chisholm said, stepping back a little so Mr Poole could close the door again.

'It'll be a stampede if we wait,' he replied. 'Do that and you'll have turned ankles, spilled goods, and every sort of folderol. The energy of crowds should not be trifled with, Mrs Treadwell. Scientists say so.'

Grace made a decision. 'Well, if scientists say so, Mr Poole, who are we to disagree?' Then she turned to the store and clapped her hands.

'Ladies and gentlemen! It looks like we're going to be busy, so we're going to open early. Now remember, be calm and cheerful. I want every person who comes through those doors to get their shilling's worth of entertainment. Miss Chisholm, we're going to need more cakes. Buy everything they can give us, including the macaroons, and then biscuits will have to do after that. Mrs Briggs, if you would concentrate on the teacups. Now Mabel and Josie will be signing records over there. They're at the Metropole – can someone go and fetch them? And Miss Chisholm, on your way to the bakery, could you pop up to Lady Lassiter's office and tell her and Nikolai we're opening early?'

Grace felt that quiver in the air – the feeling of being alive from the top of your head to the soles of your feet. Constance disappeared from her mind like smoke.

'What shall I do?' Dixon was hovering near the door of the recording area.

'Stay there, Dixon, and keep the doors open so customers can have a look in and ask questions about the recordings.'

'What if they touch things?' he asked in tones of tangled panic.

'Fear not, Mr Wells,' Mr Poole said, raising a hand. 'We shall fetch stanchion ropes to keep back the throng. Marcus! Go!'

Marcus hightailed it through the shop in pursuit of the velvet ropes and brass posts.

Grace tried to sound bracing. 'We're going to let everyone in now.' She looked around at the faces in front of her – a mix of excitement and nerves. Jack was supposed to make these sorts of speeches. She decided to keep it simple.

'Don't worry, everyone, this is going to be magnificent.'

She nodded to Mr Poole, and he flung open the doors.

CHAPTER THIRTY-EIGHT

Perhaps it was the soothing presence of Ruby's quilt, but against all odds, Jack had fallen asleep in her armchair, only to be startled awake by Tom banging open the door, and the sounds of a cheer from the factory floor washing in after him.

'First ones are coming off the presses, Jack! We've got the truck out front. How many crates of the record do we need to make the first run?'

Jack rubbed his eyes. 'Four, each with ten dozen copies. Can we make it? Or we leave at quarter to four with whatever we've got.'

'Oh, this is exciting!' Ruby said, pressing the palms of her hands together. 'Jack, let's make ourselves useful. We can put the records into their sleeves as long as we handle them by the edges. It'll make another nice picture, but if Miss James catches us getting fingerprints on anything, I won't be answerable for her actions.'

'Understood,' Jack said, and saluted.

At a quarter to four exactly a final crate was loaded into the van, and Jack, Wilbur and Pete the photographer clambered in after them. Tom himself was driving, with Ruby beside him, and the factory workers spilled out to watch them go.

Jack waved at them from the open door and was cheered in return, then Tom pulled away, making him fall back heavily into the interior, but it gave the workers a laugh and he hardly felt it.

The ride became smoother as they came onto the better roads leading into the centre of town, and Jack prepared himself for his big arrival. He hoped there was a decent crowd waiting for them. Didn't need to be a mob, but enough curious visitors to fill a frame would be nice.

The truck came to a halt and Jack flung the door open, then struggled to hide his dismay. There were only a dozen people waiting to get in and the town clock was just striking four. As Jack prepared to offer a brave face to Wilbur, no matter how badly he felt in the moment, the doors sprung open. Grace and Mr Poole emerged and, to his great surprise, his wife looked very happy indeed. She turned to the small queue.

'Thank you so much for waiting! It's a *bit* of a crush in there at the moment, but hopefully we'll have some more room soon.'

'Is there still cake?' the woman at the front of the line asked darkly.

'Oodles of cake,' Grace assured her, then turned to her husband. 'We had to open early, there was such a crowd. Do you have them?'

Jack rallied. 'We do! Four crates.'

'Can you and Tom carry one directly onto the floor, open the case there and stack the shelves? That should make a good picture, shouldn't it?'

'Aye,' the photographer said, pushing his soft hat back, then he sauntered across the pavement into the shop.

'Marcus, if you could see to getting the rest into the storeroom. Ruby, lots of people want you to sign the records. Would you be happy to join Josie and Mabel at the signing table? We've put a chair out for you. And Lillian and Nikolai are standing by to sign "The Sunrise Song".'

'As long as I can have a milk shake,' Ruby said, and bustled off towards Mr Poole, beaming.

Tom tossed his key to Marcus. He and Jack slid out the first crate and carried it between them through the open doors.

Jack couldn't take it in.

He saw Dixon at the back of the room with a group of men who were peering into the recording studio; a line snaking between the shelves, which ended with Josie and Mabel seated at one of the polished café tables signing record sleeves, and now making room for Ruby to sit between them. The booths were crammed with groups of young people, heads together over the portable players; the tea urn hissed. At the cash desk, three girls were making up packets of records in brown paper, gluing Empire Records labels to them and tying them up with a handy carrying loop of string.

Everyone stopped and turned to look at him.

'"The Sunrise Song"!' Jack exclaimed. 'Recorded this morning by Lady Lillian Lassiter and His Excellency, Grand Duke Nikolai Goranovich Kuznetsov, featuring Mabel Mills, and available for your listening pleasure right now!'

They cheered.

Tom and Jack wrestled the crate downstairs and prised off the cover. Customers were grabbing copies out of their hands before they even managed to get them on the shelves.

Some hours later, Tom drove Ruby home while everybody else returned to Lassiter Court. She was tired, she said, after all the excitement.

'What a day, Ruby! Did you see how often Marcus and his crew had to restock the shelves?'

'I did, dear. I'm so terribly proud of you.'

Tom felt his chest expand. 'Thank you.'

She reached over and patted his hand. 'I'm very sorry about your mother, but I hope you remember you have other family. Agnes is so very fond of you, as are Lillian, Jack and Grace.'

'I know. I shan't complain about the luck of my heritage, Ruby. Even if it has its complications.'

Ruby sighed. 'I had my eye out for Mrs Blow this afternoon. Did she come?'

Tom shook his head.

'She will. We all find our way to where we belong in the end. You're very like your grandfather, you know, Tom.'

Tom thought of the huge oil portrait of the richly moustachioed industrialist in the library at Lassiter Court. 'Am I really?'

'Yes, he was a good man. Don't let your mother make you forget that, Tom.'

'I won't.' He swallowed. He could not bear to think of his mother yet. '"The Sunrise Song" is really marvellous, you know.'

Ruby sighed. 'What a lovely day that was, and what a lovely night it is. I can smell spring in the air. Yes, I'm very glad to have found that one. Dear, I'm a little tired. I'll just close my eyes for a minute.'

The drive from The Empire to Ruby's boarding house was not long. Tom thought about his plans for the next few days, and the next few weeks. They filled him with a great deal more excitement than his days gambling and drinking with his elder brother had done. Poor Edmund.

Ruby sighed in her sleep, and it felt like an echo of his own thoughts. The aching sweetness of 'The Sunrise Song' had got into his bones somehow; he had a fleeting sense he was too young to feel so sadly nostalgic, but under it, in the bones of it, was a certain solid joy. Empire Records. Today he had looked at those discs lined up on the polished shelves and been able to say, 'I made that.' The glow of that memory drove his mother's shade into the darkness, where it belonged.

He brought the car to a gentle halt outside the boarding house.

'Ruby? You're home.'

She didn't respond. He put his hand on her shoulder, and shook it very gently.

'Ruby? Ruby, wake up.'

Her hand, which had been lying in her lap, fell sideways onto the seat.

Tom twisted round and took her wrist between his fingers.

'Oh, Ruby! Ruby?' He heard his own voice rise and crack. 'No, Ruby! Please?'

He held his cheek to her mouth, but felt no stir of breath; her absence was sudden, absolute and undeniable.

Ruby's landlady must have heard the engine. She opened the door and Tom saw her standing on the threshold, peering out into the night, a Siamese cat weaving between her ankles. Tom got out of the car and went to her and told her. The landlady rocked back slightly, her hand against the wall, then forward into Tom's arms, crying on his chest.

After a minute, she and the cat went to the car and Tom opened the passenger door. The landlady sat on the kerb, holding Ruby's hand, keeping her body company while Tom went on foot to the pub on the corner, where he thought there might be a telephone.

CHAPTER THIRTY-NINE

'She would have wanted you to go ahead with the wedding, Lillian,' Tom said.

The weather the next morning had turned cold again. Lillian had come down to the breakfast table when the news arrived. Now she was sitting next to Tom, her arm over the back of his chair.

Jack looked around the table, his eyes dry, but with a foul emptiness in his chest. It was impossible that Ruby was gone. After the first ripple of shock had run through the room, it was Lillian who had suggested they should postpone. Jack was not sure anyone else could even start thinking about the practicalities as yet. Grace looked bereft and pale, as if she hadn't fully grasped the news. Nikolai was staring at his hands.

Dixon had left at first light to supervise the day's recordings. It seemed insane to think he was there now, arranging his microphones as Mabel and her jazz men arrived and unpacked their instruments, all in blissful ignorance of their terrible loss.

'Are you quite sure, Tom?' Nikolai asked. 'She was a very important part of this family.'

Tom was still wearing the evening suit he had put on yesterday to play for 'The Sunrise Song'. He looked older today.

'I'm more than sure. She left very detailed instructions. It's a private burial, just me and Sarah, her landlady. I'm her executor and have inherited all rights in her work.' He ran a hand through his hair. 'Her savings go to her landlady. Grace, you are to have any of her costume jewellery you'd like, with the exception of a couple of things put aside for Sarah and Mabel.' The corner of his mouth twisted into a smile. 'She's even drafted her obituary. But we are to allow Mabel to dedicate a song to her during her current season at the Metropole, if Mabel feels that would be appropriate.'

'She planned it all very carefully,' Lillian said. 'Do you think she knew her time was coming?'

'She said nothing to me,' Tom replied. 'She was a very private person in many ways.'

They all returned their gazes to the tablecloth, and Jack wondered if any of the others were, like him, considering the idea Ruby's relationship with Sarah had been deeper than they had suspected.

Grace got up suddenly and went to the window. Jack joined her and she put her head on his shoulder. It felt like a cruel, dark reflection of the moment they had listened to 'The Sunrise Song' in the rehearsal corridor.

'She was so delighted to see you on stage again, Lillian,' Tom said, 'and she thought you and Nikolai a great match.'

Nikolai patted Tom's knee. 'This pleases me very much, Tom.'

'What about your mother, Tom?' Jack asked. 'What do we do about her?'

Tom's lip curled. 'Nothing for now.'

Jack felt a pang in his chest, and held Grace a little closer.

Tom stood up. 'I'm going to the factory to break the news. You do the same for The Empire, and I'll be over this afternoon to pick up the new masters. "The Sunrise Song" is coming off the presses this morning and every one is going to be perfect. And so will the next record be, and the next.'

'Tom, dear!' Lillian protested. 'Shouldn't you rest? You've been up all night.'

'I'll rest later. Ruby would expect me to do my job, for her and for all of you, and I'm not going to let her down.'

They remained in silence as he left, and in silence as they heard his car drive away. Finally Lillian stood up. 'We can only follow his example, I think. Jack, if you and Grace don't mind waiting while I dress, we can tell everyone at The Empire together.'

The announcement went to the newspapers in time for the midday editions, and by teatime Marcus and Mrs Briggs were gathering armfuls of flowers left in tribute by the lobby doors.

Grace decided to keep herself busy by helping out in the shop, and before the end of the day it was clear to her that Ruby would not get it all her own way. Highbridge wanted a chance to remember her.

'She didn't want anything, Grace,' Tom said wearily as they ate their dinner that evening. 'I understand people need . . . something. But a service, or a tribute in the theatre? She'll come back and haunt us.'

'I rather wish she would,' Lillian said, as Hewitt cleared the soup. 'What about something very simple. Not in the theatre itself, but the lobby, perhaps. We could just ask everyone to come along at lunchtime, perhaps. No speeches or ceremony, simply an opportunity to be together and remember her.'

'It should be before the wedding,' Nikolai said.

'Yes, Thursday lunchtime perhaps,' Jack replied. 'Tom, do you think she'd compromise on that?'

He nodded, and they continued their meal in quiet.

That night Tom decided not to resist any longer. After dinner, he went to the Bricklayers Arms and sat in the saloon, where he had shared a table with Ruby and heard Sally for the first time, to listen to her second hour. The mood was subdued, and Sally sang 'The Old Oak' in Ruby's honour, with Clive accompanying her on his accordion, the instrument sounding more mournful and lost than he'd ever thought possible. The song shook him down to the soles of his feet. Strange: Sally had said it would be like singing on stage with no clothes on, but it was Tom who felt naked as he listened. Bare and bruised. He only half heard the rest of the hour, as Sally got them all settled and laughing again. Alfred paid for a round in Ruby's honour, the patrons toasted her, then turned back to their own concerns.

When Sally finished, Tom prepared to leave, and was so exhausted and sunk in his own misery he didn't realise she was approaching till she sat down beside him and pushed a glass of whisky across the table towards him.

He looked round at her. 'That's a hell of a song, Sally.'

'I know. Wish there was something I could say, Tom.'

He was terribly afraid he was going to weep. He thought about telling her about his mother, the struggles at the factory, the triumph, and the terrible finality of his loss. 'Don't say anything,' he said. 'But if you could just sit with me for a while.'

She moved a little closer to him, so their shoulders were touching, and did exactly that.

On Thursday they closed the shop at midday precisely. Everyone who worked there wanted to take their chance to honour Ruby, and when Grace came into the lobby with the staff, she found it already full of people. Tom was there, with Ruby's landlady, and the workers from the factory: Miss James, Patterson, Fossil and a dozen other faces Grace didn't recognise. Tom came over and put an envelope into her hand.

'Grace, I was looking through Ruby's notebooks and I found this. I'm sure she was thinking about you when she wrote it.'

Grace thanked him and put the envelope, unopened, into her bag. They had left all the arrangements, other than the time and place, to Mr Poole. Grace saw a black-edged notice had been put up on an easel in the lobby, normally used to announce coming attractions. A large photograph of Ruby as a young woman had been pasted to the board, and neatly inked above it, Grace read SUSANNA 'RUBY' ROWNTREE. COMPOSER, TEACHER, FRIEND. 1855–1927.

Jack and Miss Chisholm came to join her, and Jack put his arm around his wife's waist. As they watched from the back of the crowd, the Empire band leader, Mr Porter, positioned himself next to the easel, put his violin to his chin, and began to play one of the ballads Ruby had written for *Cairo Nights*. A middle-aged man, with a frayed collar, removed his bowler hat, shuffled forward to lay a posy of violets under the easel. It was a cue. More floral tributes were brought forward: primroses tied in ribbons, scatterings of forget-me-nots and snowdrops.

'What's happening?' a voice asked at Grace's shoulder. She turned to discover Stella behind her, her eyes hidden by huge dark glasses. 'Oh, Grace, it's true! I can't . . .'

Grace embraced her. 'Stella, yes, it is. When did you get here?'

'Just this minute. I went up to the house and Hewitt sent me here. Grace, how are we going to manage without her?'

'I really don't know, Stella. Where have you been?'

'Norfolk, mostly. With the viscount. What will Mr Poole say? He hates to have his lobby disarranged.'

Jack pointed through the crowd. Mr Poole and Marcus were helping to arrange the flood of flowers, putting them around the notice itself. Already the black edges of the notice were disappearing under waves of spring blooms.

'Oh,' Stella said softly. 'Oh, Ruby!'

As the bandleader played, members of the crowd continued to come forward, offer their flowers, or simply stand for a moment with their heads bowed, then move back to join their fellow mourners. Danny stood near the doors to the auditorium with Ollie in his arms. Next to him, Milly held a handkerchief to her eyes. Grace saw Tom stiffen as Sally Blow, holding hands with a little boy, came through the crowd and laid a posy of daffodils at the edge of the growing mass. Poole smiled at them both, and ruffled the boy's hair, and Grace thought of the day Ruby had thrust her songs into Sally's pockets.

An elderly man, leaning on a bamboo cane, glanced round and caught sight of Stella, then whispered something to his neighbour. She nudged the woman next to her, and the news of Miss Stanmore's presence passed through the crowd like a breeze. Porter brought his tune to a close, then saw her, too.

'Miss Stanmore,' he said, and the crowd was so quiet he hardly needed to raise his voice. 'Might you join me for a song?'

'What do I do, Grace?' Stella whispered. 'I haven't . . .'

'This is for Ruby, Stella. Do what you do best.' Grace sighed. 'Make them feel better.'

Stella inhaled sharply, then nodded. She handed her coat to Jack, then took off her dark glasses and walked through the crowd. She paused for a second, as the others had, in front of the easel, before turning to face them. She was not dressed to perform. She barely had any make-up on at all, her lips pale and her hair loose and in curls. She wore a dark shirt and long flared trousers, but that glamour she had, that strange power, still made it impossible to look anywhere else but at her.

'How many of you were Ruby's pupils?' she asked. A number of hands went up in the air. 'Me, too. I remember once when we were rehearsing for *Riviera Nights*, she said to me, "Stella, dear, you have a very nice range, but when are you going to learn to count to four?"'

A ripple of laughter ran round the room.

'Well, let's see if she managed to teach me anything. What would you like to hear?'

Members of the crowd called out the titles of various of Ruby's songs.

'What about "My First Dance"?' the man who had laid the violets called out, to a murmur of approval. Grace was surprised; it was a recent number Ruby had written for a show in Manchester – a strange, slightly alien tune with words taken from a local poet. She thought it very unlikely Stella would know it.

But Stella nodded, then turned to the bandleader. They consulted briefly in whispers, and he played a single note, passing his bow over the open string of his violin so it sounded almost like the drone of an accordion. Then Stella sang. Grace had forgotten, there was a call and response in the song when the singer asked if her lover remembered their first dance, and the lover replied that he did. As she reached the line, she paused. The audience were uncertain of their role, and the response was tentative and off-key.

Stella broke off and smiled at them and they laughed nervously. 'Now, I think we can do better than that. When I say "Do you remember, can you recall?", you reply, "I can remember, I can recall, now shall we dance again?" Let's try it.'

They did, and exchanged relieved smiles. Faces flushed; hands sought out hands.

'Much better! Mr Porter, if you would be so kind.'

They took the tune from the second verse, and this time the response filled the lobby. Grace felt the small hairs on her arms stand up. She took Jack's hand, and the next time the line came, they, Tom and Lillian, added their voices to the throng.

CHAPTER FORTY

'We were hoping to have a word with Miss Stanmore.'

It was Friday evening and a circus-based revue was receiving a warm reception from the crowd, though the animals that appeared on stage had been giving Jack a few headaches. He claimed half of them were in league with the rat. In the stage door area, Danny and Milly were working on a jigsaw of Paris by night. They hadn't noticed the middle-aged couple approaching till they were at the lobby desk. Ollie, it seemed, had judged them worthy of passing unmolested.

'Miss Stanmore isn't a-appearing at The Empire now,' Danny said. 'But I believe she is in town for the wedding of Lady Lassiter and Nikolai tomorrow. Perhaps I c-can arrange for a message.'

The couple exchanged unhappy glances. The wife had her handbag held in front of her like a shield and her fingers were shifting nervously on the short strap. The man, in a red knitted tie, looked like he'd normally be a jovial sort of chap, but his round face was somewhat crumpled.

'Oh, we just assumed. We read this morning she sang a song here and just assumed. Oh, we are fools, Jess.'

Milly put down her knitting. 'Not fools at all. It was a natural thing to think. Just that song was in the lobby, in memory of a friend of ours who recently passed, not part of a show.'

The lady didn't reply, but cast a panicked look at her husband.

'Did you serve, son?'

Danny nodded.

'Our son did, too. We lost him at Ypres.'

'And now we've lost our Ruthie, too!' the woman exclaimed, the words coming out in a rush. She turned away and fumbled in her handbag for a handkerchief. Her husband rested his hand on her arm, but kept his eyes on Danny.

'Our name is Cook, but our daughter was Tasha Kingsland. Ruth Kingsland, up this end of the world.' Milly covered her mouth with her hand. 'Now we know the newspapers print a lot of rubbish – we don't want Miss Stanmore to think we're here to make accusations.' Mrs Cook, still wiping her eyes, shook her head violently. 'But we want to know a little about our Ruthie's life before she passed, and we thought maybe if Miss Stanmore did know her, even a little bit, and her being in this part of the world . . .'

The door to the backstage area opened and Grace came down the short flight of stairs to the lobby.

'Danny, can you keep an eye out for the printer's boy? He's bringing me another stack of samples for the shop advertisements, and I know he sometimes comes this way to pet Ollie.' The terrier clambered out of his basket to sniff Grace's ankles and wagged his tail. She bent down and scratched his ears. 'Yes, you have more fans than anyone on the stage, don't you, boy?'

Then she noticed the couple.

'Oh, good evening!'

'Mrs T-Treadwell, this is Mr and Mrs Cook.'

'Tasha Kingsland's parents,' Milly added softly. 'They were hoping to see Miss Stanmore.'

Grace immediately shook their hands. 'Oh, how . . . She's not here,

I'm afraid. I'm sure Danny's told you that.'

'He has,' Mr Cook said. 'But as I said to the young gentleman, we aren't here to cause a fuss. Just want to hear about Ruthie from someone who knew her, like.'

Grace hesitated.

'Are you l-local?' Danny asked.

Mrs Cook shook her head. 'That is, we live in Hope Valley, Sheffield way. Jimmy works the trains. My sister lives in Highbridge. We wanted so much to . . . I can't imagine what her life was like. The police came up to see us and said all sorts of nasty things. Do you have children, Mrs Treadwell?'

'I do not.'

'Then you can't imagine. I haven't been able to sleep a full night since she died, all these weeks, just wondering. And people are always asking. With our lad, we never knew how he died either, but there were so many of us going through the same thing. We could lean on each other a bit. But with our Ruthie . . .' She tailed off. 'So we thought we'd call by, just on the off-chance, but we don't wish to disturb.'

'Would you like a cup of tea, Mrs Cook?' Milly said, climbing off her stool. 'I was just about to make Danny and me a cup.'

'That would be very kind of you, dear.'

'Tasha Kingsland was Ruthie up this end of the world, Mrs Treadwell,' Milly added to Grace quietly.

'I know we're only ordinary folk, and Miss Stanmore's a star,' Mr Cook said, staring at his shoes, 'but I thought in the circumstances . . .'

Grace shook herself. 'No, please don't think that Stella would think she's too grand to talk to you. I know she's been terribly upset about Tasha's death – sorry, Ruthie's. But she might not want to shock you or upset you further.'

'Can't be worse than what we're thinking,' he said.

'Please do stay and have tea. Milly, perhaps you could give Mr and Mrs Cook a tour of the theatre during the interval. I know your daughter wanted very much to be part of this world. Perhaps it might help to see a little of it?'

'Thank you,' Mrs Cook whispered.

'Please, think nothing of it. Are you staying here overnight?'

'No, heading back on the nine o'clock train, then there's a bus and you don't have to wait too long if you time it right.'

Grace pulled her notebook out of her pocket and handed it to them.

'I can't promise anything, but could you leave me your address?'

The day of Nikolai and Lillian's wedding dawned bright and clear, with only enough breeze to stir the blossoms as they drove into town.

Tom and Jack acted as witnesses to the simple register office ceremony, with Grace, Stella, Agnes and Joe accompanying them and supplying the first congratulations. When the wedding party emerged, pausing on the short flight of steps from the high Victorian doors to the pavement, quite a crowd had gathered to greet them – a mix of theatre folk and the curious citizens who had maintained a friendly and proprietorial attitude to Lillian.

Jack felt Grace take his hand as the photographer ushered them together for the official pictures, and the staff of The Empire threw handfuls of rice and ribald remarks at them.

'Keep smiling, Jack.'

He gritted his teeth. 'Yes, dear.' Then he nodded to his right. 'Look at that.'

Danny was in attendance, wearing his uniform and with Ollie at his side, but standing close by him, with her arm through his, was the wardrobe assistant, Milly.

'Do you think there's something there?'

Grace smiled. 'I'm sure of it. I went to have tea with him the other day, and Milly was working at her sewing in the lobby. And look at Ollie.'

Jack peered a little. The terrier was wearing a white satin bow tie

attached to his collar, and looked positively smart. Jack could swear that
the dog's eyebrows had been trimmed.

'Too fancy to chase rats now.'

'Too clever to try and deal with a theatre rat. He's still excellent at
spotting interlopers at the stage door, though.'

Jack sighed and, rather than just plaster a smile on his face, made a
valiant attempt to actually be happy for Lillian. He counted his blessings
while the cheers and snaps of camera shutters continued. He was married
to the best woman in the world, he had a job he loved – a fact he was
rediscovering since the advent of Bridget Chisholm – and the launch
of Empire Records had given his life a new focus and interest. He was
surrounded by people he cared for . . . and Nikolai.

Something caught his eye. At some distance, on the other side of the
square, a quartet of men, marked out by their military bearing, appeared
to be watching them.

'Jack?' Lillian had turned and was looking up at him from the lower
step she occupied with Nikolai. 'Shall we head back to the house?'

She looked lovely. She was wearing a lavender ensemble, which looked
fashionable without appearing girlish, and her hat – a sort of spring bonnet
affair – was trimmed with fresh lilacs. She looked like the personification
of a hopeful spring. Jack felt a pang. Why shouldn't she enjoy a little
romance?

'Yes, of course.'

He put his fingers to his mouth, and produced a piercing whistle which
made his wife and mother duck and cover their ears.

'To Lassiter Court, my friends, for sausage rolls and champagne!
All welcome!'

'Much better!' Grace said, and kissed him firmly on the cheek. The
military-looking gentlemen were forgotten.

It had been a bold plan to have the reception in the gardens of Lassiter
Court during an English spring, but Nikolai claimed he was descended

from a weather god, and was always blessed with sunshine when he needed it. Jack was inclined to be sceptical, but Grace pointed out that there were awnings out for shade or shelter, and the French doors were flung open all along the terrace so they could retreat if the weather turned against them. It didn't.

The borders around the immaculate lawn were thick with daffodils and bluebells, star-gazers and hibiscus. The hedges were scattered with hawthorn blossom, and the silver birches marking the edge of the pleasure gardens at the rear of the house were shivering with a haze of fresh green growth. Roses and sprigs of baby's breath had been wrapped around the guy-ropes supporting the awnings, and the scattered tables were dressed in white linen. The buffet table itself groaned with silver serving dishes that steamed slightly in the spring air, and the wedding cake – four tiers of it, thick with sugar icing – had a table all to itself.

The car carrying Lillian and Nikolai took the scenic route, so by the time they arrived, the guests were lining the drive and crowding round the front of the house to cheer the newly-weds' arrival. Silver trays crowded with champagne flutes were carried out by phalanxes of serving men – Jack thought he recognised some of them from the Metropole – and on the other side of the house, the string players of The Empire's band were earning a few extra shillings working through their repertoire on the terrace. Nothing but an occasional breeze ruffled the crowd, and the garden filled with the sound of friendly conversation, laughter, and the smell of hot pastry and cold champagne.

After a pleasant hour or so, Jack saw signs of activity round the steps to the terrace and the string quartet put up their bows. Lillian ascended from the lawn, assisted by her new husband. Standing at the top of the steps, with the doors to the house open behind her, she raised her voice and asked for quiet.

Jack emptied his glass and held it out to a passing waiter, who carried a linen-wrapped bottle icy with condensation. It was refilled to the brim.

'My dear friends, I am so happy to welcome you all here today. I once thought my theatre days were over, but I was proved wrong when Jack joined us. I was just as sure that my days of romance were over, too, but I have, as you see, been proved wrong again.'

The crowd laughed, and Jack noticed people glancing at him. The looks seemed friendly enough.

'I am a very lucky woman, discovering in a few short years a son I had thought lost forever, who turned out to be a natural theatrical impresario, and proved his good sense by marrying Grace. I then met and fell in love with a man whose genius is almost equal to theirs . . .' Nikolai made a face, a sort of pantomime of displeasure, and Lillian laughed. 'Well, there are two of them, darling!'

Nikolai shrugged extravagantly, and a ripple of amusement passed through the guests.

'I am delighted to announce on this, my wedding day,' Lillian lifted her glass. 'That you will all get the opportunity to experience first-hand the talent of the man I have married this morning. I learnt last week from dear Miss Chisholm, that thanks to a little trouble in the Company of the Chartered Players, the New Empire has a gap in the programming in six weeks' time. Jack, forgive me for not discussing this with you, but I've consulted with Agnes, and we decided, my dear Nikolai, this is the very best wedding present I could offer you.' She turned to him. 'Nikolai, for a fortnight, the theatre is yours.'

Lillian knew how to deliver an applause line, and everyone else raised glasses and cheered and clapped while Nikolai mimed surprise, gratitude and pleasure like a hero in a fairground puppet show.

Jack was aware of keeping his smile plastered to his face, while his emotions collapsed behind it – the way the front wall of a house stays in place while a sink hole consumes the rest. He was aware of a distinct buzzing in his ears. People were *still* clapping.

Grace, who must have crossed the lawn with some haste, but with complete discretion, appeared miraculously, inevitably, at his side.

'What did she say? Grace, am I dreaming, or did Lillian just announce that she's handing over my theatre to Nikolai for two weeks?'

Grace laughed, beamed, and patted his arm as if he had said something charming.

'Yes, yes she did. What could go wrong!'

'I suppose,' Jack's face was getting sore, his muscles were having to work so hard to keep the grin in place, 'that now is not the time to remind Lillian, with passion and conviction, that replacing *Susie's Gadabout Gals* with Nikolai "the Red" Kuznetsov is going to make us a laughing stock at best?'

She smiled and nodded. 'Well, he is also one of our best-selling artistes thanks to "The Sunrise Song". We've sold the whole of the first run and we've barely been open a week. And you just made up that name yourself. But now is most certainly not the time to take it up with Lillian. You'll have to wait until they get back from their motor trip to the Lakes.'

Jack polished off his champagne in a single gulp. He didn't even taste it. The waiter, however, seemed to have developed a telepathic understanding of his needs almost on a level with his wife's. It was almost instantaneously refilled. 'Could I write a passionate and firmly worded note and pop it in the car?'

'Absolutely not.'

It was somewhere in the gap between the glass being filled, and being empty again – within a minute or so – that the military-looking men made their entrance. The four of them were wearing suits, but they had a look of shared purpose which made them an unmistakable unit. Lillian and Nikolai were still on or very near the steps, receiving handshakes and backslaps.

'Is this more entertainment?' Grace asked. 'Jack, this isn't anything to do with you, is it?'

Jack shook his head. Nikolai and Lillian had spotted them now as they crunched along the gravel path towards the couple. Nikolai took a step forward to stand between them and his wife.

'Stay here, Grace,' Jack said, setting down his glass and walking slowly across the lawn towards them. There was a general shuffling in the crowd. Danny was moving forward, too, as were Mr Poole, Tom, Dixon Wells and Joe Allerdyce. The rest retreated a little.

The oldest of the men came to a halt directly in front of Nikolai and held up his hand. The men behind him stepped out into a wide stance, their hands clasped behind their backs.

Nikolai said something to him, and the man said something back. Jack couldn't understand the words, but he guessed neither the question nor the response were particularly friendly.

The leader switched to English.

'By order of His Majesty, King Kiril III of Marakovia, I, Vladimir Taargin, ambassador to his country, am here to deliver notice to the His Excellency, Grand Duke Nikolai Goranovich Kuznetsov of Marakovia. Sir, as a member of the royal family of our nation, you are required absolutely to seek the permission of the king before entering into any marriage. You have not done so. As a member of the royal family, you are required to marry a woman of equal status to yourself. You have not done so. I demand, on behalf of your cousin the king, that you annul this travesty of a union immediately.'

Nikolai stared at him, then carefully set down his own champagne glass on the edge of the terrace. The silence was such that they all heard, quite distinctly, the clink of glass on stone. Then he looked Vladimir Taargin in the eye. He seemed, as Jack watched him, to grow, putting his shoulders back, his amiable smile vanishing. Another glamour, he thought – an ancient magic possessed by actors, musicians and nobility. They could, at will, exert a sort of gravity, a charisma, which radiated out from them in pulses, like shock waves.

'Or what?' Nikolai replied.

Taargin seemed unfazed. 'Your exile will become permanent. Your friends, such as you have, will shun you. You will be stripped of all your titles, land and possessions, and any hope you harbour of reclaiming your standing in your country will be lost forever.'

'And I was afraid it was actually something bad,' Nikolai drawled. 'Now leave, Taargin. My wife and I have some celebrating to do.'

Jack was within arm's reach of them now.

'Here, here!' Stella called out from the middle of the crowd, cupping her hands around her mouth, and several people around her applauded.

Taargin looked round, just long enough for his sneer to register with the guests, then returned his gaze to Nikolai and spoke more quietly.

'You have a future at home once you have grown out of your idiotic political beliefs. It's in your blood to rule. But not if you do this.'

'I am fifty-three years old, Taargin,' Nikolai replied. 'I have grown into my beliefs, not out of them. And I would rather take up residence in a ditch, than in a palace controlled by fascists like you and His Majesty's brother.'

Taargin screwed up his mouth. 'Perhaps your mother was not the model of behaviour she pretended to be. Only the son of a whore would give up his place in the family to marry an actress who made her living on her back.'

The man next to him laughed.

Jack threw the first punch. He took two steps forward and struck a straight jab to the man's jaw, knocking him back into the arms of the men behind him.

The three men behind Taargin broke ranks, making a grab at Nikolai and Jack. Nikolai parried a blow aimed at his head and caught its thrower with an uppercut. Jack elbowed the first one in the kidneys. The man, who had a terrifying look in his eye, took a step back, then tried to launch himself forward again. He found he could not. Joe Allerdyce had taken a firm grip on the collar and hem of his jacket and, with a twist of his considerable bulk, he spun the man and sent him sprawling across the grass.

Taargin launched himself towards Jack, landing him a vicious blow to the side of his head that sent him stumbling backwards. Half the crowd retreated still further, shrieking or making appalled tutting noises, according to their proclivities, while the others launched into the melee with a will. Jack, staggering slightly, found himself steadied by Tom, and so was in time to observe his wife throw a scotch egg at one of the Marakovians with the speed and force of a fast bowler. Ollie was growling and tugging on the trouser leg of another, then let out a yelp as his quarry counterattacked with a sharp kick.

'Bastard!' Danny exclaimed, lifting his walking stick and jabbing it hard into the offender's stomach.

Taargin was approaching Lillian, his arms at his side and his fists balled. She had taken a step up the terrace and was staring down at him with utter contempt. Nikolai turned from his first victim and slapped the ambassador across the face.

'Good show!' Jack shouted instinctively.

Taargin roared, turned and charged Nikolai, grabbing him round the shoulders, and they crashed backwards. The crowd scattered away from them, Nikolai tripped over the guy-rope, and they went down together, straight into the wedding cake. Taargin had his hands round Nikolai's throat, ignoring the storm of sugar and crumb raining down on both of them. Nikolai struggled to dislodge him, then Fenton Hewitt stepped forward and delivered Taargin a stunning blow with a silver tea tray.

Grace's work with the scotch egg seemed to have inspired the guests. The other men were now being bombarded with food. Taargin staggered to his feet and made a lunge at the butler. Jack intervened, stepping forward to shove the man off course. He spun round, regaining his balance quickly, and jabbed at Jack's flank. Jack deflected the blow, blocking with his right forearm, but the punch had the force of a steam engine. Jack punched upwards and made connection with his opponent's iron jaw, but the man hardly flinched and his eyes, as he turned them on Jack, flashed with a murderous fire.

Jack didn't even see the blow coming, just felt its thunderous impact on the side of his head. The world spun and staggered as he fought to stay upright. The shrill alarm of a police whistle cut through the air and his swimming senses. He had a vague impression of the Marakovians cowed by vol-au-vents, icing smeared over best jackets and coats, Ollie's indignant barking, and a policeman holding firmly on to Tom's arm, before discovering another policeman had hold of him and he was being propelled out of his home and into the back of a police van.

CHAPTER FORTY-ONE

The constabulary of Highbridge had the sense to keep the Marakovians and the Lassiter Court mob, as the duty sergeant referred to them, apart. Jack, when his senses were fully returned, found himself slouched between Nikolai and the butler on a hard wooden bench. Tom had made a pillow of his jacket on the bench at right angles to theirs and promptly gone to sleep. Jack suspected that, in his days as a young dilettante about town, he'd spent time in the cells before, such was his easy familiarity with the place.

Jack decided that now he was a criminal, he could at least undo his tie. He could feel his eye beginning to swell, and his feeling of sickness had subsided only to be replaced by a pulsing headache. He groaned.

Nikolai looked at him with concern. 'Vladimir was a boxer at the military academy. Most of the young men there fought with sabres, but he always preferred his fists.'

'He could win the bareknuckle fights on Liverpool docks.'

Jack noticed a cut above Nikolai's eye. It was still oozing blood. He withdrew his handkerchief and passed it to his mother's new husband. He took it with a nod of thanks and held it to his forehead.

'Yes . . . this blood, though, I think, is from a cake plate. Years fighting in France and I left without a scratch, and so my fetching facial scar will come from an English garden party.'

Jack laughed, then flinched. 'Still, we acquitted ourselves pretty well. Hewitt, I've never seen a man so handy with a tea tray.'

'I played a great deal of cricket in my youth, sir. It's all about taking the correct stance,' the butler replied with a sniff.

'So you are acquainted with that Vladimir?' Jack asked Nikolai after they had all considered this for a moment.

Nikolai removed the handkerchief and observed his own blood on it with a sigh, before refolding it and setting it on his knee. 'I am. The present king is a good old gentleman, a little befuddled by the modern world, and I am very fond of the Crown Prince, Stefan. The king's brother, Andrei, however, is not a man I admire. He thinks to unite our country through hatred of others – to turn the discontents and fears of our people outwards. I heard him speaking, not the king, in that ridiculous decree Vladimir read today.'

Jack rested his head against the painted brick wall. He had always assumed jail cells would be dank and foul-smelling, but the Highbridge police station cells were, if not comfortable, at least clean. They smelt of the same brand of carbolic soap which Mrs Briggs used to mop the backstage corridors.

'Were you really supposed to ask for royal permission before you married, sir?' Hewitt asked. Jack realised he had never seen Hewitt sitting down before. It didn't seem proper.

'Yes, my friend. According to the law in my land. But it is an old and foolish law. I am nowhere near the throne. If Prince Stefan dies before he has children of his own, the crown will pass to Andrei, and he has three sons and five grandsons. The crown has a great deal of people between me and it. It is an excuse, that is all, for barring me from my country.'

'Are they all drama critics?' Jack said, speaking softly in an attempt to stop the pain in his head finding some new level of excruciating.

'Ha! That is amusing. You are not happy with me having your theatre for a fortnight, Jack?'

Pain bounced him into honesty. 'Not entirely.'

Nikolai seemed unabashed. 'It is only two weeks. And perhaps I will surprise you.'

'I am not sure I'd ever feel quite right again, were I to be exiled from England,' Hewitt observed.

'Exile, permanent exile, was always a possibility. I feel it, Hewitt, I do. But I am not afraid of it. I would rather be here, free, than there denying my beliefs and watching men like Vladimir Taargin teaching my countrymen to hate.'

A whistle and a distant rattle of keys alerted them to the arrival of the sergeant. He observed them slowly through the bars, then turned the key and swung open the gates.

'Evening, gentlemen. Now, I have it on good authority – the authority of Lady Lassiter, in fact – that you will not take this as a general licence to throw your fists about.' Jack sat up, trying to give the impression of an obedient Labrador. 'But you are to be released without charge.'

Tom swung himself upright and yawned as if he'd had a particularly refreshing nap.

'Afternoon, Bert! How are Lottie and the kids?'

'All very well, sir—'

'That's smashing,' Jack interrupted. 'The kids and our being released, I mean, but what is happening to the ambassador and his chums? Damn it, they came uninvited to Lillian's wedding!'

'I believe that they were not the first to employ fisticuffs, however,' Bert said, raising an eyebrow. Jack avoided his gaze. 'Well . . . We had a word with them about bursting in to other people's nuptial celebrations in such an insulting manner. My constable has put them on the train back to London, and they have been strongly advised not to return.'

'Is that it?' Jack asked.

'We had a telegram from London,' Bert said, fiddling with the keys.

'Apparently locking up a group of Marakovians, including the ambassador, while they are planning a royal visit, is frowned upon.'

'Think we've seen the last of them, then?' Tom asked. His jacket had miraculously avoided getting cake on it, or getting crumpled when he used it for a pillow. He looked as if he were about to step out of his tailor's, not a prison cell. He put out his hand and Jack was hauled to his feet. He was sure he looked as bad as he felt, and he felt particularly rough.

Nikolai was pale, and the gash on his forehead made him look paler, but he got to his feet unaided, tucking Jack's handkerchief in his pocket.

'I fear we have *not* seen the last of them.'

Hewitt straightened his already straight tie. 'Then I shall keep the tray handy.'

Nikolai paused, studying the sergeant. 'You have a most interesting face.'

Bert rubbed it with his hand. 'Do I, sir? I am glad it pleases you, I suppose.'

'It does,' Nikolai said, putting a hand on his shoulder. 'I intend to put you in my play.'

'What? Base a character on the sergeant, do you mean?' Jack said, feeling his head pulse.

'No!' Nikolai said. 'I want Bert himself on stage. Bert, you are the first member of my company.'

'Am I, sir?'

'You are. Please call in at The Empire and leave a note of your availability for rehearsals with that funny little man who lives in the ticket box.'

'You mean Mr Poole, and it's box office,' Jack said, struggling to keep up. 'Do I understand you mean to use amateurs in your production?'

'Absolutely!' Nikolai declared. 'The use of amateurs, local people known around the town, is a key part of my theatrical philosophy.' He slung his jacket over his shoulder. 'We have begun.'

'Amateurs,' Jack murmured to himself as they emerged from the station to find Lillian and Grace waiting for them by Lillian's touring car. Stella had brought her sports car, and leapt out of it to offer Hewitt a kiss on the cheek and a lift back to the house with her and Tom. Hewitt consented to both.

'Amateurs,' Jack said again, more loudly as he clambered into the back of Lillian's tourer.

'What's that, darling?' Grace asked, settling in next to him, then touching his forehead. 'You've got the most awful bump.'

'Perhaps that's it,' he replied, trying to cram his long legs into the available space, 'because I could have sworn I heard Nikolai say he intends to fill our stage with amateurs.'

'I did say that.' Nikolai kissed his wife, then got into the front seat and drummed his hands on the dashboard.

'Amateurs, Nikolai?' Lillian said doubtfully as she started the car.

'Exactly. My method involves forming a drama around the people of a place – a place like Highbridge.' He looked at his new wife and smiled fondly at her. 'Lillian, my love, you must trust me. I am not finding a play I like by a clever writer, then finding people to play the roles. I find the people, and we form the drama together.'

'It sounds very unusual, Nikolai,' Lillian replied.

'It is. But you people put on a "pantomime", so I do not understand for a moment why my little experiment should make you so nervous. But I do not ask you to trust me, my dear. You may have your doubts. Then, in six weeks' time, you will see what sort of man you have married.' He twisted in his seat. 'Has the party continued in our absence?'

Grace smiled. 'It has. When we left the house, Joe and Agnes were retrieving the top tier of the wedding cake and searching for the cake forks in the shrubbery. The party has turned into a sort of scavenger hunt.'

Jack stirred uneasily. 'You continued with the party? Shouldn't you have been crying into tiny white handkerchieves over us, or something?'

'We were confident you'd be resolute,' Grace said. 'And don't worry, there's still a lot of champagne left.'

'I couldn't let a little thing like my husband being carted off to gaol ruin the day, Jack,' Lillian said, and Nikolai laughed.

'Oh, I wish Ruby were here,' Grace said. 'She would love a good food fight.'

She looked out of the window, and Jack wound his fingers around hers. 'We all do, Grace.'

She thumbed a tear away from her eye. 'Did I tell you that Tasha Kingsland's parents came to the theatre yesterday afternoon?'

'That was the poor girl who died, wasn't it?' Lillian asked.

'Yes, they were looking for Stella. I took their address, but I haven't dared speak to her about it as yet.'

'After the way she ran off last time, that's not surprising,' Lillian said, turning the car into the drive leading to Lassiter Court. 'She's promised to be here to see Nikolai and me off tomorrow. Perhaps it's time to see if you can get to the bottom of what happened, Grace.'

CHAPTER FORTY-TWO

By mid-morning the following day, Lassiter Court was quiet
again. The awnings had been taken down, rolled up and put
away; the plates and cake forks, glasses and errant spoons had
been retrieved, washed, polished and returned to their proper cabinets
and drawers. Lillian and Nikolai had left for a short tour of the Lakes,
and Tom had gone to the factory. Meanwhile, Dixon and Jack returned
to The Empire: Dixon to polish the lathe and check his microphones;
Jack to supervise the arrival of the new show and make sure none of the
circus performers had left any of their charges behind.

Stella had waved Nikolai and Lillian off, wearing a fur-trimmed silk
dressing gown, then returned to bed for an hour or two. Grace took a
book out into the garden and waited for her.

A little after eleven Stella emerged onto the terrace in her dark glasses,
and a very daring pale green trouser suit that swung around her ankles.

'Grace,' she called out and waved, then walked swiftly along the
path to Grace's bench among the roses and lavender. 'Darling, I
am packed and ready to fly away, but Hewitt can't find my car key.
I locked it up when I arrived. Have you seen it at all? It's on a little
Tiffany key ring.'

Grace adjusted her posture slightly, feeling the key in question shift in her pocket.

'Yes, I have. But I shan't give it to you, Stella. Not until you have a proper conversation with me.'

Stella removed her glasses and slipped them into the pocket of her long silk top.

'Grace, don't be ridiculous. If you want me to apologise for not taking the stage at Christmas – very well, I am sorry. Though it turned out very well in the end. But give me the key.' She put out her hand.

'I said I wanted a conversation, not an apology, Stella. Mr and Mrs Cook, Tasha Kingsland's parents, came to the theatre on Friday. They'd like to see you.'

Stella blinked rapidly.

'That won't be possible. Now stop being a little idiot and give me my key.'

She snapped her fingers and extended her palm again. Grace noticed her fingers were shaking a little.

'No,' Grace replied, lifting her chin. 'Not until you explain to me exactly what happened, and why you've left the stage. And don't tell me it's the press, because they haven't written a word about you in months. Your agent has rung me twice telling me about the offers you've received, but says you haven't responded to any of her telegrams or phone messages.'

'It's none of your business,' she snapped. 'Now give me the key!'

'You came here. You made it my business, Stella. Now tell me the truth.'

Stella made a grab for Grace's wrist and she recoiled in shock and surprise, confounded by the sudden violence of it. 'Stella, get off!'

'Just give it to me!' Stella had a dancer's strength, twisting Grace's wrist fiercely and yanking it to one side with one hand, while making a dive for her pocket with the other.

'Stella, stop it! Have you gone mad.'

'Give me the bloody key, you silly cow!'

'That hurts!' Grace tried to pull away and stand up, but Stella pushed her back against the bench.

'Stella, stop at once. I'm pregnant!'

Stella gasped and released her. 'Grace! I . . .' She took a step back and Grace turned away, rubbing her wrist. It was very red, and the pain was enough to bring tears to her eyes. 'I wouldn't have. Does anyone know?'

'No, not yet. Not even Jack. I want to wait as long as possible to tell him, so don't breathe a word.'

Stella swallowed, then straightened her back.

'Of course I won't. My congratulations . . . Now give me the key.'

'No.' Grace had meant to be calm, gracious, with her friend, but was ashamed to find her voice now came in a sort of childish wail. 'No, I shan't, Stella. You can't make me. You're my best friend. I've lost Ruby, and I've lost you, too,' the words kept coming. '. . .because you won't tell me the truth. And don't you dare tell me you wanted to leave the stage, because the only time I've seen you happy since that girl died is when you were singing for that crowd at Ruby's memorial. You've simply been playing at being Stella when we see you – terribly shocking and carefree, but I know the difference. So no, I won't give you the bloody key.'

There was a moment of silence, then Stella sat down heavily on the bench next to Grace.

Grace was still rubbing her wrist. 'You weren't in love with her, and I know you aren't slinging cocaine—'

'No, I'm not.' Stella's voice was low, and seemed to be coming from a long way away.

'A girl, Sally Blow, came to talk to Ruby just after you left.' Grace pictured herself that day, every inch the modern woman of business, and now here she was on the bench feeling hurt and as small as a schoolgirl. 'She so wanted to be at the theatre. She was already part of the family, and I think she was a little in love with Tom, but she blames her husband's death on the Lassiters, and she said working at The Empire would be betraying him. And I believed that . . . I believed how thinking she was betraying him would poison everything. And I thought of you. Of how you've been.'

Stella was shivering, a quiver that came up through her bones and seemed to shake the air out of her lungs.

'Stella, was it something like that? Stella, what did you do?'

The beautiful lower lip trembled, then Stella put her head in her hands, pulling her fingers though her platinum blonde hair, shaking so hard it seemed she would break apart while Grace watched.

'You're making me tell you?'

'Yes, I am.'

'Very well. But you won't like it. We lost a girl in the chorus of my show – she left to get married. I told Tasha about it myself in the club. Anyway, she auditioned for the part. My producer was going to give it to her, but I told him not to.'

Grace's hand fell into her lap. 'Oh, Stella. Why?'

'I don't even know,' Stella gasped. 'It was just a moment. I was feeling old and tired and . . . You don't know what it's like, Grace, all these girls snapping at my heels. They are so eager and admiring, and so bloody young! You see the directors and the producers. They looked at her like they used to look at me! As if they were hungry. And Tasha wasn't a great dancer, or a perfect singer, but she was so eager and alive and young. And just in that moment, I couldn't quite bear it anymore. I made a face and said she was too green, and the producer said, "You're the star, dear," and hired someone else. And that was that! Such a small thing, Grace.'

Grace breathed in slowly.

'And she was so disappointed!' Stella went on. 'She thought the audition had gone well, and it had. So when she found out, she came to see me – came to pour out her heart to me, because I was her friend! And I was *so* bright and encouraging, such a *good* pal, but of course it was me who'd done it to her. Then the next day she was dead. And now her parents want to see me. I can't, I simply can't . . .'

Grace turned towards her. 'Stella, that was a terrible thing to do.'

'I know! For Christ's sake, I don't need you to tell me that!' Stella lifted her face to the sky. 'I felt awful when she came to see me. Why do you think I haven't been able to set foot on stage since? It's all tainted. I'd rather die than go up there, have people look at me, tell me how wonderful I am, after doing that.'

'I understand,' Grace said, and she did. 'You still have to see her parents.'

'Grace . . .' Stella turned towards her; the shaking had lessened, but Grace could still hear it in her voice as she inhaled. 'I can't possibly. It would kill me.'

'For God's sake, Stella. No, it wouldn't, and yes, you can! It will be hard and humiliating, and they'll probably curse your name forever, but there's nothing physically preventing you from doing it. And you must!'

'But I've given up the stage.'

'And how has that helped anyone?' Grace said. 'It's all very well for you to decide your own punishment. Leaving the stage – yes, very dramatic, but it's not really up to you, is it? Stella, you're coming with me to see her parents tomorrow, or I will never speak to you again. It's as simple as that. And if you think for a second you're getting your key back before then, you're dreaming. I'll lock you in your room if I have to.'

Stella was quiet for a long time. It seemed to radiate out of her, silencing the birds, the darting of the insects. 'You can be very hard, Grace. I forget that about you.'

'I contain multitudes,' Grace said, a little sulkily, then put out her hand. Stella covered it with her own and the birdsong returned.

CHAPTER FORTY-THREE

On the drive the next day Stella said very little, only stared out of the window at the grey-green slopes of Hope Valley. Grace had sent a card to the Cooks, advising them of their intention to visit. Stella had been quiet all evening, her air one of weary resignation. When Jack asked what had happened, Grace only shook her head, and he had the sense not to press.

'This will be unutterably grim,' Stella said at last.

'Probably,' Grace conceded. 'You're not here just to confess, though, Stella. They want to know something about how their daughter spent the last months of her life.'

'Perhaps I should cover that before I admit I practically drove her to her death.'

'Yes,' Grace said, changing gear. 'Let's do it that way round.'

The road dipped as they approached the town – rows of soot-stained terraced houses that wove along the side of the valley. Below them, Grace could see the railway leading from the mines to the coast, and above the houses were neatly partitioned squares of land. Allotments for the workers, Grace presumed, filled with new growth.

Grace slowed to a crawl, then turned up a short terrace at ninety degrees to the main road. Above them the hillside was catching the early afternoon light, painting it yellowish grey and green, with stone walls running up it like veins on the back of a hand, and the shadows of clouds dashing across them.

Grace stopped the car and pulled on the handbrake.

'Here we are.'

Stella cast one more glance at her, miserable and reproachful, and opened the door.

The card must have reached them. Mrs Cook stood on the threshold, wearing a neat dark red skirt and a plain blouse, with an old-fashioned cameo pinned at her throat. Grace introduced Stella, but Mrs Cook hardly looked at them, whispering her greetings, then ushering both women into the cramped front parlour.

Mr Cook was already on his feet waiting for them, as was another man – a tall middle-aged man with large eyes and sandy hair. He wore a dog collar and reminded Grace of her uncle's basset hound.

'This is Reverend Cooper,' Mr Cook said, introducing him. 'Thank you for coming.'

Grace shook hands. The parlour had flowered wallpaper, faded where the sunlight struck it, and the space was dominated by a round table covered with oilcloth. The top of the large chest of drawers was draped with tasselled embroidery work and crammed with photographs, vases and glassware. The heavy-looking clock on the mantelpiece was flanked by large photographs – a formal studio shot of a very young man in uniform on one side, and on the other, a professional shot of Tasha Kingsland, looking up at the camera with a finger coquettishly resting on her chin.

Mr Cook asked them to take a seat at the table and his wife brought in the tea tray. It was obviously their best: matching teacups heavy with gold detailing and a slightly awkward sugar bowl with a gilt spoon. Grace hoped she and Stella would prove worthy of it.

'I'm so terribly sorry about Ruthie, Mrs Cook,' Stella said simply as she received her cup.

'You called her Ruthie, Miss Stanmore?' Mrs Cook looked up with a pleased smile. 'And please call me Jess. It said in the papers she was known as Tasha in London.'

Stella nodded. 'She was for the most part, in the clubs where she worked and so on, but some of her friends called her Ruthie, too – me included. Grace said you wanted to know a little about her life in London.'

Jess nodded. 'It's driving us half-mad, not knowing. Mrs Treadwell said maybe we'd be shocked by what you have to say. But we know the world's changed a lot since we were young.'

'Though we thought we were wild enough,' her husband said, smiling at her.

The basset hound looked between them. He seemed vaguely disappointed in them both.

'We lived a rather topsy-turvy existence,' Stella said. 'We theatre people tend to be night owls.'

Her voice was gentle, and Grace felt herself relax. Some corner of her had been scared that Stella would be defensive, and play up her cynical 'woman of the world' act. This was not the 'good country girl' of the interview with the detectives from Scotland Yard, either. It was Stella at her best – a little sad, a little amused, kind. With a slight shock, Grace realised she wasn't playing any part at all. This was simply Stella being herself.

She remained silent as her friend talked about the clubs, the strange life which turned day into night. Whatever life Ruthie had lived in this house, 'Tasha Kingsland' would get up at lunchtime, run errands, take classes or attend auditions in the afternoon, then nap before going out to work as everyone else was heading home. Stella described, in great detail, the lodgings Tasha had, the people she roomed with, its nearness to Hyde Park. How excited Tasha had been to see the king ride past one morning.

'She said he tipped his hat to her,' Stella added, and Mrs Cook wiped her eyes.

'Oh, she'd have liked that.'

'Sounds like she was having a high old time,' Mr Cook said. Then the vicar cleared his throat.

'I can only hope,' he said, 'that Ruth's tragic end will serve as a warning to other young ladies. I have listened in horror – grief and horror – as you have described this life of sin in the fleshpots of the capital. How can you not see the desperate moral turpitude of your existence?'

Stella was staring down at the tablecloth, but when she looked up again, she didn't look guilty or afraid. Her smile glittered. 'It's funny. I might have been inclined to agree with you yesterday, but telling Mr and Mrs Cook about it today, I've been remembering all the fun we had, and I realise I've been describing freedom. A girl making her own living and her own choices.'

'A terrible living and immoral choices!'

'I've always wondered, Reverend,' Stella said. 'Why did God give us bodies and music, if he didn't want us to dance?'

Mr Cook looked between Stella and the vicar. 'Freedom? That would have been our Ruthie. Both of them, her and her brother, they were after an adventure from the day they could toddle.'

'Peter?' Stella said, smiling at him. 'She talked about him a lot. One of the other girls tried to get her to go to a séance, to see if they could contact him. She laughed, said he wouldn't want her to bother him, as if Heaven was what he thought it was, he'd be busy playing cricket.'

'It is a great pity she will never see him there,' the vicar growled.

Mr Cook stood up. 'Thank you for stopping by, Reverend, but it's time for you to be off now.'

The divine looked confused and seemed to be on the point of protesting, but Mr Cook's expression did not give the impression he was open to debate. He got to his feet and tucked his chair under the table. 'Repent, Miss Stanmore,' he said. 'I'll see myself out.'

'Repent yourself,' Stella murmured, just loud enough to be heard.

The front door closed, and Mr Cook stood in the doorway between the parlour and the hall for a moment, as if to check he'd gone. 'I can see why you and our Ruthie got on, Miss Stanmore. That's just how she would have handled the canting old bugger.'

'Jimmy!' his wife complained.

'Now, Jess, you know I'm right. He wasn't even invited today, just decided he should be here when Jess told him you were kindly paying us a visit.' He picked up his pipe, and Stella snapped open her handbag and produced her cigarettes. 'He stands up there shouting about fleshpots and sin, and you can see plain as the nose on your face he's dying to give them a go himself.'

'Please do call me Stella.'

'Now you can get that cake, Jess. She baked it for you, ladies, then hid it when he turned up.'

Mrs Cook looked a little shy and a little pleased and ducked out of the room, returning with a saucer for an ashtray and the promised cake.

'He does have his ways,' she said, 'and any sweet stuff, he eats so much there's none left for us who made it.'

The cake was excellent, and Grace was suddenly glad that the vicar had been there after all. Once he had gone, they all felt like confederates.

There was a thumping footstep in the hall and a small child, no more than three, tumbled into the room.

'Judith!' an exasperated female voice called in the background. The child half stumbled, half ran towards Mrs Cook, obviously gleeful to have got away from the owner of the voice; then she caught sight of the strangers and became suddenly shy, hiding behind Mrs Cook's chair.

A young woman followed her into the room. 'I'm sorry, Mam. She's learned how to open the kitchen door on her own, the little monster.' She looked at Grace and Stella. 'I'm Rebecca, Ruthie's sister.'

Stella got up and kissed Rebecca on the cheek, then returned to her seat and began playing peek-a-boo with the child while asking Rebecca if she was still planning to be a nurse. Rebecca blushed and said that yes, she was.

Grace felt her throat close up as she watched the child's expression shift from wary to curious to delighted. She toddled over to Stella and took hold of her skirt with her fat little hands, then looked up and laughed, bobbing up and down on her knees.

Grace rested her hand on her stomach. *Please, be real. Please don't disappear on me like the others.*

'She's lovely,' Grace said, afraid she'd been staring too long. 'Is she yours?'

Stella picked up the child and sat her on her lap, bouncing her up and down. 'She's Ruthie's.'

Mr Cook noticed Grace's confusion. 'Our Ruthie was a widow, Mrs Treadwell. Her husband worked with me on the trains, killed in the shunting yard a month after Judith was born. So Ruthie handed me and Jess the baby and said to me, "Dad, I've tried life your way, now I'm off to try life my way."'

'We're glad to have her,' Mrs Cook said. 'She's kept us going these last months with her ways.'

Grace nodded and smiled, and felt her insides crumble. All these women, like Lillian and Tasha, who could just have a baby, then walk away, while she – who could hardly bear the longing for a child – could not bring one living into the world. And now there was Stella, who had never wanted children at all, so easy and natural with this toddler, getting all her smiles. The miserable unfairness of it undid Grace, but she just had to sit there and endure it. *No good deed goes unpunished*, she thought, and pressed her fingernails into her palm to stop herself crying. Would her own almost baby feel her distress and give up on her? Is that what had happened to the others?

'I suppose, we take comfort, too, that Ruthie was so happy when she died, what with getting a place in the chorus,' Mrs Cook said as her daughter led Judith away again.

Stella's face froze. Grace looked at her hands, clenched so hard in her lap now, the knuckles had turned white.

'But, Mrs Cook,' Stella said, 'she didn't get that job. After she auditioned for the vacancy in the chorus in my show—'

'Oh, she got a better one!'

Mrs Cook stood up, fetched a folded sheet from behind the clock and handed it to Stella, but Stella shook her head. Grace reached over the tea table and took it. The handwriting was round, like a schoolgirl's.

'Dear Mam and Dad,' Grace read out loud. 'Have to write quick to get the evening post, but have to tell you this IMMEDIATE. You remember I wrote to say the audition went nicely? Well, today I went to Mr Gardener's office to enquire, and they said how I hadn't got it and I was so upset. Honestly, I could have just curled up on their doorstep and died. I went straight round to see Stella, Miss Stanmore, and she was ever so sweet to me. Gave me a five-bob note, too, said to buy myself something sweet on the way home, have a cry, and then get on with it the next day. So I came home, and Nancy said there was a telegram come for me. It was from Mr Gardener himself! Said there was no place for me in Stella's show, but that he had a place for me in his new revue. I should have stayed home! Oh, but think of it. I shall be on the stage at last, and not just filling in. I'll be part of it all from the start. More tomorrow, must dash.'

'Oh,' Stella said. 'Grace, my producer just put her in another show.'

'Now, my dear,' Mr Cook said. 'I'm sorry you thought she was sad the night she passed.'

'I . . . I did,' Stella gasped. 'I'm so, so glad she was excited. But—'

Grace interrupted, handing back the letter. 'But nothing. Of course it's a tragedy she didn't get to be on stage, but it's a comfort she was about to go on.'

Mrs Cook passed her hand lovingly over the folded page. 'It is that, Mrs Treadwell. It is that.'

Stella shook her head. 'She could have got in my show. But I got jealous. I told my producer not to hire her.'

The Cooks stared at her, and the old-fashioned clock ticked away the long moments of silence. 'You, Stella?' Mrs Cook said at last. '*You* were jealous of Ruthie.'

Stella nodded.

'Well!' Mr Cook gasped. 'Our Ruthie. To think she was good enough to make you jealous. I wish she'd known that. It would trounce the king tipping his hat, wouldn't it, Jess?'

'It would indeed.'

And that was that. The visit continued while Grace sat quietly, letting the others talk about Ruthie to their heart's content, until she looked at her watch and saw it was time for them to leave if they were going to get back to Highbridge before midnight.

A long series of goodbyes and thanks followed. Mr Cook took little Judith in his arms and walked up the hill a little way with Stella as the sun sank, to see if they could spot the pony in the field at the end of the road, while Mrs Cook and Grace said their goodbyes on the doorstep.

'Thanks for bringing her, Mrs Treadwell. It's meant the world to us.'

'Of course.' She looked up the road, where Stella and Judith were pointing into the field and laughing.

'That'll be coming to you soon,' Mrs Cook said.

'Children?' Mrs Cook nodded. 'I hope so, but, I've had problems in the past.'

Mrs Cook patted her arm. 'I've been a midwife twenty years, and more than that, I have a sense, dear. Never failed me yet. Ask anyone round here.' She looked Grace up and down very carefully. 'You'll carry this one. Due middle of August, aren't you?'

Stella was very quiet on the way home.

Grace didn't interrupt her thoughts, or react when she saw Stella wipe her eyes from time to time.

They were approaching the outskirts of Highbridge before she said anything at all.

'This is going to sound awfully foolish, Grace,' she said. 'But I wish they hadn't been so kind to me. I suppose I should be all carefree and happy again, but I still feel like I betrayed her.'

Grace flicked on the lights of the car, but it seemed to make the dusk more complete around them.

'You did. When the next girl comes along who is better than you or prettier than you, be kind to her anyway.'

Stella gasped, then started to cry properly. Grace decided it would be best to let her get it out of herself before returning to Lassiter Court. She turned away from the house and up the dale, following the twisting road up past the Lassiter Enterprises shed, then up onto the hill overlooking them. The dale looked magical in the moonlight, washed in silvery greys and greens by the full moon. Occasional lights twinkled from farms and villages in the neighbouring valleys, and far beyond, Highbridge cast a pale glow up into the sky. Grace felt a peace entering her bloodstream, as if she was drawing something from the soil.

'There, I've done,' Stella said eventually. 'Take me home before I freeze to death.' She pulled her fur wrap around her shoulders. 'The little girl was sweet, wasn't she? I said they could write to me.'

'She was.' Grace pressed the ignition button and took the car out onto the road again. She wondered about what Mrs Cook had said. Somehow a little of the woman's confidence had entered Grace's bloodstream. She dared, very briefly, to hope.

'I suppose I'd better start reading some of those plays my agent has sent me,' Stella said. 'I'll leave tomorrow, if you'll return the key. Unless you can write me something new, Grace? I know Ruby left a great pile of tunes for you.'

Grace shook her head. 'No, the fox is still getting in the way.'

'The fox?'

'It's my name for Jason de Witte,' Grace said.

Stella looked thoughtful, but didn't reply, and they finished the drive back to Lassiter Court in silence.

*

Her car key restored, Stella left the next day – a little pale, perhaps, but calmer.

'Thank you,' she said simply to Grace as Hewitt loaded her cases into the car. 'I'll call my agent, and, if you'd like, I'll tell her I'll be happy to record for Empire Records.'

'I've held off recording anything from *Rivera Nights* in the hope you'd say that,' Grace admitted, as they crossed the gravel and Stella lowered herself into the driving seat. She ran her fingers over the wheel.

'I shall miss Ruby terribly,' she said, 'and I know that's only a fraction of what you and Tom must feel.'

'You could write me long letters, Stella.'

She laughed heartily at that. 'Good God, no, but I'll spend a fortune on telephone calls until we see each other again.'

CHAPTER FORTY-FOUR

Jack concentrated very, very hard. Every fibre of his being was taut. He was so attuned in that moment to every possible sound, the slightest noise, he felt briefly godlike.

'Good God, Treadwell! Are you ill?'

The moment passed. He rolled over and looked up at Dixon's concerned face staring down at him from the threshold of his office.

'Good afternoon, Dixon. No.'

'Then why are you lying on the floor like that?'

Jack crossed his ankles and put his hands behind his head. 'I have been listening for Harry, Dixon. Your friend is tormenting me. I'm fairly sure he's using the electrical conduits in the floor space to make his way around the theatre. More than that, when I'm at my desk, he makes a sneak approach and squeaks at me from under the floorboards.'

Dixon sat down beside him and crossed his legs. 'So I assume Nikolai is still refusing to tell you anything about his upcoming production?'

'Yes, he damn well is. I can't stand it. I'll try and cheer everyone up with *Whoops, Away We Go* at the end of June and *Twelve Miles Out*, which is coming in for the second half of July, has been getting excellent notices in London. I can make plenty of noise about *The Seaside Revue* coming in for August, but approaching us is this terrifying white space in the diary which simply says "Nikolai's Play".'

'Little Sam says he's working very hard.'

'Pfft,' Jack replied, examining the ceiling. 'He could be doing anything.'

Dixon pulled a cigarette from his case and lit it, then lay next to Jack.

'Did you want anything in particular, Dixon?' Jack asked.

'Oh, yes, I was wondering . . . With a nice girl . . .' He lowered his voice to a whisper. 'A nice girl one has had a few lunches with, for example – might it be appropriate to ask her out for a picnic?'

Jack hauled himself up on one elbow. 'Oh, are you asking Miss Chisholm out? Yes, a picnic is perfect. Hewitt will provide you with an excellent hamper. Take the bus out to Garthwaite. It stops at the pub, and there's a lovely spot by the river.'

Dixon frowned. 'Will she say yes?'

'Won't know if you don't ask her.'

Dixon nodded, conceding the point.

Miss Chisholm appeared at the door at that moment, smoothing down her hair. 'Mr Treadwell, I'm back from lunch . . . What on earth are you doing?'

Jack scrambled back to his feet. 'Listening for rats and discussing picnics.'

The phone rang in the outer office. Miss Chisholm cast them a slightly worried look and went to answer it while Jack hauled Dixon to his feet.

'All going well downstairs, though?' he asked.

'Yes.' Dixon pulled at his cuffs. 'Grace says Stella can come up again next week to record, and has a little time later in the summer, too. Apparently her agent's a dragon. How is the' – he waved a hand – 'money side of things going?'

'Nicely,' Jack replied. 'We'll take on another couple of girls in the shop next month, and the milk shakes are becoming quite the thing. Did Tom tell you he's selling wholesale to shops in Sheffield and

Newcastle already? The terrifying Mr Fossil is turning out discs of exceptional quality, we're told.'

'He mentioned something, I think. Oh, and I've been talking to Mr Porter about using more musicians, and he was wondering about a classical list. Nothing too heavy, but what about a few string quartets, or a sonata or two?'

'Will people like that?'

Dixon nodded earnestly. 'Perhaps not the young ones who come in to the shop in the afternoons, but older people, who like to come in early while it's quiet.'

Jack remembered the quartet which had played on the terrace at Lillian's wedding. 'Why not? We have enough in the kitty to give it a try.' He paused. 'Dixon, have you written to your mother recently?'

'I get the train into Sheffield and send a postcard once a month to say I'm well.'

Jack folded his arms and leant against the desk. 'I do understand why you might be at odds with your father, but you're fond of your mother and sister, aren't you?' Dixon conceded he was. 'Then write them a proper letter. Send them a few records!'

'I can't do that,' Dixon said simply. 'If I sent them records they'd know where I am. And I don't think Mother would want me to be here.' He paused. 'But I could say I have a job, and so on.'

'Yes, do that. It's what mothers want most, I've discovered. Just an idea of what we're up to and our general state of well-being. Forgive the avuncular advice, Dixon.'

He was rewarded with one of those miraculous smiles. 'I like it, Jack. People only give you advice if they care about you.'

'I'm not entirely sure that's the case,' Jack began, but Dixon had already put his hands in his pockets and, whistling, left the room.

'Nikolai, I am your wife and your employer!'

'Yes, isn't it marvellous? Now, go away, please. I shall see you at supper.' The rehearsal room door was shut in Lillian's face. She stared at it. It opened once more, and Nikolai leant out to put a piece of paper in her hands, kissed her on the forehead, then shut the door again.

Lillian's day was not going particularly well. Nikolai, who had once been so voluble about his dramatic ambitions, had stopped talking to her about his work entirely.

Jack was waiting in her office. He raised an enquiring eyebrow, and she shook her head.

'But we have to know some time, Lillian! We have programmes, posters to print! An audience to find! For crying out loud, he opens in two weeks.'

'I'm well aware of that, Jack.'

He brandished a heavy-looking volume at her. 'This is Danny's day book. You wouldn't believe the number of people Nikolai has coming in for rehearsals. How much are they all being paid? All I know is that he's insisting on tuppenny tickets for the stalls for the whole run, and for the whole theatre on opening night! Honestly, Lillian, what is your husband playing at?'

'Well, he's doing something!' She handed him the piece of paper. It read *The Seven Trials of Septimius Grey. Conceived and performed by The Highbridge Theatre Collective.*

Jack ran his hand through his hair. 'That's it?'

'That's it.' Lillian crossed her legs and looked sideways out of her window across the yards and back alleyways of the city.

'And he's still insisting on the "special prices"?'

She nodded, and heard Jack sigh. 'Very well. I shall do what I can.'

'You both look terribly mournful,' a voice said from the doorway, and they turned to find Agnes, wearing an emerald cape that almost reached her ankles and a hat with a bobbing peacock feather. 'Nikolai's play, I presume. Go away, Jack, I need to speak to Lillian.'

Jack took the piece of paper and left.

'Do you want tea, Agnes?' Lillian asked, as Agnes settled on the chair Jack had just vacated.

'No. I've come to tell you I think the visit here in July will go ahead. But this little detour to Highbridge will not be announced until the tour is already underway. Then arrangements will be made. David has come up with some nonsense story to give the Marakovians, to build a little leeway into things. Nikolai should make sure he is available on perhaps the twenty-seventh, and certainly the twenty-eighth of July. Put something on here. A concert. Stefan wants to hear you sing "The Sunrise Song". Apparently it's become incredibly popular in Marakovia.'

'I see. Yes, we can manage something. But who is David?'

'The Prince of Wales, dear.'

'I see,' Lillian said, looking down at the green leather top of her desk. 'Agnes, how do you get word of these things when Nikolai cannot?'

'Old school friends, Lillian. The fascists think we're gossiping old women, and one learns to work useful information into a jam recipe with a little practice. The censors get bored and don't realise what they're reading.'

Lillian smiled. 'Nikolai is afraid Stefan coming to meet him is a sign of weakness.'

'It possibly is. He obviously has few allies in the palace beyond some old ladies like me. But when one is weak, one should ask for help, don't you think? Stefan needs Nikolai's advice. He's taking some risks to get it.'

'Is there any more news out of Marakovia? I know the papers are writing terrible things about Nikolai.'

'The king's brother grows more authoritarian and more powerful every week.' Agnes stopped and leant across the table; the peacock feather in her head swooped and bobbed. 'You are having the Marakovian papers sent to you?'

Lillian sighed and shook her head. 'We don't need to. Someone has been kindly sending them to us all year, especially the ones with photographs. At the Metropole, at the Playhouse . . . and their notices of our turn at the pantomime were something special. Actually, I'm only guessing that, as Nikolai wouldn't translate it for me, but I saw the cartoon. They had a lovely shot of Nikolai leaving the police station after our wedding. God knows how – I didn't even see a photographer.'

Agnes frowned at her. 'Lillian, do you understand what you are saying?'

'I thought I did, Agnes,' Lillian replied, 'but judging by your expression, I suspect I'm missing something.'

'Dear girl! You're supposed to be the sensible one. Someone in Highbridge has been spying on you, and sending the information back to the Fascist sympathisers in Marakovia.'

'Oh,' Lillian said, more shocked than she had expected. 'Do you think Nikolai knows?'

'Probably. Perhaps he's another of these husbands who run around in elaborate rings while attempting not to worry us.'

CHAPTER FORTY-FIVE

The approaching opening night of Nikolai's play *The Seven Trials of Septimius Grey* was causing a buzz in town, but it was not the sort of buzz that Jack liked. He liked whipping up some excitement, scattering fairy dust, offering gossip and glamour to the newspapers in the run-up to a show, like an uncle cramming too many iced buns down the throats of his nephews and nieces. He wanted his audience giddy and excited, ready to be pleased before they even got inside the auditorium.

The energy radiating out from The Empire in the run-up to this particular show felt much darker. Nikolai allowed no photographer to take photographs of the set, no interviews with the accidental stars who would be appearing, and even the dress rehearsal would be closed. The posters announced only the dates, the eye-wateringly low prices, the title, and the legend *CONCEIVED AND PERFORMED BY THE HIGHBRIDGE THEATRE COLLECTIVE*.

And now it seemed the whole backstage crew, from wardrobe to the paint shop, were in on the conspiracy to keep him and Lillian in the dark.

Wilbur pushed Jack's pint over to him. 'So what's he doing?'

'I don't know! That's the entire point! But yesterday I found the whole backstage crew coming out of the rehearsal rooms. They were all pink in the face and chattering like magpies, but as soon as they saw me, they buttoned their lips and wouldn't tell me anything.'

Wilbur shrugged. 'And the cast?'

'I don't know that either! All I know is that people turn up at the stage door at all hours claiming to be part of the production.'

'And what does Ollie do?'

Jack supped deeply. 'I think he's as confused as I am. Danny says he's taken to sleeping on the other side of the counter. It's as if he's refusing to take responsibility for deciding between Nikolai's interesting amateurs and every potential burglar who might be helping himself to the family silver.'

'Keep much family silver in the theatre, do you?'

'No, Wilbur, we don't. But it's the principle. I don't like not knowing what's going on in the theatre, and it's rattling me.'

Wilbur leant his back against the bar. 'Things are getting tense at Lassiter Enterprises, you know?'

'Oh yes?' Jack said. 'I thought all that nonsense was out of the way last year.'

Wilbur frowned. 'Men and women wanting to earn enough to keep a roof over their heads isn't nonsense, Jack. The General Strike might have fizzled out, but no one was left any happier. Tom has encouraged his men to unionise, and they're talking about it to workers in the other sheds. And I think the rumours about Kelly and his men working with Constance Lassiter to prevent her people unionising are true.'

Jack sucked his teeth. 'Really? Poor Tom.'

He paid for their drinks, and they moved away to a corner table under one of the windows.

'I hear Tom's doing well,' Wilbur said. 'Word is he works like a Trojan, and treats his people properly. Plenty of people saying it's a shame he doesn't run the whole company.'

Jack studied his beer. 'Not for publication, Wilbur, but it seems Constance has been secretly at work to make our lives hell since the New

Empire opened. Grace and I think she might be a little mad.' He told Wilbur some of the details. 'She was planning on sabotaging the shellac, too, the night before we opened the shop. Luckily Joe Allerdyce had put two and two together, and gave us a warning.'

'You caught someone?'

Jack hesitated, finishing the rest of his beer. 'We changed the locks,' he said quietly.

'And what will you do about Constance?'

Jack ordered them both another pint, then watched them being poured, his elbows resting on the table, watching the light from the leaded windows sparkle on the nut-brown polish. 'That'll be up to Tom, though I'm not sure he knows it yet.'

CHAPTER FORTY-SIX

Grace entered the theatre for Nikolai's first night, looking her best on her husband's arm, and full of happy expectations. The happiness lasted until the moment she spotted Jason de Witte propping up the circle bar.

She came to a full halt and stared. 'Jack, that's Jason de Witte!'

Her eyes were immediately hot, and she bit her lip.

'That sloppy-looking man at the bar? God, I had no idea Nikolai's reputation as a serious playwright would bring up a critic like him. I'll have him thrown out.'

'No, it would be too humiliating. I suppose the Crown Prince touring England in the summer has got them interested in Nikolai's work.' Panic was making Grace's lungs tight, and her legs felt shivery. 'I'll go straight to the royal box. I can hide there.'

'Let me make a scene, Grace. Could this be another of Constance's tricks?'

'I don't care. No, don't you dare make a scene.' She looked up to find her way blocked by Agnes and Joe. Agnes was turned away, greeting one of her young admirers, so it was Joe who saw the colour of Grace's face, and frowned.

'Evening! What's the matter, Grace?'

Agnes heard and turned towards them.

'Jason de Witte is here,' Jack said. 'Grace won't let me punch him.'

'I think I'm going to be sick,' Grace said. 'Jack, he's seen us. He's coming over!'

Agnes moved slightly, so she was between the critic and the deeply criticised.

'Buck up, my girl. He's only a man.'

'People will see us talking, Agnes. It's humiliating.'

'And what would they see, these people? They'll see you behaving in a civilised fashion to a man who behaved in a very uncivil way towards you. If this is Constance's work, it's vital you don't give her the satisfaction. Now, deep breaths and smile, Grace.'

She moved aside and Grace smiled.

'Ah, Mrs Treadwell,' De Witte said as he approached, bowing slightly over his pint and staring at her figure. 'I hear you pulled off a pantomime.'

'Mr De Witte,' Grace said, and introduced Jack without her voice shaking.

'And Grace is writing another play, of course,' Jack said.

Why did he have to say that? Grace thought.

'Really?' De Witte said, and sipped his beer. 'I suppose if it amuses you to write these little things in the privacy of your own home, no one can stop you. But I hope you won't be inflicting them on the general public.'

It felt like a slap, but it was such a monumentally unpleasant thing to say, the sting of it faded almost immediately into a sort of stupefied shock. She felt Jack tense, and squeezed his arm.

'I'll always clear the Playhouse schedule for Grace if she writes something for me,' Joe said before she could reply herself. 'I'm Joe Allerdyce.'

De Witte offered his hand and Joe stared at it. 'No, I shan't take your hand,' he said after a moment. 'I don't know what passes for manners in London, but piss-poor rudeness tied up in a ribbon of wit is still piss-poor rudeness. I'd not sully my skin touching yours, and I spent the first years of my working life mopping up the lavs in the cheapest bars in the arse end of Highbridge.'

De Witte gaped like a fish. 'I . . .'

'Leave, Mr De Witte,' Agnes said. 'Leave at once.'

He swallowed, then turned back to the bar.

'I thought,' Grace said to Agnes, watching him disappear back into the crush, 'I was supposed to speak to him in a civilised fashion.'

'That was civilised,' Agnes said. 'And better than he deserved.'

'The look on his face,' Jack said gleefully. 'Joe, I owe you a steak supper.'

Joe was still looking after him. 'That, my lad, you can have, gratis and for free. What a rat of a man.'

'An insult to rats,' Agnes said.

Grace smiled, her feelings more complicated than simple pleasure at the fox's humiliation, and the five-minute bell went. 'Shall we go and see what Nikolai has for us?'

Jack's face fell at the prospect. Joe noticed and suppressed a grin. 'I suppose we must. Are you all right, Grace?'

She studied her own feelings. 'Yes, yes, I am. Thank you, Joe.'

'They've forgotten to build a set!' Lillian heard Jack hiss to his wife as the curtain lifted six minutes later. Grace shushed him.

Lillian glanced sideways and saw Jack sinking back in his chair. It appeared he would be watching the play through his fingers. The tension in her chest felt like an iron band, but she kept her professional, interested smile in place, though the first lurch she felt at what lay in front of her, was horror.

The stage was completely empty, and the back wall of the theatre, with its ragged paint over the brickwork, and various notices and old playbills, was visible. Several of the stage crew lolled against it among an assortment of random props for recent shows, stage weights and ropes. Clara Jones's old costumes were out on a rack, and a throne covered in hieroglyphs, which must have been in storage since *Cairo Nights*, was set at an angle at the back of the stage. Little Sam was sitting on it.

He tipped his cap back, clambered off and walked up to the front of the stage.

'Good evening, folks,' he said.

He had a soft voice, but it seemed to carry.

'I don't think I've ever heard him speak before,' Agnes said cheerfully.

'This evening, we, the people of Highbridge, will perform for you a tale of tyrannical outrage – a history which took place many centuries ago on a foreign shore. Any resemblance to actual rich people in this town is a total coincidence.'

He looked up at the centre of the royal circle as he said it, and the audience laughed. Lillian followed his gaze. Constance Lassiter was staring down at the stage, her eyebrows raised.

Little Sam wandered back to the throne and sat on it, half turned from the audience. Then one of the house band members walked out onto the stage, clarinet in hand, and began to play. It was a lively, bouncy sort of a folk tune, and the people in the stalls started to clap along. The lounging stagehands stirred themselves, and an assortment of men and women in the street clothes of working people poured in from the wings, dragging hampers and boxes. They rummaged in them for costumes – scraps of fabric, rich or poor – which they wrapped round their shoulders. Then they pulled the hampers to the edge of the stage and sat on them.

Mrs Giorgio, who cooked at the pie and mash shop, had plucked a scrap of fur from one of the baskets.

'Evening, all!' she declared, jutting her hip out. 'I'm Geraldina, queen of this country, and we're gathered here today to pass judgment on Septimius Grey of the Grey Trading Company. First witness, please!'

Jack was still sunk down in his seat. 'Is it a pantomime? This is a disaster – he's trying to ruin us! We can't have the theatre empty for a fortnight!'

Lillian could hardly breathe. Grace leant forward in her seat, but put out her other hand and covered Lillian's with it. Lillian wound her fingers around her daughter-in-law's, terribly grateful for the reassurance. 'I don't know, Jack,' Grace said. 'He's certainly trying something.'

The transformation which came over the stage – and the performers – was so subtly done, Lillian couldn't say when she began to notice it. Perhaps it was during one of the early comic scenes, when Lillian suddenly realised the back wall of the theatre was no longer visible. Instead, a subtly painted flat of rolling countryside, spotted with romantic-looking ruins, had replaced it. While moments of high drama played out downstage, other players disappeared, then retook their positions on the hampers in full costume. Then the hampers were gone, replaced with benches and hay bales. The queen was offered a robe in scarlet, trimmed with white fur. The throne was wheeled into position by Sam, and his seat taken by Mrs Giorgio.

But she wasn't Mrs Giorgio anymore – she was Geraldina. Half an hour into the performance, Lillian was no longer watching a group of amateur Highbridge players. They were watching the citizens of Transalina judging one of their own. Jack was sitting up now. Joe and Agnes were as still as statues.

Septimius called for justice, and a voice in the stalls called out in support. Then another and another. Lillian couldn't tell if they were plants or not. The actors on stage echoed the calls, and when the queen's guards lowered their pikes, the whole audience seemed to draw back, afraid.

'This,' Grace breathed, 'is extraordinary.'

There was no interval, yet the whole thing passed in a flash. Lillian leapt to her feet as the cast, back in the street clothes in which they had begun, lifted their arms to accept the applause. The audience, who had been weeping a moment before, were on their feet, roaring, their hands above their heads.

'You must be very proud,' Agnes whispered to Lillian.

'I honestly don't think I've ever felt like this before,' Lillian admitted. 'I think I am stupefied.' Jack and Grace were on their feet, too, and as she watched, Jack put his fingers in his mouth and whistled, then cheered again. Something dark and dreadful fell away from Lillian's heart when she saw that.

'Author, author, author!' the crowd began to chant. The applause became a steady handclap; feet stamped in rhythm and the cast joined in, too, looking off to the wings.

Then Nikolai made his appearance. He didn't strut. It was almost as if he was trying to make himself smaller. Lillian had seen him command an audience when he quelled the rising children the first day he'd come to Highbridge, and when he played King Rat. He was not doing that now. The chant of 'author' turned to one for a speech. Nikolai held up his hand, refusing at first, then conceded.

'Thank you,' he said, placing a hand over his chest. 'We are very, very glad to have this reception.' He looked round the cast, and they nodded their agreement. 'This play is about making a leap of faith. That even when we land flat on our face, such a leap of faith is worth making, so it is right that we take this chance to thank the owners of this grand theatre, and its manager, for the trust they placed in us. They haven't had a clue what we've been up to, you know!' The audience laughed. 'So please join me in thanking Mr Jack Treadwell, Miss Agnes de Montfort, and of course, my wife, Lillian Kuznetsov.'

He swept his arm out and Ruben's follow spot swung up to the box, to hearty cheers. Lillian waved, and wondered if she looked as dazed, baffled and delighted as she felt. She was sure her mascara was running after that last scene.

'The promenade bar is selling beer at the same price as the Dog and Duck,' Nikolai, continued to further applause. 'Join us. All are welcome. Now, I would like to join you, one more time, in thanking our friends . . . Ladies and gentlemen! The company!'

Grace suddenly stopped clapping and groaned, and Agnes turned and looked at her. 'Grace, are you going to be sick? There's a pot in the retiring room. Mr Poole put an aspidistra in it, but it will hold.'

Grace nodded, then left the box hurriedly, holding the handkerchief over her mouth.

'What? Grace!' Jack said, 'What's wrong with her?'

Lillian opened her handbag and removed a small packet of charcoal biscuits. 'I'm an idiot. I brought these for her, then forgot to give them to her.' She passed them to Jack and turned to the stage, applauding again. 'Give her five minutes, Jack, and then take them to her. They were the only things that helped when I was pregnant with you.'

Jack took the biscuits, and stared at them. Nikolai and the company were climbing off the stage and greeting friends in the stalls. 'She's . . .? But she's been working so hard – tiring herself out! She should have been resting. I should have been looking after her, not the shop! I read in a magazine she should make sure to get enough zinc. I'm not sure what that is, but has she been getting enough zinc? Why didn't she tell me?'

Joe was trying to suppress a laugh. He was looking directly at the stage, but his face was pink and a tear leaked out of the corner of his eye.

Agnes gave Jack another look. 'It defeats the imagination, dear.'

That broke Joe; he guffawed, and his rich rolling laughter joined the final burst of applause.

Lillian couldn't wait any longer. Leaving Jack baffled, and the others still applauding, she hurried down the stairs from the box, and into the stalls. Nikolai was in a crowd of cast and crew, but as soon as he saw her, he opened his arms and she leapt into them. He swung her in a circle, lifting her high.

'Why did you keep it all such a secret?' she said, thumping his shoulder.

He looked up at her, beaming. 'If I had told you any of those things – we will start with no set, the crew will be on stage – you would have worried more, I think. It worked, though, didn't it?'

'I'll say it did,' she said, and he gently lowered her down to the floor again and kissed her.

'Now, I believe what I should have at this point is a pint.'

CHAPTER FORTY-SEVEN

'Oh, that was wonderful,' Jack said as he and Grace came into their private sitting room at Lassiter Court some hours later. He poured himself a whisky and pulled off his tie. 'The play is extraordinary, and those notices will make it a sellout, I've no doubt. I'll give De Witte his due. He did right by the play, even after the spanking he got. I suppose his reputation would be in shreds if he did anything else. But seeing that horrible little man chopped into mincemeat by Joe! The colour he went!' His wife didn't reply. 'Aren't you happy, darling? Are you feeling ill?'

Grace took off her shoes and sat in one of the armchairs near the fire, massaging her ankles. 'No, those biscuits of Lillian's did actually help.'

He poured a whisky and took a swallow. 'Do you want one of these?'

'No, it makes me nauseous at the moment.'

He hesitated. 'How long have you known, Grace?'

'A few weeks now. Do you mind I didn't say anything? I was worried enough for both of us, and I was afraid you'd stop me helping in the shop.'

He sat down in the armchair opposite her. 'I admit, I'd have probably given it a try. I'll tell you what,' he said. I promise I shall do my best not to make a fuss, as long as you promise to tell me how you're feeling. Good or bad. Is that a bargain?'

'It is.'

He sat back in his chair, happiness running through his bloodstream with the alcohol. 'I'm glad to have seen De Witte. The horrible little man.' He looked up and found his wife was giving him that look. The look that made him feel she was peering under his skin, like a mechanic examining an engine that's making odd clanking noises. It was uncomfortable.

'Are you, Jack?'

'Yes.'

'Why?'

'Because I wanted to see him!' He hadn't even known that himself until the words came out of his mouth. 'I wanted to see for myself this man whose opinion is so much more important to you than mine, more important than Ruby's or Stella's or any of the actors and directors and producers we've worked with! What is he? How can what he thinks matter to you more than me, or the audience?'

She curled her legs underneath her and looked away.

'Well, congratulations, you've seen him.'

'Yes, and he's pathetic! He's a stupid, self-important fool! Grace, he's been this demon in your mind for months, and it turns out he's not a demon at all, just a nasty little man Joe Allerdyce made mincemeat of in twenty seconds. He's a nothing! How can you still care about the opinion of a *nothing*?'

'Because he's right!' she said. 'Just because he's rude doesn't make him wrong. Jack, you like everything! So does the audience, as long as a show has enough dancing girls and a sentimental number in the middle of act two.' She pointed at her chest. 'I have a certain facile wit, and an ability to muddle through, but I don't for one second think that anything I do is any good – not really good, I mean. And I know you don't like Nikolai, but look what he did tonight. That was good. And don't ever try and tell me you can't tell the difference!'

Jack put his hand to his forehead. 'But Nikolai's more than twenty years older than you. He's been writing and producing serious political drama for years.'

'See! You *do* know he's better, you *can* tell the difference, because you're not an idiot – though you like pretending to be one occasionally. But you bamboozle and tell me I'm marvellous, like I'm a child doing pirouettes and not falling over. That's not the standard I want to be judged by. And I let you all convince me that I was better than I thought I was! Then De Witte took everything, the worst things I've ever secretly thought about myself and my writing, and wrote it all down in five hundred and forty-seven well-chosen words, then published them in a national newspaper!' Her eyes were red. 'He was right, Jack. He humiliated me, and he was right to do it, even if he is a pathetic little man, and you all set me up for it with your flummery, and since then you've just been telling me not to worry my pretty little head over the nasty man and write another jolly play. Jack, this matters to me!'

Jack blinked at her. Confident, efficient, loving and brilliant Grace was looking at him with an expression he had never seen before. He bit his tongue. All his usual blandishments and compliments would be salt in the wound now.

'You counted the words?'

She pulled out her handkerchief and wiped her eyes. 'Yes, I did. It could be five hundred and forty-six, depending on whether you count "empty-minded" as one or two words.'

'Oh.'

She glanced at him and offered a brave half-smile, which made him feel even worse. 'Thank you.'

'What for?'

'For not telling me I'm a great writer again.'

'You know I think you are, but I realise I can't bludgeon you into agreeing with me.' He put out his hand, but she turned away again. 'I should have tried to work out why that notice bothered you so much, rather than just tell you it didn't matter.'

A crooked smile appeared on her heart-shaped face. 'Who are you, and what have you done with my husband, Jack Treadwell?'

He smiled a crooked smile of his own. 'You know how I always want to fix things?' She nodded. 'Well, I was just thinking about how when the WCs started causing trouble, I was dashing in there with another brand-new plunger, and it took Miss Chisholm to do the sensible thing and actually look at the building's insurance policy.'

'Jack . . .' There was a tremble of laughter in her voice now. 'Are you comparing me to a malfunctioning lavatory?'

'Cripes, yes, I suppose I am, but let me get to the end of this. If you want to get better, or find out why that foul little man's criticism really bit you, even when we all do genuinely think you're wonderful, you've got to take a longer view and ask someone you respect.'

She was silent for a while. 'Someone like Nikolai, you mean?'

'Yes, damn it, I suppose I do.' He took a long swig of whisky.

Grace studied him cautiously. 'Isn't that presumptuous?'

'Now you're being daft, as Mum would say. I've heard you talking with him about drama, all sorts of plays and about technical things I've never heard of. He's watched you direct. He respects you.'

She leant forward. 'And you won't make any snippy comments about it?'

'No, of course not! Why would you think . . .?' She raised her eyebrows and he stopped himself. 'I've been a bit of an arse, haven't I?'

'Yes.'

He moved to sit on the arm of her chair, and she leant her head against him. He ran his fingers through her hair. 'Such a small, elegant head, you have, Grace, and always such a lot going on in it. You do surprise me, you know.'

'Telling me to go and ask Nikolai for advice was a bit of a surprise to me, too. It was remarkable, wasn't it? What he discovered in all those people.'

'Yes, I had no idea there was such talent in Highbridge,' he said idly.

'*Full many a flower* . . .' she said. 'Jack, I may have an idea for Empire Records.'

CHAPTER FORTY-EIGHT

'A talent show?' asked Lillian. 'Yes,' Grace said comfortably, buttering her toast. She was either horribly sick in the mornings, or ravenous, and was delighted to find today was one of her hungry days. 'Or not so much a talent show, as a competition, a way of finding a new recording star for Empire Records. Someone local.'

'I have inspired you,' Nikolai said comfortably.

'Yes, you have. Well, you and Ruby. It was that poem she quoted to me.' She waved her toast in the air as she recited. '"Full many a gem of purest ray serene, The dark unfathom'd caves of ocean bear: Full many a flower is born to blush unseen, And waste its sweetness on the desert air." It's from "Elegy Written in a Country Churchyard". And, well, why should they blush unseen if we have a theatre and a bit of imagination? We could scout for talent across Highbridge ourselves, or hold auditions on Sunday afternoons in the theatre. Then have a proper show at The Empire to select the winner, and showcase a few of the singers we already have.' She swallowed quickly and waved her hand. 'Like you two.'

Nikolai looked at Lillian and raised one of his remarkably expressive eyebrows as Grace reached for more toast. 'I would like to sing with you on stage, Lillian.'

'We could have a choir to back you, and I think the instrumental section would lend itself to a waltz.'

Lillian leant forward and put her chin in her hand. 'Who would judge?'

'Stella. Harold, I think, would come up, and probably do a turn, too, and I did think we might be able to persuade Lance to come. He could duet with Stella. Josie Clarence, too.'

'I suppose Hewitt is a living example of the fact people have some surprising hidden talents,' Lillian said slowly, remembering her butler fending off Marakovians with a tea tray. Grace was looking at her hopefully. 'It will take a push, but why not? You know, there was a girl I knew in the factory, had a voice like an angel, but was too afraid to put herself forward. She might have tried something like this, though.'

'We'll have to be clever about how we promote it,' Grace said.

'And what does Jack say to this?'

'He says we'll be beset by second-grade talent, and reminds me I'm pregnant, as if I hadn't noticed, but we've come to an arrangement.'

'Well, I think it's an excellent idea, Grace,' Lillian said. 'One thing, might I suggest a date for the final? The twenty-eighth of July. It's a Thursday, and the week that *Twelve Miles Out* is playing. If we compensate the company, they will return us the night. Nikolai and I have been planning a concert, but I think your talent show would be perfect.'

'A concert? Is it for one of your charities?'

'Something like that, dear.'

'It's rather close to the date the baby should be turning up.' Grace put a hand on her belly. 'But it would give us time to plan it properly, and if you were thinking of taking back that night anyway, why not?'

Lillian looked at Nikolai again, and he smiled at her. 'You are going to have to trust us, dear, but I think we will be able to get you in some extra star power.'

'What – more than Lance?' Grace's forehead puckered into a frown.

'Yes, more even than Lance,' Lillian replied.

Grace shrugged, borne aloft on a cloud of enjoying her breakfast and a pleasant rush of loving everyone around her very much, which was so much better than the moments when she felt crushed by every breath she took, and consumed by cravings for roast chicken – which, oddly, seemed to come at the same time.

'In the meantime, Nikolai, I'd very much like your help with my writing.'

He raised an eyebrow. 'Really, Grace? Talking about writing in general terms is always most invigorating, but to critique and receive critiques, that is much more difficult.'

'It's absolutely what I want, Nikolai.'

'In that case, we can start today. Prepare your papers and deliver them to me in the morning room by lunchtime.'

'I really think you must reconsider this impulsive visit to Highbridge,' Sir Gideon said, waiting till the Prince of Wales had settled into one of the stiff armchairs in the morning room of Windsor Castle, before also lowering himself gratefully into a chair.

'Highbridge is an important town, there is no reason I shouldn't add it to my itinerary. And it's not impulsive. It might look it,' he added with a yawn, 'as it shall not be announced until after Stefan has arrived in the country, but it's not. And Highbridge will still have a couple of weeks to slosh a bit of fresh paint about. They've got plenty of factories for me to admire, haven't they? And the digs sound splendid.'

'But to go to the theatre, and watch Nikolai Kuznetsov perform, sir. It's tantamount to an endorsement of his beliefs.'

'Stefan is trying to introduce some balance, and lower temperatures politically, much as I've been attempting to do here,' the prince said coolly. 'The newspapers have been particularly unpleasant about Kuznetsov, I understand.'

'Balance! This play of his. They were like revolutionaries off to storm the Bastille, sir! That is what the reports say. And led by the sworn enemy of Marakovia, Nikolai Kuznetsov!

The Prince of Wales was dressed for golf, and Colonel Osman had noticed him glancing at his watch twice already. He finished his tea, and set down the cup and saucer on the table next to him, still half looking over his shoulder at the view into the palace gardens.

'Osman, what do you think? Stefan went through some convoluted back channels to ask me to do this, and to attend the theatre. They are putting on some sort of concert, and Nikolai and his wife will be singing "The Sunrise Song".'

'Well, Sir—' Gideon began.

'Are you deaf? I asked Osman. You brought him here and told me he's an expert on Marakovia. Lord knows, I could do with one, the briefing books from the Foreign Office have been terribly slim. Then let him "expert" me.'

Neither Osman nor Sir Gideon had been offered tea. Osman cleared his throat. 'On Kuznetsov's play, sir . . . it's an unusual piece. Very innovative staging, a cast drawn from the local populace, but I'd say its general thrust is against tyranny and pro justice for all.'

'Last time I looked, we're rather against tyranny ourselves, aren't we?'

'That's still official policy, I believe,' Osman replied, tempted into a grin. Sir Gideon huffed. 'There is no doubt that Crown Prince Stefan going to the theatre, listening to Nikolai sing "The Sunrise Song" and publicly applauding it, will be seen as a strong rebuke to the king's brother, Andrei, and his policies. I have to assume that is the plan.'

'What is this Andrei up to anyway?' the prince said, exasperated. 'They are obviously as divided as any family, but that is their problem.' He took a cigarette from the box on the table and lit it. 'The request came through private channels, and was agreed to. I shan't go back on my word because a very well-reviewed piece of theatre is making you uncomfortable, Sir Gideon.'

'Sir, I think you are right to refuse to change the itinerary, particularly over this play,' Osman said quietly. 'But I don't want to pretend there aren't some risks involved on this tour, and in Highbridge in particular.'

'Risks?'

Osman felt Sir Gideon's disapproving gaze on him. He decided to make an effort. 'As I said, this will be seen as a strong rebuke to Prince Andrei. Marakovia is a pivot point in Europe, sir. A small country of great importance, and now Crown Prince Stefan, as heir to an elderly king, is the pivot point of power in that country. His wish to visit the town where his cousin Nikolai is living, suggests he shares that man's liberal leanings. Prince Andrei is much more in sympathy with the leaders of Italy, and he has increased his power exponentially in the last few months.'

'You know, I think Mussolini makes a lot of sense sometimes. My people don't need a strong guiding hand. We're British, for goodness's sake, but those Italians! And who's to say that the Marakovians aren't the same?'

Osman sat forward. 'I disagree with you, sir.' The prince raised an eyebrow, and turned his attention from the view to Osman. 'The Marakovians do not have the experience with a constitutional monarchy we do, but under an enlightened monarch, they could become a stable democracy in time.'

'But you think there are risks?' the prince asked.

'I do not know how far Prince Andrei's allies will go if they fear they have lost control of Stefan. If he is killed, Andrei is next in line. That means a possible risk to yourself.'

'A possible assassination? That would spice things up. Well, there's a risk to me from the moment I get up in the morning, Osman. We hold the line. Stefan asked to go to Highbridge, so we'll go there.' The prince ground out his cigarette in his tea saucer. 'And you can come.'

'Me, sir?' Osman said.

'Yes, you, Colonel. I'm hereby appointing you one of my equerries. You know these fellows, their lingo and their country. I've learnt more about the place in the last five minutes than I have in the last five months. Come with me. Sir Gideon, you can remain in London.'

'But sir, royal protocol and so on, I have very little experience.'

'Then let me make this very simple for you, Colonel Osman. I am the Prince of Wales. You are not. When I tell you you are coming on this tour with me, you say "What a pleasure, sir". You then do everything you can to prevent me or my guest from being assassinated, manhandled, or, to be honest, bothered in any way. Are we clear?'

'Yes, sir.'

'Splendid.' The prince smiled at him. He had a generous smile when he wanted to employ it, and to his annoyance, Osman felt a patriotic pulse in his bloodstream. 'And remember that bit about assassinations. Key point.'

CHAPTER FORTY-NINE

The acclaim for Nikolai's play was universal. The London papers reprinted Jason de Witte's fulsome appraisal, and curious theatre critics and lovers from the capital made the pilgrimage to attend. A transfer to the West End was mooted, and Jack's and Mr Poole's days were filled with finding suitable seats for a flurry of interested VIPs, and negotiating with the employers of their disparate company to take the show to London in the spring of the following year.

Grace found her husband's preoccupation with Nikolai's play gave her more freedom than she had been anticipating. She had begun writing something, and though she was quite sure it was not good yet, Nikolai was teaching her not to expect it to be when she first set pen to paper. That helped. And working with him was difficult, but left her eager to write more – it was not as if they wrote together, or he marked her work like a schoolteacher, but he was terribly good at asking the right questions, about what was good and what wasn't.

After a chilly May, the weather was beginning to improve, and Grace announced the talent contest to the world in general. The Empire Records Search for a Star would take place on the evening of 28th July, and those who wished to perform were invited to present themselves at the theatre on the afternoon of Sunday 17th or 24th. She placed advertisements in the *Highbridge Gazette*, and gave an interview to Wilbur underlining their preference for new talent. She emphasised that the inspiration for the project was both the success of *Seven Trials* and the legacy of Ruby Rowntree.

The event would include special performances from Nikolai and Lillian with Mabel Mills, Stella performing the theme tune of *Riviera Nights* and a duet with Lancelot Drake, and Harold Drabble would also perform. Josie Clarence would sing her ballad from *Cairo Nights*, and Josie, Stella, Lancelot and Harold would act as judges. They would give their opinions of each of the potential stars, then the winner would be chosen by the acclamation of the crowd.

With the pieces arranged to her liking, Grace got on with her writing, and Hewitt and the staff at Lassiter Court made sure that roast chicken was on hand when necessary.

Agnes leant forward across Lillian's desk at The Empire. She had discovered if she wished to see Lillian alone, this was by far the best place to do that.

'The Prince of Wales has begun to find Sir Gideon a little too much. He will not now be accompanying them on any part of the tour. One of his mother's ladies-in-waiting wrote today to let me know, and I thought I'd come and tell you at once.'

Lillian felt a surge of relief. 'Thank you, Agnes, you're a good friend.'

'I'm not sure about that, but I'm making an effort to be a better one in my old age. I can't imagine, dear girl, what it is like.' She paused, weighing her words. 'What are you going to tell Jack?'

Lillian studied the blotter on her desk for a moment before she replied. 'If Sir Gideon was certain to come, I would tell him my suspicions now. But in the circumstances, I should rather wait until after Grace's baby is born. He should be looking after her at the moment.'

'If it is Sir Gideon who attacked you in '96,' Agnes said carefully, 'I cannot suppose Dixon Wells arriving here is a coincidence.'

Lillian straightened the half-written letter in front of her. 'I'm sure you're right, Agnes, but perhaps Sir Gideon was not the man. I must see him at some point to be sure, but I admit, I'm glad not to be forced to do so in the midst of Grace's talent show and a royal visit. Is the programme decided?'

Agnes nodded. 'David, Stefan and their people will stay in Joe's mansion. He is so swollen with delight at the idea, I fear for his waistcoats. On the Wednesday, they'll look at a couple of factories, including the Empire Records production shed, and Joe will give a dinner for the local dignitaries at his place. I think it might be best not to invite Nikolai to the house, at least officially. There'll be better moments.' Lillian nodded. Whatever Nikolai and the Crown Prince wished to say to each other, it would be better to do so privately, rather than under the eye of Highbridge's elite. 'Then the following day is marked as "resting" on the calendar, with the Search for a Star Pageant in the evening.' She smiled. 'When are you going to tell Grace she is putting on a show for royalty, both international and domestic?'

'She already suspects, I think. We've told her the "special guests" are not theatrical stars, so won't be taking part in the judging, but she knows the royal tour is in the area and that Nikolai is fond of the Crown Prince. She's a clever young woman.'

'The diversion into Highbridge will be announced after Crown Prince Stefan arrives in England. You had better ask Mr Poole to put aside a couple of dozen extra tickets for all the dignitaries who'll be desperate to show their faces.'

Agnes got to her feet and flicked the ribboned edges of her cape so the folds fell properly across her ample bosom, and Lillian came out from behind her desk to open the door for her.

'Of course. I shall put him on alert. He's an intelligent man himself, of course.' She began to open the door. 'But a committed royalist, so he'll keep his conclusions to himself until the palace makes the announcement. Oh, Dixon!'

She felt and repressed the familiar shudder which sometimes seized her when she met her house guest unexpectedly. He was standing in the hall with Miss Chisholm.

'Lillian,' he said seriously, 'Do you have any cold cream? I've run out, and Miss Chisholm doesn't keep any in the office. Harry's looking vexed, and I don't wish him to turn his attention to the electrics.'

'Good Lord, no, we don't want that,' Lillian agreed, recovering herself rapidly. 'No, Dixon, I don't keep cold cream in the office. Do you think Harry will wait until you can visit Bertram's?'

Dixon brightened and glanced at his watch. 'Yes, that should take me seventeen minutes.' Then he turned on his heel.

'What a very odd man,' Agnes said as he disappeared down the corridor.

'He is a little,' Lillian sighed, 'but ferociously clever. Miss Chisholm, are you looking for me?'

The secretary nodded. 'Mr Treadwell is out, Mrs Kuznetsov, and the producer of *Whoops, Away We Go* is hoping you might step into rehearsals. Temperatures—'

She was interrupted by the door to the rehearsal room banging open and the young star of the show launching into the corridor, as if propelled. 'I can't possibly work under these conditions,' she announced, then ran off down the corridor, weeping.

'. . . are running rather high,' Miss Chisholm concluded.

The director followed the star, looked up and down the corridor, then threw his papers in the air and, with a groan, strode off in the other direction.

'So I see,' Lillian said. 'Ring down from my telephone, Miss Chisholm, and tell Danny to ask Miss Halliday to wait for me.' Then she turned to Agnes. 'Try-outs before the West End run, and the directors do tend to give rather contradictory notes at this point. Will you excuse me?'

'Of course,' Agnes said. 'I shall go and spend a little money in your shop. Joe wants the latest jazz tunes, and I understand Mr Porter's new

Brahms Quintet is available. They're really very competent players, I had no idea when they just played the modern fluff.'

And the women went their separate ways.

The room above the bookshop on Charing Cross Road was uncomfortably warm, but protocol dictated they should not open the windows, and though the paper blinds did something to keep the worst of the sun off, the air felt thick, like liquid dust.

'It cannot be borne,' Taargin said. 'Despite our best efforts, the Crown Prince will visit Highbridge, and will see Nikolai perform his version of "The Sunrise Song", in full view of the press.'

'It is an insult to Andrei,' Ilya whispered. 'The Crown Prince means to hand our country to the reds.'

'A disaster for our country, 'Christian said, his voice catching, 'My family shall be murdered in their beds.'

'And mine,' Taargin agreed.

'Vladimir, I want to serve a king, not an old man who is failing in health or a boy who is the plaything of the communists,' Christian continued in an earnest whisper. 'Prince Andrei must take the throne, sir. While Stefan is here in England.'

'Andrei attends the king every day, does he not?' Ilya said, his voice as soft as silk running over silk. 'It would only be speeding on the inevitable. Suppose some terrible event overtook the Crown Prince during his visit? There are revolutionaries running amok here – radicals of the type urged on by Nikolai and his ilk. If perhaps an explosion were to, God forbid, kill the Crown Prince, the grief might kill the king. We could turn, in our grief, to Andrei.'

Perhaps it was time, Taargin thought, and a bold stroke by a man like him could remake the world. History taught such things were possible, and at times, necessary. He was ready to meet the hour.

'Prince Andrei will be in Paris next week. I shall speak to him there.'

'We need order, clarity of purpose,' Ilya said. 'A man of will. If terrible choices must be made to ensure that future, what must be done, must be done. No more, and no less. I am confident that Prince Andrei will understand, and shoulder his heavy responsibility if we do our part.'

'I agree,' Taargin replied.

'Give us our orders, sir,' Christian said, but Taargin shook his head.

'Christian, keep me abreast of anything happening at the palace. Ilya, can you find the names of people with the skills required?'

'I shall go through the files at Scotland Yard.'

'Our friend in the north will take care of the rest. Contact has been made with a personage in Highbridge who can supply what is needed. With luck, everything will be in place before this foolish diversion to Highbridge is even announced.' He stood up, his back straight. He felt heady, like a man who has reached a high peak and sees the world laid out before him. 'Good day, gentlemen.'

There was nothing particularly exciting about working in the Metropole, but Sally's attempts to get a job in one of the shops had come to nothing. She told herself to be grateful and tried not to fret over the state of her hands, or let her tiredness show.

Clive still came to the Bricklayers Arms every Friday and Saturday night, was happy with his share of the takings, and was beginning to show some flair, working something of his own into the tunes that often surprised her. It was not like playing with Ruby, but it was a great deal better than playing with George. So she sang, paid for a new patent cure which might help Dougie, and tried not to think about Tom. He'd not been in since the night after Ruby died, and she tried to tell herself that was what she wanted.

Sharps still came every Friday night and left right after her second hour – apart from one night, just before the Search for a Star Pageant was announced. Halfway through the second hour, a man dressed in a narrow waistcoat and flat cap like Sharps' own came in, leant over the table and spoke to him. Sharps left with him at once, without even looking over his shoulder at her.

Sharps was not a sentimental man. Nor a dreamer. He went to see Sally Blow sing because she had something about her which reminded him of his sister, a woman he hadn't seen in twenty years, but still thought of occasionally. Those two hours he spent listening to Sally every week didn't make him a kinder or a better man, but they stirred some memory of being loved in the last leathery embers of his soul, and he had come to value the sensation.

As soon as he was out of the Bricklayers Arms, though, he was free of it. The man who had fetched him out of the bar was a trusted lieutenant. He'd started off as a lad, lifting watches and wallets, till he outgrew that trade. He was brutal when he needed to be, but smart with it. It was a combination both Sharps and Ray Kelly valued.

They turned down the road behind the pub, and Sharps leant against the wall, one boot sole against the brick, under the fuzz of a street lamp, pulled out his knife and cleaned his nails. It helped him think.

'Tell me again, Pockets,' he said. 'Chapter and verse.'

'So our man in the number three shed, Nicky, who's been helping the occasional rifle to a better home—'

'I know him.'

'Well, he saw that greasy lad who works for Mrs Lassiter liberating something else from the stockpile. For a shipment meant to be going to Aldershot.'

Sharps raised an eyebrow. Sharps raising his eyebrow like that was often the last thing a man saw before his lights went out for good, but Pockets held steady.

'Did he now? What exactly did he see taken?'

Pockets handed him a folded scrap of paper. Sharps glanced at it, then put it into the pocket of his waistcoat. 'Good. And what did he do then?'

'Kept an eye on everything going in and out of the factories, and got some eyes on the greasy lad, too. Milner – that's what he's called.'

'And?'

'And then he got word to me, and I've come to see you. So far, those items have not left Highbridge.'

Sharps considered the pavement where the light smudged back into shadow and darkness again, folded his knife and put it back in his pocket.

'See everyone knows we're grateful for their good work,' Sharps growled. 'And get eyes out. Everywhere. And keep a close watch on strangers in the city. Watch the trains. Anything feels askew, I want to know. You hear me?'

'I hear you.'

'Something smells off. I'm going to consult Mr Kelly.'

Then he stalked off into the night, his mind buzzing with dark thoughts like flies round rotting meat.

CHAPTER FIFTY

'What are you singing?' Tom asked the next woman in the queue, a rather alarming female of a certain age, with a hooked nose and rather heavy powder on her yellowish face. They had had all sorts turn up. The news that the Prince of Wales was coming to Highbridge and would be attending the Search for a Star Pageant had meant queues of hopefuls around the theatre for the first of the audition days. Most were not very good, but Grace insisted on listening to a whole song from each of the performers who turned up. She was sitting in the front row of the stalls, her feet up on a pile of sequinned cushions from the props department, with Jack sitting next to her. Tom, who really should have been at the factory, had offered to step in at the piano when Mr Porter looked as if he was about to keel over.

'Oh.' The woman gave a little laugh. 'I'm not performing. My daughter is Baby June Dudley. I'm Mrs Dudley.'

'Oh.'

'It's ridiculous that my daughter – "the little tyke who charmed the Tyne", the papers call her – has to participate in this elimination round. I shall tell my – I mean her – agent, Mr Worton Webster, about it the moment he arrives. No doubt he will read Mrs Treadwell the Riot Act, but for the moment, we must obey our masters, I suppose. You"ll have heard of Baby June?'

Tom made a sort of non-committal noise in his throat and pretended to arrange his music.

'Yes, my daughter has that uncommon combination of talents which make for a real star. She has the voice of an angel, and can dance like an . . .'

'Angel again?' Tom supplied.

'Indeed, there is no other way to describe it. But she also has superb comic timing, and all of that brilliance is wrapped up in such God-given innocence and joy. Though, of course, nowadays recording companies only want to make records which reek of . . .' She leant over confidentially. 'S . . .E . . .X.'

'I'm sure Empire Records could make use of some innocence and joy,' Tom said, trying not to blush, and looked round Mrs Dudley in search of this little paragon. No sign of her. 'And where is Baby June?'

'I would not tire her out queuing!' Mrs Dudley replied tartly. 'She's over there, resting in the stalls.'

Tom peered out over the seats, searching for a little girl. There was none. Only a sulky-looking young woman of at least twenty with her hair in straw-coloured ringlets and a dress covered with pink ruffles.

'And has Baby June been on the stage long?' Tom asked.

'She's fourteen,' Mrs Dudley said crisply. 'Come, June dear!'

Baby June approached slowly down the aisle. She slouched terribly.

'I can't breathe with this thing round my chest,' she grumbled at her mother as she stomped onto the stage.

Mrs Dudley looked round quickly and Tom pretended to be busy with his music again.

'Shush, June! Now, even if this is just a little sing-through, remember – eyes and teeth, eyes and teeth!'

June's heavily powdered face transformed into an odd grimace that Tom supposed was technically a smile, but made him think of an illustration of a vampire.

'Baby June Dudley?' Grace said from the stalls. 'We're ready when you are.'

June thrust a sheet of music at Tom, and he played the opening bars.

'This the sort of tempo?' he asked as Mrs Dudley bustled off stage.

She lisped a couple of lines about being 'Daddy's Little Girl'. Tom went pink. She was in tune, though, and Tom suspected there was a decent voice under there. He looked up at her, noting her mother was at a safe distance.

'Look, you'll not get past Mrs Treadwell with that act. Can you play it for laughs? And sing out properly.'

June's fixed smile was replaced by a spark of genuine interest. She nodded, and Tom gave her the bars again. Her voice, when she came in, became knowing, and a little desperate, and at once the horrible dress and curls became funny. Tom played with pleasure, enjoying the genuine power of the girl's voice without the lisp. When they finished, they turned towards Grace and Jack. Grace raised an eyebrow, but Jack nodded. Another slot on the running order filled, though turning the song onto its comic edge meant it was now positively dripping with S.E.X.

Baby June was the highlight of the afternoon, but Tom stayed to the end. Sally didn't come. Tom told himself that she might be waiting till the following week, and went home feeling heavy and slow.

After the second day of auditions, Grace was happy they had a decent show. She worked on the bench under the window, by the half-light of the long summer evening and the extra illumination cast by their now powerful sign, while Miss Chisholm typed away at her desk. The noise of the keys, Grace found, was strangely soothing.

There was one slot left to fill and two possible acts to choose between, neither of which filled Grace with enthusiasm.

Someone tapped at the door, and as she looked up, Tom and Stella came in.

'Stella, darling! You're back in town. But you know the show isn't till Thursday?'

Stella laughed, and dropped down on the bench next to her.

'Of course I know that. Have you got all your acts yet? Good evening, Miss Chisholm. You're working horribly late.'

Miss Chisholm pulled the page from her typewriter and tucked it into a folder on her immaculate desk. 'Good evening, Miss Stanmore. I'm just off, as it happens. There are a couple of messages on Mr Treadwell's desk,' she said to Grace. 'But nothing urgent.'

She put on her coat and hat and wished them goodnight.

'I have no idea how we ever managed without her,' Grace sighed as Miss Chisholm left. 'I'm just deciding on the last act now. So why are you here, Stella?'

'Oh, signing record sleeves, and recording a couple of new tunes with Dixon. Then I thought I'd pop up to Hope Valley and see the Cooks. If I'm very, very good, do you think Mr Poole will give me guest tickets for them for Thursday?'

Grace ran her hand over her stomach. The baby seemed to like Stella's voice, and squirmed like a delighted eel whenever she was nearby. 'Stella, you're starring in the show. Of course Mr Poole will give you tickets.'

'Did she come today?' Tom asked, coming further into the room.

'Sally Blow?' Grace shook her head. 'I'm sorry, Tom. She didn't.'

He sat down opposite the two women in one of the straight-backed office chairs and glowered at the carpet. 'But she has to,' he said. 'She's brilliant. And she's refusing this chance because of me.'

'Because of her husband, really,' Grace said.

'What's this?' Stella asked.

Grace explained to her about Sally's husband: how she had said the fear of betraying her husband had tainted the idea of being at The Empire.

'It was her saying that which made me determined to have it out with you, Stella.'

Stella leant against the edge of the window, so the light from the sign cast a subtle silver over her. 'So it was because of this Mrs Blow that, instead of living a life of misery, I have a lovely new show, and only have to put up with Mrs Cook teasing me about being jealous of Ruthie occasionally?' Grace nodded. 'Not that I was that jealous – just a very little. Once. Is this Mrs Blow any good?'

'I told you, she's brilliant,' Tom said.

'Yes, but you're obviously in love with her, Tom, so I'm ignoring that.'

Grace laughed, not unkindly. 'I've never heard her sing, but Ruby sent one of her pupils to be her accompanist, and gave her a couple of songs.'

Stella arched an eyebrow. 'Then she has to be in it. Hold your final slot for her.'

'But Stella, if Sally really doesn't want to be on our stage—'

'Not as if you gave *me* any chance in the end. Grace, listen to yourself, do! Ruby gave this woman a song! She didn't do that for just anyone. Please. Let me do this. For you and her, and for Tom, too.'

'Very well,' Grace said. 'I'll hold the slot. She lives at the Bricklayers Arms on Victoria Road. And if you can't get her, you'll simply have to do another solo yourself.'

'I'll endeavour to give satisfaction one way or another,' she said, shaking her curls. The baby twisted joyfully under Grace's heart.

CHAPTER FIFTY-ONE

S ally had seen the advertisements, of course. She read the *Highbridge Gazette*, like everyone else, and most of the pub regulars had mentioned it, too. The day of the first audition she had spent in the park with Dougie, and the second with Noah's parents and his brother in Sheffield. Even after Clive got his share, the tips were healthy enough for her to take a trip every month or so, if she also kept her hours up at the Metropole. Dougie flourished under their fussing. The summer was easier on his chest, but she dreaded winter coming again. She set aside her shillings, promising this time that if it got bad, she would take him to the doctor, no matter the expense.

On Tuesday morning, then, after she finished her hours at the Metropole, she took the tram home and climbed the hill with a feeling of relief. The question of whether she would try out or not was settled. She would not step on that stage. Not feel the weight of Tom watching her. Not when his family had left her boy without a father.

She let herself in at the side door and called out a hello to Belle and Alfred. She had her foot on the bottom stair, thinking of the small tasks and duties she aimed to get done in the rest of her day, when Belle called out.

'Can you come into the saloon for a minute, Sally?'

Her heart froze in her chest. Belle's voice was just like Mrs Parsons' had been when she'd been let go from the grocer's. Did Belle and Alfred have nieces who were after her attic? She was already running numbers in her head, thinking what a room in one of the lodging houses up the road would cost by the time she pushed open the door into the saloon.

Stella Stanmore was sitting on one of the benches facing the bar, a cup of tea on the table in front of her. Belle and Alfred, looking somewhere between starry-eyed and terrified, sat opposite her.

'Look who's come to visit you, Sally!' Belle squeaked and then, without waiting for a reply, got to her feet and scurried out of the room, dragging her husband behind her, and blushing and mumbling as Stella thanked her for the tea.

Sally blinked. She looked a lot healthier than when Sally had seen her at Christmas – much more like the photographs in the magazines – but here she was, in full colour. Her ice-blonde hair was done up with a diamond clip, and her dress was patterned over with large red and black triangles.

'Have we met, Mrs Blow?' Stella asked. 'I think not, but you look familiar.'

Sally stayed where she was. Just looking at Stella made her feel as if she had dirt under her nails, her working dress and blouse suddenly getting shabbier under Stella's gaze.

'I was holding the basin for Mrs Briggs,' Sally said simply. 'The day everyone got sick.'

Stella nodded and waved a hand at the stool. 'Of course. The day I ran away like an awful coward and hid until my friends made me see sense.' She fluttered her eyelashes. 'Won't you sit down?'

Sally found she'd rather stay where she was. 'What are you doing here, Miss Stanmore?'

'I've come to fetch you, Sally. For the Search for a Star Pageant. And do call me Stella.'

'I've done with The Empire, miss. I told them all that weeks and weeks ago.'

Stella sipped her tea. 'Yes, yes, I've heard all that. Grace told me. But I've chosen to ignore it. Did you know I'm going to be one of the judges? And that the Prince of Wales will be attending?'

Sally shifted her weight, then decided she'd sit after all. She'd been cleaning since seven in the morning and the soles of her feet were starting to burn. She set down her bag and basket and settled on the stool.

''Course I've bloody heard! The *Gazette*'s been blaring it every day for a fortnight, and even Belle and Alf are putting up bunting, and he won't be coming anywhere near here.'

'But you aren't interested in performing for the Prince of Wales?'

Sally frowned. 'Prince is neither here nor there. I can't go on that stage. When I think what Noah went through . . .'

She looked down, her voice getting choked, at the lattice shadows across the top of the table.

'He didn't tell you anything about the problems he was having himself, did he?' Stella said softly. 'And he was proud of you, wasn't he?'

Sally felt a bubble of sorrow in her throat. 'He was so young,' she said with a gasp. 'Only twenty! He should be there when I sing, not Tom. It's not fair.'

'No,' Stella said, her eyes clouding. 'You're right about that. He'd want you to sing, though, wouldn't he? And maybe he'd like to see his son raised by a man like Tom Lassiter.'

'That's . . . There's nothing . . .'

Stella waited, but Sally couldn't put the words into a shape.

'Look, Sally, I'm sure you loved Noah very much, and I'm sure The Empire did feel tainted after you found out what happened to him. But isn't there something else? Are you afraid, Sally? You've had to keep your chin up and carry on for all these years since Noah died.'

How did she know to say those words, Sally thought, feeling it like a punch.

'Maybe just making do and having the dream is better than getting this close and not making it? Have you dreamt about it – that moment of being applauded on a stage like that? Are you afraid that failing would be worse than not trying?'

Sally couldn't say anything to that. 'I didn't audition.'

'Ruby Rowntree gave you a song. You don't need to audition.' Stella sighed. 'I did something terrible recently. Not anyone else. Me. And then I found out that most of my suffering was self-inflicted. I've come to believe the dead don't want us to suffer, Sally. Not the ones who cared for us. They're cheering us on.'

Stella reached into her neat leather purse and pulled out a card, then laid it on the table.

Sally read it. 'You are cordially invited to attend the Empire Records Search for a Star Pageant. To be judged by Stella Stanmore, Harold Drabble, Josie Clarence and Lancelot Drake, in the presences of Their Royal Highnesses the Prince of Wales and Crown Prince Stefan of Marakovia.'

Names had been filled in, and Sally recognised Mr Poole's lovely handwriting. Belle, Alfred and Dougie, and Mr and Mrs Blow.

'I'm not on it,' Sally said, looking up.

'No, you'll be backstage waiting for your turn!' Stella said, laughing. 'Bring Noah's parents. The Empire isn't to blame for your husband's death. And I'm quite certain he'd want you to be there. Arrive by five, please.'

CHAPTER FIFTY-TWO

The decision had been made that Nikolai would not attend the dinner with Crown Prince Stefan and the Prince of Wales, and Grace, so near to her due date now, had decided to stay at home with him and Dixon. Tom drove Stella, and Jack drove Lillian in her touring car.

'Will she come tomorrow, Stella?' Tom asked.

'Sally?' Stella asked. 'I hope so.' Then she turned her head and looked out of the car window as the summer evening unrolled over the fields lining the route from Lassiter Court to Joe's palace. 'Agnes tells me Joe's been fretting about the menu all week. Is your mother attending?'

'She is,' Tom said. 'Also a bishop, the mayor and the chairman of the chamber of commerce, so Constance won't even spare us a look.'

Joseph P. Allerdyce greeted them at the door, shining with polish and pride. Joe's sons, the children of his first marriage, were in attendance, and ran Joe's messages and instructions to the kitchen and waiting staff, while Agnes steadied his nerves and made sure he actually enjoyed himself.

The prince, who jogged down the stairs when they were all assembled, reminded Jack of Lancelot Drake, who would arrive tomorrow afternoon to take part in the judging. It was not simply that he was good-looking – though he was, with thick blond hair and a strong jawline – but he had a certain sort of magnetism, a mysterious ability to draw the eye. He accepted the bows and courtesies due to him, then stuck his hands in his pockets, grinned, and flirted outrageously with everyone in the room, from Agnes to Stella, Joe to the bishop.

Crown Prince Stefan, when he made his appearance, was a different kettle of royal fish. He was much younger than Jack had expected – hardly out of his teens – and was dressed in a quasi-military uniform which seemed to swamp him entirely. That number of medals on the chest of a young man whose military experience most likely consisted of sitting on a horse, while soldiers marched around in front of him, was a little much. He had an unfortunately narrow chin, and skin as pale as dirty milk.

The Prince of Wales was standing next to Jack as the Crown Prince descended the curving stairs, flanked by two men with snow-white moustaches, and high collars on their military jackets.

There was no sign of Vladimir Taargin, and Jack did not spot among the entourage any of the other men who had created a fracas at the wedding.

'What's he like, Sir?' Jack asked as they observed Stefan descending.

The prince shrugged. 'The Crown Prince? Oh, pleasant enough. Green, though, and rather unsure of himself. I think his people are hoping he'll pick up a few tips on the whole princeing lark from yours truly. You've heard the king's brother is a bit of a case?'

Jack nodded. 'A little, from Nikolai Kuznetsov, sir.'

'Ah yes, the rabble-rouser. My equerry Osman mentions him a lot. He is my personal expert on all things Marakovian.'

'Every home should have one. Any particular insights, sir?'

The prince chuckled. 'No. In my not uninformed opinion, it will all depend on the magic moment when Stefan becomes king. Some people . . . Well, it sort of settles on them and they flower into it. Others crumble. Too early to know with poor Stefan. I have no doubt he loves his people and country, and takes becoming king very seriously, but he lacks a certain sense of style, and a sense of style is helpful when you have to go around being head of state. I only just persuaded him to stop wearing his sword to dinner.'

'Too militaristic, sir?'

'Too cumbersome. He kept tripping over it, which does not inspire confidence. And he's lonely. Couple of his friends who were supposed to come on this trip were held back at the border. Visa problems. They sent a pair of stiffs who seem to belong to Prince Andrei's camp. Stefan resents them. But "sulky" is not a good look on a royal.'

Jack nodded, watching the Crown Prince being introduced to Constance Lassiter. She performed a deep curtsey which suggested practice. 'And how were your visits today, Sir? Are you enjoying Highbridge?'

'Yes, and I like this house.' He looked around at the white walls, high windows, and carefully placed modern artworks with real pleasure. 'Stefan and I are having a bit of a rest tomorrow, and Joe has offered us the use of his tennis court. I'm also looking forward to your pageant.'

'And today?'

'Good parts and bad. That woman has a rather slippery way about her.'

'Constance Lassiter, you mean?'

He nodded. 'I ummed and aahed my way through a lot of machinery, but then we went to that record place of yours, and that was a great deal more jolly!'

'It's Tom's factory, sir.'

'Oh, yes – smart boy. We were shown the microphones, and Stefan and I both recited poetry into them. They cut a disc of it right there, and before we'd finished our tea and cake we both had a copy to take home.'

'Might we sell that, sir?'

'Ha! Nice try, Treadwell. My most fearsome equerry had them scrape the master before we left. But I can assure you there were some very fetching pictures taken of me listening to records and standing outside with the Empire Records sign in shot. How's that?'

'Very good of you, sir.'

The prince polished off his cocktail. 'Now, how is your wife? I'm sorry not to meet her. I understand she's on the point of having a baby, but will be running the show tomorrow. Is that correct?'

'It is, sir!'

'I'm very well briefed.'

Dinner was excellent, and soon after pudding the Crown Prince thanked his host and retired to bed. His entourage scattered to their quarters, and the majority of the guests offered obeisance to the Prince of Wales and departed with his blessing – including Constance, who, Jack believed, had not spoken to her son all evening. Then Jack thought of Ruby. Tom hadn't lacked for love in the end.

'You don't want to go to bed, do you?' the prince complained. 'I was assured you were theatre folk.'

'Certainly not, sir,' Agnes said. 'A friend of Lillian's has recommended a late evening cocktail called the Second Wind. Shall I have Joe's people whip up a batch?'

'Oh, do, Agnes. And Miss Stanmore, might you entertain us again?'

'I can do that and have a cocktail, thanks to these darling new gramophone records, sir. Joe, dear, will we wake Prince Stefan if we have some music?'

'Doors and carpets thick as castle walls,' Joe replied. 'Play whatever you like.'

The cocktails proved worthy of their name. Half an hour later the Prince of Wales was dancing with Stella, Joe with Agnes, and Lillian with her son. The equerries had to make do with dancing with each other. Everything everybody said seemed terribly witty.

'Is Grace sorry not to come?' Lillian asked. 'It's quite a thing to have a party with the Prince of Wales.'

Jack swung her round. 'She laughed when I suggested it. No, I think she's happier at home. She's been trying to get as much of the new play done as she can before the birth, as well as putting together the show.'

They fell into an easy rhythm, a simple foxtrot that kept them out of the way of the prince's more flamboyant moves.

Jack saw Lillian was looking down and smiling. 'Very well, Lillian, I admit it. You were right about Nikolai, and so was Grace. From what she tells me, he can be terribly critical, but she seems absolutely thrilled about it.'

Lillian shrugged. 'When I was dancing on stage, dear, people telling me what an angel I was felt very nice, but it was nothing to compare with a really great dancer telling me how to improve.'

He nodded. 'He's a great writer. I'm beginning to think you're the lucky one in that marriage.'

She laughed – a deep throaty laugh with her head thrown back. 'Are you happy with the pageant, Jack?'

He nodded. 'We have a nice selection of acts. Stella is insisting on holding a spot for Sally Blow. If she doesn't show, we'll simply give Stella an extra number. Are you looking forward to performing?'

'I am. I have a stunning dress, and Grace has arranged for a group of quite charming schoolchildren to sing the final chorus with us.'

'Excellent. Now all I have to worry about is Harry. I know he and Dixon are in cahoots, but I don't trust him. He comes and squeaks under my desk whenever it's quiet. Does he ever do that to you?'

'No, dear, he knows he won't get a rise out of me.'

'The way you all talk about him is infuriating sometimes. He's a rat!'

'A theatrical rat,' Lillian said.

'And now you're laughing at me!'

'Well, of course I am.'

A whistle sounded shrilly in the darkness outside. They all turned towards the sound, which was coming from the lawns.

'What the . . .?' Joe said. They could hear shouting now, too. 'Agnes, if you'd be so kind.'

Agnes opened a small panel on the wall behind the gramophone and flicked a pair of switches. The lawns between the wide windows

and lake were immediately flooded with light. There were a number of
men outside, indistinct in the distance, but the noises and postures all
suggested violence.

'If you would stay here, Your Highness?' a chestnut-haired equerry said.

'Don't "Your Highness" me, Osman. We're all going.' The prince
picked up his dinner jacket and picked up a lit cigarette from the ashtray
as Joe pushed open the French windows, and the whole party walked
across the neatly trimmed lawn.

It was the Marakovians. One of the older moustachioed ones had the
Crown Prince by the arm and was hectoring him. Two of the younger
ones were holding another man between them. He looked up as they
approached. His hair was dishevelled, and his nose was bleeding.

'Nikolai!' Lillian cried out, kicking off her heels and running towards
him in her stockinged feet.

The other moustachioed man stepped between them.

'Kuznetsov was discovered in an attempt to kidnap Prince Stefan!' he
shouted at her. 'Torn from his bed. Dragged into the woods!'

'Poppycock!' Lillian said.

The man between her and her husband looked alarmed.

'Prince Stefan,' Joe said very slowly, and loudly enough to drown out
further discussion, 'as I'm sure he'll confirm, asked my butler about the
best path to take from the house to the woods. Something about wanting
to hear a nightingale, I understand.'

'And why were we not informed?' the man still holding Prince Stefan's
arm asked.

Joe blinked at him and blew over the glowing end of his cigar before
replying. 'Because the prince is a grown man and can go birdwatching
whenever he bloody chooses.'

'You do seem well wrapped up for someone ripped from their bed,
Stefan,' the Prince of Wales said conversationally. 'Couldn't sleep?'

The Crown Prince hesitated. 'Yes, that's it, David. It is as Mr Allerdyce
said. I thought a little night air, then I ran into cousin Nikolai. My people,

I think, misunderstood the situation. Torstein,' he said, freeing himself from the man who held his arm and speaking with a little more confidence, 'you misunderstood.'

'But this man is trespassing,' Torstein said, pointing at Nikolai.

'Wrong again,' said Joe. 'Nikolai is a friend. As such, he's always welcome here. He was not invited to dinner, as per your instructions, but that does not make him a trespasser.'

'Most certainly not,' Agnes added as Joe blew a stream of smoke into the chilly night air. 'Good evening, Nikolai.'

'Good evening, Agnes, Joe,' Nikolai replied.

'Well, that's all sorted out, then,' the Prince of Wales said, rubbing his hands together. 'Shall we have another drink?'

'I think my husband and I shall return home,' Lillian said. Osman had fetched her shoes from further up the lawn. She stepped into them.

'I'll drive you both, Lillian,' Jack said.

She looked pale, but perfectly composed again in the moonlight.

'Joe, thank you for a wonderful evening. Absolutely superb food,' Lillian told him.

'Very well, but Stella,' the prince said in a tone of appeal, 'you and Tom will stay up with us a little longer, won't you?'

'Of course, sir,' Stella said promptly.

'And you, Stefan,' the prince added kindly. 'If you cannot sleep, perhaps you would like to join us?'

'I'm sure His Highness is exhausted,' Torstein said through gritted teeth as the younger Marakovians released Nikolai. He walked stiffly over to Lillian.

'I . . . I am tired,' Stefan said, then straightened up a little. 'Goodnight, cousin Nikolai. I am glad we had the chance to speak, and I look forward to the performance tomorrow.'

Nikolai looked at him. 'I, too, am glad we had a chance to speak. I wish you well, from the bottom of my heart.'

*

'Stefan was observed leaving the house,' Nikolai explained. He was sitting in the back seat with Lillian and had a handkerchief held to his nose. 'We met as arranged, but we only had a few minutes.'

'I'm just glad you aren't hurt any worse than you are, Nikolai,' Lillian said softly.

'Lillian . . .' His voice became soft, and Jack stared fixedly out of the windscreen at the road in front of him. The night air was full of the scents of summer: ripening hay and dog roses. 'Stefan is young, but he knows these dictatorial impulses of his uncle and his supporters are wrong. He has withstood great pressures from them, in silence, unsupported, isolated.'

'It's good you were able to meet,' Lillian said sincerely. 'It must have made a great difference to him.'

They were within the grounds of Lassiter Court now, the headlights turning the grasses lining the road silvery. 'The king is in poor health,' Nikolai continued with some hesitation. 'Lillian, Stefan asked me if I would be willing to return to Marakovia to act as his advisor when he comes to the throne.'

Jack heard Lillian gasp – a shocked exhalation – as he brought the car to a halt in front of the house and switched off the engine.

'But, Nikolai . . .' Lillian said. 'No! We live here. Jack is here. Grace is about to have a baby.'

'My dearest, I know. Lillian, the first months of Stefan's reign, when it comes, will be busy, and dangerous in Marakovia. I must do as I am asked and assist him, but for some time at least, you should remain here.'

'What? Nikolai, you mean to desert me?'

'Only for as long as I can bear it. I cannot refuse to go. I cannot take you with me.'

'You *married* me,' Lillian exclaimed. 'There were vows, Nikolai!'

'You and I are never parted, Lillian, never,' he said fiercely, taking her hands. 'I shall be your husband, proudly so, every day until my death. But exile is a terrible thing. Let me make my country safe for you, and then let me teach you to love it as I do. We will come back to Highbridge, again and again, for months at a time until your grandchildren wear you out, but I made another vow, when I was eighteen, Lillian. To serve my king, and my prince. Please, do not make me betray it.'

Lillian pulled her hands free, opened the door and slammed it behind her, then marched into the house without saying anything else. Nikolai reached for the handle.

'Wait, Nikolai,' Jack said, and he paused. 'Give her a few moments. You just dropped a bombshell there. Wait for the ringing in her ears to stop before you try and talk to her.'

Nikolai leant back in his seat and sighed. 'Military talk. I forget, sometimes, you served in the Great War, Jack.' Jack said nothing, but just listened to the tick of metal as the engine cooled. 'It is to prevent such things happening again that I must go back.'

Images of the trenches – a sudden wave of compounded horrors – passed in front of Jack's eyes, then faded. 'Do you really think one man has the power to stop that?'

'No, of course not,' Nikolai said with a deep sigh. 'But I must do whatever I can. Stefan will need help negotiating our strange times at home and abroad. He has asked for mine.'

'The Prince of Wales said something about the moment he becomes king being the important one,' Jack said.

'He is probably right. Hopefully that will not be for some time. I hope I reinforced the song of his better angels this evening, but he is terribly alone. We forget sometimes, among our friends, the loneliness of kings.'

In the distance an owl hooted, then the silence gathered around them again. Jack glanced at his watch. 'It's been five minutes. Probably safe to go and talk to Lillian now. Any longer and it will look as if you're avoiding her.' The moon was high in the night sky, and full, shaming the stars. 'You do love her, don't you?'

'With all my heart.'

'I'd lead with that. Then how you'll have her join you as soon as possible, how you'll look forward to the months you'll spend in Highbridge.'

'That is good advice. Thank you, Jack.'

'Get her to forgive you before tomorrow evening. The waltz section of "The Sunrise Song" will not go well if she hasn't.'

Nikolai laughed softly, climbed out of the car and followed his wife. Jack watched him go inside, switched on the engine again, and returned to Joe's mansion.

CHAPTER FIFTY-THREE

Sharps consulted first with Mr Kelly, then steps were taken. Given what they had learnt, they knew the sort of person they were looking for. In the days leading up to the arrival of the Prince of Wales in Highbridge, the members of Kelly's gang quietly ceased their usual activities. Debtors got an accidental day or two of grace. The working girls found they could set their own hours, and keep more of what they earned. Young men of means looking for a chance to gamble illegally looked in vain. Instead, the web of Kelly's workers became a web of watchers.

They found the man they were looking for on the day of the pageant, heading quietly for the station in the thin hours of the early morning. He was intercepted, and Sharps himself drove him up to the Dales cottage where Ray Kelly, the spider at the centre of it all, was waiting.

Sharps developed a certain grudging professional respect for the man over the course of that long day. It was late before he gave up the information Ray was asking for. Sharps sent two of his people to lay the man in his final resting place, and carried the information back into Highbridge himself.

*

Tom could not stop himself. The acts who were to perform had to arrive at the theatre by five, and when Sally hadn't arrived by four, he went down to wait at the stage door. The weather was warm – a little too warm for comfort – and the air heavy.

Stella seemed supremely confident Sally would come, but the passing minutes were an agony for Tom. The town clock struck the quarter, then the half-hour, and he began to feel a crushing sensation in his chest which meant the end of hope. He didn't care about the pageant, not in this moment, but if Sally did not come tonight, any chance of her looking at him favourably as a suitor would be done with. The decision was one and the same to her. It was certainly possible she would do the show, and then turn him down flat, but if she came, he would at least be able to hope.

He heard footsteps and looked up, but the silhouette at the gate was of a boy, not a woman. It took him a moment to recognise Clive, his accordion case over his arm, and he felt himself stand, lifted to his feet with hope.

And there she was, walking into the yard in her long grey coat with her bag over her arm.

'Tom!' she said as she spotted him. 'What are you doing here among the bins? Clive, you go in, let Mrs Treadwell and Miss Stanmore know we've come.'

Clive trotted past Tom with a wink, but he didn't notice; he was too amazed by the fact that the rough yard, with its summer weeds softening the edges, its bare brick walls with a handkerchief of blue sky visible above the slate roofs, had been transformed into a romantic fairyland by the presence of Sally Blow.

'I was waiting for you, of course.'

She came towards him. 'I almost didn't come, even after Miss Stanmore turned up at the pub. But guess what she did?'

'What?' Tom said, and without thinking quite what he was doing, he took her hand. She allowed it.

'She only sent Lancelot Drake to see Noah's parents. He told them the whole story, and drove them to Highbridge. Said to come and collect me and get me here, and that's just what they did. Now, how do you think Stella knew to do that?'

'I don't know. She's had a strange time this year. I've always thought she was terribly wise, but I think it's made her wiser.'

Sally looked suddenly serious. 'Tom, they're talking about you at the pub.'

His mouth went dry. 'And what are they saying?'

'That you're a good boss. That you work as hard as they do and the pay is decent.'

'I want to be like my grandfather,' he replied with a sigh of relief. Then he grinned, struck by a very pleasing thought. 'He married a singer, you know.'

He was still holding her hand and risked squeezing it, very gently, as he spoke. She looked a bit shocked, then pink.

'He married Lillian Lyons, you daft thing. She was a star already. I mop floors.'

'But I know you're a star, Sally.'

She blinked a couple of times, then glanced at the stage door. 'Well, Stella has landed me in it now, hasn't she? What am I to do? This frock is all wrinkled from the dresser, and Clive knows the song, of course, but—'

'The band has the music,' Tom blurted out, still astonished by the miracle of her hand in his. 'Ruby's arrangement. And Milly will run an iron over your dress. You've plenty of time, you're on after Stella in the second half.'

She withdrew her hand finally. 'You never! Tom, what are you and Mrs Treadwell trying to do to me, putting me on after her?'

'It's the right place for you,' Tom said, mourning the loss of the hand, but sure of his ground as far as the billing went. 'And for the song. You can carry it, Sally, you know you can.'

'In the pub, maybe . . .'

'Just be yourself, Sally.'

She looked unsure, then flashed him a quick grin. 'Fine. Well – here goes nothing. I can't believe Lancelot Drake fetched Mr and Mrs Blow. I saw him, the night that the theatre opened again after the fire. He gave me the rose out of his lapel before he went in.'

Tom felt a lightness shivering through his bones. 'You are chosen for greatness, Sally Blow.'

'I suppose we'll see,' she said. Then she lifted her chin and opened the stage door.

'And I love you very much,' he added as the door swung to behind her.

Sir Gideon received the telegram in the late afternoon, and his first call was to the Royal Air Force. His second was to the Marakovian embassy.

'No, I will not wait until tomorrow and I will go in person. This is not the sort of news one delivers over a crackling phone line. Taargin can come or not as he sees fit, but I have an aircraft standing by and I will make use of it. We will call at the embassy on the way.'

The show would begin at half past seven. Sally, once she'd been greeted by a beaming Grace, was ushered into a large dressing room normally shared by the chorus, and was introduced to the other acts. There were half a dozen of them, including her. Milly ironed her dress, and Ollie toured the room, allowing all those who wished it to scratch his ears for luck, before trotting back to the stage door and his basket.

Ruben, the stagehand, told them the audience was due to be let in, and the receiving line arranged for the princes. The applause in the auditorium when the princes appeared in the royal box, they heard for themselves. Sally began to feel a bit sick.

'Here.' Baby June thrust a powder compact at her. 'Put some of that on or you'll look like death out there.'

'Thank you,' Sally said, taking it. Her face looked very pale and ordinary in the mirror. She stole a look sideways at June, who had heavy blue eyeshadow and eyelashes that looked like they were made of paper. Baby June pulled a cigarette case from her little wicker basket and started smoking.

'Sorry about Mother fussing,' she sighed. 'She gets anxious.'

Mrs Dudley had spent the hours between their arrival and now in a twitter of nerves. She had been exhaling loudly and at random intervals, muttering to herself about lighting cues, and starting up so often and so suddenly from her seat with some vital thought she needed to share, all of the pageant competitors had begun to look strained.

'Where is she?' Sally asked.

The powder did help a bit. She pinched her cheeks to put some colour into them and handed the compact back to June. She dropped it in her basket.

'Oh, with our agent, Worton Webster, in the audience. They had to be in their seats before the princes came in.' She blew out a long stream of smoke and for a moment her painted face showed something like real distress. 'They're evil, both of them.'

'What, your mother and your agent?' June nodded. 'Oh, love, I'm sorry to hear that. Don't you like being on the stage?'

June looked at her. 'I did, when I was little. Then my dad left. He set up with the grocer's widow down our street and Mother went a bit mad after that. I've got two little brothers at home. All this. . .' she pointed at her outfit, 'pays for their schooling.'

'They must be done with school soon!' Sally covered her mouth. 'Oh, sorry . . .'

June chuckled. 'Youngest is doing engineering. He's graduating end of this year and marrying a nice girl from our village. Second they're hitched, I'm leaving all this and me and her are going to set up a little business.'

'That sounds lovely. What business is that?'

June leant in close to her, whispering, her pink lips almost brushing Sally's ears. 'Grocer's!'

Sally giggled again. 'But won't you miss performing?'

June shrugged. 'I will. But the last few years – skipping around in frills and grinning for the old men? No. I shan't miss that. And Mother will never let me act my real age. It'd remind her she won't see fifty again. Most fun I've had this year was when that piano player got me to play it for laughs at the audition. Handsome fella.' Sally guessed she meant Tom, and found herself blushing, but Baby June was looking off into the distance. 'Maybe I should play it like that this evening.'

'Of course you should! Sounds like the sort of thing Harold Drabble would like, and he's a judge.'

Baby June tilted her head to one side and fluttered her eyelashes. 'Ooh, where's my tiffin?'

Sally almost choked laughing that time.

'Beginners, please . . .' Grace, clipboard in hand, called from the far corner of the room.

'When are you on?' Sally asked.

'Middle of the first half,' June replied. 'You?'

'After Stella in the second.'

'Oh, poor you, following Stella Stanmore!' June said, grinding out her cigarette with her heel.

Sally's slight feeling of sickness intensified as the opening bars of the first number, a Lancelot Drake and Stella Stanmore duet, drifted from the stage.

CHAPTER FIFTY-FOUR

'Three minutes, June!' Grace called out.

From what Sally could hear, the show was going well: lots of applause, some boos and cheers as the judges gave their opinions of the first act, and a lot of laughter.

'Break a leg,' June said to Sally over her shoulder, then skipped off towards the wings. Grace and Sally watched her go. Then Grace grimaced and leant suddenly against the wall. 'Mrs Treadwell?' Sally went over to her, shielding her from the view of the rest of the room. 'Are you ill?'

Grace said nothing for a minute. A bead of sweat appeared at her hairline and she'd gone very pale. 'I can't be having the baby now!' she hissed. 'It's not due for three weeks.'

'My Dougie was early,' Sally said, putting an arm round Grace's waist. 'I think they make up their own minds about this sort of thing, without consulting our plans.'

'But I've got the show to run!' Grace said, her voice even again as the worst of the contraction subsided. 'It could be hours, couldn't it?'

'It could, or it might be a lot quicker than that. Are any of the dressing rooms free?'

'Number four,' Grace said.

'Let's get you there, then. Shall I send for Mr Treadwell?'

'No, wait for the interval. It'll cause a fuss.'

With Grace leaning against Sally, they went slowly down the corridor. Baby June's music became louder as they got closer to the stage. She was obviously doing the comic version and waves of laughter followed the music. Tom was watching from the wings, his arms folded, and he was smiling. Sally's heart squeezed a little at the sight of him caught in that soft glow of light.

'Tom,' she hissed. He turned and his eyebrows shot up, then he walked down the corridor towards them. 'Sally? Grace, what's happening?'

Grace thrust the clipboard into his hands.

'You . . . run . . . show. Get . . . Lillian, Stella and Jack . . . at . . . interval.'

'Dressing room four,' Sally added, leaving him looking slightly stunned.

Baby June's act ended with a crash on the cymbals as she dropped into the splits, showing up her voluminous bloomers and with her hands under her chin. The audience cheered her and Stella came out from behind the judging table to kiss her on both cheeks.

Tom swallowed and looked at the sheet. Two minutes of comments from the judges, then Harold would close the first act. Well, he was on stage already, so didn't need fetching. Then Tom cursed under his breath. He would need to bring up the house lights from this side of the stage, but Stella would be exiting stage right, and probably heading straight to the royal retiring room to spend the interval with the aristocrats. He looked around.

'Miss Chisholm,' he hissed, seeing her moving quietly between the flats. He thought for one minute she was going to ignore him, but he beckoned vigorously and she walked quietly round the back of the stage to join him.

'Take position stage right, please,' he said, 'and the second she comes off stage, send Stella to dressing room four.'

'But—'

'Please, Miss Chisholm,'

She blinked. 'Yes, of course, Mr Lassiter.'

'Then go and fetch Jack from the royal retiring room.'

He must have conveyed something of the urgency of the situation, as Miss Chisholm was a little white around the lips.

Stella sat back from the judging table, which was elevated stage left, where Lancelot Drake was also sitting. Harold descended down the short light-bulb-lined stairs that Little Sam had built for them.

'Good evening, Highbridge,' he said, lifting his arms above his head, and the crowd cheered him, then he turned towards the royal box. 'And a special good evening to our right royal friends. Comfy up there?'

The Prince of Wales cupped his hands to his mouth, as Ruben swung the softer spot on to the box. 'Very! Harold, where's your tiffin?'

The theatre exploded into laughter. Stella leant in towards Lance, a delighted smile directed at the crowd. 'Why are they laughing, Lance?'

'The ineffable mystery of royalty, my darling,' he replied, applauding. 'Though the Prince of Wales is rather a peach.'

'You mean my new friend, David?' Stella replied, fluttering her eyelashes.

'Be a good girl, Stella. You're too young for him, anyway. My understanding is he likes older women. Talking of which, I think Baby June is the hot favourite after that turn.'

'Just you wait, Lance.'

'You really think Mrs Blow is that good?'

'I wouldn't have made you drive via Sheffield if I didn't.'

'It was rather fun. Mr Blow and I talked fishing.' He folded his arms and sat back, ready to enjoy the rest of Harold's act.

Grace breathed in through her nose and out through her mouth. Sally held her hand and talked pleasant nonsense about her son Dougie to distract her. He sounded like a nice boy, but it was not quite enough to mitigate the effects of labour.

The spasm passed, just in time for Stella and Lillian to arrive.

'Sally!' Stella exclaimed. 'What on earth are you doing here?'

'Helping me,' Grace said. 'I'm afraid my baby is making an early entrance.'

Jack tumbled into the room and dropped down to his knees. 'Grace, I'll take you to hospital at once.'

'Don't you dare,' Grace gasped. 'This could take hours. You're hosting royalty, Jack.'

Sally squeezed her shoulder. 'It's a crowd in here now, I'll leave you to it, Mrs Treadwell. Good luck.'

'Thank you, Sally,' Grace said, briefly covering her fingers with her own. 'Break a leg.'

'What about Mrs Cook?' Stella said. 'She's a midwife, and she and her husband are here as my guests.'

'Would Mr Poole know them?' Sally asked.

'Yes,' Stella replied. 'I introduced them to him.'

'Then I'll go and fetch them,' Sally said.

'Shouldn't I go?' Lillian said. 'Sally, you should be preparing for your number.'

'I'm prepared,' she said, 'and I think you'd draw a bit of attention, Mrs Kuznetsov, particularly in that dress.'

Lillian glanced down at the close-fitting gold sheath she was wearing. 'You may be right, Sally, thank you.'

'Bugger royalty!' Jack said. 'Are you sure a doctor and a hospital aren't the thing?'

Grace thought briefly of the grey-faced doctor whose lugubrious manner had made her rather dread any encounter with him during her pregnancy. 'No, I want Mrs Cook, and please hurry!'

Another wave of pain shot through her. It felt as if something was trying to tear her bones apart.

Sally headed out.

'Lillian, do go and be charming to the royal party,' Jack said, still holding on to Grace's hand tightly.

'Yes, please do, Lillian!' Grace said. 'Tom will handle everyone backstage.'

'If you are sure,' Lillian said, hesitating on the threshold; then, as Grace gave her a determined nod, she left.

'Grace, what on earth should I do?' Stella asked.

'Never marry!' Grace said through gritted teeth. The spasm passed, and she began to breathe a little more easily. 'Water, please, Stella.'

Stella fetched a glass and Jack held it to Grace's lips. In what seemed like a few minutes – and an age – someone knocked softly at the door.

'Stella? You there?'

'In here, Mrs Cook!' Stella called out. Tasha Kingsland's mother tentatively opened the door. She took one look at them and became very practical.

'I said round August, didn't I? Bit early, but never mind. Now, Mr Treadwell, dear, that nice man who made tea at the stage door? Will you get him to get the kettle on?' She picked up a couple of clean towels from the back of a chair. 'Off you pop, Mr Treadwell. A "Do Not Disturb" sign on the door might be a good idea. And have them leave the hot water outside and knock when it's ready. A basin would be useful, too.'

'Should I stay?' Stella asked as Jack kissed his wife, then left to follow orders.

'Oh, no,' Mrs Cook said, shaking her head, 'you don't want to see this!'

Stella hightailed it out of the room as quickly as Jack had done.

'Why? What can't she see?' Grace said, suddenly afraid. 'What on earth is going to happen?'

Mrs Cook patted her hand in a very reassuring manner. 'Nothing that hasn't happened millions of times before, my love. Now let's see where you're at.'

*

Tom saw the comings and goings from his spot in the wings. He glanced at his watch and rang the five-minute bell just as Jack emerged, looking profoundly baffled, from the number four dressing room.

'How is Grace?' Tom asked.

'Having a baby,' Jack replied. 'It looks awful.'

'Mr Lassiter?' Tom turned to see Danny coming up the corridor towards him. 'There's a man at the stage door asking to see you.'

'Danny, I can't possibly—'

'Danny!' Jack interrupted Tom. 'Grace is having the baby. Hot water to dressing room four.'

'Of course, Mr Treadwell. Mr Lassiter, I really think you'd better come.'

Tom thrust the clipboard into Jack's hands. 'Here, Jack, keep yourself occupied. Stella is introducing the fisherman with the voice of Caruso on curtain up.'

Then he turned and followed Danny.

CHAPTER FIFTY-FIVE

Sharps was leaning up against the wall at the entrance to the yard, paring his nails with a long knife. The yard did not look like a fairytale bower anymore.

'I know you,' Tom said as he left the stage door and approached cautiously. 'You're Kelly's man, who comes to hear Sally sing.'

Sharps straightened up and returned his knife to the pocket of his waistcoat.

'I am. Is it true she's singing here tonight, in your show?'

'She is.'

Sharps sniffed. 'You're soft on her, aren't you?'

Tom wondered – briefly – about lying, but some instinct told him the best way to survive an encounter with a man like Sharps was to be honest.

'I am. Very.' Sharps nodded, but offered no further comment. 'Is that why you asked for me? To talk about Sally?'

Sharps shook his head. 'No, I'm here to tell you you've got a bomb on the premises.'

Jack was clutching the clipboard so hard, he suspected he'd carry the scar of it for days. The fisherman was on stage now, head back, arms out, filling the auditorium with his powerful baritone. From where he stood, Jack could see the royal box. The Prince of Wales and Crown Prince Stefan were at the front, both watching with pleasant smiles on their faces as the fisherman's song swelled to a climax.

Jack risked a glance over his shoulder in the direction of dressing room four. He was not a religious man, but he began to pray anyway.

'What in God's name do you mean, a bomb? Are you blackmailing us?'

'We are not. I've had information certain items have gone missing from Lassiter shed number three, where your mother cooks up military items. A pair of shells, to be exact. I've spent the day in conversation with a gentleman, not part of our organisation, who we discovered in town, and he might make use of such things.'

'And he just told you he'd planted a bomb?'

Sharps raised an eyebrow and Tom blushed. He wondered, feeling suddenly a little ill, what Sharps had been cleaning out of his nails.

'Mr Kelly has his faults, but he's fond of the royal family.' Sharps shrugged. 'Wouldn't have bothered stopping anyone just trying to shoot that Marakovian, but there's limits.'

'Do you know where it is? We must evacuate.'

'Under the royal box. And it's too late for that. It's on an electrical switch. If whoever paid for it to be put in there sees you evacuating, they'll flick it and . . . *boom*. Got to do it quiet, like.'

'Was it . . .? Mr Sharps, is my mother behind this?'

He sniffed. 'Someone asked her for a pair of shells, Lassiter, and she handed them over quick, like, and without consulting us. What the person who bought them from Mrs Lassiter told her, I couldn't say.'

'What a pair of lungs!' Harold declared. 'Though, I must say, I'd wanted a song that was a wee bit saltier.'

The audience laughed.

'He can cast his nets in my direction any day!' Josie said. 'But we have two more acts for you. First, a husband and wife duet, and after them, our very own Stella Stanmore will be performing her hit from one of her early successes, some years ago – *Riviera Nights*—'

'Cat,' Stella said, keeping the smile on her face, while Lance snorted with laughter.

'Then our last contender! Mrs Sally Blow.'

As the violinist and his wife entered to warm applause, Tom grabbed Jack's arm, pulled him further into the darkness of the wings, and told him what he'd just heard from Sharps.

'Might it be another trick of your mother's?' Jack asked. 'Have us evacuate the theatre in the middle of a performance attended by the Prince of Wales? It would dwarf the rest of the mischief she's achieved.'

'No, Jack. I honestly believe this is real.'

Jack reached for the fire alarm, but Tom shot out a hand and gripped his wrist. 'Stop, Jack, it's on a switch. Any sign of an evacuation and it will be triggered at once. We need to deal with it in secret.'

Jack swallowed and breathed in slowly.

'Who arranged this, Tom? Who got the shells from your mother and planted them here?'

'I didn't stop to ask,' Tom admitted.

'Understood. Get up to the follow spot, Tom. Tell Ruben to keep as much light as possible off the royal box and I'll go in myself. Stella's on next, so most of the audience will be looking at her. Have you seen Dixon? I'd give my right arm for someone who really understands wiring at this moment.'

'Not since the interval. Mr Poole waylaid him as we were about to come back in.'

'We'll have to rely on what I can remember of basic training, then. Now go. Send Danny up here to run the show till I'm done.' Tom turned away. 'Tom! If something goes wrong, if I don't make it . . .' Jack looked towards dressing room four.

'I'll look after them, Jack.'

Jack walked up the staircase as casually as he could: just a theatre manager keeping an eye on things during a very important performance. He approached the door to the royal box and rested his fingers on it for a moment, then turned the handle. He slipped through the door and crouched down, just behind the chairs in which the Crown Prince and the Prince of Wales were sitting, amid a crowd of equerries and exactly over the spot he believed the bomb to be.

'Good evening, Your Highnesses, gentlemen. Please keep your attention on the stage, and try not to react to what I'm about to say. A man has just turned up at the theatre with a warning a bomb has been planted under your feet.'

There was a moment of silence, and the prince asked in a quiet drawl, 'What manner of man? Is it likely to be a prank?'

'A known criminal, sir. Who has a patriotic streak. Perhaps while the lights are directed away from you, we could ask you to step out?'

'Did the gentleman say the bomb is on a switch, or a timer?'

'A switch, sir.'

The prince gave a quick shake of his head. 'Even if Stefan and I made it out before it was blown, there would be casualties.'

'That is a possibility, sir.'

'Army man, aren't you, Treadwell?'

'Yes, sir.'

'Then find it and disarm it, while Stefan and I stay exactly where we are at the front of the box and enjoy Miss Stanmore's performance.'

Jack could see the beads of sweat starting out on Stefan's collar. The Prince of Wales slung his arm casually around the back of his chair.

'Calmly does it, Stefan,' the prince said. 'Let Treadwell do what he's doing and concentrate on this lovely girl. Did you meet her at dinner yesterday?'

'I need room to open the trapdoor,' Jack said.

One of the Prince of Wales's party slid quietly off his chair and knelt by Jack. 'I'm Osman, and an army man, too,' he said in a whisper. 'Torstein, if you and the others could leave as discreetly as possible . . . I'll assist you, Treadwell.'

'Enchanted,' Jack said between gritted teeth, 'but the rest of you – hop it.'

'That's hop it by royal command,' the prince added.

Opening the door as little as possible, the royal entourage – all bar Osman – slipped silently into the corridor.

Jack's muscles contracted. He rolled back the carpet and gently lifted the trapdoor. The Prince of Wales moved his chair closer to Stefan and leant forward, trying to give Jack cover.

It was real. Horribly, unquestionably real. Jack found himself staring at a pair of metal cylinders with wires spiralling down into the darkness from a firing cap fitted into the snub nose of one cylinder.

'Anything interesting?' the prince asked.

'A pair of shells, sir.'

Jack closed his fingers around the wires.

'Steady, even pressure,' Osman said, taking off his jacket and laying it on the floor. 'Pull the wires out and hand the shells to me, and don't let the exposed ends touch as they come free. That's important.'

'All going well, Treadwell?' the prince asked. 'Because I'm pretty sure we should be dead by now.'

'Just one moment, sir.'

Jack pulled, very gently. As he felt the sucking resistance, he wondered, vaguely, if the theme to *Riviera Nights* Stella was singing on stage would be the last song he heard on Earth. He wished his wife and child a blessed life. Then pulled a little harder.

The wires popped out and Jack caught them in the palm of his hand, his fingers separating the wires, then set them down carefully, back in the hole, away from the shells.

The song, and life with it, carried on.

Jack lifted the first of the shells out, passing it sideways to Osman, who placed it onto his coat, then the second.

'Clear,' Jack murmured. The Crown Prince seemed to slump a little.

'Good show,' the prince said clearly.

'Why *aren't* we dead, Treadwell?' Osman whispered. 'Miss Stanmore is an excellent singer, but anyone who cared to look this way must have seen there was something up. Why didn't they blow it?'

Jack peered into the void. Moving the shells had dislodged the wires a little. Just beyond where they had disappeared into the darkness, they had been gnawed through.

'Harry,' Jack said very softly.

'What's that?' the prince asked out of the side of his mouth.

'The wires, sir. They've been chewed through. Possibly by a rat who likes to torment me, but appears to have his tiny heart in the right place.'

'A royalist rat and a patriotic hoodlum on the same night? How utterly marvellous. May we return to enjoying your excellent show again, Treadwell?'

'Please do,' Jack replied. He stood up and Osman passed him the shells, wrapped in his jacket. 'I'll lock these in the safe in my office.'

'I'm happy to watch the rest of the show in my shirtsleeves,' Osman replied, quietly retaking his seat. Jack cradled the shells very carefully in his arms, then looked towards the follow spot, from where, he was quite sure, Tom would be watching in an agony of fear, and gave a thumbs up.

When Ruben's spotlight swung up to highlight their enthusiastic applause for Stella, the royal box was packed with equerries and uniforms and royalty, just as it should be.

Jack carried the shells into his office and placed them in the safe, closing the heavy door on them and spinning the dials, then walked out into the corridor again. He tried to lean against the wall, but his legs went out from under him, and he found himself sitting untidily at the top of the stairs.

Mr Poole appeared at the bottom of the flight and jogged up a few steps. 'What on earth is happening, Mr Treadwell?'

Jack held up his hand and lifted his head. 'Mr Poole, I will tell you all, but not now. Would you do me a very great favour? Could you check how Grace is?'

'I only saw her a moment ago. Mrs Cook says she's doing nicely. We have visitors. The Marakovian ambassador has turned up with a bloke from the Foreign Office, Sir Gideon Wells! He's Dixon's father. They flew up from London in an aeroplane and you'll never believe it, but from what I overheard . . .' Mr Poole looked at Jack – his exhaustion and pallor – and decided not to add to it immediately. 'I shall enquire backstage. And our new guests are in the shop. They'd like to see the princes as soon as the show ends.'

CHAPTER FIFTY-SIX

Tom made it back down to the wings in time to take the clipboard from Danny as Stella's final verse began, and went to fetch Sally. He walked down the east corridor to the large dressing room and there she was, sitting next to Baby June, the star of the first half, with Clive. He was in shirtsleeves, but someone had run a comb through his hair and managed to get his face clean.

'Sally?'

'Break a leg,' said Baby June, blowing smoke into the air.

'Thanks,' Sally said, standing up. She seemed, Tom thought, reasonably calm, just that slight shimmer coming off her he'd got used to sensing in some performers. Not nerves so much as anticipation – a readiness, like a greyhound in the traps.

Clive went ahead of them, his accordion over his shoulder. Tom breathed slowly and his heart began to slow to something like its usual rhythm.

'Sally,' he said, pausing in the shadows, just beyond the reach of the light washing from the stage. 'I'm so very glad you came.'

She looked at him. A quick smile. 'I am, too, I think. I hear you've let the men at your factory form a union.'

Alive. Better make use of the days, then.

'The women, too. And . . .' The idea became clear in his head even as he spoke. 'And I'm going to take over the whole thing, you know. Lassiter Enterprises. No more Ray Kelly, no more starvation wages. Everyone who works for us will be able to unionise if they want.'

She studied him in the half-light. 'I'm glad to hear that, Tom. It will be a better place, Highbridge, if you take charge. I'm proud of you.'

On stage, Stella was talking to the crowd, '. . . and now here is a singer I know you've all been waiting to hear from. Yes, I went to the Bricklayers Arms to fetch her myself!'

'Proud enough to marry me?' Tom asked.

Sally gasped. 'Oh, Tom . . .' Her eyes glistened. 'I don't—'

'Tell me when you've won,' he said, and took a half step back as Stella finished the introduction.

'Yes, Your Royal Highnesses, my lords, ladies and gentlemen, please welcome, with Clive Goodwin on the squeezebox, it's the Rose of Highbridge, Sally Blow!'

Lillian appeared at his shoulder. 'Everything all right, Tom?'

'Yes. Someone planted a bomb in the royal box, but Jack defused it. But I think now everything is going to be perfect.'

'I . . .? What . . .?' Lillian steadied herself against the wall. 'Jack defused a bomb? Good God, who planted it?'

'Lillian, I'm going to worry about that in a few minutes' time, but for now, I'm going to watch Sally Blow set the world on fire.'

The applause carried Sally out of the wings. As Stella returned upstage to her seat next to Lancelot Drake, the lights dimmed, leaving her and Clive in a single golden beam. The little motes of dust sparkled in the air in front of her.

This was not like the pub.

She had a sense of the crowd, the great breathing mass of them, but beyond the first row, she couldn't see any faces. She didn't need to see much more than that row, though. There was Dougie, his cheeks pink and his eyes shining, sitting between Belle and Alfred. Belle was holding his hand. And next to her, Mr and Mrs Blow, who looked as excited as Dougie. The applause died down, and somewhere in the depths of the theatre someone coughed.

'She did come and fetch me – Miss Stella, I mean,' Sally said. 'Alfred the landlord – he's sitting down there – almost had a heart attack when she walked into the saloon bar.'

A warm ripple of laughter ran through the auditorium.

She shielded her eyes and turned towards the judges. 'How did you know about that Rose of Highbridge thing, Miss Stella?'

'Belle told me!' Stella called back.

'That's Alf's wife,' she said. 'I should have known.' Then she felt it: the audience settling, coming towards her, all attention. 'Belle and Alf are both here tonight, with my little boy Dougie, and my late husband's mum and dad. My dress all right, Dougie? 'she asked.

'It's not crinkly!' Dougie shouted, which got another laugh.

'Oh, thank you. A nice girl backstage ironed it for me. I had to stand there in my smalls while she did it. But the print's nice, isn't it? End of the line from Fenwick's.'

And she was ready.

'Now, Miss Ruby Rowntree did the arrangement of this song for me and Clive here. It's a sad one, so get your handkerchieves out.'

Jack still had his head in his hands. The door to the royal circle opened a little way along the corridor, and Agnes peered out.

'Jack,' she hissed, 'what are you doing lounging about? Do come in a moment! That girl Sally's on the stage. You have to see it.'

He pulled himself to his feet, and followed her in.

'Come on then, Clive,' Sally said, nodding to the boy. 'Let's give them the song.'

Clive pulled on the accordion, and the long rasp of it seemed to ease its way through the whole theatre, running up the aisles and climbing like a tendril up the gilded columns and over the curve of the roof, nestling among the crystals of the chandelier, and making them hum.

When I feel the cold, when the mist
runs down the hills, the ghost of Johnny D

She began over the steady, open drone of the accordion. The silence was absolute.

'My God, she can hold them,' whispered Jack.

His body still felt the weight of the shells in his arms, but somehow, as Sally sang, nothing else mattered. He knew Grace was all right. He knew the prince was safe, and for the next few minutes he was in the place he should be. There was magnetism, and an ease of being around Sally which made him feel as if he was part of the song, just like she was – that he, her, the music and that slow melody, with the accordion just rippling behind it, were all part of one whole.

Then she glanced down into the pit and the orchestra came in and Jack thought his heart might explode in his chest as she put up her arms and began the chorus.

Oh what use your fairy gold,
what use grape and grain,
when my chance to have a heart that's full
can never come again?

Grace squeezed Lillian's hand while she passed on some garbled version of events she had had from Tom.

'Who would do such a thing?' Grace panted.

'Not long now, Grace, you're doing well,' Mrs Cook said. 'Perhaps we could save the bomb talk till afterwards? It's like trying to deliver a baby in Piccadilly Circus in here.'

'Of course, Mrs Cook,' Lillian said calmly. 'These fascists who don't want a new king with Nikolai advising him, I imagine.'

'But how?' Grace said, gritting her teeth. 'They would need access to The Empire! They would need to know every nook and cranny.'

Lillian fetched a cushion and tucked it under Grace's head.

'Darling, I know you're fond of him, but do you think . . . perhaps Dixon? He arrived after Nikolai, and knows that impossible language—'

'No, it can't be, Lillian. How could it?'

Lillian hesitated. 'Dixon's father is not a good man.'

'When did *you* meet him? Mr Poole said he'd only just arrived.'

Lillian's world swam suddenly in front of her eyes.

'Dixon's father is here?' Lillian said.

'Yes, he came with news . . .'

Another spasm shook Grace into silence.

'Lillian,' Grace said through gritted teeth as it passed. 'Go, you're due on stage any minute!'

Tom appeared at the doorway, and peered round carefully. 'Lillian? They're about to play your introduction.'

'Tom, how . . . did . . . Sally do?' Grace said, panting between words.

'Piccadilly Circus,' Mrs Cook muttered.

'Wonderful,' Tom said simply. 'The judges are lavishing her with praise right now. It's a triumph, Grace.'

'Goodgoawaynowbothofyou,' Grace hissed and Mrs Cook ushered them both out of the room.

Tom led Lillian towards the stage.

'Sally was incredible, Lillian. I've never seen anything like it. How's Grace?'

'Mrs Cook is looking after her. She said something about Sir Gideon Wells being here?'

'Yes!' Tom saw her face and frowned. 'Do you know him? It turns out he's Dixon's father. The one who threatened the poor chap with asylums and caused him to run away in the first place. He's with the Foreign Office. He and a Marakovian with a fearsome moustache are in the record shop, apparently. Flew up from London. Mr Poole says the King of Marakovia is dead. Presumably they'll have to get Stefan back . . . Lillian, are you all right?'

The children who would join Nikolai and Lillian for the final chorus were gathered, wide-eyed and overexcited around her husband and Mabel Mills in the wings. Nikolai looked around at her and smiled.

'Does Nikolai know about the king?' she asked.

Tom looked suddenly aghast. 'No, I haven't said . . . Should I? Lillian, I'm so sorry. Can we go on?'

She looked down, smoothing the heavy gold lamé of her dress.

Her grandchild was being born, her son had just narrowly escaped a bomb, and somewhere in the theatre, whoever had planned to blow them up was wondering at the failure of their plans. Grace was right: whoever had placed it there must know the theatre well, and she had believed they were all friends, all family here. And the King of Marakovia was dead. That meant her husband – her romantic, brilliant, dashing husband – would be leaving her to steer that country through dangerous waters. And Colonel Sir Gideon Wells was here. She could not be sure, she told herself, but those fragments of her attacker – and of Jack – she'd seen in Dixon, and the rumours Agnes's network had offered up, made her think it was very likely he was the man who had forced himself on her when she herself was hardly more than a child.

Can I go on? Out of the corner of her eye she saw the picture of her, Jack, Grace and Agnes outside the rebuilt theatre, and made her decision.

I am Lillian Kuznetsov, wife of His Excellency, Grand Duke Nikolai Goranovich Kuznetsov, I am Lady Lassiter, widow of Sir Barnabas Lassiter. I am the mother of Jack Treadwell. I am Lillian Lyons, star of the Paris stage, and 'Our Lil', touring the north-west with a ragtag family of Vaudeville players. I am a girl, sweeping the factory floor and dreaming of another life. She glanced at the mirror screwed to the wall behind the empty prompt desk. She was a little pale, but otherwise as she should be. She checked her teeth for lipstick.

'Of course we go on. Make sure the children don't miss their cue. Now, let's finish the show.'

The orchestra began to vamp the introduction and Nikolai came towards her, his hand outstretched.

CHAPTER FIFTY-SEVEN

Tom watched them from the edge of the stage. Nikolai sang the first lines of 'The Sunrise Song' in Marakovian in honour of the Crown Prince, then switched to English as Lillian joined him. Mabel entered stage right, to a warm round of applause, and added her trumpet line to the melody. Nikolai and Lillian began to dance, Lillian with her head back and her arm out, the edge of her gown hooked to her wrist so the gold shimmered and rippled around her, and Nikolai, assured and graceful, carrying her around the floor, his expression one of unfeigned admiration for his wife.

The chorus of children came on, and Lance, Stella and Harold and Josie descended like kindly gods from their judging platform to join the throng. Lance and Stella waltzed together around Lillian and Nikolai, while Harold twirled with Josie, a broad smile on his face.

After the final verse, the competitors joined them on stage: the fisherman and Baby June, a romantic tenor and an operatic soprano, the violin couple and, of course, Sally Blow and Clive with his accordion, his sharp, serious little face lightened by the smallest of smiles as he ran his fingers over the keys. Sally looked off stage, caught Tom's eye and smiled.

*

Sally looked back out at the audience. The steady glow which had begun when she stepped out on stage for her number, and had become a full roaring flame as she sang, was still burning. She felt as if she must be ablaze with it now.

She was on stage, not to sweep it down after someone else had performed, but by her own lights, and sharing it with Lancelot Drake and Stella Stanmore.

Mr Porter signalled the smashing, raucous and uplifting chords which ended the song, and as the applause and cheering crescendoed, Stella and Lance, Harold and Josie came to the front of the stage.

Stella stepped slightly upstage of them, her long silvery gown swinging round her ankles, and she lifted her arms.

'Your Royal Highnesses, my lords, ladies and gentlemen, we have one final, crowning delight for you this evening. You've heard what we think – now it's your turn. It's time for you to vote on your favourite act of this evening, and let us know who the next recording star of Empire Records will be.'

'Now,' Lance said, stepping forward, 'we're a modern lot, here at The Empire, so I'm delighted to say we have the most up-to-date equipment to help us out. Little Sam, if you wouldn't mind?'

The children parted, and Little Sam – all six feet of him – appeared, hauling a contraption on a trolley that looked as if it had been stolen from the fairground: all light bulbs and candy stripes. Sally laughed, delighted, and covered her mouth, glancing down at Dougie in the front row. He was beaming.

'Yes,' Lance went on, leaning forward and mock serious, raising one elegant eyebrow. 'The Empire Theatre's own clap-o-meter! Cheer the acts you like, and roar your heads off for your favourite, and it will be most scientifically recorded right before your very eyes.'

He stepped back and Josie, in blue chiffon, stepped up.

'Ready, Sam? So, without further ado, let's hear it for Mr Fairweather!'

The clap-o-meter glimmered, the bulbs chasing their way around its curved edge and the arrow shot up and hovered pointing straight at the roof. Josie announced the next act and the arrow wavered around the same angle. When she announced Baby June, though, it tilted over halfway and the lights flickered on and off in excited pulses.

'Baby June Dudley, coming out ahead!' Josie announced.

Sally looked across the stage at Baby June, who smiled, pouted and waved.

Then Harold announced the next names. Sally felt a strange buzzing in her ears. The violinists got about the same as the tenor, then the fisherman came close to Baby June. Then it happened.

'And now, my lovelies! What do you say to our girl, the one and only Rose of Highbridge, Sally Blow?'

The auditorium exploded with cheers. Dougie, Belle, Alfred and Mr and Mrs Blow leapt to their feet, and half of the audience with them. The clap-o-meter shot round to the far side of the dial in a blaze of white light and ringing bells.

'We have our answer!' Harold called. 'Your Royal Highnesses, ladies and gentlemen, the search for a star has found its winner – Mrs . . . Sally . . . Blow!'

Chin up, Sally Blow.

Sally lifted her eyes and tried to take it all in, caught in the deluge of it. She was hugged from all sides. She ruffled Clive's hair, and found herself steered to the middle of the stage, deafened by the noise, and then Lancelot Drake was, with a bow, presenting her with a whole bouquet of roses.

'I think you'd do very well in these new talking pictures,' he said to her with a flash of that devastating smile.

Sally looked again at Tom, standing in the wings, appearing as baffled and happy as she felt.

'Yes,' she mouthed to him, and he put his hands to his heart. Then she looked at Lancelot Drake; he was wearing that same smile he'd worn outside the theatre that night three years earlier. 'I'll discuss it with my fiancé, Mr Drake,' she said.

'We'd better give them another song,' Stella laughed, 'or they'll never go home.'

A strange electricity ran along Tom's arms and legs – a shivering, shimmering delight. He heard the door open behind him and turned round to see Mrs Cook talking to the wardrobe assistant, Milly. Even in this haze of happiness, with Mr Porter beginning the introduction to 'When the One You Love Loves You', he registered something in the set of their bodies which concerned him.

'How is Grace doing, Milly?'

Milly looked pale in the shadows, but smiled tightly at him. 'I need more linens. Mr Treadwell won't be leaving the building, will he?'

'Of course not,' Tom replied. 'Should I fetch him?'

'Not yet,' Milly said, then disappeared back into the gloom.

CHAPTER FIFTY-EIGHT

Once the applause for the encore had subsided a little, the door to the royal box opened. The Prince of Wales, smiling broadly, emerged first, but as soon as he was out of sight of the auditorium the smile disappeared.

Jack struggled to his feet.

'Your Highness, Sir Gideon Wells has come up from London with urgent news. He's in the shop downstairs, with Vladimir Taargin from the Marakovian embassy.'

The prince raised an eyebrow. 'Will the excitements of this evening never cease? Can we get there discreetly, Treadwell?'

'Yes, sir.'

'In that case, lead on. If Taargin is there, I presume they need us both, Stefan.'

The Crown Prince put a finger to the collar of his military-style jacket, to loosen it a little. 'David, an attempt was made on our lives. Shouldn't we call the police?'

'Indeed it was. We'll get to that in a minute. Presumably Mr Treadwell does not want to have a pair of shells in his office indefinitely.'

'They're secure for now. This way, sir.'

Jack led them down the stairs, and through the back entrance to the shop, which opened directly off the lower promenade.

The shop was in partial shadow. The only lights illuminated a group of tables just outside the recording rooms. Jack saw a man who looked like a taller, uglier version of Dixon, and the man who had insulted Lillian at the wedding.

Both men got to their feet and bowed.

'Stay with us, Treadwell,' the prince said over his shoulder.

'What are you doing here, Taargin?' Stefan asked. 'You were told not to come to this city.'

Taargin looked as if he had seen a ghost, glancing between the princes in horror.

'In the circumstances . . .' Sir Gideon murmured.

'What circumstances?' Stefan asked.

Taargin began to speak haltingly in Marakovian.

'Osman, what's happening?' the prince asked, lighting a cigarette.

Osman inhaled sharply through his nose, then began to translate. 'He is saying the King of Marakovia is dead.'

'Bloody hell,' the prince said quietly.

The young Crown Prince had gone very pale. 'My father?'

Taargin dropped clumsily to one knee.

'No! Get up! There is some mistake. My father was in good health.'

'Damn,' the prince said softly, then cleared his throat. 'Stefan, it is shocking news . . .'

'No . . . I . . . Where is Nikolai?'

The door from the corridor opened, and the man himself came through it and approached the pool of light in which the new king was standing. Lillian, shimmering in her gold evening gown, followed him.

'Nikolai!' Stefan cried. 'They say my father is dead.'

Nikolai hesitated, then walked into the room and knelt down. 'Your Majesty.'

The two men who had manhandled Nikolai the previous evening also knelt, their heads bowed.

The Prince of Wales sighed. 'I think we had better give them some privacy.' He waved at his equerries. 'Osman, gentlemen, with me. Show us your recording studio, Treadwell, while they get themselves sorted out. You, too, Sir Gideon.'

Jack, still hazy about how he was putting one foot in front of the other, showed them into the musicians' den and turned on the light, vaguely aware Lillian was following them. In the sudden pale yellow glow, they discovered Dixon hunkered on a stool in the corner. He got to his feet as the party entered.

'Jesus,' the prince exclaimed, then recovered. 'Dixon, I remember you from the factory. What on earth are you doing in here in the dark?'

'Hiding from me, I expect, sir,' Gideon said, his voice dripping with contempt. 'I'm sorry to admit it, but that is my son. He ran away from his mother's house months ago. Sends postcards.'

'He's over twenty-one,' Jack said, walking over to Dixon and standing next to him. 'So it's more accurate to say he left.'

'Dixon . . .' They all turned. Lillian had closed the door behind her, and through the viewing window Jack noticed Nikolai was standing again, and had his arm around Stefan's shoulder. 'Dixon, why did you come to Highbridge?'

She looks like some ancient goddess standing there in her gold dress, Jack thought. He should have asked her to act as hostess at the old restaurant – if she'd dressed like that, they'd have had a full house every night, whatever the cooking was like.

Next to him, Dixon sighed very deeply and looked at Lillian. 'The picture of you and Jack in the newspaper,' he said quietly. 'You looked kind. And I recognised you.'

'How?' She turned from Dixon to Sir Gideon. The prince and Osman exchanged curious glances. Jack felt his blood begin to slow and thicken in his veins.

'My father had a picture of you,' Dixon said. 'When I was little. He had a drawer of them in his desk. Postcards, and portraits. Lots of beautiful girls. I told my mother about them – I thought they were nice. But she threw them out. And Father beat me.'

Sir Gideon tutted.

'Then I saw the picture in the newspaper, and I knew you from the picture. Lillian Lyons – artiste. Then I realised Jack has eyes just like my sister. I didn't understand what the pictures meant when I was little. But I understand now. Or at least, I suspected. I wanted to come here and see.'

Jack heard a rushing in his ears. He looked between Sir Gideon, Dixon and Lillian. She was staring at Sir Gideon with an expression of such disgust and contempt, he was surprised the ground around the man's feet didn't burst into flame.

'Lillian,' Jack said. 'Is that man my father? Is he the man who raped you?'

'Yes,' Lillian said.

Jack launched himself across the room at Sir Gideon, but Osman intervened, hauling him backwards.

'For God's sake!' Sir Gideon said. 'This is slander from an actress and a feeble-minded child.'

'You are not a good man,' Dixon said very quietly. 'I had to get away.' He turned to the prince in appeal. 'He kept threatening me with doctors, so I came here, and I thought the doctors wouldn't be able to commit me if I'd shown I could hold down a job and be useful. I was going to tell you – tell you both – about the picture, but I was afraid you'd send me away, Lillian, if you knew.'

The prince was still considering them all, blowing cigarette smoke through his nose.

'Nonsense,' Sir Gideon said. 'Your Highness, I'm so terribly sorry you have to listen to this. My boy is in an unfortunate state. The sooner we can get him the care he needs, the better.'

The prince held up his hand. 'Treadwell, stop fighting Osman. He's not going to let you attack Sir Gideon, though I understand the temptation.' It took an effort of will of which Jack had never thought himself capable, but he stopped, his fists balled.

'Sir, this is nonsense—'

'Gideon, I've had a trying evening already,' the prince went on. 'You're making it worse. Osman, now you've pacified Treadwell, take note . . . If any attempt is made to confine Dixon Wells, you will let it be known that the Prince of Wales considers this young man to be of sound mind. That should scare any of them off from signing any committal orders.'

'Your Highness,' Gideon began. 'You can't possibly believe—'

'And yet I do,' the prince replied crisply. 'You have a reputation, Sir Gideon, and it is not a good one. I believe Dixon, and I certainly believe Lillian, not to mention,' he looked between Jack and Sir Gideon, 'the evidence of my own eyes.' He turned to Lillian. 'Mrs Kuznetsov, what would you like me to do with him? Given the years that have passed, I fear a criminal prosecution might be impossible. But whatever I can do, I will.'

Lillian inhaled sharply, then slowly closed and opened her eyes. Jack stared at her and several slow seconds ticked by. Then she replied, with the smallest hint of a smile.

'Exile, sir.'

'Very well.' The prince put out his cigarette and lit another. 'Sir Gideon, absent yourself. Go tonight. At once. Osman will manage whatever needs to be managed here. Leave for London, then find a job as far away as is humanly possible from England. Kenya, perhaps, or Canada. I'll give you a month to make the arrangements, if that is acceptable to Mrs Kuznetsov.'

Lillian nodded.

Sir Gideon rocked backwards a little, his hand reaching towards the wall for support. 'No, no. This is ridiculous! You do not have that power, sir.'

The prince studied the end of his cigarette. 'No, not as such, but I can make your life bloody uncomfortable if you remain on these shores.' He glanced up, a brittle anger in his eyes. 'You will go. Treadwell, I will not let you beat him, but do you have anything you wish to say to your father before he leaves?'

Jack was caught up in the mysterious sensation of things coming together and falling apart at the same time. The line of Sir Gideon's jaw, familiar from his own shaving mirror; the kink in his hair, an inch from his scalp, which seemed to resist the blandishments of brilliantine: it was terrible to see his own familiar features distorted by that superior sneer, the purplish nose of a drinker and the unhealthy redness of his skin.

'Dixon may be my brother, sir, but that man is not my father. My father raised me in a village twenty miles from here, and is buried in the churchyard next to his wife.'

The prince studied him for a long moment. 'Seems he did a decent job of it. Gideon, get out of my sight. And go quickly, before I release Treadwell and he kicks your arse over the threshold, as is his right, and which I'm sure would be very satisfying.'

Sir Gideon walked stiffly over to the door. Lillian faced him for a second then, without lowering her eyes, stepped aside to let him go.

CHAPTER FIFTY-NINE

J ack put out his arms and Lillian came towards him.

'Lillian, darling, I'm so sorry.'

He pulled his handkerchief from his pocket and gave it to her, and realised his own hands were shaking.

His mother carefully wiped her eyes.

'How is Grace?' he asked.

'She seemed to be managing very well before I went on stage.' She turned to the prince. 'Grace is having the baby.'

'Good Lord.' The prince blinked.

'And Tom and Sally Blow are engaged, Jack.'

Jack settled his arm around her shoulders and pulled her closer to him. His heart was thudding in his chest – a mix of revulsion and relief, making him shudder. 'Good for them. You were magnificent then, Lillian. I wish Nikolai could have seen you. I'll tell him in great detail, when he's done shoring up the new king.'

'Thank you, sir,' Dixon said to the prince. 'I don't want to go to an asylum. He just wants to control my money, you see.'

'Really? How ghastly. Glad to be of assistance, Mr Wells,' the prince replied. 'One rarely has a chance to make use of one's princely powers, so it's rather fun taking them out for a run. Treadwell, I realise it's a busy evening, but I really think we should discuss who tried to blow us up. Don't think I've done anything in particular to offend recently, though there's always the occasional anarchist who tries to take a pop at me or someone else in the family just to make a general point.'

Osman smoothed down his shirtsleeves. 'I'm afraid it was an attempt on Stefan, sir. I have no doubt that when they learnt that, in spite of months of them trying to poison him against Nikolai, he had arranged a visit here and a meeting, they decided to act.'

'King's death came at a very convenient moment, didn't it? And did you see Taargin's face? I don't think he was expecting us to stroll in. Sticky.' The prince peered out through the viewing window. 'Right, well, we'd better broach the subject with Stefan himself.' He opened the door. 'Come along, everyone.'

'Jack,' Lillian said, laying a hand on his arm, 'I'm so sorry you had to find out this way.'

He drew breath. Every nerve jangled and his skin felt clammy and cold. 'I meant what I said, Lillian. I was raised by good, kind people who I loved, and who loved me. Do you think Sir Gideon will leave the country? I'd happily never think of the man again.'

'I hope so,' said Dixon as he shuffled past them. 'Life will be much more pleasant for my mother and sister.'

CHAPTER SIXTY

Tom and Sally stepped out of the stage door into the yard, and looked around into the shadows.

'Mr Sharps,' Tom said, stepping forward and peering into the darkness where the glow of the gaslights did not reach.

One shadow detached itself from the rest, and Sharps stepped into the light where they could see him, though his cap kept his face in shadow.

'Didn't hear no boom,' he said. 'I suppose you found it, then?' Then he touched his knuckle to the brim of his hat. 'Mrs Blow.'

'Good evening, Mr Sharps.'

'We found it,' Tom said. 'Thank you.'

Sharps smiled. 'And I see you won, Mrs Blow, judging by them flowers.'

'Yes,' Sally said simply. 'I did.'

'Sally has agreed to be my wife,' Tom said.

A slight stiffening in Sharps' posture was, at first, the only sign he'd heard. 'Treat her properly, Mr Lassiter.'

'I will. And I'm giving you notice – you and Mr Kelly. I intend to take over from my mother, and when I do, any and all connection between Lassiter Enterprises and yourselves will cease. On the hour. Is that understood?'

Sharps came towards him in long easy strides, but Tom did not flinch. As soon as he was an inch away from Tom's face, Sharps stopped.

'I could kill you in a heartbeat, boy,' he growled.

Tom met his gaze. 'I don't doubt it, Mr Sharps. But I don't see what good it would do you either.'

Sharps laughed – a low rasping sound like gravel bouncing off slate.

'True. Your mother's been running hot, Lassiter, sending off our product to theatrical types in London. Fetching police up here. Then selling shells to foreigners, attracting more trouble. Mr Kelly is happy to disengage. Willing to draw a line under it, if you are.'

'I am.'

'You still be singing in the pub, Mrs Blow? Or are you too high and mighty for that now?'

'I'll be there tomorrow night, as usual,' Sally said calmly. 'Not about to let Belle and Alf down, not after all their kindness to me and Dougie.'

A flicker of a smile crossed Sharps' thin lips. 'I'll be seeing you then.'

'Mr Sharps?' Tom said as he turned away.

'What? I've got things to do, Lassiter.'

'Who bought the shells from my mother, and hired the bomb-maker?'

Sharps scratched behind his ear. 'He wasn't very chatty by the time I'd finished getting the rest out of him, and he didn't get a name. A woman. Wore red gloves.'

Dixon had not been absolutely sure Jack was his brother when he arrived in Highbridge, and had then been absolutely sure he would be asked to leave if the truth came out. But Lillian and Jack appeared to be directing all their anger at Sir Gideon.

He followed them into the main body of the shop. His father had gone, vanished like King Rat in the pantomime. He thought about Lillian dressed as Fairy Bow Bells, bopping him on the head with her wand, and glanced sideways at her. He looked round at the gold and green decorations, and a prince had become a king here. That was like a fairy tale, too.

'How are you, Your Majesty?' the Prince of Wales said to the new King Stefan of Marakovia. 'We will, of course, bend every sinew to get you home as soon as possible. Anything at all you need, only ask. And of course, I offer my condolences, and on their behalf, the condolences of the King and Queen.'

Stefan still looked pale, but nodded. 'Thank you, David. Nikolai will be coming back with me.'

Nikolai looked at his wife, his dark eyes clouded with worry. She managed to smile at him, leaning against Jack.

Someone knocked at the door connecting them to the theatre.

'Come in,' the prince said, and it opened.

Miss Chisholm entered. She was wearing her coat, her handbag held in front of her. 'A telegram for Vladimir Taargin,' she said, bobbing a quick curtsey to the prince. She crossed the shop floor till she was standing in the midst of the Marakovians, her back to the new king, opening her bag.

'Jack!' A voice echoed through the open door. It was Tom's, cracking with urgency. 'Jack! It was Miss Chisholm!'

'You are not my king,' she said, turning and letting the bag fall to the ground.

'I'm not anyone's king. . .' the Prince of Wales began, lifting his hands. He watched as the snub-nosed pistol Miss Chisholm held swung towards Stefan. Nikolai grabbed him, pulling him aside as the gun cracked.

'For Andrei!' she said, and pulled back the trigger again. Taargin, standing inches from her, did nothing.

For Dixon, the world seemed to break into a number of small and distinct pieces: Tom's shout; the first earsplitting crack of the gun; Lillian starting forward; Jack holding her back; the click as Miss Chisholm drew back the trigger once more; the sensation of movement as Dixon found himself leaping forward, stepping up onto one of the chairs, then throwing

himself down, catching Miss Chisholm's arm, knocking the muzzle up
towards the roof as the gun exploded again.

There was a moment of silence. Dixon's ears were ringing. Then Tom
helped him up. Miss Chisholm was now speaking in Marakovian with
a blistering rage, hissing into his ear in that half-remembered language
about weakness and destiny. The men accompanying Stefan were
shouting, too. Time was elastic – the infinite moment it took the gun to
fall to the floor; the millisecond as Tom kicked it away – and suddenly
Osman had hold of Bridget. She fought them, kicking out, growling like
an animal, then, seeing it was useless, slumped.

'Who the hell is *she*?' the prince said, then turned to the more chinless
of his equerries. 'Actually, I don't care. Get her locked up somewhere, or
stand guard over her or whatever, then do call the police. I want her in a
cell. And I think we may require a doctor for Colonel Osman.'

'It's just a scratch, sir.'

'Why does everyone always say that? Nevertheless . . . Stefan, are you
whole?'

'I am,' Stefan said. 'His Excellency, Grand Duke Nikolai Goranovich
Kuznetsov, saved my life.'

Taargin began to protest in his own language. Stefan held up his hand.

'In English, please, as a courtesy to our hosts.'

Taargin cleared his throat. 'Nikolai Kuznetsov was stripped of all his
titles!'

Stefan stared at him. 'I think in the moment, my friend, you might
have forgotten whom you are addressing.'

Taargin flushed bright red.

'I . . . Yes, sir.'

Dixon watched as Bridget was led away. The fight seemed to have gone
out of her entirely. Nikolai was sitting, a little in the shadows. Being shot
at seemed to have made Stefan more, rather than less, sure of himself.
He nodded, and Dixon sat down rather sharply on one of the chairs, and
Jack and Lillian came and sat next to him.

Stefan nodded, then cleared his throat.

'We will, with your agreement, David, spend the night at the home of Mr Allerdyce, as arranged. I will return home in the morning, before the death of my father is announced to the press.' He paused, looking at his highly polished shoes. 'David, Mrs Kuznetsov, Mr Treadwell, we are profoundly in your debt. May I ask, if it is at all possible, that the events of this evening, as they pertain to me, are kept confidential? We shall discuss what to do with that woman, and . . .' his eyes travelled significantly over Taargin, 'whoever we discover her to have been in league with.' He pulled out a chair and sat down.

The Prince of Wales nodded to his remaining uninjured equerry, who scuttled off to find the transport.

'Tom,' Jack said wearily, 'pass the word, will you? Anyone who knows anything about bombs or guns is to stay quiet. And please, I'd be grateful for any word of Grace.'

The Prince of Wales, watching Stefan, leant up against the table next to where Dixon and Jack were slumped in hard-backed chairs.

'There, I think Stefan's getting the hang of it. You know, strictly speaking, you shouldn't sit down in the presence of a member of the Royal Family who is standing.' Dixon began to struggle up, but the prince laughed softly, and pushed him back down. 'I think in the circumstances, Mr Wells, I'll allow it.'

As Tom left, Milly came in and looked round. 'Mr Treadwell? Is Mr Treadwell here?' Her voice sounded high and urgent in the gloom of the shop.

'I'm here, Milly.'

'Oh, thank goodness. Please, Mr Treadwell. Grace needs you right this minute.'

Jack didn't ask permission, or bow to his shop full of royalty. He left, his sharp stride breaking into a run as he reached the door which led back to the theatre.

'Poor devil,' the prince said. 'Well, I wish them both the best of luck.'

Dixon looked round, surprised at the lack of reaction from Nikolai to the last few minutes. He was still in a chair in the shadows, his chin on his chest, unmoving. Lillian must have thought the same thing; she took a step forward, her hand outstretched.

'Nikolai?' she said.

Dixon had never heard a name spoken in that way – so full of love, and so full of dread.

Stefan put his hand on Nikolai's shoulder, then pulled back his dinner jacket. His white dress shirt was soaked in blood. 'Get me something to stop the bleeding,' the King of Marakovia snapped, as Lillian started forward with a groan.

CHAPTER SIXTY-ONE

Tom and Sally were crossing the stage, heading towards the dressing rooms, when one of the other things Sharps had said – just before the red gloves – stirred itself out of Tom's memory and presented itself to his conscious mind. It stopped him in his tracks, and he was still standing, blinking on the spot where Sally had been when she said 'yes' to him, when above him, Mr Poole appeared through the doors from the promenade bar.

'Tom!' he called out, waving down at him. 'Is everything all right? I'm a-flutter!'

'Everything's fine, Mr Poole.'

He pressed his hand to his forehead. 'Thank heavens! We're all up here. Harold is doing a turn, and I think Lance is going to do a number from his new "talkie". We're all staying till we have news of Grace. Is Mr Treadwell all right?'

Tom struggled for a moment to think clearly.

'Yes, yes, he's fine. I'll join you in a minute. Mr Poole, can you pass the word? Anyone who knows anything about the shenanigans is to keep mum. And Miss Chisholm has . . . gone away.'

'Shame! Yes, I'll close the loop on the chatter.'

'And, Mr Poole . . . is Stella there? I'd like a word with her in private. In the lobby.' He turned to Sally. 'Do you mind going up ahead of me?'

'Think I'll cope.' She kissed him briefly on the lips and walked off. 'And I'll stay quiet.'

Mr Poole gave him the thumbs up, and Tom took the side door through the wings, then walked up the central aisle of the stalls. Sally had agreed to marry him. He would be a father to Dougie, a regular at the Bricklayers Arms as well as the Metropole; he would loosen his mother's grip around Lassiter Enterprises. He would make records. Ruby would be proud of him – and all of that could begin very soon.

The theatre exuded a sort of exhausted goodwill, as if the last pleasures of the crowd were still sinking into the carpet, taking their place among the crystals of the chandelier, making them shine. He went into the lobby to find Stella, a beautiful silvery wraith, coming down the stairs towards him.

'Congratulations! I'm so pleased about you and Sally. Oh, Tom, what is it?'

He put his hands in his pockets. 'Stella, who did you get your drugs off in London?'

She gasped, and blinked at him.

'I . . . I know it will sound awful, Tom, and I'd rather you didn't tell Grace, but . . . Jason de Witte. Most of us did. His stuff was always much nicer than the rest.'

'He was Tasha Kingsland's supplier, too, wasn't he?'

She nodded, her hand resting on the marble newel post at the bottom of the stairs.

'Stella, did you buy the drugs off him with cash?'

'No, I didn't. That seemed so sordid. He would just hand out little packets in exchange for . . .' Her voice trailed away.

'Gossip,' Tom said wearily. 'Any titbits or anecdotes you had. You know why he wanted them, Stella? Because he was feeding them all back to my mother. Anything about the London theatre she could use to cause problems for The Empire. And using him to spread nonsense about The Empire in London. My mother was sending him cocaine from Ray Kelly's smuggling operations. I think he's been using Lassiter Enterprises to distribute it across the north of England. That's why Jason de Witte took the trouble to write a horrific notice of Grace's play.'

'Oh,' her eyes widened. 'Oh, no!'

'Did you hear about Archibald Flynn's tax problems and pass that on?'

'Yes . . . Oh, Tom, what should I do?'

'Call those detectives and tell them the truth, Stella. And let me deal with my mother.'

'Tom! Stella!' Poole called down the stairs, his voice an octave higher than usual. 'There's an ambulance arriving! Who is it for?'

SIX MONTHS LATER

Lillian was thinking of the first night of Nikolai's play when the organ music started. It had been, she thought, a perfect evening: his power and passion so fully on display, his talent, his zest for life. She was very, very proud of what both her husbands had achieved, and deeply grateful she had married Nikolai, whatever pain loving him had also brought her. As the full and thunderous chords rang out, making the ancient stones of the cathedral tremble, she stood. It was right to be here in the city her husband had spoken of so often. It was right to witness this moment.

His Majesty Stefan V, King of Marakovia, led the procession, preceded only by a flock of priests, and his train was carried by a dozen page-boys in floppy white cravats. Behind him were four men in civilian dress, with short cloaks hanging from their shoulders. One carried a sword, another a shield, one an orb and one – His Excellency, Grand Duke Nikolai Goranovich Kuznetsov – a crown.

'Lillian, Nikolai looks like Count Dracula,' Tom whispered, and Lillian had to bite her lip to stop herself laughing. Sally tried to frown at him, but her eyes were dancing, too.

The wound that Nikolai had received on the night of the talent show had not been fatal. Within a day, he had been cursing his doctors and insisting he was well enough to travel; within a week, he had left for Marakovia.

Tom and Sally had been married three months now, and Tom was in the process of removing Lassiter Enterprises from his mother's hands. It had been announced to the press that Edmund's health had worsened, so Constance would retire to Switzerland to be near her elder son. How Tom had loosened his mother's grip over the business, Lillian was not certain, but she was sure that the return of Darien Burnside, Jack's awful assistant, who had visited Edmund in Switzerland, had been part of it. Presumably Darien would be able to testify, if asked to do so, that Edmund was in no condition to support or veto his mother's business decisions, no matter what she had been telling the board. Then, she suspected, Tom's hand had been strengthened by the arrest of Jason de Witte. They had opened the *Illustrated London News* in early September to find a picture of him, head sunk, standing between two police officers whom Grace identified as Orme and Hatchard. The humiliation of that man had been a pleasure to witness, even at second hand. Evie Wilkins – known in London as Evangelista D'Angelo – a doyenne of the West End stage and Lillian's oldest and closest friend, had even driven up to Highbridge to give them an account of De Witte's arrest in person. They had chosen to apprehend him in the middle of a gala where half of the West End were present to watch. 'Took the champagne glass out of his hand and put cuffs on him mid-barb,' Evie told them. She had impersonated his horrified goldfish gape on and off all evening, till they were all laughing too hard to speak. Even Grace, who had been trying, Lillian thought, not to enjoy De Witte's downfall excessively had succumbed to laughter in the end.

Dear Grace, Lillian thought. The early arrival of her daughter had caused even Mrs Cook some moments of anxiety, but while Lillian left the theatre in the ambulance with her husband, terrified he might die, little Ruby Treadwell was born, healthy and whole, backstage. Lillian was shocked, and a little delighted, to find she was immediately, abjectly, in love with the child, and grateful beyond belief to discover Tom and Grace had no immediate plans to leave Lassiter Court. Indeed, they would be masters of it whenever she was in Marakovia with Nikolai.

It occurred to Lillian, with a shock, that if Edmund eventually succumbed to his injuries, Tom would inherit the baronetcy and Sally would become Lady Lassiter. Dougie peered round his mother and caught Lillian's eye. She winked at him, and he grinned back.

Once Nikolai had passed, there followed any number of military types, and then a bunch of working people, nicely dressed, with great ribbons on their shoulders, carrying the tools of their trade, from hammers and hoes, to sewing baskets and cooking pots. Sally was glad she had a good view of them through the ceremony, because it was long and in Marakovian, and it was fun to try and guess what everyone was from what they carried.

'She's a teacher!' Sally whispered to Dougie. 'That's a slate and she's got a piece of chalk on a string.'

'Shush, you two!' Tom said, gently. 'Honestly, can't take you anywhere.'

'All right, Mr Lassiter, sir.' She was quiet for a couple of minutes, admiring the engagement and wedding rings on her finger. 'What about the wicked uncle, Andrei? Is he here?'

'No, he retired to the country due to his ill health.'

'I bet he did.'

The choir started up, and Sally settled, her arm round Dougie's shoulders, listening to the strange harmonies. Not her sort of tune at all, but nice nevertheless. She glanced along the row. Dixon was there, looking unhappy because they had insisted he wore a new coat. The Prince of Wales himself had been quite firm about it. Jack and Grace sat next to him. Jack and Grace's little girl, Ruby, was a sweetheart. Stella was at the end of the row, missing four days of her latest show to attend the coronation, and to flirt with the Prince of Wales.

There were more prayers.

Sally let her thoughts drift back to Highbridge and the new town house she and Tom had just bought in a square on the west of the town centre. It was near the recording studio and still only two tram stops from the Bricklayers Arms where she still sang once a week, and Dougie's school.

Tom had told her everything that had gone on that night after Grace's baby was born. The involvement of Bridget Chisholm had really shocked him. It had shaken Jack, too, and Dixon, and for a moment there everyone had fretted about things at The Empire going off the rails again, with no Miss Chisholm, and Jack and Grace tied up with little Ruby. Lillian had stepped into the breach, saying she was grateful to have something to think about while Nikolai was away. She'd even managed to hire a new assistant before Jack's office got into too much of a state.

By and large, the whole matter of the evening had been hushed up. Miss Chisholm, they thought, had been arrested, but Mr Poole said there was not a breath of anything in the papers, and whenever Jack rang up Colonel Osman, he was told nothing and was referred to someone called Barrington-Smythe, who had replaced Sir Gideon, who also told him nothing but managed to be ruder about it. They had learnt, through sheer persistence, that Miss Chisholm was not called Miss Chisholm at all, but was the daughter of a close ally of Taargin's – Ilya something or other – who had married an English girl before the war. Taargin was still an ambassador, but not in England.

As far as the world knew, Crown Prince Stefan had received news of his father's death and returned home immediately, supported a few days later by his cousin, Grand Duke Nikolai Goranovich Kuznetsov. Stefan had landed at the northern border and ridden on a horse, like an old-fashioned knight, through the country to the capital while heralds pronounced the news of his father's death and his succession. In every town or village he passed through, he invited the people and landowners to join him. By the time he arrived at the capital, with Nikolai by his side, he was at the head of a mass of thousands of his people. It was probably around that time, Sally guessed, that his uncle started to feel a touch peaky.

There was a movement in the row. Stella was getting up and moving along the side of the cathedral. Sally looked at her order of service. It didn't help her much, being all in Marakovian, but she guessed what was coming when she saw (Kuznetsov/Rowntree/ something or other) Lancelot Drake y Stella Stanmora c Mabelou Millsou. Shame Lillian and Nikolai weren't singing it, but perhaps that would have been pushing the more conservative citizens of Marakovia too far. Sally didn't think she'd ever enjoy hearing "The Sunrise Song" as much as when she had listened to it in the theatre, knowing in her bones she'd won the competition and would marry Tom, but this was something else. Lancelot and Stella had a full orchestra backing them. Their voices and Mabel's trumpet echoed upwards, weaving through all the ancient stone arches and battering at the stained glass. It sounded like a sweet wind sweeping over a field and seemed to tease the tassels of the military men, and rattle the jewels in the coronets of the aristocrats clustered near the new king. Then the new king smiled, possibly at their attempts to sing the song in the original Marakovian, and suddenly everyone was smiling.

The parties after the coronation lasted deep into the night. Jack tucked little Ruby up in her cot and kissed her head. Grace was at the dressing table, already in a nightgown and brushing her hair.

'Do go out again, Jack,' she said. 'We'll be perfectly all right and I'm too shattered to change my dress again.'

He looked out of the window; the night sky was bright with bonfires and the fireworks were still sparkling in the night sky over the castle.

'You want to, don't you? Go and find Lillian and dance with her.'

'Do you think I'll be able to manage the theatre without her for a while?' he asked.

'Naturally you will, without Constance working through her collection of nasty tricks. But for the moment the king still needs Nikolai, and Nikolai and Lillian have been missing each other terribly. So go and dance with her while you have the chance.'

He flopped down on the bed. 'You can be brutally practical sometimes.'

He rolled over to admire his sleeping daughter again. 'Did you ever read that note that Ruby left for you? The one Tom found?'

'Yes. I look at it every day before I start work.' She reached into her evening bag and pulled out a sheet of paper, then handed it to him.

'You even travel with it?' he asked, flicking it open.

'Obviously.'

Have faith, Grace, it read. *There are always more tunes, more songs, more stories.*

'Apparently simple, but perfectly balanced and very well phrased. Very Ruby. I miss her,' Jack said, handing the note back to her.

'We all do,' Grace replied, tucking it carefully away.

'And does the De Witte notice still bother you, Grace, when you work?'

She frowned slightly. 'It bothers me a lot less, Jack. Not because Constance bribed him to do it, but just because I think I'm getting better as a writer. I have at least the courage to try and become better now. That feels like an achievement.'

'And you've forgiven Stella?'

'Of course. She felt much worse about it than we did. I never expected her to cut that man dead just because he'd given me a bad notice. He was far too important. How on earth could she have known what was going on? And she'll be a very indulgent godmother to baby Ruby just to make up for it.'

'Brutally practical again, I'm very proud of you.' He rolled off the bed and put on his jacket. Grace turned her face up to be kissed. He obliged.

'By the way, King Stefan has bought you an amusing present, so remember to be amused when you get it.'

'What is it?' he asked suspiciously.

'A case of Marakovian cold cream. I say it's for you, but obviously it's really for Harry.'

Jack let out a bark of laughter. 'I welcome it. I've already removed everything vaguely resembling a rat trap from the theatre. Did you hear about Dixon's postcard?'

'From Italy? With a four leaf-clover and no signature? Yes, it must have been from Miss Chisholm, don't you think?'

'I'm certain of it. Discreetly removed from England and Marakovia. No trial in exchange for no fuss.'

'A little like Tom sending his mother to Switzerland.' She put down her hairbrush. 'I dread to think what she'll be plotting there. You know, when I was younger, I used to think I knew what was going on in the world because I read the newspaper. I must have a word with Wilbur. Now, go and dance with your mother.'

He turned the handle, then stopped, and looked back at his sleeping child and his beautiful wife. Nikolai had arranged for a room with a balcony, a decanter of whisky in every room, heavy glasses and comfortable chairs.

'Actually, darling, I can dance with Lillian tomorrow. I think I'd rather watch the fireworks from here, with you and Ruby.'

She grinned. 'Oh good! I mean, you can still go, I meant that. But Tom and I were looking through some of Ruby's tunes, and I think I have quite a good idea for a new show. Do you want to hear about it?'

He took off his jacket again and fetched the whisky.

'I'd like that very much.'

ACKNOWLEDGEMENTS

Gosh, here I am writing the acknowledgements for my second novel. How exciting! As I'm sure you know, every production relies on a team of expert, enthusiastic and creative people toiling tirelessly in the wings and backstage to make any production come to life, and of course the same is true of this or any novel. So here are the cast of players I wish to thank for their wonderful support, hard work, humour and skill. Nothing happens without them and I am hugely indebted to you all, and unlike in most productions here there is no star, featured or ensemble billing. You are all top turns to me!

To everyone at my publishers, Bonnier Books UK. Thank you so much for everything you do – this is truly a team effort. Thank you specifically to Sarah Benton, MD at Bonnier Books UK, for always championing me, and to my editor, Claire Johnson-Creek. To Clare Kelly for helping to spread the word about my books so wonderfully far and wide and to Natalia Cacciatore for the creative and brilliant marketing. To Laura Makela, Chelsea Graham and the rest of the audio team for helping to bring my words to life, to Jenny Richards for another beautiful cover design, to Alex May and everyone in production for turning it into an actual real book, to Vincent Kelleher, Stuart Finglass, Stacey Hamilton,

Stella Giatrakou and the rest of the incredible sales team. Thanks to my copy-editor, Steve O'Gorman, and my proofreader Gilly Dean. There really are so many of you involved and I really appreciate your love and support for my books.

Thank you to my endlessly supportive agents at Curtis Brown: Gordon Wise, Alastair Lindsey-Renton, Helen Clarkson and Sarah Spear, as well as Elliot Prior and all at the Maskell Clarkson Renton office.

My huge thanks also go to Imogen Robertson for really understanding The Empire and my characters.

And last but certainly not least, I'd like to thank each and every one of you who has picked up this book – whether in physical form, ebook or audio. None of this would be possible without you, and I'm eternally grateful.

Love,
Mxx

LETTER FROM THE AUTHOR

Hello my lovelies!

Oh! the joy I felt returning to the world of The Empire, catching up with the characters we feel we already know so well, and meeting the new members of our cast of players. I missed them and couldn't wait to get started on this new adventure.

The challenges faced by the Theatre nearly 100 years ago are no different from those we face now. Finding plays and musicals that excite and entice an audience to come through the doors and into the hallowed auditorium is a huge challenge. Finding stars, featured players, ensembles and technical staff to populate the roles and fill the stage is the key to any production's success. Making sure the building runs smoothly and the people working in it are as happy and fulfilled as possible and most importantly finding new ways to keep audiences entertained and keep them coming back for more time after time is ultimately the most important requirement for any theatre.

The roaring twenties were a time of huge change for the theatre world and the country in general. As ever political, economic and social challenges were enormous and no area of life in Great Britain was immune to these, so it was great fun weaving the characters in Highbridge into the tapestry of those issues Britain and Europe faced at this time.

Love, life, death, intrigue, egos, triumphs, disasters, talent and troublesome rodents were and still are what make the magical world of The Empire and indeed every theatre all over the world, go round . . . and I bloody love it. It's my world and I rejoice in the fact that I get to share it with you once again. There really is no business like show business.

I would love to ensure you're the first to hear about my writing, upcoming bookish events, cover reveals or even a few cheeky giveaways. That's why I set up my readers' club, Behind the Curtain. You can sign up here: https://bit.ly/BehindTheCurtainBall to become part of the Behind the Curtain readers' club. It only takes a few moments to sign up; there are no catches or costs. Bonnier Books UK will keep your data private and confidential, and it will never be passed on to a third party. We won't spam you with loads of emails, just get in touch now and then with news about my books, and you can unsubscribe any time you want. And if you would like to get involved in a wider conversation about my books, please do review *A Backstage Betrayal* on Amazon, on GoodReads, on any other online store, on your own blog and social media accounts, or talk about it with friends, family or reading groups! Sharing your thoughts helps other readers, and I'd love to hear what you think.

So, places please ladies and gentlemen. The lights are dimming. The curtain is about to rise once again at the glorious Empire Theatre.

With my love

DON'T MISS MICHAEL BALL'S GLITTERING DEBUT . . .

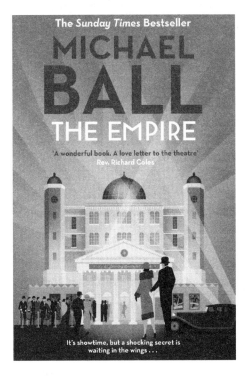

The *Sunday Times* Bestseller

MICHAEL BALL

THE EMPIRE

'A wonderful book. A love letter to the theatre'
Rev. Richard Coles

It's showtime, but a shocking secret is
waiting in the wings . . .

WELCOME TO THE EMPIRE THEATRE

1922. When Jack Treadwell arrives at The Empire, in the middle of a rehearsal, he is instantly mesmerised. But amid the glitz and glamour, he soon learns that the true magic of the theatre lies in its cast of characters – both on stage and behind the scenes.

There's stunning starlet Stella Stanmore and Hollywood heartthrob Lancelot Drake; and Ruby Rowntree, who keeps the music playing, while Lady Lillian Lassiter, theatre owner and former showgirl, is determined to take on a bigger role. And then there's cool, competent Grace Hawkins, without whom the show would *never* go on . . . could she be the leading lady Jack is looking for?

When long-held rivalries threaten The Empire's future, tensions rise along with the curtain. There is treachery at the heart of the company and a shocking secret waiting in the wings. Can Jack discover the truth before it's too late, and the theatre he loves goes dark?

AVAILABLE NOW

TAKE A PEEK BEHIND THE CURTAIN IN MICHAEL BALL'S MAGICAL MEMOIR . . .

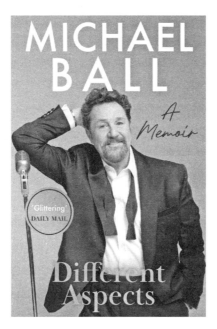

In 1989, a young Michael Ball landed the lead role in the musical Aspects of Love. It was a moment that changed his life forever. It was the first time he worked with legends of the stage like Andrew Lloyd Webber and Trevor Nunn; it was from that show that came his smash hit song, Love Changes Everything, which rode high in the charts for 15 weeks; it was then, also, that he first met his long-term partner Cathy McGowan and battled back against the stage fright that had threatened his career.

Over three decades later, Michael returns to a new production of the same show where he made his name, definitely older, possibly wiser, and with a lifetime's worth of stories to tell. In *Different Aspects*, Michael takes us backstage inside the making of a West End hit, while diving back into memories to explore that moment in his twenties when the world was at his feet and his life changed beyond recognition.

Part exploration of the pitfalls and pratfalls of modern theatre and part exploration of his life, his career and his relationships, *Different Aspects* is the story of a life lived on the stage. There is laughter, there is tears, there is sweat and some blood, there is even some Roger Moore, although, famously, not quite enough. And through it all the show goes on.

AVAILABLE NOW